湖南师范大学哲学社会科学名家经典丛书（首批）

编辑出版委员会

主　任：李　民　蒋洪新　张国骥　刘湘溶

学术委员：（按姓名拼音排序）

匡乐满　李　民　李双元　李维琦　李育民　凌　宇
刘茂松　刘湘溶　蒋洪新　蒋冀骋　蒋坚松　蒋新苗
欧阳峣　谭双泉　唐凯麟　唐贤清　田中阳　王步标
王善平　王治来　吴家庆　谢自楚　张国骥　张楚廷
张怀承

编　委：（按姓名拼音排序）

蔡　骐　邓颖玲　何扬波　金育强　孔春晖　李培超
刘大明　刘子兰　马卫平　沈又红　王　辉　唐贤清
夏赞才　肖北庚　谢炳庚　谢志钊　张怀承　赵炎秋
钟毅平　朱咏北　朱训德

执行主编：欧阳峣

执行副主编：杨合林

湖南师范大学哲学社会科学名家经典丛书

文学翻译十讲
英中文版

刘重德　著
蔡平　译
彭长江　审校

湖南师范大学出版社

图书在版编目（CIP）数据

文学翻译十讲：英中文版 / 刘重德著；蔡平译. --长沙：湖南师范大学出版社，2018.1
ISBN 978-7-5648-2164-7

Ⅰ.①文… Ⅱ.①刘… ②蔡… Ⅲ.①文学翻译-英文 Ⅳ.①I046

中国版本图书馆 CIP 数据核字（2015）第 132036 号

文 学 翻 译 十 讲 英中文版
WENXUE FANYI SHIJIANG

刘重德　著
蔡　平　译
彭长江　审校

◇策划编辑：刘苏华
◇责任编辑：胡亚兰
◇责任校对：张晓芳
◇出版发行：湖南师范大学出版社
　　　　　　地址/长沙市岳麓山　邮编/410081
　　　　　　电话/0731-88873070　88873071　传真/0731-88872636
　　　　　　网址/http://press.hunnu.edu.cn
◇经销：湖南省新华书店
◇印刷：天津画中画印刷有限公司
◇开本：710mm×1000mm　1/16
◇印张：22.75
◇字数：306 千字
◇版次：2018 年 1 月第 1 版
◇印次：2024 年 8 月第 2 次印刷
◇书号：ISBN 978-7-5648-2164-7
◇定价：83.00 元

如有印装质量问题，请与承印厂调换。

总　序

　　兹编凡九种，皆国师至湖南师大各时期学人之所撰著，涉国学与西学多门。将以纪念我校八十华诞，观澜溯源，回眸往迹，追缅先辈；亦欲以略窥前贤治学门径，砥砺同仁，商量旧学，培养新知，探奇揽胜，再谱新篇。

　　1938年，日寇猖獗，狼烟遍地，国运迍邅。著名教育家、心理学家廖世承先生慨然以教育救国为自任，辞病父，别妻子，自上海来吾湘安化之蓝田，筚路蓝缕，以启山林，创建国立师范学院。世承先生以教员为学校之命脉，延揽人才不遗余力。其学识人格、恭谦态度又足以动人，故众多名家大师、学林翘楚不避险难，先后从四方辗转跋涉而至。钱基博、钱锺书、锺泰、谭戒甫、马宗霍、骆鸿凯、高觉敷、孟宪承、皮名举、李剑农、汪梧封、高昌运、沈同洽、储安平、雷敢、唐长孺、张舜徽、吴世昌、周邦式、谢扶雅等，或为家传独诣之士，或出鸿儒硕学之门，或来自海内外知名学府。一时俊彦云集，彬彬称盛。

　　国师以"仁爱精勤"为校训，尤重人格与道德之养成。士子风操，侠肝义胆，铮铮愕愕，沛然浩然。1944年，日寇南进，长沙失守，逼近衡阳。战事不利，警烽四起，国师师生临危不乱，处变不惊，作息有序，弦歌不辍。其独立不移、动心忍性之民族正气，于稳定当地社会人心之作用甚巨，当时即为报章所称许。及衡阳城破，学校转迁溆浦，钱基博先生犹欲独自留守，谓"非寇退危解，不赴院召，亦使人知学府中人尚有人站得起也"。孰谓书生怯弱，百无一用，须知国士一人，雄冠万夫！中华民族威武不屈之精神气概，我国师有之矣！

国师由蓝田而溆浦，由溆浦而南岳，播迁流离，殆无宁日。新中国成立初，国师并入湖南大学，1953年全国高等学校院系调整，成立湖南师范学院。1984年，湖南师范学院更名为湖南师范大学。1996年，湖南师范大学进入国家"211"工程重点建设行列。

"余既滋兰之九畹兮，又树蕙之百亩。"八十年，艰苦卓厉，弦歌鼓舞，春华秋实。今日之湖南师大，声望与日月俱来，美誉无羽翼自飞。然而，亦有可深思者。今之论大学者，皆据前辈教育家、清华大学校长梅贻琦先生之说："所谓大学者，非谓有大楼之谓也，有大师之谓也。"何谓大师？非徒积学储宝、著作繁富之谓也，必得有独立之精神与自由之思想，能引领一代，可薪火相传者也。以此衡之，今人文社科领域之著述非不富矣，而大师之称号，能当之无愧者复有几人？我校学人，能不勉哉！

兹编定名为"湖南师范大学哲学社会科学名家经典丛书"，凡选九种：

廖世承撰《教育心理学》（1925年）；

锺泰撰《中国哲学史》（1929年）；

骆鸿凯撰《文选学》（1936年）；

马宗霍撰《中国经学史》《文字学发凡》（1937年）；

钱基博撰《近百年湖南学风》《经学通志》（1941年）；

李剑农撰《中国近百年政治史》（1948年）；

杨树达撰《汉书窥管》（1955年）；

林增平撰《中国近代史》（1958年）；

刘重德撰《文学翻译十讲（英中文版）》（1991年）。

经者，贯穿布帛锦绣之纵线，能一以贯之者也；典者，典籍也，典范也。所谓经典，乃能一以贯之，代相传递，能示人以轨范、法则者也。经典并非无可挑剔，其文献资料或有未逮，其具体观点或有可商，其概念话语或已过时，然其独立之思想，独创之方法，独到之见解，独特之价值，其大本大宗，却能远绍前哲，启示后昆。故其价值不会因时过境迁而衰减，反如深泉之水，随挹随出，老树之花，愈采愈香。

是为序。

蒋洪新

Preface

I accept with pleasure Prof. Liu Zhongde's invitation to write a preface for his book *Ten Lectures on Literary Translation*. Not only have I known him since his school days at the Southwest Associated University; also, the subject of translation itself, whether from English to Chinese or vice versa, has long intrigued me as a professor of Western literature in Chinese universities and Chinese literature in American universities. For the specialist, it is true, translated works are no substitute for the original, and I have urged my students to learn as many foreign languages as possible, yet translations serve a useful purpose for the vast reading public who desires to seek world-wide knowledge in fields ranging from literature and culture to science and technology but who lacks the facility and opportunity to read books in the original language.

The art of translation is a combination of literary skills, acquired and perfected through long, persistent practice, and the knowledge of grammatical rules and linguistic principles, whose application makes for correctness and exactitude. In the "Ten Lectures", the author expounds in detail the dual nature of translation, i. e., art versus technology, with many quotations and illustrations helpful for the beginners. After dwelling upon the principles and standards of translation such as faithfulness in content, expressiveness in language, and closeness to the style of the original work, he delves into the controversial but fascinating question of literal and free translation, giving at the same time an account of the development of these two schools and their advocates in Chinese literary history. He also offers valuable suggestions on the various methods of translation and discusses its grammatical and linguistic aspects. Especially interesting to me are the last three chapters that deal with the question of literary style in translation and the problems of rendering English poems into Chinese and Chinese poems into English.

During the last several decades of my professional career as teacher, writer, and translator of Chinese and English literature, I have tackled the same problems and succeeded in producing, with the help of my friends, colleagues, and former students as contributors, a comprehensive anthology of Chinese poetry in English translation[1]. This experience enables me to appreciate in particular Prof. Liu Zhongde's introductory remarks and overall views on the translation of poetry. I agree with him that it is feasible, though difficult, to translate poems satisfactorily and successfully. Here, I just want to add that of the three schools of translation, the classical, the creative, and the free, mentioned in the chapter on "Problems of Translating Poems", the last has emerged as the most popular and attracted a majority of followers among Western scholar-translators. A new generation of competent and distinguished translators has taken over since Arthur Waley the field of Chinese-English translations, greatly extending for Western readers the horizon of Chinese poetry.

One regrets, however, that the same cannot be said of the situation in China, where there is only a meager attempt by translators to introduce Chinese poetry to Western readers. With this thought in mind, I read with appreciation and anticipation Prof. Liu Zhongde's book, which is a useful, practical guide to the methods and techniques of translation. An author of numerous articles and books on the subject and a veteran translator himself, Prof. Liu both instructs and inspires in his "Ten Lectures" future generations of translators. Its publication, I hope, will not only inform readers of the art of translation but also attract them to the work of translation itself, especially in the rendering of Chinese literature into English and English literature into Chinese, thus giving an impetus to the cultural exchanges of the East and West. I look forward to the expected influence and valuable contributions of Prof. Liu's book in this field.

Liu Wu-chi 柳无忌

Note 1.

Sunflower Splendor: Three Thousand Years of Chinese Poetry (1975), ed. by Wu-chi Liu and Irving Y. E. Lo. "Sunflower Splendor is the largest and, on the whole, best anthology of translated Chinese poems to have appeared in a Western Language." (—*The New York Times* Book Review)

Foreword

When I was unexpectedly made a teacher of translation in the 1940s, I felt like sailing on an uncharted sea without a compass. To back myself up I had only some meager knowledge of Chinese and English; I had had no training in translation, nor had I ever been groomed for a teaching job.

Like other young teachers of English, I sought help from Chinese works. I hunted in the library and rummaged in the second-hand book stores. Unfortunately, the references I found were few and the information skimpy and ill-documented. True, there had been prolonged and heated debates on literal and free translation, but the participants were more emotional and polemical than methodical and illuminating.

Disappointed with Chinese pundits, I turned to Westerners. There was Alexander Fraser Tytler with his neat principles, but his examples were all unconnected with the Chinese language and so hardly of any use to Chinese students. There was Matthew Arnold sharply critical of the old translators of Homer, but since the original was in Greek, many of his remarks eluded my understanding.

Compared with those sweating over their exercises in the classroom in the old days, the teachers and students of translation in the 1980s could call themselves lucky. In recent years, there have appeared numerous articles comparing Chinese and English; there have also been published some textbooks in Chinese on the practice of translation. Moreover, there have been introduced from abroad such theorists as Savory, Newmark and Nida, whose works are far more digestible and systematic than their predecessors. And now comes along Professor Liu Zhongde with his *Ten Lectures on Literary Translation*, the fruits of long years of research and experiments.

One thing that would soon strike the readers is the writer's extraordinary diligence and wide coverage. He has studied translation theories, old and new, with great patience. Starting from Yan Fu, he has gone through numerous works down to the 1980s. He has also dug into many volumes published abroad and emerged with brief summaries and interesting comments.

Any book on translation cannot do without examples, and here the writer has proved to be particularly helpful. While others have confined themselves to comparing isolated phrases and sentences in the source and target languages, he gives us complete passages whenever necessary. The provision of full contexts makes the meaning and style of the expressions under scrutiny much clearer to the readers, and so are the writer's remarks and observations.

In the opinion of Professor Liu, translation is at once a science and an art. It is a science because a comparison of the different language systems shows that there are rules to be followed by the translators, such as *The horse is a useful animal* should be rendered into 马是有用的动物 with the English articles unaccounted for. In so doing he is on solid ground, and his judgment can easily win general approval.

But, as pointed out in the first lecture, translation is also an art, and about art there are a multiplicity of theories. "Despite a number of treatments of the basic principles and procedures of translation," concedes Eugene Nida, one of the noted theorists of today, "no full-scale theory of translation now exists." Consequently, if there should be in the book certain ideas hard to understand or agree to, they should cause no-one to raise his eyebrows.

I thank Professor Liu, for he has given me much food for thought.

Wang Zongyan　王宗炎

Acknowledgements

The author thanks all those who have helped to make this a better book than it would otherwise have been. Among them, he is especially grateful to Professor Liu Wu-Chi, his former teacher, and Professor Wang Zongyan, his old friend, who were generous enough to write the preface and the foreword to this book and offered valuable and detailed comments on the manuscript. He is also indebted to a number of specialists in translatology, particularly to Professors Ma Zuyi, Gu Yanling, Peng Jing, Tan Zanxi, Lin Jihai, Xiao Liming, Chu Zhida and Xiong Xiling, who gave the author their precious suggestions for revision.

Liu Zhongde
Professor of English
Foreign Languages Department
Hunan Normal University

Lecture One	Nature of Translation	001
Lecture Two	Principles of Translation	015
Lecture Three	Faithfulness of Translation	034
Lecture Four	Literal Translation and Free Translation	049
Lecture Five	Commonly-Used Methods of Translation	070
Lecture Six	How to Translate English Attributive Clauses	084
Lecture Seven	Image-Rendering and Sentence-Division in Translation from Chinese into English	098
Lecture Eight	Translatability of Literary Style	109
Lecture Nine	Problems of Translating Poems	138
Lecture Ten	Translation of English Poetry into Chinese	173

Lecture One Nature of Translation

By translation here I specifically mean translating, the process of translation, in which something is translated, instead of the work translated. So far as the definition of translation is concerned, of course, it is very easy for us to copy one from a dictionary; that is, a rendering from one language into another, but that seems to be too general and simple. Various definitions have been given to translation. Now I'd like to cite some of them:

Translation is a science.

Translation is an art.

Translation is a craft.

Translation is a skill.

Translation is an operation.

Translation is a language activity.

Translation is communicating.

All the definitions mentioned above may be taken for reference because each of them is true when looked at from a certain angle.

Among them the first two are most important for they represent two schools—the school of science and the school of art. The former maintains that translating should reproduce the message of the orginal by means of the transformation of linguistic equivalence. It puts stress on the study of description of the process of translation, and the structures and forms of language so as to reveal the objective laws inherent in translating. The latter school advocates re-creating a literary work by using expressions of another language. It emphasizes the effect of translation. Lin Yutang (1895-1976) was once a representative. In his essay *On Translation* he declares that translation is an art whose success depends upon one's artistic talent and enough training. Besides these, there are no set rules for translation and there is no short cut for art.

In my opinion, both schools have their strong points and weak points so far as literary translation is concerned. Now there is a tendency to combine their theories into a comprehensive one. As a matter of fact, literary translation has a double nature. That's to say, on the one hand, it is a science with its own laws and methods and on the other, it is an art. Now let's have a further discussion of its double nature in the following.

Translation Is a Science

We say that translation is a science, because it has its own laws and methods. Take the translation between English and Chinese for example, if we want to translate well, we must be entirely familiar with the content of the original and all the knowledge it concerns. In addition, we should have a comparatively comprehensive and thorough study of English and Chinese so that we may do our work with high proficiency.

Chinese and English have their respective characteristics. True, they have similarities, for example, the word order of the subject and its predicate, of the transitive verb and its object and of the preposition and the object it governs; and at the same time, they have remarkable differences: for instance, the former has no articles but the latter has the definite "the" and the indefinite "a" and "an". Although the two languages have their respective characteristics which are not quite alike, still we can do the translation between them. It is because language is the direct reality of thought and the basic law of reality-thought-language which reflects the objective existence is in common to both English and Chinese, thus making it possible to express the same ideas and feelings in different languages. And quantities of translated works have long proved the possibility of translation.

And at the same time, we must admit that the languages in which various peoples think and express their thoughts are quite different in characteristics and usage. This is the problem that troubles the translators, including the veteran ones. No smatters can solve such a difficult problem. If one wants to be a qualified translator, one should, first of all, have a penetrating study and careful comparison of the similarities and differences between these two languages so that one may find the corresponding laws and methods in the translation between them, do translation effectively and ensure the quality of translation.

Corresponding laws do exist in translation. Take the following sentence as an example:

The horse is a useful animal.

This is a very simple sentence, and there is no question about word order. But the matter of how to deal with the two articles in the original is worth studying. Many beginners of English often, to our disappointment, translate the sentence like this:

这马是一个有用的动物

At first sight, the translation seems to be very faithful. Every word is translated into Chinese, but in fact it is one hundred percent wrong because it fails to convey the intrinsic sense of the original. No Chinese would say so in such a situation. The correct translation should be 马是一种有用的动物. Now the translation makes sense. But in order to achieve conciseness which is characteristic of the Chinese language, it ought to be further improved as 马是有用的动物. This shows that in accordance with the usage of Chinese both the definite and indefinite articles had better be omitted in the translation. By the same token, if we translate the sentence back into English, it will never do for us to render it word for word. But on the contrary, we are obliged to add the two articles required by the English usage. Of course, the English translation may also go without articles on condition that we use the two nouns in the plural form as in "Horses are useful animals".

In the course of the translation of this sentence, there are both addition and omission. They are not arbitrary, but depend on the intrinsic characteristics of the two languages under discussion. The Chinese "马是有用的动物" and the English "The horse is a useful animal" or "Horses are useful animals" are exact equivalents to each other in meaning and function. Thus the contradiction in translation gets to its dialectical unity and we may say that in the translation between English and Chinese the method of proper addition and proper omission is one of the corresponding laws, which can all be found out by a thorough and careful comparative study of these two languages.

The existence or non-existence of articles is a basic difference between English and Chinese as discussed in the above. Another basic difference existing between the two languages, as pointed out in *A Course of English-*

Chinese Chinese-English Translation by Prof. Gu Yanling and Prof. Xiong Xiling, lies in the fact that more verbs and fewer nouns and prepositions are used in Chinese than in English while more nouns and prepositions and fewer verbs are used in English than in Chinese. This phenomenon appears to be just a difference in the use of different parts of speech, but in fact it shows the special features of either language in diction, syntax, conventional ways of expression, etc. Secondly, as in the case of English, words in noun or adjective form are often used to express the idea of action, thus serving as verbs. Such words, in fact, are not very rare. Furthermore, collocations with such words, which bear the meaning and the character of a verb, as the key words, are to be found at every turn.

In order to illustrate what has just been said about the features in the above is true, let's take an example from *Theory and Examples of English-Chinese Translation* by Ti Xi et al. , which runs as follows:

Gates Avenue families carried their pails to the hydrant at the curb.
住在盖茨街的家家户户都得提小桶到街边水龙头去取水。

In the English sentence, there is only one verb, but in the Chinese there appear as many as six. Out of this comparative study, we can find another important method of translation—conversion of parts of speech.

From the analysis of the two simple sentences as shown in the above we see that even in translating very simple sentences there is so much worth studying. It goes without saying what profound knowledge and proficient skill it demands of the translator when he is to render a whole piece of writing. Anyhow, it will never do for one to translate word for word and mechanically adhere to the superficial similarities in words, phrases and grammatical structures. He must follow the scientific process from thorough understanding to accurate representation. That's to say, the translator must first comprehend the content and style of the whole work before he sets his pen to paper, and then creatively reproduce the original as it really is by using the corresponding laws and proper methods of translation in a flexible way so that the translation may be lifelike as well as intelligible.

After we have discovered the characteristics, differences and similarities of the two languages concerned, we can naturally find out their intrinsic laws and interrelation, thus bringing about some practicable methods of translation. Now we may well conclude that translation is indeed a science with its own peculiar laws and methods, a science related to lexicology, grammar, rhetoric and other branches of linguistics.

Translation Is an Art

Now let's turn to the point of translation as an art. There are quite a lot of people who lack a correct understanding of this. A popular fallacy is that translation is far easier than creation. Another fallacy is that translation is difficult to read or even unreadable. Since such misunderstandings exist, it is necessary and worthwhile for us to discuss the following questions:

1. Is translation really far easier than creation?

Writing is rather hard. That's quite true. Not everybody can write satisfactorily. A writer should have had rich experience in life and accumulated a great deal of source material.

What's more, he should be good at generalization and creation. Only thus, is it possible for him to produce a satisfactory work. And translation is not so easy as some non-professionals think it to be. We may state that it is rather difficult. A qualified translator must possess the following three qualifications:

First, he must be at home in the two languages concerned and quite familiar with their characteristics, similarities and differences.

Secondly, he must have a thorough understanding of the content, artistic features and style of the original and the historical background in which it was written.

Thirdly, he must know very well the basic principles and methods of translation and is experienced in practice.

"It often takes as long as ten days or even a whole month to establish a term in translation after repeated consideration and hesitation." This is a famous remark made many years ago by Yan Fu(1853-1921), and all the veteran translators, I think, must have shared the same feeling with him. Even Lenin(1870-1924) and Lu Xun(1881-1921) were no exceptions. Once, in order to find out a satisfactory explanation of a specific term, the former searched a minutely defined dictionary for as many as five times and the latter often broke into a cold sweat when he came across something difficult to translate. From this we can imagine how difficult it is to put a complete literary work into another language. The difficulty in translation just lies in the fact that both the content and the style are already existent in the original and as a result, you will have to do your best to reproduce them as they are in quite a different language. However great the obstacles are there in the work you are going to deal with, you can do nothing but manage to overcome them one by one. Sometimes you are even forced to produce coinages. For instance, the Chinese terms "资产阶级" and "无产阶级" were established long after the use of the transliterations of bourgeois "布尔乔亚" and proletariat "普罗列塔利亚". So is the case with the Chinese terms "民主" and "科学" through the transliterations of democracy "德谟克拉西" and science "赛恩斯". And something new took place in the syntax.

For instance, the conditional clause introduced by the conjunction 假若 and the concessional clause introduced by the conjunction 尽管 at the end of a complex sentence were remarkably unusual to the reading public when they first occurred. But now they are no longer strange to them.

Thus it can be seen that the process of translation is actually a process of re-creation and reproduction. Creation and translation have their respective difficulties and prerequisites. How can we favor one and disfavor the other?

As we all know, Lu Xun and Guo Moruo (1892-1978) were both great writers and great translators in the history of literature in China. So far as the question which, creation or translation, is more difficult is concerned, their opinion must be just and convincing. Let's listen to what they said about it.

In his *Titleless Essay* (1) in the second collection of *Qiejieting Essays*, Lu Xun says: "I have always thought that translation is easier than writing, for at least you needn't work out a plot. But as soon as you put pen to paper, you meet with obstacles. For instance, you can avoid a noun or a verb you cannot make good use of in writing, but you can't do so in translation. You will have to continue to rack your brains for it until you get dizzy as if you are feeling in your head for a key to open a box, but in vain." Even when he came to his old age, he still felt it to be difficult to do translation. He said: "The novel *Dead Souls* is very difficult to translate... as if you were doing a mere drudgery and had a hard time of it." (See *the Letter to Xiao Hong* on March 13, 1935) "I feel it to be a painful task to render Gogol. It seems as if I had an attack of some illness whenever I finish translating two chapters." (See *The Letter to Hu Feng* on June 8, 1935)[1]

In his speech *On Literary Translation* delivered at the National

Conference on the Work of Literary Translation, Guo Moruo points out: "Translation is a creative work. Good translation is equal to creation... Sometimes translation is more difficult than writing. A writer must have experience in life, but a translator has to experience what the author has experienced. And a translator must not only be proficient in his mother tongue but also have a very good foundation in a foreign language. Therefore, translation is not easier than writing at all."

To be fair, the conclusion should be as Lu Xun points out: "Creation is difficult and so is translation."[2]

2. Are translations really so difficult to read that you can hardly get through them?

Translations so difficult to read existed indeed both before liberation and after it. Strictly speaking, they are unqualified works of translation, but mere scribbles done by those who do not have the qualifications demanded of a worthy translator as mentioned under the topic *Translation Is a Science*. How could they make themselves understandable? However, such translations are rare. Among the translated works, most are good or basically good, and some of them are excellent. Among the Chinese translators quite a few are well-known, for example, Zhu Guangqian (1897-1986) and Lü Shuxiang. Their translations are so faithful and smooth that the readers feel much interested and can hardly part with them. So is the case with the successful translations in other countries. Engels (1820-1895) once praised Laura Lafargue's translation as "true and fluent". This shows that the difficulty in reading is not intrinsically related to translation. In fact, writings which are difficult to get through also exist. Whether a work is good or bad depends on the artistic level and technique of its author or translator.

Here I'd like to give two examples: one to illustrate improper translation and the other to illustrate successful translation.

Ex. 1. My hands are clean. I have no blood on them.

我的双手是清白的！它们上面没有沾满鲜血。

These two sentences are quoted from an article of translation published in a newspaper from an English article entitled *Judges Will Be Judged*.

It's evident that there are three defects in the translation of the two sentences.

The first defect is poor collocation.

The word "clean" may mean "清白" in Chinese sometimes. For instance, "He has a clean record" may be translated as "他历史清白". But according to the usage of Chinese, "清白" can never be used to describe a man's hand. As everybody knows, the word "clean" may also mean "干净" in Chinese. The translator should have chosen this meaning of the word in his translation. The correct translation of the first sentence, therefore, should be "我的双手是干净的". Besides, there is no need to change the period into an exclamation mark.

The second defect is improper wording.

"它们上面" is the word-for-word translation of the prepositional phrase "on them". The translation of the second sentence sounds somewhat unnatural. There are two ways to solve the problem. One is to repeat the noun "手". Thus, the translation will be "手上没沾鲜血". The other way is to omit the pronoun "它们". Thus, the translation will be "上面没沾鲜血". The meaning is clear enough.

Inaccuracy is the third defect.

The expression "沾满鲜血" would be all right if it were used in an affirmative sentence. For instance, one may say "那些法西斯分子手上沾

满了人民的鲜血". But it is improper to use it in a negative sentence, because the expression "没有沾满鲜血" may cause some misunderstanding. It may imply that there is, anyhow, still some blood on the hands of the person concerned. So the character 满 is superfluous.

For the reasons mentioned above and in accordance with the usage of the Chinese language, the following combination of the sentences into one is preferable:

我的双手是干净的,上面没沾鲜血。

Ex. 2. 匪军所至,杀戮人民,奸淫妇女,焚毁村庄,掠夺财物,无所不用其极。

Wherever the bandit troops went, they massacred and raped, burned and looted, and stopped at nothing.

The original is quoted from *The Selected Works of Mao Zedong* (1893-1976). The author exposes the outrages committed by the bandit troops. In the sentence four parallel phrases are used. They make the sentence terse, compact and forceful. The whole sentence is so smooth that it can be read in a single breath. The translation is well-done for it fully conveys the thoughts and feelings of the original and successfully retains the terseness, compactness and forcefulness in style. Here the translator makes use of two means. One is to use proper addition and proper omission. For instance, on the one hand, the translator purposefully omits the respective objects "the people", "the women", "the villages" and "the property", and on the other he tries to apply a rhetorical device, the formation of parallelisms with each two pairs connected by an "and". The other means is to use the transitive verbs "massacre", "rape", "burn" and "loot" intransitively. That's to say, they are used with their objects understood. Yet the meaning remains quite clear in the context. Of course, another translator may render the sentence in a different way. For instance, he may take the four transitive verbs as they are and have all their objects expressed and connected only by one "and". No doubt, such a rendering is grammatically right, but the above-mentioned stylistic characteristics of the original will be impaired to some degree.

Even the translation of the title of an essay or a book may show the translator's artistic level. Some titles are translated well, and some not. For instance, the free translation of the title of the novel *Oliver Twist* by Charles Dickens (1812-1870) as 《雾都孤儿》and that of the title of the play *Hamlet* by William Shakespeare (1564-1616) as 《王子复仇记》seem quite satisfactory for the former gives the reader a vivid image of both the hero and the background of the story and the latter tells him what the story is about although there is nothing to blame in the transliteration of 《奥列佛·推斯特》and that of 《哈姆莱特》. I have read a translation entitled 《我们是怎样过母亲节的》in a magazine. The title of the original essay is *How We Kept Mother's Day*. I venture to say that the title is very poorly translated. Two reasons can be given. One is that the English verb "keep" here does not mean "spend", but it means "celebrate". The other one is that in the narration of the author there is a note of mild satire which can be even felt in the original title, but the translator deprives the author of it by misrepresenting it. In my opinion, the title should be translated literally as 《我们是怎样庆祝母亲节的》.

From the analysis of the examples as mentioned above we can see that translation demands a broad and profound knowledge. In other words, a translator should have an understanding of literature and art, rhetoric and aesthetics; otherwise, he can hardly accomplish the task of reproduction of the original.

"All the first-class translations amount to creations".[3] That is true. Through a comparative study of some excellent translations against their originals and an earnest practice, we can find, I am sure, that "translations is an art, a bilingual art. It can reproduce the fine ideas of others just as painting does. However, it works not through color but through words, words of a different language."[4] A translator may be compared to an actor who can enter into the spirit of a character and represent him as lifelike as possible by means of his outstanding art of performance. The translator must first understand the content and style of the original thoroughly and profoundly, and then creatively and accurately reproduce it with the aid of his outstanding art of translations. Lu Xun maintained that translations must not only transmit the thoughts and feelings of the author but also contribute to the development of the reader's intelligence. "A translator must strive, on the one hand, to make his translations easy for the reader to understand, and on the other, to keep the charm and style of the author,"[5] he added.

Of the value and function of translations, Lu Xun had a high evaluation. He said, "Translations is not easier than casual creation. It has rendered service to the development of the new literature in China and done much good to the Chinese writers and readers." And he regarded translations as re-creation. According to A. S. Pushkin(1799-1837) the aim of translations is to reproduce an artistic work.

In accordance with what we have discussed in the above, now we can come to the following conclusion:

Whether a work of translations is good or bad, readable or not, it has nothing to do with translations itself; rather, it depends on the artistic level and technique of the translator. Whoever has a good command of translations both in theory and technique can, of course, offer satisfactory translations. It is because, as pointed out at the very beginning of this lecture, translations is not only a science with its own laws and methods but also an art of reproduction and re-creation.

Notes

1. *Lu Xun—An Outstanding Translator* by Guo Baoquan, *Translators Journal* No. 4, 1981.
2. *A New Way in the World* in *An Anthology of Essays Not Included in My Previous Collections* by Lu Xun.
3. *Preface* to *The Art of Translation* by Zhang Qichun, Kaiming Book Store, 1949.
4. *Introduction to Translation, its Principles and Technique* by Lu Dianyang, Shidai Publishing House, 1958.
5. *Titleless Essay*(1) in the *Collection of Qiejieting Essays* by Lu Xun.

Lecture Two   Principles of Translation

The so-called principles of translation and criteria of translation are actually the two sides of the same thing. The former lays emphasis on the translator, who should follow them while translating, whereas the latter on the reader or critic, who may use the criteria to evaluate a translation. Talking of the importance and double function of the criteria of translation, a theorist puts it quite well, saying that the criteria of translation function as a plumb-line for measuring the professional level of translation and as a goal set for translators to strive after. Hence, the formulation of definite and normal criteria of translation has a momentous bearing on its gusto and quality. In this lecture, I'd like to keep to the stand of a translator to put forth the three characters "信达切" (faithfulness, expressiveness and closeness) as a set of principles for reference.

In the recent decades, whenever the question of principles of translation is under discussion, the three characters "信达雅" (faithfulness, expressiveness and elegance) formulated by Yan Fu in his *Introductory Remarks* to his translation《天演论》are thought of and supported as the one and only maxim all translators must observe.

Yan Fu made contributions to the Enlightenment of the bourgeoisie in China. Kang Youwei (1858-1927), Liang Qichao (1873-1929), Tan Sitong

(1865-1898) and others were the leading spirits of the Reform Movement of 1898. Yan Fu was among them. "They were engaged in writing articles to found the theory of Constitutional Reform and Modernization or in translating Western works to propagate the bourgeois ideology of Europe. Besides, they founded learned societies, set up schools and published newspapers. All these things sprang like bamboo shoots after a spring rain in Jiangsu, Hunan, Hebei, Guangdong and other provinces. It produced a great impact on the traditional Chinese ideology. Many patriotic intellectuals were involved and a whole generation was influenced."[1] Although the Reform Movement of 1898 didn't last long and failed in the end, yet judging from its significance in the emancipation of the mind, it may still be said to have made some preparations for the Revolution of 1911 under the leadership of Sun Zhongshan(1866-1925).

So far as the introduction of Western works into China is concerned, the contributions made by Yan Fu were most remarkable. His translation of the first two chapters of T. H. Huxley's *Evolution and Ethics and Other Essays* entitled《天演论》was first carried in the *National News*(《国闻报》), which started publication at Tianjin in 1897. "Shortly after the Sino-Japanese War of 1894-1895, the big powers began to occupy various ports of China by force, which badly upset the Chinese people. The translation expounded the generally acknowledged truth of the law of the jungle, the survival of the fittest and the preservation of species through unceasing efforts. The book brought a new hope to people who had felt disappointed and disheartened. It became popular with the whole country and was regarded as the best of the translated works. It played an important role in the Reform Movement. The Shanghai *News of Current Affairs*(《时务报》) and the Tianjin *National News* held the leading position of public opinion respectively in the South and North. The influence of Yan Fu's thoughts was no less than that of Liang Qichao's."[2]

But the three principles formulated by Yan Fu for translation, especially some of the methods related with them, seem to be not one hundred percent applicable to the work of translation today. It is necessary to make a re-evaluation of them. In my opinion, we should neither negate nor affirm them as a whole without any criticism or revision. The correct attitude towards them is to accept them critically and absorb what is still useful to us. For convenience sake in our discussion, some extracts from the first three points of Yan Fu's *Introductory Remarks* to his translation of Huxley's work will be made as follows:

1. In translation there are three difficulties, namely, faithfulness, expressiveness and elegance. It is already very difficult to achieve faithfulness. Without expressiveness, mere faithfulness would mean work to no avail. This shows that the latter is quite important in translation... The translation must express the profound meaning of the original. As for the order of words and that of sentences in the original, there is no need for the translator to stick to them. He may make some change where necessary. But in meaning, the translation must conform to the original. I label this book of mine not as a translation but a transmission of ideas so that I may easily develop and elaborate the ideas therein. In fact, my method is not orthodox...

2. Substantives in English are often immediately explained by postpositive attributive words, phrases or clauses... and sentences are then constructed by adding the necessary parts to make the meaning complete. The syntax of the English language is not quite like that of the Chinese. In the former, sentences may contain as few as two or three words or as many

as scores or even hundreds. If the complex sentences were translated word for word, they would become unintelligible. If improper omissions were done, the original meaning might be impaired. In this case, the translator must have a thorough comprehension of the sense and spirit of the whole text. Then he will be able to render it well and satisfactorily. As for those texts that are hard to understand themselves, he will have to give supplementary remarks where necessary so as to render the corresponding foregoing statements understandable. This is done to achieve expressiveness, or rather faithfulness.

3. *The Book of Changes* says that faithfulness is the first thing in wording. Confucius(551 B. C. -479 B. C.) states what speech requires is only expressiveness. Again he said that language without literary grace can not go far and wide. All these three requirements as mentioned above are indispensable both to writing and to translating. Thus elegance must be achieved in addition to faithfulness and expressiveness so that the translation may go far and wide. Besides, it is easy to achieve expressiveness in translating the profound meaning and refined words by means of the vocabulary and syntax used before the Han Dynasty, but difficult to do that in the so-called vulgar modern language...

From the above three quotations, we can easily see that Yan was erudite in scholarship, elegant in diction and much experienced in translation. But so far as the methods of translation put forward by him are concerned, judging from the present point of view, some of them are not applicable to the translation in its true sense. Let's have a further discussion of them:

First of all, we'll talk about the nature of his translation.

Just as Yan Fu recognized himself, his "translation" of Huxley's book was merely a transmission of ideas, a method he described as "not orthodox". That is to say, his so-called translated work is not worthy of the name of translation in the strict sense of the word. It can only be called incomplete translation or editing-translation. It will become evident as soon as we have a look at the original and translation of the first sentence of the Introduction to the book.

The original:

It may be safely assumed that, two thousand years ago, before Caesar (100 B. C. -44 B. C.) set foot in southern Britain, the whole countryside visible from the windows of the room in which I write, was in what is called "the state of nature."

Yan's translation:

赫胥黎独处一室之中,在英伦之南,背山而面野,槛外诸境,历历如在几下。乃悬想两千年前,当罗马大将恺撒来到时,此间有何景物。计惟有天造草昧,人功未施。

In Yan's translation, we can find that there are both the change of person—the change of the first person "I" into the third person "Huxley" and the addition of meaning as "罗马大将(the Roman general)," "背山 (with hills at the back)" etc. It is impermissible to do so for the strict translation, especially for the translation of literary works. Otherwise, unfaithfulness would be caused.

Secondly, the question about the order of words and that of sentences.

One is not altogether inexcusable to make some changes in the order of words and that of sentences when necessary while doing the so-called editing-translation. But so far as true translation is concerned, it is only permissible to make some changes in the word order in accordance with the intrinsic laws existing in the original and target languages, e. g.

Out rushed the man and his wife. (Jespersen)

那个人和他的妻子冲出去了。

If we don't make a thorough change of the word order in this simple English sentence, we can hardly render it into legible Chinese. As to the order of sentences, we must be quite careful. If it means the order of clauses in a complex sentence, it will have to be rearranged sometimes, e.g.

Gone are the days when they ran wild in our country and lorded it over the people.

他们在我国胡作非为、对人民称王称霸的日子已经一去不复返了。

If it refers to sentences with full stops (logically speaking Yan Fu must have meant such sentences), in my opinion, the order of such sentences shouldn't be changed at will and there isn't much necessity to do so, because a sentence with a period at the end can express a complete meaning in any language. So long as you translate sentence by sentence, a coherent paragraph will be made. Of course, you should have the whole text in mind at the same time.

The principle that the order of sentences shouldn't be changed at random is always true when applied to the translation from English into Chinese. But as you do translation from Chinese into English, you will have to take into consideration the feature of well-knitness of English sentences and may well change some commas, semicolons and colons into full stops where necessary. Since space is limited, only one example is given as follows:

我们的民族将再也不是一个被人侮辱的民族了,我们已经站起来了。(毛选五卷第一篇《中国人民站起来了》)

Ours will no longer be a nation subject to insult and humiliation. We have stood up. (*English Version of the Selected Works of Mao Zedong*: The

Chinese People Have Stood Up).

Judging from the feature of the structure of the English syntax, it is all right for the English version to divide the original one sentence into two. Otherwise, looseness in sentence construction might arise. However, the order of the two English sentence remains the same as that of the two clauses with no conjunction in the original Chinese. On the contrary, there is, sometimes, the necessity of combining some simple English sentences into one Chinese sentence, e. g.

We have utterly lost touch. We have nothing at all to say. We gaze at each other as dumb animals gaze at human beings. (*Seeing People Off* by Max Beerbohm.)

These three sentences may have the following two different translation:

1. 我们完全失去了联系。我们根本无话可说。我们就像不会讲话的牲畜呆呆地望人那样地你望着我我望着你。

2. 我们完全失去了联系,根本无话可说,就像不会讲话的牲畜呆呆地望人那样地你望着我我望着你。

The first is a sentence-by-sentence translation and the second a combination of the three original sentences into one. Both are faithful to the content and read smoothly. But comparatively speaking, the former seems and sounds wordy whereas the latter concise. It's because the same subjects are seldom repeated in accordance with the Chinese usage except for an emphasis on purpose.

Thirdly, the question of making supplementary remarks where necessary so as to render the corresponding foregoing statements understandable.

Yan Fu said this in his *Introductory Remarks* and put it into practice in the process of "translating" Huxley's work. For instance "罗马大将"(the

Roman general) and "背山" (with hills at the back) did appear in his so-called translation of the very first sentence of the book. Besides, the reader can often find inserted in his "translation" "Yan's note", which expresses his own points of view and constitutes a personal style of his. But so far as true translation is concerned, such a method should not be adopted. No matter how difficult the original is, the translator must first have a thorough comprehension of the sense and spirit of the whole text and then translate it as it is. And at the same time he must always pay enough attention to the coherence of the text, namely, the coherence between sentences and paragraphs so that the translation may read as an integral whole. Whenever he comes across words or expressions which are really difficult to reproduce as they are, footnotes may be added to have them further illustrated. As for "the translator's note" inserted in the text of translation, it's unnecessary at all.

Fourthly, the question of what kind of language is better in translation.

About this Yan Fu maintained that the vocabulary and syntax existing prior to the Han Dynasty should be used in translation and he was as good as his word in his practice because he thought that only by so doing could it be easy to better express the profound meaning and refined words and help the translation go far and wide. This viewpoint of his is somewhat subjective for we know that things are constantly developing, and so is the language which varies with things. The Chinese language had already developed into the modern vernacular in which *Water Margin* and *A Dream of the Red Mansions* were written respectively by Shi Nan'an (c. 1296-1370) and Cao Xueqin (? -1763 or 1764) long before Yan was born. The minute description of the scenes and vivid depiction of the characters in the above two literary masterpieces are quite well-known to the reader. It shows that the modern Chinese vernacular is very expressive. What Yan translated was a work written in modern English. Why should he have chose the vocabulary and syntax prevailing before the Han Dynasty in his translation? Couldn't the modern Chinese vernacular express such profound meaning of such refined words as in the *Evolution*? But in fact the modern complicated things and ideas can be better expressed in the modern Chinese vernacular instead of the classical Chinese. Therefore, Qu Qiubai (1899-1935) said: "Translation calls for the absolute correctness and pure Chinese vernacular, thus introducing the language of new culture to the reading public." (See *Correspondence on Translation*, *The Complete Works of Lu Xun*, Vol. 4) Furthermore, some new terms must be coined, such as "无产阶级" for proletariat and "人民民主专政" for people's dictatorship, especially the names for chemical elements. Could they be found in the classical Chinese language? Take the term "社会主义" (socialism) for example. It appeared in *Xinmin Cong Bao* (《新民丛报》) in 1902. The Science Press retranslated Huxley's book *Evolution and Ethics* in the modern vernacular Chinese for the reading public and published it in 1971, for nowadays not so many readers can understand Yan's translation fully, to say nothing of appreciating it. His use of the classical Chinese demonstrates that he was rather conservative on the question of language. He once wrote in a letter: "My translations are not intended for school-children, but for scholars who had read a lot of ancient books. I am ashamed to follow the style of writing in which articles have been published in the press."

Although there is something unsatisfactory in the three-character principle put forward by Yan Fu, yet judging from the historical background we should acknowledge that he was an outstanding forerunner in the field of translation and made great contributions both in theory and practice. The shortcoming found in his principle is due to his historical limitations. The analysis and criticism as made in the above aim at better absorbing the essence of his theory.

So much for Yan Fu's three-character principle. Here I would like to introduce the three "laws of translation" formulated by Alexander Fraser Tytler(1749-1814), an English theoretician, in his *Essay on the Principles of Translation*:[4]

1. The Translation should give a complete transcript of the ideas of the original work.

2. The style and manner of writing should be of the same character with that of the original.

3. The Translation should have the ease of the original composition.

Strictly speaking, the ideological content, the linguistic representation and the stylistic characteristic of a piece of literary writing constitute an integral entirety, and a literary translation should be an accurate reproduction of it as a whole. But for convenience, the whole may be divided into three aspects—content, representation and style. It's not only practicable but also reflects the actual process of translation which is being done by a serious and dutiful translator.

This process of translation consists of three steps:

The first step. The translator should read the whole piece of writing carefully, try to grasp the ideological content the author wants to express and make clear not only the literal meanings but also the implications between the lines.

The second step. Owing to the fact that not all the usages of the two languages concerned are alike, there may be the following different cases in wording: (1) Sometimes the translator can find expressions which are entirely equivalent to each other, e. g. the English idiom "Strike while the iron is hot"and the Chinese "趁热打铁". (2)Sometimes he has to change the image. For instance, the English idiom "as lean as a rake"had better be translated as "骨瘦如柴"instead of the literal rendering "瘦得像耙", for the former retains the vividness of expression by substituting one image for another and conforms to the usage of the target language whereas the latter goes against it though the original image is kept. (3) Sometimes the translator will have to make a change in the surface value of some words so that he may get a suitable representation which can express their true implication. For instance, the English proverb "Every dog has his day"can only be flexibly rendered as "人人都有自己得意的时候", the preferable "dynamic equivalence", according to Eugene A. Nida, for the original. If we should translate the proverb word forword, naturally, it would not make sense at all.

The third step. The translator must have a good grasp of the author's portrayal of his characters and style of writing. Only thus can he have a reliable basis for his choice of words and making of sentences. Both the choice and arrangements of words and sentences are based on the comparatively satisfactory reproduction of the original images and style. That is to say, the same words should be rendered in different ways according to the status of characters and style of writing in the original. Take the English saying "More haste, less speed"for example. If these words are said by a less-educated character or a writer with a simple style, you may well render them as something like"越快就越慢". If they are said by a well-educated character, you'd better render them into the classical Chinese expression "欲速则不达". Otherwise, the original images and style will probably be impaired.

A conscientious and responsible translator must get fully prepared for translation through these three steps before he sets his pen to paper. If he does not take the three steps into consideration, and begins his translation word for word as soon as he comes across a piece of writing, be can hardly succeed for he goes against the principles of translation. Just as Belinsky (1811-1848), a Russian critic, pointed out, "To be close to the original is not to change letters, but to convey the spirit of the original." And Chernyshevsky (1828-1889) said more definitely that the word-for-word translation couldn't get close to the original, but on the contrary would make it more difficult to understand. Facts have proved their viewpoints to be true.

How does the word-for-word translation come into being, L. N. Sobelev, a Russian theorist, puts it well in an essay entitled *Translate Images by Means of Images*, "The word-for-word translation is generally derived from the translator's ignorance of the translation technique and theory and his incompetence".

With regard to the principles of translation, the first two of Yan Fu's, namely, faithfulness and expressiveness may be carried forward whereas all the three laws expounded by Tytler can be accepted, for they are comprehensive and practical.

Referring to the opinions of the two theorists as mentioned above and absorbing the quintessence of their principles, I venture to propose the three characters "信达切" (faithfulness, expressiveness and closeness) as a set of principles of translation for reference, which seem more comprehensive and practical. They may be defined as follows:

1. Faithfulness—to be faithful to the content of the original;

2. Expressiveness—to be as expressive as the original;

3. Closeness—to be as close to the original style as possible.

What I mean by being faithful to the content of the original amounts to what Yan Fu meant by "the translation conforming to the original in meaning" and what Tytler meant by the law "that the translation should give a complete transcript of the ideas of the original." This is, of course, the first important principle of translation. The translator ought to convey the author's ideas faithfully and exactly. He has no right to alter the meaning of the original to suit his own taste. Lu Xun pointed out, "Translation does not tolerate any mistakes." Even for the so-called "bianyi(编译)" or "yishu(译述)" (incomplete translation or editing-translation), strictly speaking, it should not go against or deviate from the central idea of the original. It is only permitted "not to stick to the order of words and sentences" and "make some supplementary remark where necessary so as to render the corresponding foregoing statements understandable."

Having achieved his faithfulness to the content of the original, the translator must aim at making his translation as expressive as the original, for it is intended for the reading public. If one's translation is not readable and understandable, what's the use of it? It's just as Yan Fu said, "Without expressiveness, mere faithfulness would mean work to no avail."

During the debate on the principles of translation in the 1930's appeared two opposite schools. One said: "Smoothness (which is corresponding to the expressiveness as mentioned above) is preferable to faithfulness in translation". The other argued: "Faithfulness is preferable to smoothness." Following the former, a translator might sacrifice some of the content of the original. Acting according to the latter, he might make his translation not quite readable somewhere. This has been demonstrated by some of their translations. We should take it as a lesson. So long as we work hard at the practice and theory of translation, we can finally unify these two seemingly contradictory principles of faithfulness and smoothness. A great number of brilliant translators have already set good examples for us to learn from.

We may say that faithfulness and smoothness (or expressiveness) are the two rudimentary principles every translator must observe.

Only after a translator achieves the faithfulness in content and smoothness or expressiveness in wording can he further pursue the closeness in style.

Why should I not adopt the principle of elegance formulated by Yan Fu but replace it with that of closeness? It is because elegance means gracefulness, and in fact it is only one of various styles. Evidently, we should not make all our translations elegant in style. The original style must be exactly reproduced as it is. The word closeness is a neutral term which may be applied to all kinds of style. Zhang Qichun (1913-1967) discussed the various styles of the Chinese and foreign literature. He said: "Style is the art of representation... it is a revelation of individuality. For instance... the style of Li Bai (701-762) is elegant and forceful whereas that of Du Fu (712-770) profound and thoughtful."[5] The style of Henry James (1843-1916) and that of Ernest M. Hemingway (1899-1961) are also quite different. The former is wordy and obscure while the latter brief and implicit.

Of this question, Buffon (1707-1788), a French naturalist, made the well-known statement that style is the man. (Le style, c'est l'homme.) That's to say, style varies with authors. Some are elegant in style, some vulgar, some flowery and some plain. A translator should try his best to make the style of his translation as close as possible to that of the original.

Specifically speaking, if the original style is elegant, of course, the translation style should be elegant, too. If the original style is not elegant, the translation style shouldn't be elegant, either.

Style represents the essential characteristics of each writer's writing. Various writers have various styles. This is already a universally acknowledged truth. For instance, the essential characteristic of the political essays written by Lenin is to make use of allusions and stir up the reader's thinking in images and that of Lu Xun's miscellaneous essays is characteristically brief and pithy, sharp and sarcastic. The translator must strive to reproduce their respective characteristics in writing, i. e. , style besides being faithful to the original content and making his representation expressive. Only thus can his work be called translation which conforms to the principles—faithfulness in content, expressiveness in wording and closeness in style.

Now we'll have a further discussion, in the light of dialogues in literary works, of the impropriety of the character 雅 (elegance) as a common principle applied to style. It's undeniable that the dialogues of the characters either in a play or in a novel are quite different in linguistic style due to their status. Such being the case, the translator should do his best to retain the tone and manner of speaking of all the characters concerned. He should not make the vulgar elegant and vice versa. If we put all the vulgar expressions into elegant ones, the images of the characters in literary works will be greatly impaired, because the typicalness or typicality is usually reflected, on the one hand, in their actions and, on the other, in their words. Suppose in a literary work you are going to translate, you come across such vulgar expressions as "Damned, you son of a bitch, go to the devil!" How could you make them elegant in your translation? They should be rendered as they are into something like "该死,你这个狗崽子;见鬼去吧!" Otherwise, you may be criticized for being unfaithful to the original.

Generally speaking, vulgar expressions are often found in novels and plays. Sometimes, even poems can't exclude them.

We are all familiar with poems by Mao Zedong. Now let's take a quotation from him. There is a very vulgar line in his poem *The Dialogue Between Two Birds*. The line runs as follows:勿须放屁! Is the expression "放屁" itself elegant or vulgar? Evidently, it's vulgar. How should a translator render it into English? Should he turn the vulgarity into elegance? He shouldn't, of course. He has no right to do so. He is obliged to keep the vulgarity as it is. Compare the two following English versions of this line. One version is "Stop your windy nonsense!" and the other "None of your shit!" The latter is good for it is as vulgar as the line is in the original poem. So far as the former is concerned, it is not so good. Two reasons may be given for this remark of mine. One, the expression "windy nonsense" is unidiomatic. We have often come across the expression "sheer nonsense" for emphasis in English, but most probably we can hardly find such an expression as "windy nonsense". It is a coinage made by the translator. It won't be accepted by people. Two, the expression "windy nonsense" is illogical. The adjective "windy" which is suggestive of wind, means insubstantial or empty and the noun "nonsense" meaningless words or empty talk. Obviously, the adjective "windy" is redundant or superfluous. "Stop your nonsense" may be said, naturally, but it doesn't correspond to the original "勿须放屁" in style because it is not so strong or emphatic as the original.

Concerning style, Jonathan Swift (1667-1745), a famous English writer, gave style a very concise definition:

"Proper words in proper places make the true definition of a style." What he said is applicable to writing, and to translation as well.

A translator must work hard at the closeness to the original style and the reproduction of the original images if he wants to make his translation worthy of appreciation. But such a success is not easily achieved. We can see the difficulty in the criticism made by M. Arnold (1822-1888) of the several English versions of *Iliad* and *Odyssey* by Homer(9th-8th? B.C.):

"Homer is rapid in his movement, Homer is plain in his words and style, Homer is simple in his ideas, Homer is noble in his manner. Cowper renders him ill because he is slow in his movement, and elaborate in his style; Pope renders him ill because he is artificial both in his style and in his words; Chapman renders him ill because he is fantastic in his ideas; Mr Newman renders him ill because he is odd in his words and ignoble in his manner. All four translators diverge from their original at other points besides those named; but it is at the points thus named that their divergence is greatest..."[6]

It is not easy to satisfactorily realize the three principles of translation—faithfulness, expressiveness and closeness, indeed. But they should be put into practice by every possible means. Otherwise, the goal of the translation that reproduces an artistic work as Belinski pointed out can never be attained. Only by satisfactorily realizing these principles mentioned above can the translator come up to the standard set by Belinski: "Translation is an art which perfectly reproduces a literary work of another nation in one's own native tongue." Only by so doing can the translation be faithful to the original.

If he hopes to satisfactorily realize the principles of faithfulness, expressiveness and closeness, a translator of literature must have enough linguistic and literary attainments. As early as 1852, N. A. Dobrolyubov (1836-1861), a Russian critic, pointed out, "It goes without saying that the language he wants to translate from is the one he must have a good command of. That's to say, he should master the minute distinctions of words in meaning and allocation and those of the small particles which are of no much importance themselves. Besides, he must be versed in the target language. He can write it not only easily and fluently but also correctly and gracefully. He can make use of all the wealth of the target language and avoid its incorrect wording and impure vocabulary while exactly conveying the original ideas. As a result, the reader can hardly find anything stiff in the translator's work." From the critic's remarks, we can see that a literary translator must, on the one hand, have a thorough grasp of a foreign language and, on the other, be proficient in his mother tongue. What's more, he should possess some knowledge of linguistics and literature. In his essay entitled *Struggle for the Realistic Translation*, Ivan Kashkin says that a translator "must first of all make clear the basic rhetorical features of the authors through a literary analysis theoretically and point out their linguistic characteristics through an analysis from the angle of linguistics. And then the decisive step is to choose the necessary means of expression according to the yardstick of literary requirements..."

In the course of the realization of the three principles, it is extremely difficult to achieve "the closeness to the original style". However, we translators should meet difficulties head on instead of shrinking back from them. Mao Zedong pointed out long ago, "It is not easy to learn a language well. The mastery of it calls for hard work." We can imagine how difficult it is to translate satisfactorily, for it is related to two different languages, the original and the target. In his speech at the National Conference on Literary

Translation held at Beijing in 1954, Mao Dun (1896-1981) said that the translator should make a strict scientific study of the original work and that this is a must while translating it. And at the same time, in the process of translation, he must be careful and serious in the choice of words and making of sentences and in the coherence of the whole text in accordance with the principles of faithfulness, expressiveness and closeness so as to retain the charm and style of the original.

To sum up, the Trinity Principle of Faithfulness, Expressiveness and Closeness I put forward in this lecture actually constitutes an organic entirety, because "closeness" always exhibits itself in the style. In "closeness" lie "faithfulness" and "expressiveness" and vice versa. "Faithfulness" is the prerequisite of "expressiveness" and "closeness"; "expressiveness" the representation of "faithfulness" and "closeness"; and "closeness" the very picture of "faithfulness" and "expressiveness". This three-in-one principle can never be overemphasized.

Notes

1. Yang Tongliang and Wang Junyi, *Comments on Qi Benyu's Article* entitled *Patriotism or National Betrayal*, *Guangming Daily*, Dec. 1, 1976.
2. Fan Wenlan, *Modern History of China*.
3. Yan Fu, *A Letter to Liang Qichao on His Translation of Inquiry into the Nature and Causes of the Wealth* by Adam Smith.
4. Alexander Fraser Tytler, *Essay on the Principles of Translation*.
5. Zhang Qichun, *The Art of Translation*.
6. Mattew Arnold, *On Translating Homer* in his book *Essays—Literary and Critical*.

Lecture Three   Faithfulness of Translation

    Faithfulness is an important question of the principle of translation. All theorists maintain that translation should be faithful to the original and no translator thinks that his translation is unfaithful to it. But in reality, some translators achieve faithfulness in their translation, and others don't. Evidently, it depends on whether the translator understands faithfulness correctly. Strictly speaking, faithfulness is the generalization of the three principles of translation—faithfulness, expressiveness and closeness. That's to say, true translation demands that the translator be faithful to the content, language and style of the original at the same time. By faithfulness to the content and style of the original the translator must be true to its whole text, not to metaphrase individual phrases or sentences. Only by thus doing, can he come up to the standard of translation which conveys not only the meaning but also the spirit of the original work. If he doesn't take this into consideration, the result will go contrary to his wishes. He could never achieve faithfulness of translation, should he lack a correct understanding of it, disregard the internal relations in the text, but mechanically sticks to the literal meaning of isolated words. Let's have a discussion of how to translate the following expressions or sentences in accordance with the principle of translation—faithfulness.

1. No, I didn't.

This is a sentence consisting of only three simple words. It looks so simple that it does not seem to be worth mentioning. But judging from the angle of translation, we should make a point of it. This expression may be used to answer either an affirmative question or a negative question. Suppose someone asks you "Did you go to see the film last night?" If you didn't, you may answer, "No, I didn't." When you are asked "Didn't you go to see the film last night?" You may give the same answer if you stayed at home. You would be wrong if you made no difference in translating the English sentence "No, I didn't ". The word "no" is defined as "不" in all the English-Chinese dictionaries. But this definition is entirely useless in the translation of the two above-mentioned answers. In the first answer, the word "no" must be omitted in the Chinese version. The proper translation should be: "我没有去" or simply "没有去". In the second, it must be thought of just in the opposite direction as "是的". Can you find the annotation "是的" in any English-Chinese dictionary? I'm sure you can't. Yet the Chinese "是的" is exactly the equivalent for the English word "no" in this specific situation.

From the discussion of the translation of this simple sentence, we can clearly realize what faithfulness is in essence and that all dictionaries are not reliable all the time. Just as Mencius (c. 372-c. 289B. C.) pointed out long ago, "It's better to have no books than to believe all of them blindly at any time." We must take a critical attitude in using dictionaries and other reference books and have our own judgment.

2. They call themselves Englishmen; and they are afraid to fight.

This is a sentence taken from one of the plays by George Bernard Shaw (1856-1950). If you translate the conjunction in its ordinary sense, your translation would be illogical and thus unfaithful to the original, because this "and" actually means "but". The proper translation should be:

他们都称自己为英国人,(而他们)却害怕打仗。

In Shaw's eyes, Englishmen are brave. No Englishman should be afraid to fight. Whoever is afraid does not deserve the name of Englishman. He looks down upon those who are afraid to fight.

3. One step further and you will be lost.

This is a commonly-used sentence-pattern. In form, it is a compound sentence connected by the co-ordinating conjunction "and", but in sense it's a complex sentence. The first elliptical clause "One step further" functions as a subordinate clause of condition and the second clause connected by "and" as the main clause of result. The sentence can be transformed as follows:

If you take (or move) one step further, you will be lost. Thus in translating this sentence, we may make use of the Chinese sentence pattern ("只要……就……")" to translate it as.

(只要)再走一步,你就完蛋。

4. I am in good health now and I can resume my work.

Just like Example 3, it is a compound sentence connected by the co-ordinating conjunction "and" in form, but a complex sentence of cause and result in sense. The "and" here is equivalent to the subordinating conjunction "so that". Therefore, the sentence really means: I am in good health now so that I can resume my work. The proper translation should be:

我现在身体很好,(因此我)可以恢复工作了。

5. I cannot keep these flowers alive and I have watered them well, too.

Similarly, we should not understand this "and" in its usual sense as "而且" or "并且". We must know that the coordinating conjunction "and" actually functions as the subordinating conjunction "though" or "although". So the proper translation should be:

这些花,虽然我也好好浇了,但仍然养不活。

Examples 2 to 5 are all sentences linked up by the coordinating conjunction "and". There seems to be some contradiction between the syntactic analysis and translation. We may solve the problem by interpreting such linguistic phenomena in the following way:

When we do syntactic analysis, we may still call the sentences compound ones connected by the coordinating conjunction "and" in grammatical structure and at the same time we must make a further explanation that the word "and" in the four sentences as mentioned above specifically and functionally introduces various kinds of clauses, for instance, in 2 it introduces a coordinate clause of contrast, in 3 a main clause of result, in 4 an adverbial clause of result and in 5 an adverbial clause of concession.

So far as translation is concerned, it is determined by the true meaning conveyed in the sentences. We should never be perplexed by the appearance of any seemingly simple word. Context and implication must be thoroughly studied and grasped. Otherwise, you might be led astray by a very simple word. In all these four sentences, if you insisted on translating the conjunction "and" as "而且" or "并且" as usual, on the one hand you couldn't make yourself understood and on the other it clearly shows that you don't quite understand the sentences. How can you talk of the faithfulness of translating them?

6. It never rains but it pours[1].

There is a "but" in the sentence. How do you explain it? Does it still mean "但是"? No. It is equivalent to "unless" or "if... not", introducing a subordinate clause of condition. The sentence may be used in two different senses. In its literal sense, it refers to weather and means that it never rains unless it pours(if it does not pour). It may be translated as

不下则已，一下就是倾盆大雨。

In its metaphorical sense, the sentence refers to misfortune and means that misfortunes do not come singly, in other words, one misfortune comes on the neck of another. It may be translated as

祸不单行。e. g.

John fell ill, then his brothers and sisters all fell ill. It never rains but it pours.

约翰病了，接着他的弟兄和姐妹都病了。真是祸不单行啊！

7. The boy sat down to do his homework when he saw his playmate coming.

Generally speaking, "when" is a subordinating conjuction introducing an adverbial clause of time. But here in this sentence its meaning and function are equivalent to "and then suddenly". That's to say, the word "when" actually introduces a coordinate clause. According to the characteristic of terseness of the Chinese language, we had better omit "and then". However, it's preferable to have the implication of the suddenness in the occurrence of the succeeding event expressed in our translation so that the spirit of the original may be fully conveyed. The sentence should be translated as "那个男孩坐下去做家庭作业，突然看见自己的玩耍伙伴来了。" In the first clause, the predicate verb "sat" is in the past tense. Sometimes, the predicate verb is in the past progressive. For example, I was writing a letter when the light went out. The corresponding Chinese is "（当时）我正在写信，灯突然熄了"。And the phrasal verb predicate "be about to do something" is often used in such a sentence pattern, e. g. They were about to start when it began to rain heavily. The corresponding Chinese is "他们正要动身,突然下起雨来了".

One sentence more to illustrate the special use of the conjunction "when":

Augustus returns and is about to close the door when the voice of the clerk is heard from below.

This sentence quoted from a play written by George Bernard Shaw is of the same sentence pattern as just discussed above. What we should pay attention to is the use of the present tense. Why should the predicate verbs be used in the present tense? It's because they are used in the stage directions of that play. As you know, all stage directions are represented in the present tense. We may translate the sentence like this:

奥古斯塔回来,正要关门,突然从下面传来了那个办事员的声音。

In the three following sentences, please observe how to translate the who-clauses.

8. Don't you feel it strange that she should be so much ungrateful to Jack, who did so much for her when she was in poverty?

In form, the who-clause in this sentence is a non-restrictive attributive clause introduced by the relative pronoun "who", but in sense it is an adverbial clause of concession. The relative pronoun "who" is functionally equivalent to "although he". Thus the sentence may be rendered as follows:

虽然杰克在她穷困时帮了她那么多的忙,她却对杰克如此忘恩负义,难道你不觉得奇怪吗?

9. Some teachers of English will be engaged from America who should strengthen our teaching work.

In form the who-clause in this sentence is a restrictive attributive clause for there is no comma to separate the relative pronoun from its antecedent, but in sense it is an adverbial clause of purpose. "who should" is equivalent to "so that they might". The sentence may be translated as:

我们将从美国聘请一些英语教师来加强教学工作。

10. Her refusal to obey him greatly incensed him who had never met that kind of opposition before.

In form this who-clause is a restrictive attributive clause, too, but in fact it functions as an adverbial clause of reason. The relative pronoun "who" may be replaced by "as he". Thus the sentence may be translated as follows:

她拒绝服从他,这使他大为生气,因为他从来没有遭到过那样的反对。

All the above who-clauses are a special kind of attributive clauses. They are called semi-adverbial by R. W. Zandvoort in his book entitled *A Handbook of English Grammar*. In my opinion, we may also call them adverbial-attributive clauses. The term means that in function they are adverbial clauses and in form they are attributive ones.

11. For the moment, we are discussing nothing but the adoption of agenda[2].

Someone put the sentence into Chinese as "我们目前讨论的是通过议程,决非其他的什么". What do you think of the translation? Is it quite right? Not quite, I think, because it does not sound idiomatic in Chinese. The problem lies in the fact that the translator has not a profound understanding of the idiomatic English expression "nothing but". The expression is interchangeable with the adverb "only". It corresponds to the Chinese "只是" or "只不过是". For instance, the Chinese sentence "他只不过是个白痴" may be translated by means of the corresponding expression "nothing but" as "He is nothing but an idiot". The No. 11 sentence may be improved like this:

我们目前正在讨论的只(不过)是通过议程。

12. The origin of the shells was Portuguese: that is to say they came from Portuguese Guinea or Guinea (Bissau).³

Consider how to translate the conjunction "or" in the sentence. You would commit a mistake if you translate the word "or" as "或" or "或者". Why? Because Portuguese Guinea and Guinea(Bissau) refer to one and the same country instead of two different countries. The word "or" here means "namely" (即). Thus the sentence should be rendered as

这些炮弹的来源是葡萄牙,也就是说,它们来自葡属几内亚即几内亚(比绍)。

13. We can only wonder why it should be claimed it (the draft) has a history of a whole week behind it.

Consider how to translate the word "should". If it is translated as "应该", the tone of surprise will be lost. As we know, when "should" is used together with "why", it often expresses surprise in tone. Its equivalent in Chinese is "竟然" or "居然" or "偏偏". The sentence may be rendered like this:

为什么竟然(有人)说草案拖了整整一个星期之久,对此我们不能不觉得奇怪。

14. An old dog like him never barks in vain. Whenever he barks, he always has some wise counsel worth listening to.

Think it over how we should translate the expression "old dog". First of all, we must know the word "dog" has both a commendatory sense and a derogatory sense. If you call someone old dog in England, it means you praise him as an old hand or an expert. If you call someone as a running dog, it means you scold him. The same is the case with the Chinese characters "牛"(ox) and "马"(horse). When you describe someone as "千里马"(a winged steed) or "识途老马"(an old horse knowing the way) or "人民的老黄牛"(people's old ox), it is commendatory. When you talk of him as "当牛当马"(serving as an ox or a horse) or "牛脾气"(bullheaded or pigheaded or as stubborn as a mule), it is derogatory. Sometimes, people may even call themselves by the names of such animals. For instance, in one of his poems Lu Xun describes himself as "俯首甘为孺子牛(Head bowed, like a willing ox I serve the children)". When others praise you as "老马识途"(an old horse knowing the way), you may modestly answer "马齿徒增"(merely advanced in age). The English word "dog" and the Chinese characters "马"(horse) and "牛"(ox) are all used in a metaphorical sense. Thus the two sentences may be translated into something like this:

像他这样的老狗是从不乱叫的。一叫他总有高见值得一听。

From this we can see that when we do translation, we must take social customs and metaphorical use of words into consideration.

15. All is not gold that glitters.

Although the clause "that glitters" is separated from the antecedent it modifies, yet it is a restrictive attributive clause. Pay attention to the special use of the adverb "not". If we translate the two words "is not" in this sentence in the same way as we render them in such sentences as "This is not a book" and "He is not a worker", we would produce an illogical statement as "闪闪发光的东西都不是金子" because the adverb "not" here in this sentence is in its special use as a word of partial negation. Thus the sentence should be put into Chinese properly like this:

闪闪发光的东西并不都是金子。

That's to say, among all the things that glitter, some are gold and some aren't.

16. He did not come to see her.

This sentence may be translated two different ways when it stands alone. One way is "他没有来看她". The other is "他并不是来看她的", which implies that he came not to see her, but to do something else. The sentence should be said in a falling tone in conversation when it means "他没有来看她" and in a falling-rising tone when it means "他并不是来看她的". The different meanings of the sentence are determined by context in writing.

17. I'm sorry, but I disagree with you all.

The words before the conjunction express an apology. How do you think we should translate the word "but" following a statement of apology? If you take the Chinese usage into consideration in such a case, the best way of translating "but" is not to translate it at all. So the proper Chinese version for this English sentence should be as follows:

对不起,你们大家的意见,我全不同意。

Such is the case with the sentence "Excuse me, but can you tell me how to get to Sloane Square?" You may deal with the word "but" in the same way as mentioned above. Furthermore, you must be more flexible in translating this sentence. In my opinion, you may render it either as 请问,去斯隆广场怎么走? or as 劳驾,请您告诉我去斯隆广场怎么走。

18. As time wore on, the *old* hunger brought him to his *old* despair.

This instance and its two proper versions of translation are offered by a professor. Now let's have a study of how to deal with such a sentence. If one should translate it mechanically like this:

随着光阴的消逝,那老饥饿又把他带到他的老绝望。

it would sound very awkward and unpleasant. Sometimes, it is necessary for the translator first to get rid of the influence or interference of the superficial lexical meaning and syntactic structure and then to give a happy representation both in wording and in construction so that the true spirit and literary flavor of the original may be reproduced. Thus the above mentioned English instance may be properly rendered as follows:

A. 挨过了一段时间之后,旧日的忍饥挨饿的滋味又引起了他旧日的绝望。

B. 挨过了一段时间之后,往昔的饥饿痛苦又使他陷入往昔的绝望心情之中。

Either A or B is well done and, as a result, reads naturally and smoothly.

The concrete expressions or sentences which are worth discussing are too many to enumerate. Here I give a score of expressions or sentences in the hope that the reader may draw inferences about other cases from them. Even from this small number of instances, we are already able to see that in order to fully realize the faithfulness of translation, a translator must (1) profoundly comprehend the actual linguistic situation, (2) dialectically apply the corresponding laws inherent in the two languages concerned, (3) take into consideration what kind of readers you are translating for, (4) handle the contradiction between the syntactic structures and the actual implications in a flexible way, (5) have a good command of the special uses of the common words "and", "or", "but", "when", "who", etc., (6) put idiomatic expressions into equivalent or similar ones, (7) make a point of the different practices in representation, (8) grasp the methods of translating images, using literal translation or free translation or transformation, (9) distinguish partial negation from complete and pay enough attention to the various ways of translating such negative sentences as double negation, pleonastic negation, multiple negation and cumulative negation, which constitutes a source of trouble for translators. (10) reproduce the spirit and tone of the original, (11) see to it that his translation is logical, natural and smooth and (12) weigh and consider repeatedly so as to achieve better and better results.

In short, it is quite essential for a translator to take into consideration many things, such as meaning, function, tense, logic, literary form even in dealing with some sentences or lines of literature. We can easily imagine what an all-round consideration we should have when we translate a whole article or a whole book.

In order to make the translator better and further realize the faithfulness of translation, I'd like to quote a passage from the book *Mother and Her Boarders* by Rosemary Taylor and Lü Shuxing's translation of it for reference:

But then a few days later Mr. Sawyer came to Mother, his face beaming, and said they'd be leaving for Michigan the next day. And Mrs. Sawyer looked radiant, too, and for the first time gobbled up her dinner like a little pig.

Afterward she took Mother into her room for a long talk.

"What do you suppose struck them?" Father asked Mother when they went to bed. "All this time they couldn't leave, just had to stay here, and now they're off in this awful hurry, it sure is a mystery."

"No, it isn't," said Mother, "She told me why. She's going to have a baby."

"Oh, she is. Well, that's good. That'll cheer her up. But it's still no reason for this hasty exit."

"I think she's a little crazy," said Mother. "She told me she had to stay here until she got pregnant, that if she went away before, she knew she would not get pregnant."

"Of all the loony ideas!" snorted Father. "Couldn't she get pregnant back in Michigan? Any particular magic in this house?"

"Maybe," said Mother.

Father pondered on that. "What do you mean by 'maybe'?"

"Well... Rose Kane is going to have one."

"Oh, well, that's fine."

"And," added Mother, "We are, too."

"Great jumping grasshoppers!" cried Father. "Why don't you tell a fellow?"

可是过不了几天,索先生满脸春风的⁴来找母亲来了,他说他们再过一天就回密希根去了,索太太也是一团高兴,吃起饭来也一口等不及一口,像一只小猪。

吃过饭她把母亲请到她屋子里去谈了老大半天。

"你看他们怎么回事?"睡觉的时候父亲问母亲。"一向以来他们只是不愿意走,只是非住这儿不可,这会儿说走就走,真是怪事。"

"不,一点儿也不怪,"母亲说,"索太太告诉我来着,她怀了娃娃了。"

"哦,原来如此,这是好消息。她从此可以快活起来了,可是也不必这么急于要走哇。"

"我看她有点神经,"母亲说。"她告诉我,她当初打定了主意,非在这儿怀了孕不走,她说她若空着肚皮走了,以后就不会再怀孕了。"

"也没听见过这种傻话!"父亲鼻子里哼了声。"她在密希根就怀不了孕吗?咱们这个房子里有仙气吗?"

"也许,"母亲说。

父亲想了想。"你这个'也许'是什么意思?"
"这个……甘太太也有了。"
"喔! 有意思。"
"再还有,"母亲随随便便的找补一句,"咱们也有了。"
"乖乖龙底东!"父亲直叫唤。"你怎么不直爽点儿说哇?"

Just as the Chinese saying goes, the falling of one leaf heralds the autumn. After a careful review of Lü's translation against the original, we may say that he has fully realized the principle of faithfulness and come up to the standard set for translation. The reasons may be given as follows:

Firstly, he successfully conveys the thoughts and feelings of the author, thus preserving the content of the original.

Secondly, the language of his translation is as expressive as that of the original.

Thirdly, the translator is close in style. The original is in the style of lively, popular and plain colloquialism, and so is the case with that of his translation. What's particularly well-done is in putting the exclamation "great jumping grasshoppers" as "乖乖龙底东" by making use of the dialect of North Jiangsu, which does not only agree with the status of the character and the situation of the dialogue but also fully expresses the great joy of a husband who hears such good news. If the exclamation should be mechanically rendered into something like "蹦跳的大蚂蚱", it would become a laughing-stock.

However, strictly speaking, there are still two points which may be improved. One, Mr. Sawyer, Mrs. Sawyer and Rose Kane should have been rendered as 索耶先生、索耶太太 and 罗斯·凯恩(Rose Kane). There's no much need to make them sound as names of Chinese people. Two, the question "Why don't you tell a fellow?" should have been rendered literally as "你为啥不告诉人家呢?", which is closer to the original tone. As you know, "a fellow" which is in the third person singular, means "me" here. In other words, it refers to the speaker himself. In Chinese, there is also such a linguistic phenomenon. That's to say, the third person "人家" or "别人" may replace the first person just like the English expression "a fellow".

Well, now let's come to the conclusion that a translator must conscientiously take heed of the principle of faithfulness or seriously observe the three-character principles—faithfulness in content, expressiveness in language and closeness in style.

Notes

1. M. T. Boatner, J. E. Gates, et al., *A Dictionary of American Idioms*, 1975.
2. *Journal of UN Documents Translation.* No. 1.
3. *Idem.* No. 3.
4. The character "的" was then used as a marker for both an adjective and an adverb.

Lecture Four　　Literal Translation and Free Translation

Disputes over the method of literal translation and that of free translation have a long history in China. The first dispute took place in the course of translating the Sanskrit Buddhist scriptures into Chinese. Dao'an (道安, 314-385), one of the well-known monks of the Qian Qin State during the East Jin Dynasty, was the representative of those who firmly advocated literal translation. Although he knew nothing of Sanskrit and did not take part in translation personally, yet he was in charge of the work and put forth the criteria for the translators to follow. Since he feared that free translation might not be true to the original, he advocated strict literal translation so as to be faithful to the content. Works done under his direction were typical of word-for-word translation in which no alteration was made except accidental changes in word order.

But Kumarajiva (鸠摩罗什, 344-413), one of Dao'an's contemporaries, firmly advocated free translation. He was versed in both Sanskrit and Chinese. All his translations were done in accordance with the usage of the Chinese language. He made either addition or omission where he thought necessary in order to better convey the sense of the Buddhist sutra. His translations went far and wide and exerted a great influence over Chinese philosophy and literature.

This dispute lasted until the time of Xuanzang(玄奘,602-664), a very famous monk and great translator of the Tang Dynasty. He did not make any assertion whether he was for or against literal or free translation. Yet people labeled his translation as "new devices for translation", which was essentially a flexible way of making good use of both literal translation and free translation. He could already apply addition and omission and other means in dealing with various linguistic phenomena so as to keep the meaning and spirit of the original. Besides, Xuanzang took a very serious and responsible attitude towards his translation. He worked hard all the time, setting a brilliant example for his contemporaries and coming generations.

The experience of Xuanzang in the translation of the Buddhist scriptures is worth summing up. For instance, Xuanzang advocated transliteration for polysemous words as 薄伽, the original of which has six different senses, for things which did not exist in China, e. g. 阎浮树(a kind of tree) and for other terms which could not be rendered exactly. Moreover, he employed the following methods while translating the scriptures according to the sum-up made by P. Pradhan(柏乐天), and Indian scholar, and Zhang Jianmu(张建木), a Chinese scholar: (1) addition(补充法), (2) omission(省略法), (3) transposition(移位法), (4) division or combination(分合法), (5) substitution(假借法), (6) restoration of nouns for pronouns (代词还原法).[1] Some of the six methods are related to accidence and some to syntax. Daoxuan(道宣,596-667), one of his contemporary theorists, spoke highly of his translation, saying:

"All the present translations of Sanskrit scriptures are done by

Xuanzang. It is he alone that determines the meaning of the original. And the words flow out of his mouth just as they come from under the pen of a master. His translation is accomplished the moment the clerks finish recording his words."

As pointed out by Luo Xinzhang, Xuanzang understood the Buddhist doctrine and had a good command of both Sanskrit and Chinese. He often used the method of literal translation, but he did not give up at all that of free translation when and where he thought it necessary. And Luo quoted from Liang Qichao (梁启超, 1873-1929): "Xuanzang made a perfect combination of literal translation and free translation. None ever did better than he in such work."[2]

In his paper entitled *Translated Literature and Buddhist Scriptures*(《翻译文学与佛典》) Liang added, "So far as the style of translation was concerned, the focus lay in the gain or loss of literal and free translations... Since new versions appeared daily, 'jade and stone' were mixed up. Then their desire for truthfulness became stronger and stronger and as a result literal translation was much more valued than free translation. It went so far that the translations were difficult to read and understand. Thus, in response to this, arose a reaction, which made the advocacy of free translation get the upper hand of that of literal translation. At last, the two methods got well blended and combined, which brought about a new style of translation. These might be the stages translators should go through, and the prosperity of Buddhist literature provided a full demonstration of it." The words of Liang as cited above may be deemed as a very valuable summary of the process of the development of literal and free translation in China and of their mutual complementation, which consequently gave birth to Xuanzang's "new devices for translation".

The facts mentioned above are about the dispute over literal translation and free translation and its development in the period of introducing the Buddhist sutra. Such a dispute occurred again in the 30s of twentieth century. Quite a lot of people aired their views. Some were for free translation, such as Zhao Jingshen(赵景深), who went so far as to say "Rather to be smooth(in language) than faithful(in thought)", and some for literal translation, such as Lu Xun(鲁迅), who diametrically opposed Zhao by openly declaring "Rather to be faithful(in thought) than smooth(in language)". Both statements are opinionated words when taken as practical or observable principles of translation, for everybody knows that a qualified and satisfactory translation must be not only faithful in thought but smooth in language, which is the minimum demand of a translator.

However, there were quite a few scholars whose arguments are still very valuable for reference in the study of this subject. Now let's take the arguments of Mao Dun(茅盾) for example. First he made a distinction between literal translation and the "dead" (mechanical) translation. His points of view are as follows:

Superficially speaking literal translation means "not to alter the original words and sentences"; strictly speaking, it strives "to keep the sentiments and style of the original". The meaning of the same word used in a sentence is often somewhat different from its definition in a dictionary. You must try to find a corresponding and appropriate expression for it when you translate something literally. It would be "dead" translation if you should mechanically move the definition into your translation regardless of whether it is well-collocated or not in the target language. The "dead" translation won't be quite intelligible because words lose their proper places. Some readers mistake "dead" translation for "literal" translation.

That's a great confusion. Mao Dun was sure that theoretically literal translation was not wrong at all.³

Secondly, he gave a definition of literal translation. He thought that the so-called literal translation was not necessarily word-for-word, neither a word more nor a word less. Since the organization of words in Chinese is different from that in a Western language, it is actually impossible to achieve word-for-word translation in most cases. Zhang Songnian(张崧年) once made an experiment of word-for-word translation and eventually it proved a failure. The definition of literal translation was "not to distort the true features of the original work". Suppose there were two versions of one and the same original—one was a word-for-word translation lacking the original spirit whereas the other a non-word-for-word translation which in the main reproduced the spirit of the original. How should we judge the two versions? According to Mao Dun, the latter could be called literal translation in its true sense.⁴

Fu Sinian(傅斯年) also supported literal translation. His reasons are:
"The thought of the author can't be independent of language. If we want to retain the author's thought, we must retain his grammar at the same time. If we change the original tone into a different one, what is expressed is surely not the author's thought. Therefore, literal translation is the way ' to keep true features'. We should follow it in our translation. It's impossible to do literal translation word for word all the time owing to the fact that Chinese and Western languages are quite different. But it's possible to carry it out sentence by sentence. That is because the order of sentences is exactly that of thought."⁵

During the heated dispute of 1930s between the school of literal translation and the school of free translation, Lu Xun was a staunch advocate of literal translation, but he didn't object to any unavoidable free translation. In fact, he proposed both faithfulness and smoothness as the main criteria to be observed in translation. His open declaration that he would prefer faithfulness to smoothness was aimed at opposing Zhao Jingshen's onesided advocacy of "preferring smoothness to faithfulness". But in his practice, as Li Ji(李季,1922-1980) pointed out, Lu Xun did never set literal translation against free translation and repel it though he put emphasis on the former. Just on the contrary, he held that the method of free translation might be used where and when necessary. And Li Ji cited Lu Xun's own words in the *Preface* to his translation entitled《小彼得》as a convincing proof:

"It is not quite proper for foreign language learners... to begin their translation with children's stories, for they are apt to rigidly adhere to the original text and dare not translate it in a free way so that the translation is very difficult for the children to read. The manuscript of《小彼得》had this kind of shortcoming. Thus I revised it on a large scale while reading and correcting proofs. As a result, the translation became more smooth than before." (*The Complete Works of Lu Xun*, vol. 14, p. 237)

Another convincing proof given by Li Ji that Lu Xun did not oppose free translation was found in Lu Xun's *Brief Preface* to his translation of the work *On Art*,《艺术》, in which Lu Xun said:

"Biology, physiology, psychology, physics, chemistry and philosophy, etc. are touched upon in the book... to say nothing of aesthetics and scientific socialism. All these subjects are not among my attainments. As a result, the translator feels there are many obstacles in the course of translation... Much time has been spent, yet the translation turns out to be a dry and difficult book... If there is someone who devotes himself to the study of the book, it is better for him to reorganize the sentences, make the terms easy to understand and render it in such a free way that the translation may be close to interpretation. " (*The Complete Works of Lu Xun*, Vol. 15, p. 175)

In Lu Xun's translation, Li Ji concluded that the method of literal translation and the method of free translation were merged. He merely regarded the former as primary and the latter as supplementary. [6]

Here I'd like to say a few words about the dispute over the same question of literal translation and free translation in the West, where it is quite interesting to find that there were different opinions on these two methods. For instance, in ancient times, Saint Jerome (c. 347-419/420 B. C.) advocated that in translating literary works free translation should be used while in translating the Bible literal translation should be used. Marcus Tullius Cicero (106-43 B. C.) stated that he translated as an orator instead of an annotator and did not approve word-for-word and sentence-for-sentence translation. In modern times, the controversy continued in the West just as in China. I'm very glad to discover that it has been developing in the same direction. In other words, more and more people have come to nearly the same understanding that literal translation should be adopted as the primary method and free translation as the secondary or supplementary.

Having made a further study of the two historical disputes over literal translation and free translation, I once more find that the two methods handed down by our predecessors are not out-of-date at all as some people think them to be, but still remain greatly helpful to translators if they have a better understanding of the essence of literal translation and free translation and make the best use of them in a flexible and realistic way. I am going to expound my viewpoints in the following.

On the one hand, literal translation and free translation have been "twin sisters" ever since the work of translation came into being, which is historically true both in the East and in the West and, on the other, the successful experience gained by our forerunners, such as Xuanzang and Lu Xun, should be inherited and developed. Now it is time for us to give a comparatively accurate and comprehensive definition to the two methods of translation.

Literal translation may be defined as having the following characteristics:

Ⅰ. Literal translation takes sentences as its basic units and the whole text into consideration at the same time in the course of translating.

Ⅱ. Literal translation strives to reproduce both the ideological content and style of the entire literary work and retain as much as possible the figures of speech and such main sentence structures or patterns as SV, SVO, SVC, SVA, SVOO, SVOC, SVOA formulated by Randolph Quirk, one of the authors of the book *A Comprehensive Grammar of the English Language*.

Examples for Literal Translation

1. A. Still waiting here? Seems you have waited a long time. B. Have to wait. C told me he would come, and I have something to tell him. It won't wait.

A:还等在这儿？好像你已经等了很久时间。B:不得不等。C 对我说他会来,我也有件事要告诉他,那可不能等。

2. He walked at the head of the funeral procession, and every now and then wiped his crocodile tears with a big handkerchief.

他走在送葬队伍的前头,还不时用一条大手绢抹去他那鳄鱼的眼泪。

The two above examples are borrowed from the essay *Literal Translation, Free translation and Word-for-Word Translation* by Feng shize (冯世则).[7] But the slight modification of the first example is made by the writer. From the two examples we can see the fact that not only the meaning and tone of the original are well conveyed in the translation but also the sentence patterns and the figure of speech successfully reproduced.

What is free translation then? It may be defined as a supplementary means to mainly convey the meaning and spirit of the original without trying to reproduce its sentence patterns or figures of speech. And it is adopted only when and where it is really impossible for translators to do literal translation.

Ex. 1. No admittance! (one-member sentence)
闲人免进。(SV)
Ex. 2. It rains cats and dogs. (SVO)
大雨滂沱。(SV)
Ex. 3. Where there is a will, there is a way. (complex)
有志者事竟成。(simple)
Ex. 4. It's an ill wind that blows nobody good. (complex)
对于某些人有害的事可能对于另外一些人有利。(simple)[8]

The sentence patterns are changed and in the translation of Ex. 4 the figure of speech disappears as well.

No matter what method you may use, the prerequisite is that you must be able to carry out the principles of faithfulness, expressiveness and closeness. Only when you keep the meaning and spirit of the original sentence structure and/or its figure of speech can your translation be regarded as proper literal translation; otherwise it is merely "dead" or mechanical translation. Similarly, only when you change the sentence-structure and/or the figure of speech but make no addition to or omission of the original meaning at will can your translation be regarded as proper free translation; otherwise it's merely "random" translation.

When you decide to translate something, first of all you must read it carefully from the very beginning to the very end. Never set your pen to paper until you have a thorough understanding of its content and at the same time a full grasp of its style if it is a piece of literary work. In the course of your translation, you may make use of literal translation on condition that your translation is both readable and intelligible to the readers when you keep the sentence-structure and/or the figure of speech of the original. For instance, "Mary is a worker" may be literally translated as "玛丽是个工人", "John studies very well" as "约翰学得很好" and "Though the colonialists were armed to the teeth, yet the local people still dared to fight with them" as "虽然殖民主义者武装到了牙齿,但当地人民仍然敢于同他们战斗".

But in quite a number of cases literal translation alone won't do. Then you'll have to master the true meaning and spirit of the original and render it properly in accordance with the characteristics of the two languages concerned. For instance, "Practice makes perfect" may be translated freely as "熟能生巧" or "业精于勤". Another instance: It goes very much against the grain with me that the name of the witness should ever be suppressed. (J. Galsworthy) Using the method of free translation, the compilers of *The Dictionary of English Idioms* translate the sentence like this:

"不发表证人的名字,实在大大地违反我的本意。" This translation is well done. First, "go against the grain with somebody" is an idiomatic expression which means "be contrary to one's inclination". Therefore, it can's be translated word for word. Secondly, the predicate verb in the that-clause is in the passive voice. The compilers change it into the active so that it reads more idiomatically to the Chinese readers.

From this we can see that we must proceed from reality, namely, concrete syntactic construction and/or rhetorical means when we do translation. That's to say, those sentences and/or figures of speech it is better to translate by means of literal translation should be done literally and those it is better to translate by means of free translation should be done freely. It is impossible for one to translate an article or a book using only one method of translation, so one must take a flexible attitude in order to avoid stiffness and unintelligibility. As a matter of fact, sometimes one has to combine the two methods in translating even a single sentence, e. g.

1. Every dog has his day.

人人都有得意的日子。

2. The oppressed people in the world would rather go through fire and water to fight against imperialists and colonialists than be turned round their little fingers.

世界上被压迫人民宁肯赴汤蹈火同帝国主义者和殖民主义者进行斗争,也不愿任人摆布。

In the translation of Ex. 1, the sentence pattern (SVO) is the same as in the original, but the image is changed from "dog" into "man". In the translation of Ex. 2, the syntactic construction is reproduced. There are two metaphors. The first metaphor "go through fire and water" gets basically retained while the second disappears. Evidently, the translation of the two above sentences is neither one hundred percent literal nor one hundred percent free. It's a combination of both literal translation and free translation.

Either literal translation or free translation has its limit. It would become absurd once it goes too far. Beyond its limit, literal translation would make laughing stocks such as "牛奶路", the mis-translation of "the Milky Way" and "躺在自己的背上", the "dead" or mechanical translation of "lie on one's back". Their correct translations should respectively be "银河" or "天河" and "仰卧" or "仰面躺着". Beyond its limit, free translation would be wide apart from the original. Take Lin Shu (1852-1924) for example. He translated more than 150 literary works. He made a great contribution to our country in introducing foreign literature into China, indeed. But as far as translation itself is concerned, what he did is not quite worthy of the name. His "translation" can only be called "half translation and half rewriting". First, he did not know any foreign language himself, but relied on others' interpretation of the original. He not only made much addition and omission in content but also even changed the form of what he "translated". This being the case, how could we expect him to be fully faithful and true to the original? Secondly, he did his translation in the classic Chinese language all the time. With regard to Lin's translation, Mao Dun said that double distortion was unavoidable. The co-operators interpreted the original in colloquial Chinese to Lin. There might be more or less distortion in their interpretation. Then he wrote down in classic Chinese. There might occur some more distortion. [9]Though Lin Shu was nescient of foreign languages, he was voluminous in rendition. Imperfect as his versions are, he left us a kind of translation device—annotation, which promoted the dissemination of foreign literature in China in those years.

Two instances more to illustrate literal translation and free translation. Generally, whether we should use literal translation or free translation depends upon the interrelation between the source language and the target language. Take English and Chinese. They have similarities and dissimilarities in their ways of expression. We may adopt the proper method of translation in accordance with concrete situations and context. There may be three cases: A. being necessary to adopt literal translation; B. being necessary to adopt free translation and C. being necessary to adopt a combination of the two.

There are sentences which can be translated in various ways, e. g.

1. It means killing two birds with one stone.

As an isolated sentence, it may be rendered in the following three ways:

A. 这意味着一石二鸟。(literal translation)

B. 这意味着一举两得。(free translation)

C. 这意味着一箭双雕。(combination)

Although A does not sound quite idiomatic, it retains the original images "stone" and "birds" and at the same time it is comprehensible and fresh. In B the original images are lost, yet the true meaning and spirit of the sentence is well expressed. In C, images are replaced: "stone" by "arrow", and "birds" by "vultures", which still give a vivid picture to the readers and the translation reads very fluently. All the three translations are readable and comprehensible. Which is best depends on the whole context and the style of an article or a book where the sentence is.

2. 你不要班门弄斧了。

Three different ways of translation may be provided:

A. Don't display your axe at Lu Ban's door. (literal translation)

B. Don't teach your grandmother to suck eggs. (free translation)

C. Never offer to teach a fish to swim. (free translation)

All the three translations may be accepted. But which is the best? It depends on the actual situation. If your translation is intended for Chinese readers, you may well adopt the method of literal translation. If it is intended for foreigners, you'd better use the method of free translation so that they might easily understand what you mean; otherwise, you will have to make a detailed note about the allusion because they neither know who Lu Ban was nor understand what is meant by displaying one's axe at a person's door.

The foregoing discussion shows that either the advocation of literal translation as the sole method or the advocation of free translation as the sole method is unavoidably one-sided because it does not conform to the reality of the translation between the two languages which have both similarities and dissimilarities. Usually, it's impossible for one to translate every sentence of an article or a book literally. Nor is there any necessity of translating every sentence freely. The correct attitude should be: When you translate sentences which are similar in structure and/or in figure of speech in the two languages, literal translation should be used; when you translate sentences which are dissimilar in structure and/or figure of speech, free translation should be used; and when you translate sentences which are partly similar and partly dissimilar in structure and/or figure of speech, the two methods should be flexibly and cleverly combined. We must always keep in mind that methods of translation are to serve the purpose of fully carrying out the principles of faithfulness, expressiveness and closeness.[10]

Therefore, in the course of translation, we should never forget the principles of faithfulness, expressiveness and closeness and we must try our utmost to achieve them in our wording, sentence and paragraph-making with the whole text in view. Take the following sentence for example. "Nixon was smiling and Kissinger smiling mere broadly. "This sentence is quoted from the book *Life of Kissinger*. It's not so easy to translate. First, we can't translate the verb "smile" simply as "笑" because the Chinese character "笑" means both smile and laugh whereas the English word "smile" is only corresponding to the Chinese phrase "微笑"; secondly, the adverb "broadly" must be taken into consideration along with the verb "smile", or else you can hardly find a proper equivalent for "broadly" out of English-Chinese dictionaries. Considering the fact that biography is generally a literary form of writing, this sentence may be rendered as "尼克松满面春风,基辛格更是笑容可掬". As you know, both "满面春风" and "笑容可掬" are Chinese literary expressions to illustrate one's happiness revealed on the face.

In a word, the adoption of method of translation depends on the actual sentence-structure and/or the figure of speech and on the demand of the principles of faithfulness, expressiveness and closeness. My view of literal translation and free translation may be boiled down to one concise conclusion that the two methods are indispensable and supplementary to each other with the former as the primary and the latter as the secondary and ought to be adopted in a flexible and realistic manner.

Why should I regard literal translation as the primary or basic method in general? It is because it will help make our translation much easier to accomplish the following three purposes:(1) being faithful to the original in ideological content,(2) reflecting the scene and flavor of the foreign country concerned and (3) absorbing the new ways of expression. Translation is a linguistic activity which demands objectivity instead of subjectivity from the translator and literal translation is an effective means to achieve this end. But at the same time we should know that literal translation is not the sole and universal method for it has its own limitations. Whenever it won't work owing to the linguistic, racial, customary, cultural or historical factors, naturally we must at once turn to the secondary or supplementary means—free translation for help so that we may effectively get out of the trouble we meet with.

In order to demonstrate that my conclusion does conform to the reality and inherent laws of the translation between English and Chinese, particularly the translation from English into Chinese, I'd like to translate the last part of the story *The Black Rock Coffin Makers* by Louis L'Amour as an experiment and make an analysis of the translation to show what percentage literal translation, free translation and the combination of both respectively amount to. And in my translation I'll mark each sentence by either lt (literal translation) or ft (free translation) or comb (combination of both).

The original[11] of the selected passages and their translation are contrasted as follows:

Tucker's street was more crowded than usual when they rode up to Ashton's office and swung down. Jim Gatlin pulled open the door and stepped in. The tall gray-haired man behind the desk looked up. "You are Ashton?" Gatlin demanded.

他们骑马到艾什顿事务所跃身下马时,塔克镇街上比往常更拥挤。(lt)吉姆·加特林拉开门走进去。(lt)坐在办公桌那里那位苍白头发的人抬起头。(lt)"你是艾什顿吗?"加特林问。(lt)

At the answering nod, he opened his shirt and unbuckled his money belt. "There's ten thousand there. Bid in the XY for Cochrane an' Gatlin."

艾什顿一点头,他就敞开衬衫,解开钱袋。(comb.)"这里有一万。(lt)是为科克伦和加特林购进 XY 农场出的钱。"(comb.)

Ashton's eyes sparkled with sudden satisfaction. "You're her partner?" he asked. "You're putting up the money? It's a fine thing you're doing, man."

艾什顿的眼睛突然闪出满意的神色。(comb.)"你是她的合股人吗?"他问。(lt)"你出这笔钱?(lt)你在做好事啊,伙计。"(ft)

"I'm a partner only in name. My gun backs the brand, that's all. She may need a gun behind her for a little while, an' I've got it."

"我只是名义上的合股人。(lt)我的枪用来维护农场所有权,就是这样。(comb.)她可能暂时需要一支枪保卫她,我也刚好有一支。"(lt)

He turned to Doc, but the man was gone. Briefly, Gatlin explained what they had found and added, "Wing Cary headed for town now."

他转身向多克,但那人走掉了。(lt)扼要地,加特林说明了他们发现的情况,并补充说:"温·卡里现在就来镇上。"(lt)

"Headed for town?" Ashton's head jerked around. "He's here. Came in twenty minutes ago!"

"就来镇上?"(lt)艾什顿摇了摇头。(ft)"他在这儿。(lt)二十分钟以前来过!(lt)"

Jim Gatlin spun on his heel and strode from the office. On the street, pulling his hat brim low against the glare, he stared left, then right. There were men on the street, but they were drifting inside now. There was no sign of the man called Doc or of Cary.

吉姆·加特林急转身,大步离开事务所。(lt)在街上,他把帽檐拉低,避免刺目的阳光,左看看,右看看。(comb.)街上有人,但他们此刻都在漫步回到户内去。(comb.)没有多克或卡里的踪影。(basically lt)

Gatlin's heels were sharp and hard on the boardwalk. He moved swiftly, his hands swinging alongside his guns. His hard brown face was cool, and his lips were tight. At the Barrelhouse, he paused, put up his left hand, and stepped in. All faces turned toward him, but none was that of Cary. "Seen Wing Cary?" he demanded. "He murdered Jim Walker."

加特林的马靴敏捷而坚实地踏在板道上。(ft)他走得很快,双手随着两支枪前后摆动。(lt)他结实的棕色面孔表现镇静,嘴唇紧闭。(comb.)他在那家廉价小酒店门前停下来,举起左手走进去。(lt)所有的面孔都转向他,但就是不见卡里。(comb.)"看到温·卡里吗?"他问。(lt)"他谋杀了吉姆·沃克。(lt)"

Nobody repled, and then an oldish man turned his head and jerked it down the street. "He's gettin' his hair cut, right next to the livery barn. Waitin' for the auction to start up."

没人应声,然后一位老人转过头来,向街上努嘴示意。(comb.)"他正在理发,就在马车店隔壁。(lt)在等拍卖开场。(lt)"

Gatlin stepped back through the door. A dark figure, hunched near the blacksmith shop, jerked back from sight. Jim hesitated, alert to danger, then quickly pushed on.

加特林退出门来。(lt)一个模糊的人影,靠近那家铁匠铺弯腰站着,往后一缩便不见了。(lt)吉姆警惕危险,停了一下,接着迅速前进。(lt)

The red and white barber pole marked the frame building. Jim opened the door and stepped in. A sleeping man snored with his mouth open, his back to the street wall. The bald barber looked up, swallowed, and stepped back.

那根红白相间的理发店标杆标明了那坐木屋。(lt)吉姆打开门走进去。(lt)一个正在睡觉的人打着鼾,口张着,背向临街墙。(lt)那个秃顶理发师抬起头,吸了口气,向后退。(lt)

Lecture Four Literal Translation and Free Translation

Wing Cary sat in the chair, his hair halftrimmed, the white cloth draped around him. The opening door and sudden silence made him look up. "You, is it?" he said.

温·卡里坐在椅子上,头发理了一半,围着白布。(comb.)开着的门和突然的沉静使他抬起头。(lt)"是你,对吗?"他问。(ft)

"It's me. We found Jim Walker. He marked your name, Cary, as his killer."

"是我。(ft)我们发现了吉姆·沃克。(lt)他划下了你的名字,卡里,是谋杀者。(lt)"

Cary's lips tightened, and suddenly a gun bellowed and some thing slammed Jim Gatlin in the shoulder and spun him like a top smashing him sidewise into the door. That first shot saved him from the second. Wing Cary had held a gun in his lap and fired through the white cloth. There was sneering triumph in his eyes, and as though time stood still, Jim Gatlin saw the smoldering of the black-rimmed circles of the holes in the cloth.

卡里的双唇紧闭,而且突然枪响了,什么东西击中吉姆·加特林的肩膀并使他像陀螺一样转了一下,打得他侧着身子倒向门口。(lt)那击中的第一弹使他未中第二弹。(ft)温·卡里原来在膝部放着一支枪并隔白布开了火。(lt)他眼睛里流露出一种胜利的狞笑,而且好像时间停止了走动,吉姆·加特林看见白布上两个洞眼烧焦的边缘还在冒烟。(comb.)

He never remembered firing, but suddenly Cary's body jerked sharply, and Jim felt the gun buck in his hand, He fired again then, and Wing's face twisted and his gun exploded into the floor, narrowly missing his own feet.

他不记得开了火,但突然卡里的身子剧烈地抖动了一下,同时吉姆感到枪托在手里。(lt)于是他又开了一枪,温的脸抽搐起来,枪也响了,打进地板,差一点儿打中自己的脚。(lt)

Wing started to get up, and Gatlin fired the third time, the shot nicking Wing's ear and smashing a shaving cup, spattering lather. The barber was on his knees in one corner, holding a chair in front of him. The sleeping man had dived through the window, glass and all.

温开始站起来,加特林第三次开枪,那颗子弹射穿了温的耳朵,打碎了刮脸剃胡须用的杯子,肥皂泡沫也溅掉了。(comb.)在一个屋角里,那个理发师跪着,拿起椅子挡在前面。(lt)正在睡觉的那个人也早已冲开玻璃窗逃走了。(ft)

Men came running and Jim leaned back against the door. One of the men was Doc, and he saw Sheriff Eaton, and then Lisa tore them aside and ran to him. "Oh, you're hurt! You've been shot! You've...!"

人们跑着来了,吉姆背靠着门。(lt)其中有一个是多克,他还看到了司法行政长官伊顿,接着是莉莎把他们扯开,向他跑去。(basically lt)。"哦,你受伤了!(lt)你已经被打中!(lt)你已经……"(lt)

His feet gave away slowly, and slid down the door to the floor. Wing Cary still sat in the barbershop, his hair halfclipped.

他的脚慢慢站不住了,他从门上滑到地上。(comb.)温·卡里仍然坐在理发店,头发剪了一半。(lt)

Doc stepped in and glanced at him, then at the barber. "You can't charge him for it, Tony. You never finished."

多克走进来,望了他一眼,然后望着理发师。(lt)"你不能要他的理发费,托尼。(comb.)你没理完!(lt)"

There are altogether 64 sentences in the selected material. 42 of them are rendered by means of literal translation($65.5^+\%$), 8 by means of free translation(12.5%) and 14 by means of the combination of both($22^-\%$). Of course, this percentage does not apply to all materials for translation. But, anyhow, it convincingly proves the truth that we should use the method of literal translation and the method of free translation in a flexible and realistic way and with the former as the primary and that it would be absolutely wrong to favor one and disfavor the other.

Notes

1. *A Short History of Translation in China* by Ma Zuyi, 58 – 60, China Translation and Publishing Corporation, 1984.
2. *The Self-made System of Theories of Translation in Our Country*, a preface written by Luo Xinzhang to the book *An Anthology of Essays on Translation* he compiled, published by the Commercial Press in 1984.
3. "*Literal Translation*" and "*Dead Translation*" by Mao Dun, *Novels Monthly*, Vol. 13, No. 8, 1922.
4. *Literal Translation, Smooth Translation and Distorted Translation* by Mao Dun, *Literature*, Vol. 2, No. 3, 1934.
5. *Some Remarks on Translation Books* by Fu Sinian, *New Trend*, Vol. 1, No. 3, 1919.
6. *Contributions Made by Lu Xun* written by Li Ji, *Translation Journal*, January, 1952.
7. *Literal Translation, Free Translation and Word-for-Word Translation* by Feng Shize, *Translators Journal*, No. 2, 1981.
8. The four examples and their translations are cited from *The Dictionary of English Idioms*, The Commercial Press, 1972.
9. See Note 4.
10. *Free Talks about Translation* by Liu Zhongde, 45 – 47, The Shaanxi People's Publishing House, 1984.
11. The material is selected from Louis L'Amour's collection of short stories entitled *Law of the Desert Born*, Louis L'Amour's Enterprises, Inc., 1983.

Lecture Five   Commonly-Used Methods of Translation

Talking of the various concrete methods of translation, of course, they are too many to enumerate and exhaust. Here I'm going only to introduce several commonly-used ones:

Ⅰ. Corresponding sentence patterns(句型对应)

Everybody knows that it is a very good method of learning English to make a good command of corresponding sentence patterns and the situations of their use. So far as translation is concerned, a mastery of them is an indispensable basic training, because it not only makes you quick in response but also ensures that your translation will conform to the usage in syntax. The corresponding sentence patterns are numerous. A few examples will be given below.

1. *As soon as* he came to Changsha, he paid a visit to Yuelu Academy.

If you are familiar with various sentence patterns, at the sight of this English sentence you will naturally think of the corresponding Chinese pattern "……一……就……" and promptly and correctly translate it into Chinese like this:

他一到长沙,就访问了岳麓书院。

2. 你书读得越多,你就会越有学问。

"……越……越……" is a Chinese sentence pattern. Its equivalent in English is the pattern "The more... , the more... ". Having a good grasp of the corresponding pattern, you will feel it quite easy to render the sentence as:

The more you read, the more learned you will become.

3. But for your help, we could not have accomplished our task in time.

"But for... " is an English sentence pattern, whose Chinese equivalent is "要是没有……" or "要不是……". Thus the sentence may be put into Chinese as:

要是没有你的帮助,我们便不能按时完成任务。

4. 他直到成年才开始读书。

"……直到……才……" is a Chinese sentence pattern, the equivalent of which in the English language is "... not... until... ". The sentence can be translated as:

He did not start to read until he came of age.

Making use of this pattern, see to it that the negative word "not" is followed by a verb of momentary action.

The examples given above are enough to show the importance of sentence patterns in the work of translation. In the course of our study, we must at all times compare, analyze, sum up and bear in mind the sentence patterns of the foreign language we are learning and those of our mother tongue so that we may achieve good results when we are engaged in translation.

Ⅱ. Rearrangement of word order(词序调整)

We have often to rearrange the word order when we translate from English into Chinese. It is because the two languages have each their own characteristics. For instance, attributive phrases and clauses usually follow the words they modify in English whereas they usually precede the modified words in Chinese. Englishmen and Americans prefer to put the adverbials of time and of place at the end of a sentence while we Chinese people often have them at the beginning. If these two kinds of adverbial coexist in a single sentence, the adverbials of time usually follow those of place in English, but they are exactly in the reverse order in Chinese. In English sentences, the possessive pronoun often goes before the noun it stands for and the personal pronoun appears in the subordinate clause previous to the main clause. However, nouns are always mentioned first in Chinese sentences. The above characteristics and other ones not yet mentioned here necessitate the rearrangement of word order in the translation between the English and Chinese languages, e. g.

1. The suggestion *put forward by the teacher* was accepted by his students.

教师提的建议被学生接受了。

2. The National Science Conference was held *in Beijing in 1977*.

全国科学会议是一九七七年在北京举行的。

3. When *he* was twelve, *Mark Twain* lost his father.

马克·吐温十二岁时失去了(他)父亲。

4. In *her* novel *Jane Eyre* Charlotte Brontë gives a very vivid description of the ill-treatment of the girls at Lowood.

夏洛特·布朗蒂在(她的)小说《简·爱》里生动地描绘了罗伍德学校女学生受虐待的情形。

5. *His* sympathy for the Chinese revolution and his friendship for the Chinese people gained *Edgar Snow* many enemies.

埃德加·斯诺,由于对中国革命同情并对中国人民友好,引起很多人对他的仇视。

Ⅲ. Conversion of parts of speech(词类转换)

The conversion of parts of speech is also one of the commonly used methods, e. g.

1. The *use* of bacteriological weapons is a *clear violation* of the international law.

使用细菌武器显然违反国际法。

The English nouns "use" and "violation" are converted into the Chinese verbs "使用" and "违反", and as a result the English adjective "clear" is converted into the Chinese adverb "显然". Of course, the sentence is still intelligible if we render it word for word without conversion of parts of speech like this:

细菌武器的使用是对国际法的明显违反。

But anyhow it sounds not so natural as the foregoing translation.

2. At the meeting, some *were for* the proposal and others *against* it.

会上,有的赞成那个提议,有的反对那个提议。

The English construction of "v. to be + a preposition" is converted into the Chinese transitive verbs.

3. He dialed the *wrong* number.

他拨错了电话号码。

The English adjective "wrong" which modifies the noun "number" is converted into the Chinese adverb "错" which modifies the predicate verb "拨"。

From the three examples, we can already see the usefulness of the conversion of parts of speech. We should make a flexible use of it when necessary. Sometimes, we find there are translations, which don't read naturally. One of the reasons may be that the translator stubbornly sticks to the original parts of speech and tries his utmost to retain them.

Ⅳ. Proper addition or omission(恰当增减)

In many cases, it is neither possible nor necessary to translate word for word. In the process of translation we will often have to make proper addition or omission of some individual words in accordance with the corresponding laws inherent in the two languages concerned. But meanwhile we should see that the "proper" addition or omission is quite different from the "random translation" because the former aims to retain and better express the original meaning whereas the latter is subjective and irresponsible to the original text. Please observe what proper addition or omission is in the following examples:

1. We don't *retreat*, we never have and never will.

我们不后退,我们不曾后退,我们也永远不后退。

The verb "retreat" appears only once in the original, but its Chinese equivalent "后退" thrice. Some additions are made in the translation, but they are quite necessary and proper(not random at all) so far as the true meaning of the original is concerned. If we put the Chinese sentence back into English, then some omission must be made according to the usage of the English language.

2. John got up very early *in* the morning. He put on *his* jacket,(*his*) trousers *and* (*his*) shoes, sat down *at* (*his*) desk *and* began to do *his* homework.

清晨约翰起得很早。他穿上夹克、裤子和鞋,就在书桌那里坐下来开始做家庭作业。

In the translation, the prepositions "in" and "at" and the second conjunction "and" are all omitted. As for the 3rd person possessive pronoun "his", it may appear once or even five times, but the corresponding Chinese

"他的" is usually unnecessary to be expressed in the translation. If we do back translation, we must have all the omitted words expressed so as to make the English sentence grammatic and idiomatic.

Ⅴ. Necessary repetition(必要重复)

Englishmen and Chinese are quite different in handling the same concept or action expressed by a noun or a verb. The Englishmen often adopt substitution and the Chinese repetition. We should repeat the foregoing nouns or verbs while translating from English into Chinese and substitute the previous nouns or verbs with pronouns or pro-verbs while translating from Chinese into English, e. g.

1. A functionary in the leading post must be able to discover *problems* and good at analyzing and solving *them*.

领导干部必须能够发现问题,并善于分析问题,解决问题。

2. Parents should not only love their *Children* but(also)help *them* and educate them.

父母不仅应当爱护自己的子女,还应当帮助自己的子女,教育自己的子女。

In the two English examples, the nouns "problems" and "children" appear only once but in the Chinese sentences the two corresponding nouns "问题" and "子女" occur three times so as to be more specific.

3. The *grammar* of Russian is much more complicated than *that* of English.

俄语语法比英语语法复杂得多。

4. The *silks* of China are better and cheaper than *those* of any other country.

中国的绸缎比任何其他国家的绸缎都价廉物美。

In the two English examples, the nouns "grammar" and "silks" are replaced by the demonstrative pronouns "that" and "those" in order to avoid repetition but in the Chinese sentences the demonstrative pronouns can't be used in this way. The same nouns have to be repeated.

5. He *studies* English as hard as she *does* Chinese.

他学英语跟她学汉语一样用功。

6. A. I *appreciate* this film very much.

我很欣赏这部电影。

B. So *do* all the young people.

所有青年人都很欣赏(这部电影)。

In sentences 5 and 6, the prop word "do" is used to respectively replace the preceding verbs "studies" and "appreciate" in English whereas in Chinese the same verbs are repeated.

Ⅵ. With the help of "有人"(someone or some people...)(借助"有人……")[1]

We can make use of the Chinese sentence pattern "有人……" to overcome the difficulty in literally translating such English patterns as "It is (or was) thought (or other similar verbs) that...", e. g.

1. *It was thought that* he was a good teacher.

当时有人认为他是个好老师。

2. *It was believed that* she would never come back again.

当时有人相信她永远都不会回来了。

3. *It is announced that* there will be a new film tomorrow.

有人通知明天放映新影片。

4. *It is maintained that* the criminal should be punished sternly.

有人主张这个罪犯要严加惩处。

Ⅶ. By means of either "祝"or"愿"(祝、愿咸宜)[2]

We may render the English sentence pattern introduced by "May" expressing wish by means of the character "祝" or the character "愿", e. g.

1. *May* you enjoy a splendid health!

祝(愿)您(你)健康!

2. *May* you come back with merits!

祝(愿)您(你)立功归来!

3. *May* the favorable wind accompany you!

祝(愿)您(你)一帆风顺!

4. *May* success attend you!

祝(愿)您(你)成功!

Ⅷ. Making use of extraposition(利用外位)[3]

We know that a sentence usually consists of several parts. When the part of subject, attribute or object of the English sentence is so long that it's not easy to arrange the translation according to the original syntactic structure, we may make use of extraposition to solve the problem. By extraposition we mean that we may first render the part of subject, attribute or object and place it at the very beginning of the translation and then repeat the meaning it contains through the Chinese pronouns "这" or "这些" or "其", which somewhat resembles the English relative pronoun "whose" with the foregoing clause as its antecedent and introduces the not yet expressed parts into the translation, e. g.

1. ... it may be advisable *in the course of the consultations to envisage yet another alternative, namely, that we should consider this question as the fourth item on the agenda and the question of Korea as the third.*

……在磋商过程中设想另外一种可供选择的方案,即我们把这个问题作为议程上的第四个项目来审议,而朝鲜问题则作为第三个项目,这可能是可取的。

In this sentence, the part of subject begins with "in the course" and ends with "as the third", but its head word is simply the infinitive "to envisage", which has its adverbial and objects. The whole part of subject is rather long, so the translator first puts it into Chinese and places it at the beginning of his translation, and then renders the grammatical subject "it" as "这" and its predicate. If the part of the real subject is comparatively long in the sentence pattern "It + v. to be + adj. + infinitive phrase or that-clause", the above method may be adopted. Otherwise, we may render the sentence like this: "real subject + predicate introduced by the grammatical subject it". Take for example the following sentence:

It is quite necessary (important) for technical personnel to master a foreign language.

技术人员掌握一门外语十分必要(重要)。

2. The questions of *international security*, *the invitations of representatives of the two parts*, *disarmament*, *substantive consideration of the question of the sea-bed* are the questions to be considered in this anniversary session.

国际安全,邀请两个部分的代表、裁军、海床问题的实质性的审议,这些都是在这届(周年)纪念会议上要审议的问题。

So far as the subject "the questions" is concerned, it is rather short in the sentence. But when taken into consideration together with its modifier, the of-phrase which contains several objects functioning as appositives to the subject, it makes a fairly long subject group. Therefore the translator first makes use of extraposition to translate the appositives and places them at the beginning of his translation, and then employs the Chinese expression "这些" to sum up the preceding subjects on the one hand and on the other to introduce the predicate of the whole sentence. As a result, the translation is not only intelligible but idiomatic.

3. We feel that the proper procedure *to resolve the issue of which items should follow it* is through consultation.

我们认为,要解决接下去应是哪些项目这个问题,其适当程序是通过协商。

In the sentence, the infinitive "to resolve" is an attribute modifying the subject of the that-clause, "the proper procedure". It will make a considerably long part of attribute combined with its object "the issue" and the relative clause modifying the antecedent. Consequently, the translator first renders this part of attributive as an extraposition immediately after having done the main clause and then uses the character "其" (something like a relative pronoun) as a link to refer back to "the issue" and usher "the procedure" into the translation, hence an idiomatic Chinese sentence.

Ⅸ. Mutual transformation of affirmative and negative expressions(正、反转变)[4]

There are affirmative and negative expressions both in English and in Chinese. Some English words, phrases or sentences of affirmative expression may be transformed into Chinese words, phrases or sentences of negative expression, or vice versa.

A. From affirmative into negative(正说反译)

1. Verbs

(1) If the weather *holds* a couple of days, the plane will take off.

要是天气三两天内保持不变,飞机就起飞。

(2) Such a chance was *denied* me.

我没有得到这样一个机会。

2. Adverbs

(1) We may *safely* say so.

我们这样说万无一失。

(2) The subversion attempts proved *predictably* futile.

不出所料,颠覆活动证明无效。

3. Adjectives

(1) It would be most *disastrous* if even a rumor of it were given out.

甚至只要有一点风声泄漏出去,其结果就不堪设想。

(2) His refusal is not *final*.

他的拒绝并不是不可改变的。

4. Prepositions

(1) This problem is *above* me.

这个问题我不懂(或:我解决不了)。

(2) It was *beyond* his power to sign such a contract.

他无权签订这种合同。

5. Conjunctions

(1) The guerrillas would fight to death *before* they surrendered.

游击队员宁肯战死,也不投降。

(2) He'd rather die standing *than* live kneeling.

他宁肯站着死,也不愿跪着生。

6. Phrases

(1) The islanders found themselves *far from* ready to fight the war.

岛民们发现自己远远没有做好作战准备。

(2) When Philip missed the last bus, he was *at a loss to know* what to do.

菲利普误了最后一班公共汽车,茫然不知该怎么办。

7. Clauses or sentences

(1) He was 75, but *he carried his years lightly*.

他七十五岁了,可是并不显老。

(2) *My guess is as good as yours.*

我的猜测并不比你高明。

B. From negative into affirmative(反说正译)

1. He *carelessly* glanced through the note and got away.

他马马虎虎地看了看那张便条就走了。

2. *Don't lose time* in posting this letter.

赶快把这封信寄出去。

3. *The significance of these incidents wasn't lost on us.*

这些事件引起了我们的重视。

X. Translation of passive voice(被动译法)

It is universally acknowledged that there are two kinds of voices: active and passive. The passive voice is much less used in Chinese than in English. Let's make a comparison and analysis of the following abridged original and translation:

Child Laborors in a Country

In a certain country, millions of working-class children are forced to work as child laborors. Child labor is mostly used in agriculture. It is reported that more than eight hundred thousand children are hired on plantations and farms. They are cruelly exploited by the monopoly capitalists.

...

Child laborors are badly treated by the big farmers. They are made to do what is usually done by grown-ups, but they are paid very much less. In one county in a state of that country, as many as 4,000 children are forced every summer to go and work for the capitalists. They are made to work in the burning sun from seven o'clock in the morning until four in the afternoon...

In recent years monopoly capitalism has been hit harder and harder by economic crises. More and more children have been hired to work in factories and on farms, because the monopoly capitalists are trying very hard to keep the wages low.

...

某一个国家的童工

在某个国家,有数百万工人阶级的子女被迫当童工。童工劳动大多用于农业。据说有八十多万儿童受雇于种植园和农场,受着垄断资本家的残酷剥削。

……

童工受着大农场主的虐待。他们被迫来干通常是成年人干的工作,但收入却少得多。在某州的一个县里,每年夏季竟多达四千儿童被迫为资本家劳动,从早上七点直到下午四点都不得不在烤人的太阳下做事……

近年来,垄断资本主义已经遭到经济危机的越来越严重的打击。越来越多的儿童被雇到工厂和农场劳动,因为垄断资本家正在极力设法使工资保持低水平。

……

The above-quoted English material consists of three passages, eleven sentences. All sentences but one are in the passive voice. Yet the material reads naturally and fluently. The translation would sound quite awkward if we should mechanically render all the predicates in the passive voice by the Chinese passive-voice formula "aux. v. 被 + main v.". In the cited translation the translator overcomes the awkwardness by means of (1) the aux. v. 被(corresponding to English aux. v. be) plus the main verb; (2) the alternative form of passive voice "受" or "遭到"; (3) the idiomatic expression "据说" (equivalent to "be" + said or reported), (4) exchange of voices, such as "收入" meaning "receive" in exchange for "are paid", "不得不……做事" in exchange for "are made to work". The several means of treating the voice as mentioned above are not concoctions but corresponding laws inherent in the two languages concerned.

Notes

1. *Translation—Its Principles and Technique* by Lu Dianyang, 137 – 138, Times Press, 1958.
2. Ibidem, 160.
3. *The Application of Extraposition in Translation* by Xu Shenghuan, *Journal of UN Documents Translation*, No. 2.
4. *A Course of English—Chinese Translation* by Zhang Peiji et al. 103 – 110, Shanghai Foreign Language Education Press, 1980.

Lecture Six　　How to Translate English Attributive Clauses

In English, there are three kinds of complex sentences, namely sentences containing attributive clauses which function as adjectives; sentences containing subject, object, predicative or appositional clauses which function as nouns and sentences containing adverbial clauses which function as adverbs. Among them sentences of the first kind are most difficult to translate. In this lecture we are going to have a discussion of such sentences. First of all, we must know that in Chinese there are attributes which are often translated in the form of attributive clauses in English, e. g.

这就是说,我们不但要把一个政治上受压迫,经济上受剥削的中国变为一个政治上自由与经济上繁荣的中国,而且要把一个被旧文化统治因而愚昧落后的中国,变为一个被新文化统治因而聪明先进的中国。[1]

The corresponding English version is as follows:

In other words, not only do we want to change a China *that is politically oppressed and economically exploited* into a China *that is politically free and economically prosperous*, we also want to change the

China *which is being kept ignorant and backward under the sway of the old culture into an enlightened and progressive* China *under the sway of a new culture.* ²

Secondly, we must know that whether a sentence is smooth or awkward does not depend on whether it is long or short, but depends on whether it is well organized or not. The above example is rather long, yet it is smooth both in the original and in the translation. On the contrary, the following two sentences are not so long, but their respective translations might sound very awkward if we couldn't handle them properly.

1. My plan, which I have used many times, is very simple.

﹡我的我已经用过它多次的方案是很简单的。

2. Toward evening, we stopped at an inn, where we passed the night.

﹡傍晚,我们停在一家我们在那里过了夜的旅店。

No doubt, the Chinese versions of these two sentences both sound awkward because they, on the one hand, violate the law and methods of translating various kinds of attributive clauses and, on the other, do not conform to the Chinese usage. The attributive clauses in the above English sentences are both non-restrictive. In accordance with the proper law and methods of translation and the usage of the Chinese language, they should not be translated word for word as they are in the original and be placed before the words they originally modify, and at the same time there is no need to get the subjects of both attributive clauses expressed in the Chinese translation. Thus the proper translation of the two English sentences should be like this:

1. 我的方案,已经用过多次,很简单。

2. 傍晚,我们停留在一家旅店,在那里过了夜。

As a result, the complex English sentences each with an attributive clause have now been transformed into two simple sentences each with a compound predicate.

From this analysis, we can see that a translator ought to forever observe the laws and methods of translating various kinds of attributive clauses. Grammatically, attributive clauses are divided into two classes: restrictive and non-restrictive. But in translation we must add three classes, namely, semi-adverbial clause as the author of *A Handbook of English Grammar* R. W. Zandvoort calls it or adverbial-attributive clause as I name it.

Class I   Restrictive Attributive Clause[3]

The restrictive attributive clause is used to restrict the meaning of the antecedent it modifies. It has three characteristics: (1) It is placed after the antecedent; (2) Generally there is no comma to separate the clause from the antecedent it modifies; (3) The clause forms an indispensable part of the sentence it belongs to in meaning. If you should drop the attributive clause, the sentence might change its meaning or even become senseless, e. g.

1. This is a book (that) I like best.
2. This is the book (that) I like best.

Without the attributive clause, the first sentence can still stand as an independent simple sentence, but there is a great change in meaning. As for the second, it will no more make sense, for none could understand what you mean by saying "This is the book" without any proper context or conversational situation.

In translating sentences of this kind, generally speaking, we should place the attributives before the words they modify in Chinese. Here I call simply attributives what are corresponding to attributive clauses in English, for in Chinese such modifiers are not necessarily in the form of clauses all the time. Sometimes, they may be either in the form of phrases or in the form of words. This applies to all the following Chinese sentences.

1. This is *the place where the workers' and peasants' Red Army made the crossing in* 1934.

这就是工农红军1934年渡江的地方。

2. A. Do you know *the man who spoke to your father yesterday*?

你认识昨天对你父亲讲话的那个人吗?

B. No, I don't know who he is.

不,我不晓得他是谁。

3. Here is *the man you are looking for*.

你正在寻找的那个人就在这儿。

4. *Everything he said* seemed quite reasonable.

他说的话似乎都很有道理。

5. That is *the first book of the kind I have ever come across*.

这是我碰见的第一本这样的书。

6. She made a list of *all the articles there are on the subject*.

她把有关这个题目的现有的一切文章列了一个单子。

7. There is no *difficulty we can't overcome*.

没有我们不能克服的困难。

8. This is *the problem which remains to be solved*.

这就是那个尚待解决的问题。

9. That's *the way they study*.

这就是他们学习的方法。

10. Who is *the man you visited yesterday*?

你昨天访问的那个人是谁?

11. *Such people as they are* will never do that sort of thing.

像他们那样的人永远都不会做那种事情。

12. Have you got *the same pen as I bought last week*?
你已经得到像我上周买的那样的钢笔吗?

In general, such attributives in Chinese are also placed before the words they modify as mentioned above. But in some particular cases, as in those sentences whose main clauses are of the "there is (or are)" pattern, either kind of word order—the attributives placed before the words they modify or the attributives placed after them sounds all right, e. g.

(1) But there are still *people who have failed to memorize the lessons of the past*.

(2) How many *students* are there in your class *whose homes are in the countryside*?

Compare the two Chinese versions of each of the original sentences in the following:

(1) 但仍然有人没有记取过去的教训。

但仍然有没有记取过去教训的人。

(2) 你们班上有多少同学家在乡下?

你们班上家在乡下的同学有多少?

Both versions are grammatical. Yet the former, the so-called pivotal sentence pattern, it seems, sounds more natural, and thus it is preferable.

Class II Non-restrictive Attributive Clauses

The non-restrictive or continuative attributive clauses are used to give further or supplementary explanations to the words they modify. Generally, there is no need for antecedents and attributive clauses to chang places with each other. That's to say, the same word order may remain in the translation from English into Chinese. This applies to sentences from 1 to 8. e. g.

1. Someone proposed the name of *Mr. Smith*, *whom we elected as representative*. (= and we elected him...)

有人提史密斯先生的名,我们选他当了代表。

2. Last week I saw *Modern Times* with Charles Chaplin playing the leading role, *which I think one of the most amusing films*. (= and I think it...)

上周我看了查理·卓别林主演的《摩登时代》,我认为是最有趣的影片之一。

3. *His article*, *which I have just read*, is very instructive.

他的文章,我刚才读过,很有教育意义。

4. Westminster Abbey, which is one of the oldest churches in Great Britain, contains the graves of many famous Englishmen.

威斯敏斯特教堂,大不列颠最古老的教堂之一,里面有许多知名英国人士的坟墓。

5. It rained *all night and all day*, during which time the ship broke into pieces. (= and during that time...)

雨整整下了一天一夜,在那段时间里,那条船破碎了。

6. Jack is *a scholar*, *in whose study there are lots of books*. (= and in his study...)

杰克是个学者,他书房里有很多书。

7. *John won the race*, *which made him very happy*. (= and it...)

约翰赛跑获胜,这使他很高兴。

8. *The relations between China and the United States of America have been improved*, *which will contribute to our four modernizations and world peace*. (= and it...)

中美两国关系已经得到改善,这将有利于我们的四个现代化和世界和平。

In all such attributive clauses, we may change the relative pronoun into a personal pronoun and connect it to the main clause by the conjunction "and". But there are two cases in the order of clauses. (1) the order may remain if the attributive clause is originally placed after the main clause (sentences 1,2,5,6,7 and 8); (2) the and-clause will have to be shifted to the place after the predicate of the main clause if it is originally inserted between the subject of the main clause and its predicate (sentences 3 and 4). As to the order in the Chinese versions, it remains just as it is in the original sentences.

So far as the method of translating these sentences is concerned, all such attributives are placed after the words they modify. But the disposal of the relative pronouns are not quite alike. (1) They are usually omitted in the Chinese version when used as subjects or objects (sentences 2,3,4); (2) They must be translated when used as other parts. In sentences 5 and 6, "which" and "whose" are both used as attributes. (3) Sentences 7 and 8 have their own characteristics; First, the relative pronoun is always the word "which" and what it stands for is not a noun or noun phrase but the whole main clause; secondly, it always serves as the subject of the subordinate clause and it may often be rendered as the Chinese character "这".

Class Ⅲ Semi-Adverbial

The following attributive clauses are named semi-adverbial by R. W. Zandvoort in his work entitled *A Handbook of English Grammar*. The term signifies that such clauses are attributive ones in form, but adverbial ones in function and sense. Yao Shanyou calls such clauses as "formally attributive clauses functioning as adverbial ones in sense" in his *English Grammar*. They may be translated into Chinese as adverbial clauses expressing cause, purpose, condition, etc. e. g.

1. *Premier Zhou who was busy all day long never knew what* fatigue was. (who = though or although he)

周总理虽然整天很忙,却从不知疲倦。(concession)

2. *My uncle, who will be seventy tomorrow,* is still a keen sportsman. [4] (who = though or although he)

我伯父虽然明天就满七十岁了,但仍爱好运动。(concession)

3. *Envoys* were sent *who should strengthen our international position.* (who should = so that they should)[5]

派了使节,以便加强我们的国际地位。(purpose)

4. *Anybody who should do that* would be laughed at. (who = if he)

无论是谁,只要做那种事情,都一定会受到嘲笑。(condition)

5. For further particulars you had better apply to *my brother, who has paid particular attention to the subject.* (who = because he)

关于细节,你最好询问我弟弟,因为他对这个问题特别留意。(cause)

All such attributive clauses can be placed after the words they modify in the Chinese version and connected to them by "虽然","以便","只要" or"因为" etc. Meanwhile, the subjects of the subordinate clauses may be omitted in translation as in examples 1,2,3,4, if they refer to the same persons as those of the main ones; otherwise, they should be retained in the Chinese version as in example 5.

Sometimes, the subordinating conjunction expressing cause may be omitted in the Chinese version, and the relation between cause and result can still be felt by the reader. e. g.

6. *Out teacher, who is getting old*, will soon retire. (who = as he)

我们的老师,越来越老,不久就要退休。(cause)

7. *The people's war in Russia, which inflicted heavy losses on Napoleon's army*, incensed *the conqueror, who had never met that kind of opposition anywhere in Europe*. (which = because it; who = as he)

俄国的人民战争,使拿破仑的军队受到重大的损失,激怒了这位征服者,(因为)他在欧洲任何地方都从来没有遭到过那样的反抗。(cause)

Class Ⅳ   Attributive Clauses Introduced by Relative Pronoun "As"

When the word "as" alone is used as relative pronouns in the attributive clauses, there may be five cases[6] with its antecedents.

Here only three of them will be illustrated. Please pay attention to the function and translation of the word "as" in the subordinate clause.

Ⅰ. The word "as" standing for the concept of an action in the clause

1. *To write a dull book*, as any poor writer could do, was unworthy of him.

写一本枯燥无味的书,这是任何一个蹩脚的作家都会做的,但对他来说,是不相称的。

2. It is absolutely wrong *to think foreign languages useless*, as quite a few people did before.

认为外语无用是绝对错误的,不少人过去有这种想法。

In sentence 1 the word "as" stands for the concept expressed by the infinitive phrase "to write a dull book" and in sentence 2 for that expressed by the infinitive phrase "to think foreign languages useless". The phrases both serve as the subject, and thus the word "as" is a relative pronoun, which functions as the object of a verb to do. In such sentence patterns, the Chinese word "这" or expression "这种" may be used to translate the relative pronoun "as".

II. The word "as" standing for the concept which may be inferred from a similar noun or noun phrase in the main clause.

In such sentence patterns, the relative pronoun "as" may be translated in Chinese as "这"(Ex. 1) or "这种"(Ex. 2).

1. No many young people wish to be *scientists*, as (= scientists) it is possible for them to be on condition that they work hard.

现在许多青年都想当科学家,在自己刻苦努力的条件下,这是大有可能如愿以偿的。

2. His grandfather was *a simple-mannered man*, as (= simple mannered man in its plural form) the large-hearted and large-minded men are apt to be.

他祖父质朴大方,慷慨而心胸开阔的人也往往是这样。

3. He seems *a foreigner*, as (= a foreigner) in fact he is.

他似乎是个外国人,事实上,他也是个外国人。

III. The word "as" standing for the concept expressed by an adjective in the main clause

1. He was not *sick*, *as* (= sick) some of the other passengers were.

他并没有病,其余乘客有些人倒是病了。

2. He thinks her answer *incorrect*, *as* (= incorrect) it probably is.

他认为她的回答不正确,她的回答大概也是不正确的。

There are two common characteristics in the second and third use of the word "as": (1) "as" serves as the predicative in the subordinate clause; (2) there is a verb to be in the clause where "as" functions as a relative pronoun. You may either use "这" or "这样" or repeat the foregoing noun or adjective to represent "as" while translating such sentence patterns.

Class V   Attributive Clauses to Be Treated in Unusual Ways

Ex. 1. In short, we are for a world *in which every people, rooted in their national cultural values, will be receptive to the abundant benefits of other nations.*

一句话,我们赞成这样的世界:每个国家的人民都扎根于自己的民族文化宝库之中,又汲取其他国家的丰富滋养。[7]

Ex. 2. But it has the big disadvantages that we have no large and disciplined army of socialist leaders *who understand the objectives in all their complexity*, and *who have clear ideas about how to promote the movement towards them.*

但它的一大缺点是使我们缺少这样一大批受过训练的社会主义领导人,他们懂得我们目标的全部复杂含义,并且明确地知道怎样才能推动运动朝着这些目标前进。

Ex. 3. He unselfishly contributed his uncommon talents and indefatigable spirit to the struggle *which today brings them (those aims) within the reach of a majority of the human race.*

他把自己非凡的才智和不倦的精力无私地献给了这种斗争,它今天已使人类中大多数人可以达到这些目标。[8]

All the restrictive attributive clauses in the three examples are not translated in the Chinese structure ending in the character "的" and placed before the words they modify, but rendered as post-positioned explanatory clauses. And at the same time, the English articles before the antecedents should be converted into the Chinese modifiers "这样的" as in Ex. 1, "这样" as in Ex. 2 or "这种" as in Ex. 3 in order to show the close relation between the words to be further explained and the clauses which aim to make a further explanation of the original antecedents; we have treated the restrictive attributive clauses in the three above examples in such an unusual way, either because there are more than one restrictive attributive clause as in Ex. 1 and Ex. 2, or because the restrictive attributive clause is rather long as in Ex. 3. If we should translate them as we usually do, the Chinese versions would sound unnatural and unidiomatic.

Ex. 4. He liked his sister, *who was warm and pleasant*, but he did not like his brother, *who was aloof and arrogant*.

他喜欢热情愉快的妹妹,而不喜欢冷漠高傲的哥哥。

Ex. 5. But his laugh, *which was very infectious*, broke the silence.

但他富有感染力的笑声打破了沉默。

The above-mentioned two attributive clauses are non-restrictive in from, but they are all rendered as premodifiers just like restrictive ones. It's because they are short and closely related to their antecedents. They would result in a loose sentence construction and a choppy context in case we should translate them as we usually do nonrestrictive attributive clauses.

Ex. 6. We are peoples *that have inherited ancient wisdom, that know the worth of biding one's time and recognized opportunity for combat.*

我们的人民继承了古代的智慧,懂得如何等待并善于抓住战机。

Ex. 7. In a word, a true revolution is one *that is devoted to human progress in all domains and that makes human progress the supreme and final object.*

总之,真正的革命,致力于人的全面发展,并以此作为行动的最高指标。

Ex. 8. We live in a world *where relations between states are relations of forces.*

在我们所处的世界上,国家之间的关系是力量对比的关系。

In examples 6, 7 and 8, all the attributive clauses are restrictive, but they are translated in special ways: In the first two, they are transformed into predicates of the Chinese sentences with the omission of relative pronouns after the main clauses are compressed into noun phrases serving as subjects of the predicates mentioned above. In the third, the main clause is compressed into an adverbial phrase while the restrictive attributive clause transformed into the SVA Chinese version with relative adverb already blended in the adverbial phrase at the very beginning of the sentence.

Ex. 9. He had talked to vice-president Nixon, *who assured him that everything that could be done would be done.*

他同副总统尼克松谈过话。副总统向他担保,凡是能够做到的都将竭尽全力去做。

Ex. 10. He is with his youngest son, *who is accompanying him on his lecture tour in China.*

他带着小儿子。小儿子陪他在中国进行巡回演讲。[9]

In these two examples, the actors and sufferers of the action are of the same number and sex. If, in the second clause of the Chinese version, we do not repeat the nouns functioning as antecedents in the original, the reader will not be able to make clear who is the actor, because there is not the so-called relative pronoun in the Chinese language. Since the nouns have to be repeated, the better way out is to make the second clause independent, which seems more natural and idiomatic in Chinese.

The methods of translating the several kinds of attributive clauses as discussed above are not complete at all, but they are fairly typical. They may be helpful to beginners if they properly take them for reference.

Notes

1. Mao Zedong, *On New Democracy* (Chinese version).
2. Mao Zedong, *On New Democracy* (English version).
3. Part of the English example sentences in this class are cited from *A Practical English Grammar* by Zhang Daozhen.
4. This English example sentence is quoted from *A Handbook of English Grammar* by R. W. Zandvoort.
5. English example sentences from 3 to 7 are cited from *English Grammar* by Yao Shanyou.
6. See the book entitled *A Study of the Uses of the English Word "As"* by Liu Zhongde, Hunan People's Publishing House, 1979.
7. Exx 1,2,6,7,8, Ma Zuyi, 1980, *On the Technique of Translation from English into Chinese*, Jiangsu People's Publishing House.
8. Exx 3,4,9,10, Lu Hongmei, *On the Translation of English Attributive Clauses*, read at the Discussion of Contrastive Study and Translation between English and Chinese, held in Jiangxi, July, 1990.
9. Ex 5, Gu Yanling and Xiong Xiling, 1989, *A Course of English-Chinese Chinese-English Translation*.

Lecture Seven Image-Rendering and Sentence-Division in Translation from Chinese into English

Naturally, there are quite a lot of questions worthy of discussion in the course of translation from Chinese into English. But in this lecture the author will only have a talk about the question of how to render images and that of how to make sentence divisions found in the essay entitled *Oppose Stereotyped Writing* by Mao Zedong. [1]

I How to Render Images

Images and figures of speech are essential components of the literary language. But they can also be found in some thesis and speeches. The language in Mao Zedong's works is rich in images and figures of speech, which the American writer Anna Louis Strong commended long ago. So far as his essay *Oppose Stereotyped Writing* is concerned, it abounds with images and figures of speech. Ten of them are quoted and a comparison and analysis made so as to find out some universally applicable rules for reference.

Lecture Seven　Image-Rendering and Sentence-Division in Translation from Chinese into English

1. 如果我们连党八股也打倒了,那就算对于主观主义和宗派主义最后地"将一军",弄得这两个怪物原形毕露,"老鼠过街,人人喊打",这两个怪物也就容易消灭了。

If we destroy that (referring to the stereotyped party writing) too, we shall "*checkmate*" subjectivism and sectarianism and make both these *monsters* show themselves in their true colours, and then we shall easily be able to annihilate them, like "*rats* running across the street with every one yelling, kill them! Kill them!"

2. 中国是一个小资产阶级成分极其广大的国家,我们党是处在这个广大阶级的包围中,我们又有很大数量的党员是出身于这个阶级的,他们都不免或长或短地拖着一条小资产阶级的尾巴进党来。

China is a country with a very large petty bourgeoisie and our Party is surrounded by this enormous class; a great number of our Party members come from this class, and when they join the Party they inevitably drag in with them a petty-bourgeois *tail*, be it long or short.

3. 说理的首要方法,就是重重给病患者一个刺激,向他们大喝一声,说"你有病呀!"使患者为之一惊,出一身汗,然后好好地叫他们治疗。

The first thing to do in this reasoning process is to give the *patient* a good shake-up by shouting at him, "You are ill!" so as to administer a shock and make him break out in a sweat, and then to give him sincere advice on getting treatment.

4. 我们有些同志喜欢写长文章,但是没有内容,真是"懒婆娘的裹脚,又长又臭"。

Some of our comrades love to write long articles with no substance, very much like the *foot-bindings of a slattern* long as well as smelly.

5. "对牛弹琴"这句话,含有讥笑对象的意思。

The saying "*to play the flute to a cow*" implies a gibe at the audience.

6. 何况这是党八股，简直是老鸦声调，却偏要向人民群众哇哇地叫。

What is worse, he is producing a Party stereotype *as raucous as a crow*, and yet he insists on *cawing* at the masses.

7. 党八股的第五条罪状是：甲乙丙丁，开中药铺。

The fifth indictment against stereotyped writing is that it arranges items under a complicated set of headings, *as if starting a Chinese pharmacy*.

8. 主观主义和宗派主义的东西，表现在党八股式的文章和演说里面，却生怕人家驳，非常胆怯，于是就靠样子吓人，以为这一吓，人家就会闭口，自己就可以"得胜回朝"了。

But those who write subjectivist and sectarian articles and speeches in the form of Party stereotypes fear refutation, are vey cowardly, and therefore rely on pretentiousness to overawe others, believing that they can thereby silence people and "*win the day*".

In this sentence, Mao Zedong quotes the saying "得胜回朝" which means that a general wins the day (or the field) and comes back (or returns) to the court. But the translator retains the first half of the saying "得胜" (win the day) and gives up the second half "回朝" (return to the court). In my opinion, it is better to render the saying literally as "win the field and return to the court". We have three reasons: First, the saying itself as a whole is translatable; secondly, the literal translation is contextually intelligible; and thirdly, it accords with the principle of keeping the original images. We should be quite careful about images or figures of speech and try our best to keep them as much as possible for the sacrifice of them would cause more or less impairment or loss of them.

9. 俗话说："到什么山上唱什么歌。"又说："看菜吃饭，量体裁衣。"

As the sayings go, "Sing different songs on different mountains" and "fit the dress to the figure and fit the appetite to the dishes".

In this sentence, the translator uses not only the method of literal translation to keep the images, e. g. "Sing different *songs* on different *mountains*" and "fit the *dress* to the *figure*" but also the means of flexible translation by which "dishes" is still of literal translation whereas the image "appetite" an exchange for that of "rice".

10. 党八股的第四条罪状是:语言无味,像个瘪三。上海人叫瘪三的那批角色,也很像我们的党八股,干瘪得很,样子十分难看。如果一篇文章,一个演说,颠来倒去,总是那几个名词,一套"学生腔",没有一点生动活泼的语言,这岂不是语言无味,面目可憎,像个瘪三吗?……我们很多人没有学好语言,所以我们在写文章做演说时没有几句生动活泼切实有力的话,只有死板板的几条筋,像瘪三一样,瘦得难看,不像一个健康的人。

The fourth indictment against stereotyped Party writing is its drab language that reminds one of a *Piehsan*.² Like our stereotyped writing, the creatures known in Shanghai as "little piehsan" are wizened and ugly. If an article or a speech merely rings the changes on a few terms in a *classroom tone* without a shred of vigour or spirit, is it not like a piehsan, drab of speech and repulsive in appearance?... It is because many of us have not mastered language that our articles and speeches contain few vigorous, vivid and effective expressions and *resemble not a hale and healthy person but an emaciated piehsan, a mere bag of bones.*

In this example, the rendering of images and figures of speech is done not only by means of literal translation as "resemble not a hale and healthy person" but also by means of flexible translation as "classroom tone" in which the image of a student or a scholar is replaced by that of a classroom. Besides, transliteration is used, e. g. "piehsan".

To sum up, four methods of rendering images and figures of speech are found in this article and they may be applied both to the translation from Chinese into English and to that from English into Chinese.

The first is the method of literal translation. It makes up 90% in the 10 above examples. This shows how important literal translation is in rendering images and figures of speech. Just as Lu Xun pointed out, it could retain the "sentiment" and "charm" of the original.

The second is the method of transformation of images. It still makes the language vivid and lively although it transforms the original images into new ones. There are two cases: partial transformation as "fit the appetite to the dishes" and entire transformation as "a mere bag of bones".

The third is the method of free translation to convey the meaning the original images contain. We must be careful not to overuse it lest it should impair the images and lose them, thus depriving the language of vividness and liveliness. Sometimes it is unavoidable. However, we must see to it that the true meaning the original images contain is fully conveyed. For instance, the translation of the Chinese saying "逼上梁山" as "to join the rebels as the last resort" is well-done. But generally we ought to do our utmost to retain the images or at least replace them by other appropriate ones in order to make the language vivid and lively. Now let's have a discussion of how to translate the Chinese saying "同声相应,同气相求". If we should adopt the method of literal translation to retain the original images, the non-Chinese readers would feel it hard to understand their true metaphorical sense. If we should adopt the method of free translation to express the meaning they contain, it would become dry and lifeless. In accordance with the principle of making the translation as picturesque as the original, here we may apply the method of exchange of images to put the above Chinese saying into the English "Birds of a feather flock together". Both expressions mean "Like attracts like".

The fourth is the method of translation, e. g. the translation of "瘪三" as "piehsan". When we use transliteration, we must pay attention to its intelligibility. For instance, the transliteration "piehsan" is intelligible enough because the author of the original makes clear what a piehsan is like in the context. Otherwise, we will have to give proper footnotes to the transliterations so that the foreign readers may understand them. Though this method is seldom used, accounting for only 10% in the examples, yet it is indispensable. In fact, it has already a long history, e. g. the transliteration of feudalistic term "衙门" as "yamen" and that of "叩头" as "Kowtow" or "kotow" which can be found in dictionaries compiled and published in UK and USA.

II How to Make Sentence Division

Owing to the fact that Chinese and English belong to different language families, there are dissimilarities in the use of some punctuation marks. For instance, Chinese has the mark dun(、), whereas English has not such a mark. There is not any mark between the personal name and the family name of a Westerner, but we must insert a mark like a full stop as soon as they are translated into Chinese. Its only difference from a period is in its place which is a little higher than the position of a full stop of a sentence. Take the transliteration 威廉·莎士比亚 of William Shakespeare for example. Here I would like to go into the usage of commas and periods.

Commas are much more often used in Chinese than in English while periods are much more often used in English than in Chinese. That's to say, sometimes commas (occasionally semi-colons) in the Chinese original have to be changed into periods in the corresponding English version. As a result, the Chinese sentence will become at least two sentences. which naturally brings about the question of sentence division. Make a comparison between the sentences selected from the same essay and the sentences of English version:

1. 因为长而且空,群众见了就摇头,(comma)哪里还会看下去呢?

Because the articles are long and empty, the masses shake their heads at the very sight of them. (the period replacing the comma in the original) How can they be expected to read them?

2. 延安虽然还没有战争,但军队天天在前方打仗,后方也唤工作忙,(comma)文章太长了,有谁来看呢?

Although there is as yet no fighting here in Yen'an,³ our troops at the front are daily engaged in battle, and the people in the rear are busy at work. (the period replacing the comma in the original) If articles are too long, who will read them?

3. 比如军事指挥员,(comma)他们并不对外发宣言,但是他们要和士兵讲话,要和人民接洽,(comma)这不是宣传是什么?

The military commanders, for instance. (The period replacing the comma in the original) Though they make no public statements, they have to talk to the soldiers and have dealings with people. (again the period replacing the comma in the original) What is this if not propaganda?

4. 提出问题,首先就要对于问题即矛盾两个基本方面加以大略的调查和研究,才能懂得矛盾的性质是什么,(comma)这就是发现问题的过程。

To pose the problem, you must first make a preliminary investigation and study of the two aspects of the problem or contradiction before you can understand the nature of the contradiction. (the period replacing the comma in the original) This is the process of discovering the problem.

5. 要解决问题,还须作系统的周密的调查工作和研究工作,(comma)这就是分析的过程。

In order to solve the problem it is necessary to make a systematic and thorough investigation and study. (the period replacing the comma in the original) This is the process of analysis.

6. 拿洗脸作比方,(comma)我们每天都要洗脸,许多人并且不止洗一次,洗完之后还要拿镜子照一照,要调查研究一番,(loud laughter)生怕有什么不妥当的地方。

Let us take washing the face to illustrate the point. (the period replacing the comma in the original) We all wash our faces every day, many of us more than once, and inspect ourselves in the mirror afterwards by way of "investigation and study" (loud laughter) for fear that something may not be quite right.

7. 其结果,往往是下笔千言,离题万里,(comma)仿佛像个才子,实在到处害人。

Often the result is "A thousand words from the pen in a stream, but ten thousand li away from the theme". (the period replacing the comma in the original) Talented though these writers may appear, they actually harm people.

8. 总之,不看实际情形,死守着呆板的形式、旧习惯,(comma)这种现象,不是也应该加以改革吗?

In short, there is a disregard for actual conditions and deadly adherence to rigid forms and old habits. (the period replacing the comma in the original) Should we not correct all these things too?

9. 所以我劝这些同志先办"少许",再去办"化",不然,仍旧脱离不了教条主义和党八股,(comma)这叫做眼高手低,志大才疏,没有结果的。

I would therefore advise these comrades to begin just a little change before they go on to "transform", or else they will remain entangled in dogmatism and stereotyped Party writing. (the period replacing the comma in the original) This can be described as having grandiose aims but puny abilities, great ambition but little talent, and it will accomplish nothing.

10. 有些天天喊大众化的人,连三句老百姓的话都讲不来,(comma)可见他就没有下过决心跟老百姓学,(comma)实在他的意思仍是小众化。

There are some who keep clamouring for transformation to a mass style but cannot speak three sentences of the common people. (the period replacing the comma in the original) It shows they are not really determined to learn from the masses. (the period replacing the comma in the original) Their minds are still confined to their own small circles.

11. 孔夫子提倡"再思",韩愈也说"行成于思",(comma)那是古代的事情。

Confucius advised, "Think twice". And Han Yu said, "A deed is accomplished through taking thought." (the period replacing the comma in the original) That was in ancient times.

12. 鲁迅说"至少看两遍",(comma)至多呢?

Lu Hsun[4] said, "Read it over twice at least". (the period replacing the comma in the original) And at most?

13. 把国际主义的内容和民族形式分离起来,是一点也不懂国际主义的人们的做法,(comma)我们要把二者紧密地结合起来。

To separate internationalist content from national form is the practice of those who do not understand the first thing about internationalism. (the period replacing the comma in the original) We, on the contrary, must link the two closely.

14. 但是"化"者,彻头彻尾彻里彻外之谓也;(semicolon)有些人则连"少许"还没有实行,却在那里提倡"化"呢!

But "transformation" means thorough change, from top to bottom and inside out. (the period replacing the semi-colon in the original) Yet some people who have not made even a slight change are calling for a transformation.

Each of the 14 quotations in the above forms one sentence in the original text, but it becomes more that one in the English version. Through an analysis and comparison of the linguistic data in the 14 quotations we can draw a conclusion as follows:

Generally speaking, a comma (sometimes a semi-colon though not so often) in the Chinese original may be replaced by a full stop in the English version before the following 5 categories of sentences: 1. Sentences of Interrogation, see Exx 1, 2, 3, 8 and 12. 2. Sentences of Exemplification, see Exx 3 and 6. The English expressions "Take sth. (for example or instance)" and "(Let us) take A to illustrate B" belong to this category. 3. Sentences of Generalization, see Exx 4, 5, 9 and 10. The English sentence patterns "This or That plus linking verb be", "This or That can be described (or defined) as..." and "this shows..." falls in this category. 4. Sentences of contrariness, see Exx 13 and 14. 5. Sentences of Explanation, see Ex 7. In the English version the second sentence functions as a further explanation of the first.

Since there exists the phenomenon of sentence-dividing in the translation from Chinese into English, there must be the phenomenon of sentence-combining in the translation from English into Chinese. Take the following two sentences:

There is a dictionary on the desk. It is very useful. The two sentences may be combined to form a sentence in the Chinese version like this: 书桌上有本词典,很有用。

Notes

1. The original is based on *Selected Works of Mao Zedong* published by the People's Publishing House in 1969 and the translation on the English version of his selected works published by the Foreign Languages Press, Beijing, 1965.
2. 3. 4. "瘪三""延安" and "鲁迅" should be spelt as biesan, Yan'an and Lu Xun instead of piehsan, Yenan and Lu Hsun according to the Chinese Phonetic Alphabet. But the Wade's spellings Piehsan, Yenan and Lu Hsun remain as they are so as to retain the original transliteration.

Lecture Eight Translatability of Literary Style

1. Definition of Style and Its Identification

Talking of the question of translatability of literary style, we must, first of all, make clear what style is. According to the Revised Edition of *A Dictionary of Literary Terms* (J. A. Cuddon, 1979) , style is " the characteristic manner of expression in prose or verse; how a particular writer says things. The analysis and assessment of style involves examination of a writer's choice of words, his figures of speech, the devices (rhetorical and otherwise) , the shape of his sentences (whether they be loose or periodic) , the shape of paragraphs—indeed, of every conceivable aspect of his language and the way in which he uses it. " Style may be compared to "the tone and voice of the writer himself, which is as much peculiar to him as his laugh, his walk, his handwriting and expressions on his face. " [1]

In the words of Theodore Savory, "Style is the essential characteristic of every piece of writing, the outcome of the writer's personality and his emotions at the moment, and no single paragraph can be put together without revealing in some degree the nature of its author." (Theodore Savory. 1957)²

In short, style is the man as Buffon put it: Buffon was a thinker and writer of France in the eighteenth century.

It is universally acknowledged that every writer has a literary style and that his style is reflected in his writing. As everybody knows, both Li Bai (李白) and Du Fu (杜甫) were great poets of the Tang dynasty in China, but their literary styles are different. Li's is elegant and forceful whereas Du's profound and thoughtful. So is the case with the style of Henry James and that of Ernest Hemingway. The style of the former is wordy and obscure and that of the latter brief and implicit. (张英进,1986)³

The above-mentioned instances fully testify to the correctness of the well-known Buffon eighteenth-century statement that style is the man. When a literary work which has a distinct style is read, the author may be immediately identified even if the work is published under a pen name. There is a very interesting story about Lu Xun (鲁迅). In 1918, Zhou Shuren (周树人) published a short story entitled *Diary of a Madman* (《狂人日记》) in the magazine *New Youth* (《新青年》) and adopted "Lu Xun" as his pen name for the first time. His intimate friend Xu Shoushang (许寿裳) was deeply moved and attracted by the story as he read it at Nanchang, Jiangxi. He thought that it must have been written by his friend Zhou Shuren because its content was so profound and its wording so pithy and sharp. But the name printed under the title of the story was "Lu Xun" which he had never heard of before. Then he wrote a letter to Zhou: "Have you read *Diary of a Madman*? Do you know the author of the story?" Zhou gave Xu a reply telling him that Lu Xun was his pen name.⁴

There is no doubt that different literary works have discernibly different styles. But as soon as the question of translatability of the original style is raised, people are not of the same opinion. Theodore Savory points out in his book *The Art of Translation* that some people say "A translation should reflect the style of the original" and others say "A translation should possess the style of the translator," Savory him self advocates that translation should reflect the original style and illustrates the possibility of reproducing the style of the original in the words of Liche and Moore: "Suppose that we have succeeded in writing a faithful translation of a characteristic page of Ruskin, and that we submit it for criticism to two well-educated French friends, one of whom has but little acquaintance with English, while the other has an intimate knowledge of our language. If the first were to say 'A fine description! Who is the author?' and the second 'surely that is Ruskin, though I do not remember the passage', then we might be confident that in respect of style our translation did not fall too far short of our ideal. We should have written French that was French, while it still kept the flavour of the original." [5]

2. Translatability of Style

Among Chinese translators, there are still quite a few who consider the original literary style untranslatable although many think that it should be reproduced and that it is possible to reproduce it. It seems that the question of translatability is worth further discussing. Here in this part, I'd like to introduce the arguments for the translatability of style. As for those against it they will be analyzed in the next three parts.

Translators who deem it possible to reproduce the style of the original work have a lot of valuable opinions. But because the space is limited, they can't be quoted here one by one. Mao Dun (茅盾) may be taken as their representative. In 1954, he pointed out at the National Conference of Literary Translators:

"Literary works are a kind of art created in language. What we demand of them is not merely the recording of concepts and of incidents. Besides these, they should possess artistic images which are attractive to the reader. In other words, the reader must have a strong feeling towards the characters' thought and behaviour through the artistic images portrayed in their literary works. Literary translation is to reproduce the original artistic images in another language so that the reader of the translation may be inspired, moved and aesthetically entertained in the same way as one reads the original.

"Naturally, such a translation is not purely a technical change in the form of language, but it requires that the translator realize the author's process of artistic creation, grasp the spirit of the original, find the most appropriate confirmation in his own thought, feeling and experience, and reproduce fully and correctly the content and form of the original in a literary language suited to the original style... Since the main task of literary translation lies in the faithful reproduction of the spirit and features of the original, such creative artistic translation is quite necessary. And many outstanding examples among the translations of world literature have proved that it is possible. Lu Xun's translation《死魂灵》(*Dead Souls*) written by Gogol and the translation of Pushkin's《茨冈》(*Tsygane*) done by Qu Qiubai (瞿秋白) and the latter's translations of some writings by Gorki have also proved the possibility of such creative artistic translation."[6]

Qu Qiubai's art of translation has been and is still highly valued. The greatest characteristic of his translation is his faithfulness to the original. He is so faithful that his translation is quite like the original not only in content but also in form including syntactic structures and style. He gives the reader a Pushkinian style in translating Pushkin and a Gorkian in doing Gorki. (Li Pan, 1984) [7]

As for Western translation theoreticians, there are a large number of well-known ones who firmly maintain both the necessity and possibility of reproducing the original style. For instance, Alexander Fraser Tytler (1813) says in the first chapter of his *Essay on the Principles of Translation*:

"I would therefore describe a good translation to be that in which the merit of the original work is so completely transfused into another language, as to be as distinctly apprehended, and as strongly felt, by a native of the country to which that language belongs, as it is by those who speak the language of the original work." [8]

Both the Chinese and Western theoreticians as mentioned above hold that the reproduction of the literary style of the original work is necessary and possible, still I must admit that it is really a hard task to accomplish. Take translating Homer for example. From the criticism of the various translations of Homer by Mathew Arnold (1906), we can easily see how hard a job it is to reproduce the Homerian style. To translate Homer successfully, "the translator of Homer should above all be penetrated by a sense of four qualities of his author:—that he is eminently rapid; that he is eminently plain and direct, both in the evolution of his thought and in the expression of it, that is, both in his syntax and in his words; that he is eminently plain and direct in the substance of his thought, that is, in his matter and ideas; and finally that he is eminently noble:—I probably seem to be saying what is too general to be of much service to anybody. Yet it is strictly true that, for want of duly penetrating themselves with the first-named quality of Homer, his rapidity, Cowper and Mr Wright have failed in rendering him; that, for want of appreciating the second-named quality, his plainness and directness of style and diction, Pope and Sotheby have failed in rendering him; that, for want of appreciating the third, his plainness and directness of ideas, Chapman has failed in rendering him; while for want of appreciating the fourth, his nobleness, Mr Newman, who has clearly seen some of the faults of his predecessors, has yet failed more conspicuously than any of them. " [9]

In spite of the difficulty in reproducing the original style, I quite agree to the views maintained by Dr. Nida in his *Language Structure and Translation*.

"Rather than being impressed by the impossibilities of translation," says he, "anyone who is involved in the realities of translation in a broad range of languages is impressed that effective interlingual communication is always possible, despite seemingly enormous differenees in linguistic structures and cultural features. These impressions as to the relative adequacy of interlingual communication are based on two fundamental factors: (1) semmatic similarities between languages, due no doubt in large measure to the common core of human experience; and (2) fundamental similarities in the syntactic structures of languages at the so-called kernel, core, level. " [10] It seems, then, that the principle of dynamic equivalence (or functional equivalence) put forward by Nida is worth studying for it may contribute to the reproduction of the original style in translation.

3. Analysis of the First Argument Against the Translatability of Style

What arguments have those who consider the style of the original work untranslatable then? Generally speaking, they have three arguments. Let's discuss them one by one in the following:

One argument is that different languages can't express the same style. We acknowledge that different languages bear different characteristics. As an illustration of this, we may make a comparison between the English and Chinese languages. English has articles, but Chinese does not have any such things. The possessive pronouns, conjunctions and passive voice are much more often used in English than in Chinese. The ways of answering the "yes-no questions" are sometimes different in the two languages. However, there do exist corresponding laws between English and Chinese. For instance. "The horse is a useful animal" and "马是有用的动物", "He put on his coat and his hat and went out" and "他穿上上衣,戴上帽子就出去了", "Isn't she at home? No, she isn't" and "他不在家吗? 是的, 他不在家" ——all these are idiomatic and expressive English and Chinese sentences corresponding to each other in essense and spirit. Translation would become a little easier if we bad a good command of such existing corresponding linguistic laws. All languages are basically the same in function. That is to say, they can all express thoughts, reflect life, describe surroundings, portray images, create new words and produce literary works of various styles.

As far as style is concerned, we must take the whole piece of writing into consideration instead of some particular words or expressions. Those who consider the original literary style untranslatable often try to prove their arguments with puns, poems and other things that are difficult to translate. "Broadly speaking, the cases this happens fall into two categories. Those where the difficulty is linguistic, and those where it is cultural. (Catford, 1965)"[11] But a qualified translator is usually possessed of some appropriate ways of cracking his hard nuts in translation once he is determined to translate a work. Sometimes, puns may be rendered still as puns. Zhang Guruo (张谷若) tried successfully to keep them while translating *David Copperfield*. There is no denying that some puns can't be well retained. Then the translator can convey its main meaning and add a footnote as a compensation for its lost sense, e. g.

杨柳青青江水平,闻郎江上唱歌声。
东边日出西边雨,道是无晴还有晴。
——刘禹锡《竹枝词》

    The willows are green, green;
    The river is serene;
    There's his song wafted to me.
    In the east the sun is rising;
    In the west rain is falling;
    Can you see if it's fair or foul?

This is a translation of Zhang Qichun (张其春).[12] But a footnote such as the following had better be added so that the reader may understand the poem better:

    Footnote: "晴" 〔qíng〕 here is a pun. On the one hand it means "fairness of the weather", and on the other it implies "情" 〔qíng〕, a homophone which means "love".

Other things which are difficult to translate may also be properly tackled. For instance, Qian Gechuan (钱歌川) in one of his translations cleverly rendered the Chinese pseudo-homophones "委员" 和 "桂园" into English as "committee" and "common tea" Some more examples about how to treat homophones will be given as follows:

Example One:

(This paper is our passport to the gallows. But there's no backing out now.) If we don't *hang* together, we shall most assuredly hang separately.

(这张纸片儿就是咱们上绞架的通行证。今儿个谁都不准往后缩。)咱们要是不摽到一块儿,保准会吊到一块儿。(范守义,1978)[13]

In the original the word "hang" appears twice. Hang (together) means to unite whereas hang (separately) to be hanged one by one on the gallows. It's rather difficult to keep the homophone in the translation. But the translator skilfully overcomes the barrier by making use of the two Chinese characters "摽" [biao] and "吊" [diao] which are of the same rime. Biao means unite in the Beijing dialect. Thus the original sense is preserved.

Example Two:

Julia:... Best sing it to the tune of 'light of love.'

Lucetta: It is too heavy for so light a tune.

——The Two Gentlemen of Verona, Act I, Scene II.

朱丽娅:……可是你要唱就按《爱的清光》那个调子去唱吧。

露西塔:这个歌儿太沉重了,和轻狂的调子不配。

——朱生豪译莎剧《维洛那二绅士》

The two "light's" constitute a homophone in the original while "清光" [qīng guāng] and "轻狂" [qīng kuáng] sound quite alike in pronunciation and at the same time they correspond to the original in sense. (彭长江,1987)[14]

In short, an appropriate substitute, or a dynamic equivalence as Dr.

Nida calls it, may be given for a hard-to-translate word or expression according to the needs of its context when it is really impossible to get it literally rendered. However, such words and expressions are rare to find in an ordinary literary work. They can never constitute insurmountable obstacles in reproducing the original literary style as a whole. Therefore, we may quite safely say that the point of view which takes isolated trees for a wood is not quite proper.

Everybody knows that verse is much harder to translate than prose, but it does not seem right to come to the hasty conclusion that all poems are untranslatable. In fact, there are a lot of well-rendered poems. Let's take one of them for example:

《春怨》

金昌绪

打起黄莺儿，
莫教枝上啼。
啼时惊妾梦，
不得到辽西。

A Lover's Dream

By Jin Changxu

Oh, drive the golden orioles
From off our garden tree!
Their warbling broke the dream wherein
My lover smiled to me.

—W. J. B. Fletcher

Lecture Eight Translatability of Literary Style

In the note for the poem, Lü Shuxiang (吕叔湘, 1980) made a penetrating analysis of the translation of this poem. The note runs as follows:

"The original is rimed, and so is the translation, e. g. tree and me. The English translation of the poem has a rhythm pattern in the form of weak and strong stresses corresponding to that of the Chinese original in the form of level and oblique tones. For instance, the first line may be scanned in this way: Oh dríve/the gól/den ór/ióles. The number of words in each line of the English translation is indefinite. The English lines may seem unsymmetric at first glance because an English word often contains more than one syllable, but actually they are still symmetric when the accented syllables in each line are counted. For example, the first line and the third line have each four accented syllables and the second and fourth lines have each three.

"Wording will have to be more flexible or elastic and addition, omission and alternative ways of saying things more often used when one tries to keep the poetic form in translating a poem for he is often affected by rimes and metres. For instance, the Chinese '莫教啼' is omitted in the translation and an alternative way of implying this idea is employed in the fourth line. Thus the meaning of the original poem is still faithfully conveyed. If a translation can not retain the sense and spirit of the original, it can never be regarded as well-done." [15]

As a matter of fact, there appear addition, omission and alternative ways of expressing one and the same idea in translating this poem, but they are all based upon the content of the original, and therefore they do not deviate from its artistic conception. Since the golden orioles are driven away from the garden tree, there is naturally no need to translate "莫教啼" for its meaning is already implied in the preceding line. Although "到辽西"

and "smiled to me" do not look the same in the surface structure, yet in the deep structure they both indicate the lovers' meeting in a dream so that the original poetic image is retained by means of an alternative way of expression or a dynamic equivalence. Finally, one more word about the analysis of the translation of the poem. According to any dictionary, there's only one accent on the initial letter "o" in the word orioles whereas in the scansion the two "o's" are equally stressed. This is permissible for a poet or a poem translator, for he has the so-called poetic licence, that is, freedom from the ordinary rules of language allowed in verse.

The methods of translation as mentioned above are occasionally adopted even in translating some prose writing. However, we must always bear in mind that the employment of such methods is mainly for the purpose of better conveying the sense and spirit of the original. The translation of "春怨" may be regarded as well done either in its form, wording and rhythm or in its sense, image and spirit. And what's more, the plain and tactful style of the original is in the main reproduced in the translation.

This translation is not the only example which shows that poems can be successfully rendered by a qualified translator. Examples of this sort might be quoted in hundreds. In order to prove further the truth of this claim, it seems desirable to give one more example, which reads:

《月下独酌》

李 白

花间一壶酒,
独酌无相亲。
举杯邀明月,
对影成三人。

月既不解饮，
影徒随我身；
暂伴月将影，
行乐须及春。
我歌月徘徊，
我舞影零乱。
醒时同交欢，
醉后各分散。
永结无情游，
相期邈云汉！

Last Words

An arbour of flowers and a kettle of wine：
Alas! In the bowers no companion is mine.
Then the moon sheds her rays on my goblet and me,
And my shadow betrays we're a party of three!
Though the moon cannot swallow her share of the grog,
And my shadow must follow wherever I jog.
Yet their friendship I'll borrow and gaily carouse.
And laugh away sorrow while springtime allows.
See the moon—how she glances response to my song;
See my shadow—it dances so lightly along!
While sober I feel, you are both my good friends;
When drunken I reel, our companionship ends,
But we'll soon have a greeting without a goodbye,
At our next merry meeting away in the sky.

—Herbert A. Glies

Giles has succeeded in both conveying the brevity and grace of the original poem and retaining its rimed and rhythmic form and romantic color.[16] That's Zhang Qichun's evaluation of Giles' translation of this poem of Li Bai. I agree with him in the main. But the translation of the last two lines is not quite exact. We may make some improvement of it. First, here I'd like to quote for reference the translation of the last two lines by a Japanese poet named Obata:

Let us pledge a friendship no mortal knows
And often hail each other at evening,
Far across the vast and vaporous space!

The Japanese poet's version seems more close to the meaning of the original though it sounds a little wordy. Now I venture to offer my revision on the basis of the poet's as follows:

Let's keep companions each other abiding by,
Meeting at night far across the broad and vast sky.

4. Analysis of the Second Argument Against the Translatability of Style

Another argument of those who consider the original literary style untranslatable is that translators have their own styles. It is undeniable that a good translator has his own style while writing his own work. But he knows that he should give up his own style and strive to reproduce the style of the original in another suitable literary language while translating a literary work. Theodore Savory makes a thorough and vivid exposition of this in his book *The Art of Translation*. He says: "…the translator has never allowed himself to forget that he is a translator. He is not, he recognizes, the original author, and the work in hand was never his own; he is an interpreter, one whose duty it is to act as a bridge or channel between the mind of the author and the minds of the readers. He must efface himself and allow Rome or Berlin to speak directly to London or Paris. If he feels that he has done this, he may well be proud of his achievement." [17]

In China, there are a lot of fine translated works which basically retain the original style. Take the translation of *Vanity Fair*, (《名利场》) by Yang Bi (杨必). Nan Mu (南木) sets a high value on it in one of his essays (1980). I'd like to make a brief summary of his evaluation as follows:

Thackeray raises the curtain of the fair to the reader in the tone of a typical traveling artist. In order to convey this kind of artistic conception, whether the various scenes the manager witnesses at the fair and his words and deeds or the interesting comments inserted by the author are all transplanted by the translator in a language of the same literary flavor as the original, so that there is an atmosphere of a fair prevailing in the Chinese version, thus having an artistic effect which attracts the reader to see what actually happens at the fair. What's more, the translation reads very easily, fluently and idiomatically, words being carefully chosen and sentences well arranged. Consequently, both the rich content and the humorous artistic style of the original are gratifyingly reproduced. [18]

In his comment, Sun Zhili (孙致礼, 1984) also speaks highly of *Vanity Fair* (《名利场》) by Yang Bi:

"Literature is an art of language and translation of a literary work is a re-creation of the art of language. The reason why《名利场》is universally acknowledged as a fine translation is that the translator has, on the one hand, tried his utmost to keep the charm of the original and on the other taken the law and usage of his mother tongue into full consideration. As a result, so pure, natural and colorful a Chinese translation is achieved that the reader can be inspired, moved and aesthetically entertained in the same way as one reads the original."[19]

Meanwhile, Sun points out some defects in Yang's translation. The translator impairs the foreign flavor sometimes when he seeks too much assimilation of English into Chinese. For instance, he assimilates English godfather to the Chinese 干爹 meaning adopted father and godson to 干儿子 meaning adopted son. However, one flaw cannot obscure the splendor of the jade. Yang's《名利场》may still be evaluated as one of the masterpieces that have reproduced the original style.

If a translator persisted in expressing himself in his translation without taking the style of the original into consideration, no doubt, he could hardly achieve good results. So is the case with Pope's translation of Homer. Zheng Zhenduo (郑振铎, 1921) points out in his paper that the style of Homer's epics is plain and forceful. Homer often makes use of imagination, hint and simile, but seldom employs metaphorical expressions. But unfortunately, Pope prefers to use metaphors in his translation, which runs counter to the characteristic of Homer's original language. For example, Pope says "In wavy gold the summer vales are dressed" (*Odyssey*, 19, 131) instead of "The fields are full of grains" (田里满是谷粒) and "From his eyes Pour'd down the tender dew" (*Iliad*, 11, 486) instead of "He (the soldier) wept" (这个士兵哭着).[20] Arnold, the famous English critic, criticizes Pope in his essay *On Translating Homer* for his affectation both in wording and in style, which goes against the original.

Excellent translators are just like excellent actors and actresses. Excellent actors and actresses have each their own individuality. But when they play the part of a character on the stage, they must and can immediately forget their own individuality in their performance and enter into the spirit of the character so that the role may be acted true to life. In reality quite a large number of actors and actresses are capable of sucessfully playing any role, positive or negative. Liu Xiaoqing (刘晓庆) is known to be such an excellent actress.

Besides, as the world knows, the style of singing of Mei Lanfang (梅兰芳) has been handed down and is being passed on by some of his faithful and able disciples and followers. So is the case with many other famous actors' or actresses' singing style. Similarly, the style of painting and calligraphy, etc. can all be acquired and imitated by clever and hardworking people. By the same token, the various literary writing styles can be appreciated and reproduced.

The story I've recently read in *China Daily* will further convincingly demonstrate what I have said of the acquirement and imitability of artistic styles is true. The story tells of how Liu Yinru[21] has grown up to be a successor to the well-known Master Cao in molding dough figurines:

At an exhibition held in Egypt last March, a 31-year old Chinese woman was extemporizing a dough figurine with the help of a small burin and bamboo needle. In about 15 minutes, a lump of dough had become a god of longevity three centimetres tall.

The young woman was none other than artist Liu Yinru. She was apprenticed to Cao Yice at the Beijing Artistic Figurine Factory at the age of 18. Cao, nicknamed Dough Figurine Cao, was famous for his skill at molding figurines of beauties from *A Dream of Red Mansions*.

Then Yinru sat beside her teacher everyday, watching and imitating. First she learned how to make the "Red Mansions" beauties. After that, she began to make them on her own following the traditional method. She practiced again and again, sometimes working from dawn to dusk. Through three years' effort, she had mastered dough modeling.

Unfortunately, one day, her teacher suddenly died. It was a severe blow to her, indeed. But she made up her mind to "live up to what her teacher expected of her and keep his skills alive" and her wish came true at last after years of hard work. In 1979, some of her products were shown in Beijing's Zhongshan Park. Many visitors mistook them for creations by Dough Figurine Cao, thinking he was still alive. What made them think so? It was the style, i. e. the formal and spiritual resemblance, of Cao's dough figurine molding that had been embodied in Liu's exhibits.

The above-quoted story once more vividly shows the truth that artistic style of any kind may be satisfactorily acquired and imitated. Logically speaking, how could one say that the literary writing style is an exception?

Facts enumerated in the above are quite enough for us to conclude that an adequate translator can manage to forget himself at the time of rendering a literary work written by somebody else just as an actor or actress does at the time of playing a role on the stage, and exert every effort to learn and imitate and thus reproduce the original style. Undoubtedly, it is most desirable, at least in theory, that literary works should be translated by such translators as have the same style in writing as that of the authors. But this principle can not be easily put into common practice.

5. Analysis of the Third Argument Against the Translatability of Style

The third argument of those who consider the original style

untranslatable is that there are no objective criteria for the judgement of what kind of translation is good and what kind is bad. To be sure, some isolated individual words, expressions and even sentences may sometimes be hard to judge. But as far as the wording and style of a whole piece of translation are concerned, there are still objective criteria to go by. Comparison will make clear what translation is more satisfactory. Look at the following examples:

Example One Comparison between the translation of *Jane Eyre* by Wu Guangjian(伍光建) and that by Li Jiye(李霁野).

The original: There was no possibility of taking a walk that day. We had been wandering, indeed, in the leafless shrubery an hour in the morning; but since dinner (Mrs Reed, when there was no company, dined early) the cold winter wind had brought with it clouds so sombre, and rain so penetrating, that further outdoor exercises was now out of the question.

Wu's translation:那一天是不能出门散步的了。当天的早上,我们在那已经落叶小丛树堆里溜过有一点钟了;不料饭后(李特太太,没有客人来,吃饭是早的)刮起冬天的寒风,满天都是乌云,又落雨,是绝对不能出门运动的了。

Li's translation:那一天是没有散步的可能了,不错,早晨我们在无叶的丛林中漫游过一点钟了,但是午饭之后——在没有客人的时候,里德夫人是早早吃饭的——寒冷的冬风刮来这样阴沉的云,和这样侵人的雨,再做户外的活动是不可能的了。

Mao Dun (1937) analyzes these two passages of translation as follows:

They are both literal translations, but there is still some difference in their similarity. Li has the original sentence patterns transplanted as much as possible. If we make a careful comparison between the above-given versions, we might say that Li's is closer to the original. The word "indeed", the adverb "so" and the present participle "penetrating" in the second sentence of the original are all omitted in Wu's version. This may be deemed as of no great importance. But when we read the translations against the original, we will have to admit that Li's version better represents the gentle tone of the original. Wu's words "刮起冬天的寒风,满天都是乌云,又落雨,是绝不能出门运动的了" sound lucid and lively indeed, yet we feel that a sort of meticulousness is lacking in them. [22]

The so-called gentleness and meticulousness mentioned above both refer to style. So far as the reproduction of the original style is concerned, Li's translation of this passage is evidently superior to Wu's. Mao Dun's evaluation is objective and fair. Talking of another passage, he speaks highly of Wu's translation.

Example Two Comparison between the two translations of the poem *A Red, Red Rose* by Robert Burns (1759-1796).

Original:
O my Luve's like a red red rose
  That's newly sprung in June;
O my Luve's like the melodie
  That's sweetly played in tune.
  ...
And fare thee weel, my only Luve!
  And fare thee weel awhilel!
And 1 will come again, my Luve,
  Tho' it were ten thousand mile.

This poem consists of four stanzas. Here only the first stanza and the last stanza are quoted for discussion.

> Translation One:
> 吾爱吾爱玫瑰红,
> 　六月初开韵晓风;
> 吾爱吾爱如管弦,
> 　其声悠扬而玲珑。
> ……
> 暂时告别我心肝,
> 　请你不要把心耽,
> 纵使相隔十万里,
> 　踏破地皮也要还。

The first stanza, as pointed out by Chu Zhida (楚至大, 1986), does not conform to the style of a folk song. The address "吾爱" is seldom found in ancient Chinese folk songs. It is naturally unfit to be used in translating the Scottish dialect "my Luve". Other expressions such as "韵晓风" and "如管弦" are not fit, either. And we deem it improper for the translator to describe the melody with the Chinese "玲珑". As to the last stanza, it sounds rather vulgar, while the original is plain and fresh and there is nothing like a doggerel in it at all. Besides, "心肝" is too vulgar for "my Love", and "踏破地皮也要还" does not quite tally with the original.

> Translation Two:
> 啊,我爱人像红红的玫瑰
> 　它在六月里初开;
> 啊,我爱人像一支乐曲
> 　美妙地演奏起来。

......
再见吧,我唯一的爱人,
我和你小别片刻。
我要回来的,亲爱的,
即使是万里相隔。

Translation Two is done by Yuan Kejia (袁可嘉). It not only reproduces the form of the original poem but keeps its style.[23]

Example Three Comparison between two translations of the ci (词), a form of verse, to the tune called "xiang-jian-huan" (相见欢) by Li Yu (李煜, 937-978), the last ruler of South Tang in the period of the Five Dynasties, who is good at verse writing and famous for ci.

Original:
剪不断,理还乱,是离愁,别是一般滋味在心头。

Clara Candlin's Translation:

Unsevered
Though sundered.
In chaos, yet
In order set.

This strange commotion in the heart
Is but the wanderer's woe.

—*The Herald Wind*, P. 34.

Translation by Chu Dagao (初大告):
Cut it, yet unsevered,

Order it,the more tangled—
Such is parting sorrow.
Which dwells in my heart,too subtle a feeling to tell.
—*Chinese Lyrics*,P. 7[24]

Which is better of the two versions? It is quite evident. I am sure all the readers who can appreciate the original and comprehend the translations would say at a glance that the latter is much better be cause it is more accurate in meaning and more natural in form as well.

As everybody knows, different literary works have different styles. The style of your translation must correspond; or at least, be close, to that of the original you are working at. You must always try your best to reproduce the original style in your translation as much as possible.

Strictly speaking, the ideological content, linguistic expression and stylistic characteristics of a literary work constitute a unified entity, and the translator should reproduce the three elements as a whole. But for convenience's sake, both Yan Fu and Tytler divided this entity into three components: content, expression and style. This is feasible and reflects the actual working process of a conscientious translator.

We all acknowledge that literature is an art of language. As Gorki definitely points out in his *Talk to Young Writers* literature is to create images and typical characters, and reflect real events, natural scenery and thinking processes through language. What he means is that language is an indispensable instrument in literary creation. That's to say: No language, no literature; no literature, no (literary) style.

6. Literary Point of View and Linguistic Point of View

If one wants to reproduce the original style satisfactorily, one must, in my opinion, have two points of view before he sets about his translation.

First of all, he must have a macroscopic point of view, namely, the literary point of view. The translator should always remember what he is working at is a literary work written by somebody else and try his utmost to turn his translation into a work of art which is in conformity with the thought, feeling and style of the original. Thus, the translation will be as moving and vivid as the original work and the reader may be aesthetically entertained as well.

Secondly, he must as well have a microscopic point of view, namely, the linguistic point of view. In the process of translating, all the paragraphs, sentences and words should be attentively studied so that the best expressions may be chosen to satisfy the needs of reproducing the thought, feeling and style of the original. From the linguistic point of view, style is formed by the happy coordination of paragraphs, sentences and words. Therefore, even if some individual sentences or words were not satisfactorily rendered, they would not affect the style of the work as a whole. So long as the general tone or spirit of the original is conveyed, we may say that the original style is basically reproduced.

Style can never go without language. In other words, paragraphing, sentence-making and wording are absolutely essential to style. Paragraphs, sentences and words form the basis which underlies style. Liu Xie (刘勰), author of *Wenxin Diaolong* (《文心雕龙》) , a book on writing, made clear over a thousand years ago the relationship between the paragraphs, sentences and words and the tone and spirit of a whole piece of writing. He said that sentences are made up of words, paragraphs of sentences and a whole article of paragraphs. That an article is excellent is due to its flawless paragraphs, that a paragraph is fine is due to its blemishless sentences and that a sentence is good is due to proper words.[25] This has long been the goal writers pursue and translators today should try their best to make their translations correspond, or at least, steer close to the original in style so that resemblance in spirit may be achieved. At the same time the translator should render the words, sentences and paragraphs so well that resemblance in form may be achieved. Only in this way can his translation come up to the standard.

Now I would like to deal in somewhat detail with the question of paragraphing, sentence-making and wording:

First, paragraphing. What I mean by paragraphing here refers extensively to chapters and natural paragraphs in a novel, acts, scenes and dialogues in a play, paragraphs in prose and stanzas in verse. All these must be translated in their original order. Inversion here is unnecessary and impermissible.

Second, sentence-making. Sentence-order and sentence-patterns should be kept as much as possible. The passage of Li Jiye's translation of *Jane Eyre* and the stanzas of Yuan Kejia's translation of *A Red, Red Rose* quoted above are both in conformity to this principle. But sometimes we have to make some change in sentence-patterns in accordance with the different usage of the target language. For instance, there is no need of keeping the passive voice in translating the sentence "Good-bye was said." And a change should be made in the sentence pattern in which a noun indicating time or place serves as its subject and such a verb as "saw" or "witnessed" as its predicate verb followed by a direct object. Only when we have rendered the sentence patterns flexibly where necessary can we be said to have satisfied the minimun requirement of clear expression of meaning and smooth use of language in our translation.

Third, wording. Wording here means choice of words and rhetorical devices. According to the demand of the context and style, every word must be weighed carefully and every figure of speech dealt with seriously. "As lean as a rake" is a simile. There may be two translations: "瘦得像耙" (literal) and "骨瘦如柴" (a change in image). Evidently, the latter sounds far better than the former. This shows that how important collocation is in wording. British satirist Johnathan Swift gave a very brilliant exposition of the interrelation between words and style. He said:

"Proper words in proper places make the true definition of a style."

This concise definition of style may be applied both to writing and to translation.

7. Conclusion

Now we can come to the following conclusion:

Whether a translation be good or bad, readable or not, it has nothing to do either with the original work or with the original writer; rather, it depends upon the theoretical knowledge and practical technique on the part of the translator. Whoever has a good command of translation both in theory and practice, can, of course, offer satisfactory translations. It is because translation is not only a science—a science with its own peculiar laws and methods. but also an art—an art of reproduction and re-creation.

To sum up, the thought, feeling and style will be reproduced so long as the paragraphs, sentences and words in the original or source language are faithfully, flexibly and satisfactorily transferred to the target or receptor language. Resemblance in form and that in spirit are complementary to each other. The former is the basis for the latter and the latter the crystalization of the former. The working process of a writer is from form (paragraphs, sentences and words) to spirit. That is to say, as soon as a piece of writing is completed, a certain kind of style is naturally shaped. But the process of a translator consists of two steps. First, he should carefully appreciate the tone and spirit of the whole original work through words, sentences and paragraphs and determine what kind of style it reflects both from the point of view of literature and from the point of view of linguistics. Then he starts translating it sentence by sentence and paragraph by paragraph from the very beginning to the very end, with the reproduction of the original style always kept in mind. "Faced with a passage in the original language." says Savory, "he (the translator) must ask himself:

(1) What does the author say?

(2) What does he mean?

(3) How does he say it?

This method of analysis may be applied to the paragraph, to the sentence, or even to the phrase..." [26]

Meanwhile, a translator should pay much attention to the three aspects of an utterance. Tzvetan Todorov (1970) calls them verbal, syntactic and semantic. "The verbal aspect of a text is constituted by the concrete sentences which form it. The syntactic aspect involves the interrelations of the parts of the text. And the semantic aspect involves the global sense of the utterance, the themes it evokes." [27]

The translatability of literary style of the original work has been testified and guiding principles, convincing examples and proper methods have been given. All literary translators are expected to uphold reproduction of the original style as their common goal and strive for it all their lives.

Notes

1. Cuddon, J. A. , 1979, *A Dictionary of Literary Terms*, 663. W. & J. Mackay Limited, Chatham, Great Britain.
2. Savory, Theodore, 1957, *The Art of Translation*, 54. Jonathan Cape, Thirty Bedford Square, London.
3. Zhang Yingjin, *Literary Style and Translation Judging from Modern Stylistics*, Foreign Languages, No. 1, 1986.
4. *The Meaning of the Pen Name Lu Xun in the* 600 *Anecdotes of Celebrities* compiled and published by China Youth Publishing House, 327-328, 1982.
5. Savory, *The Art of Translation*, 55.
6. Mao Dun, 1954, *Struggle for the Development of the Cause of Literary Translation and the Improvement of the Quality of Translation* in the book *An Anthology of Essays on Translation* compiled by Luo Xinzhang, 511-512, 1984.
7. Appendix I. *Li Pan Talking about the Translation Work Done During Various Dynasties in the History of China*, to the book *Free Talks about Translation* by Liu Zhongde, published by Shaanxi People's Publishing House, 1984.
8. Tytler, Alexander Fraser, 1813, *Essay on the Principles of Translation*. Everyman's Library ed. by Ernest Rhys.
9. Arnold, Mathew, 1919, *On Translating Homer*, in *Essays—Literary and Critical*. 215. Everyman's Library.
10. Nida, Eugene A. , 1975, *Language Structure and Translation*, 98. Stanford University Press, Stanford, California.
11. Catford, J. C. , 1978, *A Linguistic Theory of Translation*, 94. Oxford University Press.
12. Zhang Qichun, 1949, *The Art of Translation* published by Kaiming Book Store, 56.

13. Fan Shouyi, 1987, *Fuzzy Mathematics and Evaluation of Translation*, Chinese Translators Journal, 18, No. 4.
14. Peng Changjiang, 1987, *Phonetic Variation and Literary Translation*, Chinese Translators Journal, 18, No. 4.
15. *English Versions of the 100 Four-Lined Tang Poems* compiled and annotated by Lü Shuxiang, Note 96, The Hunan People's Publishing House, 1980.
16. Zhang Qichun, 1949, *The Art of Translation*, 196-197.
17. Savory, *The Art of Translation*, 50.
18. Nan Mu, 1980, *On the Chinese Version of Vanity Fair*, Chinese Translators Journal, No. 2.
19. Sun Zhili, 1984, *On the Linguistic Characteristics of the Chinese Version of Vanity Fair*, Chinese Translators Journal, 37, No. 10.
20. Zheng Zhenduo, 1921, *How to Translate Literary Books? Novels Monthly*, vol. 12, No. 3.
21. See the reportage entitled *Artist in Dough Is Model of Dedication*, China Daily, August 11, 1989.
22. Mao Dun, 1937, *On the Two Chinese Versions of Jane Eyre*, Translations, Vol. (New) 2. No. 5.
23. Chu Zhida, 1986, *The Translated Poems Must Resemble Its Original*, Foreign Languages, No. 1.
24. Zhang Qichun, 1949, *The Art of Translation*, 108.
25. Liu Xie: "因字而成句,积句而成章,积章而成篇;篇之彪炳,章无疵也;章之明靡,句无玷也;句之菁英,字不妄也。"
26. Savory, *The Art of Translation*, 25.
27. Tzvetan Todorov, 1971, "*The Place of Style in the Structure of the Text*", in Literary Style, a Symposium, Oxford University Press.

Lecture Nine   Problems of Translating Poems

Concerning the problem of translating poems, quite a few have done research both in this country and abroad. Some think that poems are translatable and others do not. Among those who advocate the translatability of poems there are still disputes about which is the better way, to render them in the form of free verse or to put them in that of classical poetic composition.

No agreement has been reached so far. Now I venture to express my opinion about this question so as to make a tentative approach to it.

I hold that it is possible, but quite difficult, to translate poems satisfactorily and successfully.

Why do I say so? It's because, first of all, there exist many things in common among men. For instance, they all have the thinking powers to reason logically and the feelings to express joy or sorrow, love or hatred, and possess the same nature, world and universe no matter what races they may be. In other words, all human beings are endowed by nature with the same mind which has the same function so that they can commune with one another. As a consequence, poetry, a product of the mind, is understandable, enjoyable and translatable. And secondly, the translatability of poetry has already been demonstrated by quantities of historical facts. The poems written by the well-known poets in the world, such as William Shakespeare, John Milton, Percy Bysshe Shelley, Lord Byron of England, Henry Wadsworth Longfellow and Walt Whitman of the United States of America, Victor-Marie Hugo of France, Johann Wolfgang von Goethe of Germany, Aleksander Sergeevich Pushkin of Russia, Sir Ra bindranath Tagore of India, were translated into various languages long ago and a great number of them well-done. Take the Chinese poems written by the poets of the Tang Dynasty for example. There were versions in various languages. According to the English Version of the 100 *Four-Lined Tang Poems* compiled and annotated by Lü Shuxiang, more than fifty poets were selected, inclusive of the most famous two, Li Bai and Du Fu. Their translators amount to eight including English Oriental scholar Herbert Allen Giles and British consul W. J. B. Fletcher[1]. Besides, a considerable number of modern Chinese men of letters translated their classical poems into English and had them published as *An English Version of Tang Poems* by Cai Tinggan, *An English Version of Classical Poems* by Weng Xianliang, *A New Translation of Three Hundred Tang Poems* by Xu Yuanchong. Lu Peixuan and Wu Juntao, *Selected Poems and Essays of the Tang and Song Dynasties* by Mr. Yang Xianyi and his wife.[2]

So far as the contemporary poems are concerned, we can also find lots of them translated either from a foreign language into Chinese or from Chinese into a foreign language.

Poems call for the beauty in form, sound and meaning. A translator of them should not be satisfied with the mere conveying of the ideas in the original, but must strive for the reproduction of the original beauty. To achieve this, he ought to, first of all, retain the original meaning and artistic conception and secondly, do his best to make his translation bear a certain due form, rhythm, and rime when necessary. Owing to the differences in the characteristics of various languages, it is both impossible and unnecessary for the translator to render the original poems word for word. However, he has the responsibility to try in a thousand and one ways to overcome the difficulties and even the individual untranslatabilities which may arise from the different characteristics of the original and target languages. The translator is allowed to make up the loss in the meaning of some foregoing or following words somewhere within the whole poem. What is most important for him to do in translating a poetic work is to keep its original artistic conception and style. In order to illustrate my viewpoint as expressed above in the previous lecture we have already had a discussion of the translation of Jin Changxu's 《春怨》as *A Lover's Dream* by Fletcher. Lü Shuxiang speaks highly of Fletcher's translation. He deems his translation as a great success. I have quoted Lü's analysis in detail and given my own evaluation of it. Here there is no need for me to repeat what I have said in Lecture Eight. Only a few words more should be added about the translation of this poem.

Just now I received a paper entitled *On the Style of the Author and That of the Translator* from a young friend[3], who mentions the same translation of the poem by Fletcher. Generally speaking, his opinion about the English version is affirmative. And at the same time, he points out the translator's misuse of the word lover. His reason is that the Chinese character "妾" does not mean concubine all the time. Sometimes it is used as a self-depreciatory appellation of a wife. His comments are right. Thus the title《春怨》of the original poem should have been literally translated into something like *Complaint in Spring* instead of *A Lover's Dream*. For all this, we may still say that Fletcher's translation is well-done either in its form, wording and rhythm or in its sense, image and spirit. And what's more, the plain and tactful style of the original is in the main reproduced in the English version.

Fletcher already made use of the method of compensation in translating this poem. It is, generally, an effective accommodation often employed by experienced translators to overcome the local difficulties or local untranslatabilities while translating a literary or poetic work. Addition, extension, break-up, incorporation, substitution, transposition, etc. [4] may all fall under the category of compensation. Whenever a translator can't translate some words and expressions literally, he may make use of this or that compensation method so as to better convey the spirit of the original and reproduce the style of it.

In my opinion, omission should be put in the category of compensation for addition and omission are usually relative to each other. Take the articles for example. When you do translation from English into Chinese, you will have to use omission. When you do translation from Chinese into English, you will have to use addition. So is the case with the possessive pronouns in the translation between the English and Chinese languages. I published an essay entitled *Commonly Used Translation Methods Illustrated with Example Sentences*. [5] Nine methods are summed up in it. The fourth of them is Proper Addition and Omission of Words, which, in fact, comprises the relative twins as mentioned above.

Compensation is an indispensable method to overcome the difficulties in the translation of literary, especially poetic works. The compensation in translation is to make up the semantic losses caused in the course of converting the linguistic forms of the original language into those of the target. Since translation took place, the method has been adopted, widely popularized and summed up theoretically by some people. Fayun (法云, 1088-1158), a monk of the Song Dynasty, said: "Translation means exchange—to exchange what one lacks with what one has." A scholar of Jewish descent said: "Translation fails where it does not compensate." (*After Babel*) Balhudarov, a soviet scholar, said: "The method (of compensation) is often used when no equivalents or proper expressions can be found in the target language." (*Language and Translation*) In one of his articles, the chief editor of *Babel*: *International Journal of Translation*, the organ of FIT, definitely points out that compensation is a useful way of reproducing the original. (See *Translation Unit—a Question for Research in Modern Translatology* by Luo Jinde, *Chinese Translators Journal*, No. 12, 1984).[6]

Besides the compensation method, there are still other methods of translation, which we will discuss later.

In order to further illustrate the translatability of poetry and offer some more compensation methods, here I'd like to say a few words more about Burns's poem *A Red, Red Rose*, and Yuan Kejia's translation which I cite in the foregoing lecture as a good example of literal translation. The original was written by Robert Burns, Scottish national poet. The poet was much influenced by folk songs as a child. Thus his poem has a breath of his native soil and a flavor of folk song and his poetic language is popular and fluent. Yuan's Chinese version is successful and comes up to the standard of beauty in form, sound and meaning because firstly it retains the meaning and artistic conception of the original, secondly it basically bears a form corresponding to the original: each stanza being made up of four lines and lines looking comparatively even in length, and thirdly its language is also popular and fluent, its rhythm natural and rime scheme similar: the first stanza of both being in the scheme of ABCB, the only difference in the last stanza lying in that the scheme of the original is ABAB while that of the translation becomes ABCB. In addition, the plain and lively style of the original is satisfactorily reproduced. The two stanzas are translated literally. Even so, the method of omission is used in the translation. For instance, the indefinite article "a" in the first line of the first stanza, the definite article "the" in the third line, the possesive pronoun "my" in the third line of the last stanza, the three "and's" in the first three lines and the impersonal pronoun "it" indicating distance in the last line all disappear in the Chinese version. Otherwise, the translation would sound wordy and unidiomatic.

So much for the translatability of poetry.

Why do I say that poetry is difficult to translate? The first reason is: various nations still have minor differences among the many things they share in common. For instance, in addition to the difference in their linguistic characteristics, there are differences in their local environments, social customs and cultural backgrounds, etc. The second reason is: poetry demands refinement in language, freshness in artistic conception and distinctiveness in style. In other words, it calls for beauty in form, sound and meaning. It goes without saying that the three-aspected beauty is not easy to reproduce. Here I'd like to quote Mathew Arnold's criticisms on the four English versions of Homer's *Iliad and Odyssey*, which, I am sure, may throw some light to this matter.

"Cowper's diction is not as Homer's diction, nor his nobleness as Homer's nobleness; but it is in movement and grammatical style that he is most unlike Homer. Pope's rapidity is not of the same sort as Homer's rapidity, nor are his plainness of ideas and his nobleness as Homer's plainness of ideas and nobleness; but it is in the artificial character of his style and diction that he is most unlike Homer. Chapman's movement, words, style, and manner are often far enough from resembling Homer's movement, words, style, and manner; but it is the fantasticality of his ideas which puts him farthest from resembling Homer. Mr. Newman's movement, grammatical style, and ideas are a thousand times in strong contrast with Homer's; still it is by the oddness of his diction and the ignobleness of his manner that he contrasts with Homer the most violently." [7]

In the following three more English versions of the Tang fourlined poems will be discussed to verify the difficulty of translating poetry.

《宿建德江》

孟浩然

移舟泊烟渚，
日暮客愁新。
野旷天低树，
江清月近人。

A Night-Mooring on the Jiande River

by Meng Haoran

While may little boat moves on its mooring of mist,
And daylight wanes, old memories begin...
How wide the world was, how close the trees to heaven,
And how clear in the water the nearness of the moon!

—Bynner

Lü Shuxiang points out that it is a clever device for the translator to use the English word "begin" to render the Chinese "新". Is there any other word better than that?

"In the third line, Bynner misuses the word 'was' for 'is'. Maybe, it is owing to the influence of the foregoing expression 'old memories'. As a result, the vivid view before the eye turns into a trace of the past travel and thus the charm of the original poem is lost. What a great difference the improper use of a single word makes!"

《塞下曲》

卢纶

其三

月黑雁飞高,

单于夜遁逃。

欲将轻骑逐,

大雪满弓刀。

Border Songs

By Lu Lun

III

High in the faint moonlight, wild geese are soaring
Tartar chieftains are fleeing through the dark—
And we chase them, with horses lightly burdened
And a burden of snow on our bows and our swords.

—Henry H. Hart

The compiler and annotator says: "The last two lines of the original poem mean only the intention to chase the fleeing tartar chieftains, but the translation changes the mere intention into a historical fact. The original depicts the severe cold and hardship on the border whereas the translation describes the heroism of officers and men of the royal army."

The meaning and artistic conception are essential components of a poem. The translator has only the obligation to retain them, but no right to make any alteration.

《赠别》

杜牧

其二

多情却似总无情,
唯觉尊前笑不成。
蜡烛有心还惜别,
替人垂泪到天明。

Parting

by Du Mu

II

How can a deep love seem a deep love,
How can it smile, at a farewell feast?
Even the candle, feeling our sadness,
Weeps, as we do, all night long.

——Bynner

Lü Shuxiang makes a fairly detailed analysis of this English version. He says:

"In the first line, the word 'seem' means 'to show itself' and in the fourth line the word 'do' stands for the word 'weep'."

"The translation of the first line is rather successful. The predicate 'seem a deep love' means 'make an appearance of deep love with a smile and affectionate prattle'. Can people with deep love behave so in such a case? Bynner succeeds in expressing the impossibility by means of a rhetorical question. But viewed together with the second line, what is conveyed in the English version seems not so deep as in the original for a pair of sweethearts can hardly show their deep love on their faces. How can they smile and prattle at a farewell feast? According to the translator, it is due to deep love that make them unable to smile. The original implication is more complicated for it implies that people with deep love may strike no loving attitude, nor may people without any affection strike it. The heroine seems to be, on the one hand, deep in love and, on the other, indifferent, which has been a riddle so far. Only now it turns out that she is not lacking in affection because the evidence lies in her inablility to smile only at the farewell drinking cup. Usually they, the heroine and the hero, often have a chat between them, how can they become silent all of a sudden if they were not affectionate to each other? The translator sees only the one side of the matter that people with deep love need not gesticulate as ordinary pairs do, but doesn't grasp the other side of it that the girl with deep love appears passionless while naturally revealing a passionate devotion. That's why I say the translation is not so deep as the original in meaning.

In the original, it is the candle that weeps for the heroine, but in the English version the expression "as we do" means that the candle weeps just as the parting couple. Thus what is expressed in the translation is not so delicate as in the Chinese. The translator may think since the couple can't smile at the farewell feast, naturally they have no choice but to shed tears. What does their tear-shedding signify? No doubt, it is a sign of the outburst of deep love. This constitutes a contradiction in the context of the translation. In fact, the girl at parting is neither in a position to put on a smile on her face, nor does she know how to express her deep love in a smile. She is merely able to look dejected in absolute silence.

"In short, the original poem portrays a very young girl of fourteen or fifteen with tender love. She still doesn't know how to express it. So it is quite natural for her to look innocent and shy. The feeling expressed in the translation is much more strong and mature although the English version itself may be regarded as a good poem when it is viewed alone. If we compare the original and the translation to paintings, the former seems to be a watercolor whereas the latter an oilpainting. If we compare them to wine, the former resembles something like the weak yellow Shaoxing liquor while the latter something like the strong white spirit." [8]

The above analysis is accurate and convincing. But according to one of my three principles, namely, the principle that the translation must be as expressive as the original, neither more nor less, the English version of this poem cannot be regarded as an entirely successful translation. Just as the annotator points out, it is not so deep and delicate as the original. It expresses more than the poem in Chinese.

The examples as discussed above seem already enough to show the difficulties in translating poems.

However, are there any poems which are absolutely impossible to translate? In general, I think, such poems do not exist. Even the Chinese palindromic verse is still possible to translate in meaning, but its form can't be retained as it stands. The forms will have to be more than one. Now let's see how to render the two lines of Wang Rong's palindrome on spring stroll.

池莲照晓月
幔锦拂朝风

These two lines make sense when read in the proper order from beginning to end or in the inverted order from end to beginning.

Version A in the proper order
The lotus in the pond is being shone upon by the dawn moon,
And the curtains of silk stirred by the early morn breeze.

Version B in the inverted order
The breeze is stirring the silk curtains at dawn,
And the moon shining upon the lotus pond in the early morn.

At the end of the West Jin Dynasty, poetess Su Hui weaved a piece of brocade into a palindromic verse and gave it as a souvenir to her husband sentenced to exile to the desert. This verse is much more complicated in reading. Empress Wu Zetian (武则天, 624-705) greatly appreciated it and wrote a preface for the achievement of the poetess, saying this piece of brocade is so well-woven that "the five colors match one another, the length and width of it are both eight cun and the palindromic verse on it may be read vertically, horizontally, from left to right, from right to left, from beginning to end, from end to beginning, from top to bottom and from bottom to top into more than two hundred poems." No matter how complex the palindromic verse is, all the meanings it contains can still be translated, only the translator will have to put the whole verse in various versions. No doubt, it's never possible for him to keep one and the same form as the original. For all this, none call arbitrarily allege that palindromic verse is entirely impossible to translate. It is merely rather difficult for one to translate it. As a matter of fact, difficulty has various degrees.

Now we are going to discuss how to translate poems.

Opinions vary about what is the better way to translate them. Xu Yuanchong says:

"The translators in the old edition of *The English Translations Against the Original Chinese Poems* may be roughly divided into three schools. The first school consists of the translators in the early period, who translated poems in the form of classical poetry. The school may be called classical school, whose representative was Giles. The second school consists of the translators in the late period, who translated poems in the form of free verse. The school may be called free school, whose representative was Arthur David Waley. The third school consists of the translators who creatively adapted the original into English. The school may be called creative school, whose representative was Ezra Loomis Pound. The translators abroad added in the new edition of the above-mentioned book are in the main the successors to the three schools..." And at the same time Xu points out the translators at home also belong to these three schools and have their respective representatives. [9]

So far as the development of the three schools abroad is concerned, according to Professor Wu-chi Liu (柳无忌) the school represented by Waley has become prosperous since 1950. In recent years there have appeared a lot of translated works of Chinese verse by J. D. Frodsham, David Hawkes, Burton Watson, Jonathan Chaves, Stephen Owen, James J. Y. Liu, etc., who surpass their predecessors in their achievements. And among all the works the most important and comprehensive is the collection entitled *Sunflowers Splendor* (《葵晔集》) : *Three Thousand Years of Chinese Poetry* edited by Wu-chi Liu and Irving Yucheng Lo (Indiana University Press, 1975, 1990) .

Before we review the three propositions or schools as mentioned above, I think, it is better to first give an account of what the basic features and requirements are in translation so that we may have a reliable basis or criterion to evaluate them.

"For the translator, the content of the original work is something that exists objectively, and the translator's task is to convey this something instead of anything of his own to the reader. In this sense, translation is not writing. In other words, it does not mean that the translator writes his own work, nor does it mean that he composes his own by borrowing the ideas from the original work. Should there be any understanding which runs contrary to this, it would be incompatible with the concept of translation. That is a basic feature in it. " [10] Similarly, translating poems should also bear this basic feature. That's to say, translating poems is not writing them. It does not mean that the translator writes his own borrowing the ideas from the original.

What are the basic requirements then? Cheng Fangwu pointed out long ago, "The translation of a poem must remain to be a poem. That is the first thing we should never forget. And secondly, it should be faithful to the original. " [11]

Either of the two requirements is indispensable, firstly because the original poem is a piece of artistic work both in form and in spirit and consequently its translation should also remain such a piece of work. That's to say, the poetic artistry must be retained and the beauty in form, sound and meaning sought. And secondly because the translation of a poem should be faithful to the original since translating is not creation itself. Being faithful to the original, in my opinion, means that the translation of a poem should convey the content of the original and adopt a form close to the original. Only when this is achieved can the translation be regarded successful.

I put forward the three principles[12] of faithfulness, expressiveness and closeness in 1979. Faithfulness means "faithful to the original content," expressiveness "as expressive as the original language" and closeness "close to the original style."[13] Content and form, ideological character and artistic quality or content, language and style, on the one hand, are a unified whole and, on the other, may be analyzed by means of dividing one into two or into three. So far as the translation of poems is concerned, faithfulness in content means retaining the original meaning and artistic conception. Expressiveness in language refers to the original wording being easy or difficult to read and understand. That's to say, if the original is easy to read and understand, the translation should also be easy; if the original reads difficult, the translation shouldn't run contrary. Poems vary in style. Some are popular, some are graceful; some plain, some flowery; some solemn and some humorous. The translator must strive to make his translation close to the original in style.

After we have a correct understanding of the features, requirements and principles of translation, it is easy for us to see that the proposition and method of the creative school should not be popularized for they go too far beyond the limits of translation. Please look at the following example:

The first and fifth stanzas of Longfellow's *The Psalm of Life*

Tell me not, in mournful numbers,
Life is but an empty dream!
For the soul is dead that slumbers,
And things are not what they seem.

In the world's broad field of battle,
In the bivouac of life.
Be not like dumb, driven cattle!
Be a hero in the strife!

The translation of the two stanzas by Dong Xun

莫将烦恼著诗篇
百岁原如一觉眠
梦短梦长同是梦
独留真气满坤乾

扰扰红尘听鼓鼙
风吹大漠草萋萋
驽骀甘待鞭筈下
骐骥谁能辔勒羁[14]

The gist of the first stanza of the original poem *The Psalm of Life* is "Tell me not, in mournful numbers, /life is but an empty dream!" whereas the translator insists on saying "A hundred years of life is originally like a sleep, and dreams are dreams after all, whether long or short." The scenes of the battle and bivouac and the images of the cattle and the hero in the original all disappear in the translation. The translator substitutes the battle field with the so-called hongchen (red dust), the bivouac with desert, the cattle with inferior horses and the hero with superior horses. A translation like this seems to me unacceptable for the translator irresponsibly alters the theme, scenes and images of the original poem to satisfy his own needs.

Such is the case with the creative school in doing translation from Chinese into English. Xu Yuanchong points out, "The representative translations by the creative school are found in the book of《东方诗选》(*Selected Poems from the East*). In the book the translators translate the classical Chinese poems into the new English poems of the modernist school. They expand one line into a few, and don't capitalize the first letter at the beginning of each line and put any punctuation marks at the end of it. Sometimes when they have a strong poetic inspiration, they re-create the original poem they are working at. For instance, the original Chinese poem entitled Jin Se (musical instrument painted with a beautiful brocade-like design) by Li Shangyin (李商隐, c. 813-c. 858) consists of eight lines or sentences whereas in the English version there are thirty six lines of variation." [15]

Modernist poet Pound ran wild in his translation of Chinese poetry. Yu Guangzhong feels indignant at this. He says: "Many translations of Pound are more of 'adaptation', 'recomposition' or even 'plagiaristic creation than of translation. Thomas Sterns Eliot even went so far as to state that Pound 'invented Chinese poetry', which are deceptive words not to be taken as authoritative. But the intention of some poets to put creation in translation is quite obvious". And Yu adds immediately, "I strongly dissent from such adapted 'free translation' as to express the feelings of Pound in the name of Li Bai." [16]

Strictly speaking, such adapted or running-wild translation can't be called "free translation" for the proper free translation of poems is to strive for the conservation of the original meaning, artistic conception, spirit and style, but not to alter the charm, style and features, etc. Mao Dun advocated free translation with proper restraint. He first quoted the original poem and its translation:

The original
美人卷珠帘,
深坐颦蛾眉;
但见泪痕湿,
不知心恨谁。

The translation
A fair girl draws the blind aside
And sadly sits with the dropping head;
I see her burning tear drops glide
But know not why those tears are shed.

And then Mao Dun gave his comments and put forth three restrictions for the properly restrained free translation. He said:

"The English version in the main resembles the original in its romantic charm and it is done by means of free translation … It seems that some restrictions should be placed on free translation: 1. Free translation does not mean abbreviation or omission. To abbreviate or omit a lot of the original is 'not to be taken as an example'. The translation of 《木兰辞》(*The Ballad of Mulan*) is fine, but it has the shortcoming of too much resembling abbreviation and omission. 2. Free translation must keep the romantic charm of the original, which is 'some subtle spirit' above the rhetorical techniques, the individuality of a poem that forms the most important constituent element and the most difficult, but not necessarily impossible, to convey. 3. The translation must be close to the original in style. If the original style is moving and tragic, how can it be made quiet and beautiful?" [17]

In my opinion, the rendering of poems is not necessarily done by free translation. It depends on specific conditions. We literally translate whatever is suitable for the method of literary translation. For instance, the translation of Burns's *A Red, Red Rose* by Yuan Kejia as discussed in the above is, on the whole, translated literally. Both the syntax and the surface meaning of the words remain the same as in the original. And we freely translate whatever is suitable for the method of free translation. Take the translation cited by Mao Dun for example. It may, in the main, be said to have been translated freely. There are several places where considerably remarkable alterations are made of the surface meaning of words. For instance, "卷珠帘" (rolls up the pearl curtain) becomes "draws the blind aside", "颦蛾眉" (knitting the beautiful eye-brows) "sadly…with the dropping head", "泪痕湿" (tear traces wet) "burning tear drops glide", and "心恨谁" (who the heart hates) "why those tears are shed". Still the translation reproduces the image and scene of "a beautiful girl sitting sadly in her boudoir alone". Such alternative ways of saying things as in the above imply a sort of "re-creation". However. they are quite different from the creative school's making use of a poem under translation to put over their own ideas. Viewed as a whole, the above-cited translation tries to express the content of the original—mainly the image and artistic conception and convey the spirit of the original—mainly the feelings of a girl sitting in her boudoir alone. In most cases, the translator should flexible use either the method of literal translation or that of free translation or combine both in a flexible way. Why do I say that the above translation is translated freely "in the main" instead of "entirely" for it doesn't make any change of the syntax.

So much for the discussion on the unacceptableness of the creative school's proposition and ways of doing translation.

How do matters stand with the classical school and the free school now?

At present, so far as the translation of Du Fu's poems into English is concerned, as Zhou Weixin and Zhou Yan in their essay *Du's Poems and Translation* point out, "It varies with the translators. But when roughly classified, the translators may be divided into two typical schools: the absolutely free school, and the strict school who put stress on symmetry in form. Although the two schools are different in approach and equally satisfactory in result, still they each develop in depth and constantly strengthen their own approaches in accordance with the recent tendency in their respective development so that they give birth to theories opposite to each other and produce remarkably different translations. This can be seen from the two representative works published not long ago. The former is Weng Xianliang's《古诗英译》(*An English Version of Old Poems*, Beijing People's Publishing House, May, 1985), the latter Wu Jun Tao's《杜甫诗英译》(*An English Version of Du Fu's Poems*, Shaanxi People's Publishing House, September, 1985). Both translators are experts and both works fine. However, their viewpoints of translation are opposite to each other. Weng maintains that poetry may be translated into prose. He says: 'The translation of a poem is not merely a copy of it. Whether it resembles the original lies in the spirit, not in the appearance. Furthermore, the translation should not subject to the restraint of the traditional form. It makes no difference whether it is rimed and divided into lines. It's quite free'. (*The Brief Preface to An English Version of Old Poems* by Weng Xianliang, p. 1) Wu says on the contrary. 'If you want to convey the spirit and features of the original in a considerable perfection, you must try your best to make your translation close to the original both in spirit and in features. Since the original is poetry, it is better not to translate it into prose. Since the original is rigorous classical poetry, it is better not to translate it into modern free verse.' (*Preface to An English Version of Du Fu's Poems*, P. 31)" [18]

The authors quoted in the above further make five points of comparison between the two English versions by Weng and Wu. Although they say in the above quotation that "Both translators are experts and both works fine", Yet judging from the five points of comparison, we can easily see that their praise of Wu is sincere whereas that of Weng contains some criticism in it. Now let's cite the third point of comparison as follows:

"3. Weng gives a free rein to his translation, which leads to looseness while Wu is profound and accurate in his translation, in other words, he neither overstates nor understates things. Take the translation of 《野望》 (a view in the. open) for example:

清秋望不极,迢递起层阴。
     Weng's Translation
The autumn air ought to be clear: yet
the prospect is circumscribed by dark
masses looming in the distance.
(*An English Version of Old Poems* by Weng Xianliang, P. 26)

Wu's Translation
The autumnal view is infinite for one's gaze.
And far away somewhere roll up the wreaths of haze.
(*An English Version of Du Fu's Poems* by Wu Juntao, P. 130)

"Under comparison we find that Wu strictly observes the limits for translation, so his translation is fairly to the point and there are few faults to be found in it…While Weng is so much liberal in his translation that he neglects the character '望' (view) and thus renders '望不极' (view is infinite) as 'air ought to be clear', which does not quite conform to the original." Meanwhile, the authors cite the words of Prof. Wen Yiduo to warn translators: "The translator shouldn't misuse his liberty. He must be especially careful so that he may not distort the meaning of the original."

In one word, the authors advocate the method of translating poetry in a form of certain rime scheme. They say:

"In order to better keep the charm of the original, the three-in-one method which takes into consideration the beauty in meaning, sound and form, should be adopted. The so-called three in one means: 1. The translation of words is accurate, elaborate and beautiful, the stress being put on conveying the significance in the depth of the content instead of sticking to the 'beauty in meaning' in the superficial form; 2. The 'beauty in sound' is to be expressed by means of rime, repetition and rhythm; 3. The 'beauty in form' expressed by means of symmetry and antithesis so as to make the length of sentences in the translation nearly even with that in the original. That's to say, the translator is good at combining the rhythm and meaning of words cleverly." And at the same time, they gave a translation as an example of "three in one":

《登高》[19]
风急天高猿啸哀,
渚清沙白鸟飞回。
无边落木萧萧下,
不尽长江滚滚来。

Translation

The wind so swift, the sky so steep, and gibbons cry;
Water so clear and sand so white, backwards birds fly.
The boundless forest sheds its leaves shower by shower.
The endless river rolls its waves hour after hour.

(*On the Translation of the Tang Poetry into English*, *Translators Journal*, No. 3, 1983, P. 22) [20]

As a whole, the translation of this poem is very good. But there is something worth discussing. For instance, his rendering of the expression "鸟飞回" as "backwards birds fly" doesn't seem satisfactory, because (1) "回" here is the simplified form of "迴" which means "circle" or "wheel", and (2) even if one may comprehend "鸟飞回" as "birds fly back", the adverb "backwards" still can't substitute the adverb "back" whose meaning is different from that of "backwards". In my opinion, it's better to understand and translate the expression under discussion as 'birds circle or wheel'. In order to keep the original rime, "backwards birds fly" may be improved as "birds circlingly fly" or "birds wheelingly fly."

Concerning how to translate the old Chinese or Tang poems into

English, I agree to the method of translating them with a certain rime scheme. When I wrote the paper entitled *The Principles of Translation Expounded by Theodore Savory*, I said:

"As to the question of how poetry should be translated and of whether any addition or omission can be made in the translation, Savory agrees that poetry should be translated into poetry and that the translator had better rime his translation if the original is rimed, but he does not agree to any addition or omission for the sake of riming. He holds that poetry may be translated in the form of prose poem or in the form of poetic prose when necessary. Thus it won't be subject to the limitations of the schemes of riming nor of the rules of accentuation, and as a result the ideas and feelings can be fully conveyed.

"... The translation of classical poetry in a classical pattern is naturally of a high order on condition that on the one hand the rules and forms of classical poetic composition are observed and on the other no original meaning is misrepresented. But when some specific classical poems are really so difficult and complicated that you can hardly translate them in a classical pattern so as to keep as much as possible the original ideas, situations, artistic conceptions and images in their translations, you may as well try to render them in the form of free verse. Anyhow, it is far better than sticking to the regular length of each line and the rime scheme of each poem by means of wilfully adding or omitting the content of the original in the translation." [21]

There is no lack of excellent translations of the Tang poems in the form of free verse. Take the translation He Zhizhang's 《回乡偶书》 (*Coming Home*) by Bynner for example. Now let's have an appreciation of it.

《回乡偶书》

贺知章

少小离家老大回，
乡音无改鬓毛衰；
儿童相见不相识，
笑问"客从何处来？"

Comming Home

by He ghizhang

I left home young. I return old,
Speaking as then, but with hair grown thin;
And my children, meeting, do not know me.
They smile and say: "Stranger, where do you come from?"

——Bynner

Lü Shuxiang points out, "Whether the Chinese characters '儿童' refer to the children in the family or those in the village, it seems that 'the children' may be used in either case. Besides this. the translation tallies with the original and reads like a very fine poem".[22]

Lü speaks highly of the translation of this poem in the form of free verse. His comments are objective and just, because 1. the translation in the main retains the beauty in meaning, 2. it also consists of four lines which are even as a whole judged from the number of accented syllables, which shows that the translation has taken the beauty in form into consideration, and 3. it has a fluent natural rhythm, reads smoothly and sounds pleasant to the ear, which means that it lacks no beauty in sound. Riming, of course, is an essential element of the beauty in sound in a rimed poem, but the natural rhythm a constituent too. And what's more, the simple and plain style of the original has got reproduced in the translation. "Fine translations may be produced by putting the classical poetry into free verse. There are translators abroad who have worked out fine translations of poetry in this way. Their purpose of doing so is to guard against translating the foreign classical poetry into uncorresponding national classical poetry, especially against bringing in the cliches from the national classical poetry, which may hinder the reader from feeling the breath of the original. The English sinologist James Legge's translation of the ancient Chinese collection of poems entitled *The Book of Songs* in the form of the English classical poetry is not so good as that of the ancient Chinese poetry in the form of free verse (or as what we call it 'semifree') by his fellow countryman Arthur David Waley; Of course, the quality of translation is more or less related to the personal ability and level of linguistic attainments of the translator. From this we can see that only with enough accomplishment in language can one translate poetry in a classical form and that it demands a high artistic level of one to produce better translation without the aid of an appropriate form and some corresponding scheme." [23]

In the above we have mainly discussed the question of how to translate the classical poetry from Chinese into English, and taken the improper translation of Longfellow's *The Psalm of Life* by Dong Xun in the form of five characters to a line and the successful translation of Burns's *A Red, Red Rose* by Yuan Kejia in the form of rimed vernacular free verse (or the so-called semi-free verse) as examples. There are quite a few people who have tried to translate the classical English poetry in the form of five-or seven-character pre-Tang poems. But judging from the basic principle of faithfulness to the original, such translations often present a shortcoming either of adding flowers to a brocade or of distorting the original meaning owing to riming. Wang Yizhu has the same impression of this. He says: "In our country in the earlier period Su Manshu, Ma Junwu and others used the ancient poetry form to translate the English poems. Later many followed their example and some of them translated the foreign poems either in the form of ci and qü, which are two forms of Chinese verse. Some of the translations themselves are brilliant, but strictly speaking, what we appreciate is merely the creation of the translator, for the original only functions as something of reference to them." [24]

The reasons for why it is difficult to succeed in translating the classical English poems in the form of the five-charactered old Chinese poetry or in the form of the seven-charactered are as follows:

"First, our mother tongue has developed from the classical style of writing with monosyllabic characteres as units into the modern spoken language with monosyllabic or more than one syllabic words as units. The translation of poetry with the monosyllabic characters as units evidently runs counter to the characteristics of the modern Chinese. Secondly, the syllables of the foreign languages with an alphabetic system are based on vowels. The number of syllables in a word is determined by the number of vowels it contains. But in Chinese when viewed as a mere collection of characters, a character can only make a syllable in any case. As a result, such monosyllabic characters can never well match the polysyllabic words. And thirdly, even if the corresponding lines in the translation contain as many syllables as in the original, yet the translation must be read in such a way that each group of two or three characters is recited in a breath. As a consequence, each character in the translation do not agree with each syllable in the original whether it is judged by its pause in time or by its effect in hearing."[25]

In my opinion, there is one more reason: The classical Chinese poetry is compendious and condensed whereas the classical English accurate and detailed so that they both often disagree with each other in how to express the meaning.

Bian Zhilin and others advocate translating the classical foreign poetry with dun (sound groups) as rhythm units. They say:

"Translating with dun as rhythm units conforms both to the tradition of the classical Chinese poems, songs and ballads and to the characteristics of the modern spoken language. Although Chinese characters consist of monosyllabic words, yet ours is not a monosyllabic language. We speak mostly in groups of two or three words in a breath instead of speaking word by word. Consequently, the rhythm of dun (sound groups) is very obvious in the modern spoken language. The number of syllables of each line of the classical poetry in Europe (including U. S. S. R.) is roughly regular too, but what counts is the kind and number of the metrical feet (Exceptional is the classical French poetry, which has its own way). The dun system (the internal nature of each dun and the mutual relation among the sound groups) remain to be further studied. However, the practice has proved that the dun method is flexible, achieves equivalence in form and rhythm in the translation as a whole and makes the Chinese version close to the original in effect when we use the number of dun to replace that of metric feet instead of sticking to the number of words. Both may be entirely the same in number sometimes, at least, approximate. As a matter of fact, this method during the past ten years has produced a number of comparatively successful works and revealed the possibility of its further development."[28]

The superiority of translating the classical foreign poetry by substituting the metric feet with dun (sound groups) and the regular rime scheme with an irregular one often found in the form of new poetry in modern Chinese began to come into being in China in the early 1950s. Up till now, such a method of translating the classical foreign poetry has already taken the dominant position. The publication of a series of translations by the Hunan People's Publishing House in recent years constitutes a convincing evidence of this. For instance, *Byron's* 70 *lyric Poems* translated by Yang Deyu may be regarded as the representative work of those who support the dun system. Now let's have an appreciation of one out of the 70.

She Walks in Beauty

She walks in beauty, like the night
    Of cloudless climes and starry skies;
And all that's best of dark and bright
    Meet in her aspect and her eyes:
Thus mellow'd to that tender light
    Which heaven to gaudy day denies.

One shade the more, one ray the less,
    Had half impair'd the nameless grace
Which waves in every raven tress,
    Or softly lightens o'er her face;
Where thoughts serenely sweet express
    How pure, how dear their dwelling place.

And on that cheek, and o'er that brow,
    So soft, so calm, yet eloquent,

The smiles that win, the tints that glow.
But tell of days in goodness spent,
A mind at peace with all below,
A heart whose love is innocent.

《她走在美的光影里》

她走在美的光影里,好像
　无云的夜空,繁星闪烁;
明与暗的最美的形相
　交会于她的容颜和眼波,
融成一片恬淡的清光——
　浓艳的白天得不到的恩泽。

多一道阴影,少一缕光芒,
　都会损害那难言的优美;
美在她绺绺黑发上飘荡,
　在她的腮颊上洒布柔辉;
愉悦的思想在那儿颂扬
　这神圣寓所的纯洁高贵。
那脸颊,那眉宇,幽娴,沉静,
　情意却胜似万语千言;
迷人的笑容,灼人的红晕,
　显示温情伴送着芳年;
和平的、涵容一切的灵魂!
　蕴蓄着真纯爱情的心田!

There are four commonest forms of metrical feet in English prosody. They are iambus (short long), trochee (long short), dactyl (long short

short), and anapaest (short short long). Just as the tonal patterns in classical Chinese poetry can't be transplanted in its corresponding English version, nor can the forms of metrical feet be transplanted in its corresponding Chinese version. "But in translating the classical English poetry it is possible to achieve the following two things: The first thing is to make the number of dun of each line in the translation equal to that of metrical feet in the original and the second is to arrange the rimes in the same scheme as in the original, both of which will help reproduce the musical beauty of the original (such as the even, regular and harmonious rhythm and the graceful rime scheme suiting the needs of the ideological content) as much as possible in another language." [27]

3473 lines in the translation of Byron's 70 lyric poems by Yang Deyu are all in the same rime scheme as in the original. So far as the method of dun replacing the metric feet is concerned the number of dun and that of metric feet is the same in at least more than 96% of lines. Only less than 4% of lines are appropriately adapted in the light of specific conditions. Therefore, we may say the translator has in the main realized the proposition advanced by Poet Shelley that only when the translation of poetry is in the same form as the original, can he really match up to the author.

The translator's achievements in translating the 70 lyric poems are praise-worthy. I think we must take a dialectical and magnanimous attitude towards the translation of poetry so as to have a correct understanding of the proposition that the translation of poetry should be in the "same" form as in the original. Only when one has a try in translating poems can he be aware how hard and difficult it is to do such translation.

Finally, let's have a discussion of the translation of free verse, which has prevailed far and wide in the world since its establishment by Walt

Whitman in the United States. Its main characteristics lie in that there are no strict restrictions in the division of stanzas and lines and no definite schemes in riming. In general, it is still divided into stanzas and lines, but puts more stress on internal rhythm than on end rimes, which has become the main trend of the modern English and American poetry. According to the principle of translating poems put forward by Shelley, it is better to translate the modernist English and American poetry which does not stress regular riming in the form of new Chinese poetry which does not stress regular riming, either. e. g.

Several Voices out of a Cloud
by Louise Bogan

Come, drunks and drug-takers; come perverts unnerved!
Receive the laurel given, though late, on merit;
to whom and wherever deserved
Parochial punks, trimmers, nice people, joiners true-blue.
Get the hell out of the way of the laurel.
It is deathless. And it isn't for you. [28]

Just as Marcus Cunliffe, the author of *The Literature of the United States*, points out:

"The colloquialism of this poem is exaggerated in order to startle the reader, but there are innumerable other instances of poems that employ the vernacular with unobtrusive assurance. Miss Bogan's poem was published in 1938; by then, the conversational verse of W. H. Auden showed that at least one British poet had also captured a voice-box. Perhaps his subsequent removal to the United States, and adoption of American citizenship, indicated that he felt especially at home with the American compound of polite speech and lingua fransa. " (p. 306)

Now let's have a look at the translation:

《一片云中的几种声音》
by Zhang Fangjie

来吧,醉鬼和吸毒的人们;来吧,丧失勇气的堕落者!
接受这桂冠吧,给的虽迟,却是论功行赏;给的是受之无愧的人,
褊狭的无聊人物,随风转舵者,雅人,高贵的名流。
你们都滚开,不要碰这桂冠,它是没有死亡的,也不是给你们的。[29]

In the original poem there is the exaggerated colloquialism in wording, and the full freedom in the length of lines and no rimes can be found. The translation is well-done as a whole for it's quite faithful to the original in wording, in the order of words and lines and in the ideological content. Only one point may get further improved. That is, the metaphorical sense of the word "deathless" (不朽的) should be taken in place of its surface meaning (没有死亡的) so as to make it agree with the subject laurel (桂冠). From this we can once more see how difficult it is even to translate a poem of free verse satisfactorily and perfectly.

So far as the poetic form and riming are concerned, the new poetry in China has been developed into two schools since its birth in the 1910s. One school advocates more freedom in writing and puts no stress on riming just as the modernist English and American poets. The other still maintains a certain form of good proportions and an irregular scheme of riming. The basic principle of translating such new poetry into English may be defined as follows:

The translation should also be poetry and true to the original. In other words, the translation must be faithful to the original content, as expressive as the original in language and close to the original in style. In a nutshell, the translation of a poem is wholly determined by the specific original.

Notes

1. *English Versions of the* 100 *Four-lined Tang Poems*, compiled and annotated by Lü Shuxiang, published by Hunan People's Publishing House, 1980.
2. Xu Xuanchong, 1988, *A Free Talk about the Translation of Shi and Ci into English*, *Chinese Translators Journal*, No. 3.
3. Yuan Honggeng, 1988, *On the Style of the Author and that of the Translator in Literature*, *Journal of Lanzhou University* (Social Science Edition), No. 2.
4. Concerning the methods of compensation, see Wang Enmian's *An Initial Research of Compensation Methods in Translation*, *Chinsse Translators Journal*, Nos. 2 and 3, 1988.
5. Liu Zhongde, 1984, *Free Talks about Translation*, Shaanxi People's Publishing House.
6. See Note 4.
7. See Note 5.
8. See Note 1.
9. See Note 2.
10. He Kuang, 1955, *On the Criteria of Trauslation*, *Russian Teaching*, No. 6.
11. Cheng Fangwu, *On Translating Poems in An Anthology of Essays on Translation* compiled by Luo Xinzhang, 333, The Commercial Press, 1984.
12. Liu Zhongde, 1979, *On the Principles of Trauslation*, *Journal of Hunan Teachers College*, No. 1.
13. "达如其分" (as expressive as the original in language) is the new definition given recently by the author of the lectures to the character "达" (expressiveness), one of his three-character principles (信达切).
14. The translated poem is quoted from Qian Zhongshu's *The First English Poem The*

Psalm of Life Translated into Chinese in *An Anthology of Essays on Translation* compiled by Luo Xinzhang, 244, 245.
15. See Note 2.
16. Yu Guangzhong, *Translation and Creation* in *An Anthology of Essays on Translation*, 743.
17. Mao Dun, 1922, *Some Comments on Translating Poems*, *Literary Supplement to the Current Affairs Daily*, No. 52. The original poem entitled《怨情》by Li Bai.
18. Zhou Weixin and Zhou Yan, 1987, *Du Fu's Poems and Trauslation*, *Foreign Languages*, No. 6.
19. *Deng Gao* is a qilü written by Du Fu. The last four lines are: 万里悲秋常作客,／百年多病独登台。／艰难苦恨繁霜鬓,／潦倒新停浊酒杯。
20. See Note 18.
21. Liu Zhongde, 1986, *The Principles of Translation Expounded by Theodore Savory*, *Foreign Languages*, No. 4.
22. See Note 1.
23. Bian Zhilin et al. *The Question of Artistic and Poetic Translation* in *An Anthology of Essays on Translation* compiled by Luo Xinzhang 1984.
24. Wang Yizhu, 1981, *On the Untranslatability of Poetry*, *Reference for Compilalion and Translation*, No. 1.
25. 26. See Note 23.
27. Yang Deyu, 1981, *A Postscript to his Translation of Byron's 70 Lyrics*, Hunan People's Publishing House.
28. 29. Marcus Cunliffe, 1979, *The Literature of the United Slates* (English-Chinese edition), 306-307, Today's World Press. Hong Kong.

Lecture Ten Translation of English Poetry into Chinese

I. The Influence of the Translation of English Poetry on the New Poetry in China

By English Poetry here I mean various poems written in the English language, not necessarily by British poets. The poem which was first translated into Chinese by Dong Xun during the Qing Dynasty is Henry Wadsworth Longfellow's *A Psalm of Life* (1839).

In the history of literary translation in China, Lin Shu and Dong Xun had things in common: 1. Neither know any foreign language. Yet the former translated more than 150 novels such as *Ivanhoe* (1820) by Sir Walter Scott (1771-1832) and *Uncle Tom's Cabin* (1852) by Harriet Elizabeth Stowe, nee Beecher (1811-1896) with the help of his interpreter whereas the latter did only one poem, namely *A Psalm of Life* on the basis of the Chinese version of this poem[1] by Sir Thomas Francis Wade (1818-1895). 2. Both used the classical Chinese in their translation. Owing to the fact that they could not read and appreciate the original works themselves, misrepresentations were unavoidable in their translation. However, Lin Shu had a fairly remarkable influence on Chinese new literature, but Dong Xun didn't make much contribution to it for he "translated" only one poem and committed glaring mistakes in his so-called translation《人生颂》.[1] I have just given a detailed analysis of his work in the preceding lecture. No repetition is needed here.

Like other forms of foreign literature, English poetry began to be translated by experts early in the twentieth century. In 1909 Su Manshu (1884-1918) translated *The Selected Poems of Lord Byron*, including *My Native Land—Good Night*, *The Ocean*, *The Isles of Greece*, etc. Here I'd like to quote the sixth stanza of his translation of *The Isles of Greece* against the original so that we may get a glimpse of how such forerunners as Su and others translated English poems in the form of pre-Tang poetry.

Original

'Tis something in the dearth of fame,
 Though link'd among a fetter'd race,
To feel at least a patriot's shame,
 Even as I sing, suffuse my face;
For what is left the poet here?
For Greeks a blush—for Greece a tear.

Translation[2]

威名尽坠地　举族供奴畜
知尔忧国士　中心亦以恧
而我独行谣　我犹无面目
我为希人羞　我为希腊哭

In order to make the reader better grasp the spirit of the original poem, the corresponding stanza of Yang Deyu's version[3] in modern Chinese and by means of "dun" (sound groups or modern Chinese phonetic pauses) in place of the English metrical feet is cited as follows:

置身于披枷带锁的民族,
　　与荣誉无缘,也心甘情愿;
至少,能痛感邦家的屈辱,
　　歌唱的时候,我羞惭满面;
诗人在这里有什么作用?
为祖国落泪,为同胞脸红?

Around the May 4th movement, there were more and more people who engaged in translating English poetry. For instance, in 1915 Chen Duxiu (1879-1942) translated Rabindranath Tagore's four poems from their English version and published them in the magazine *Youth* (later *New Youth*). Immediately after that, Liu Bannong (1891-1934) put *The Song of the Shirt* by Thomas Hood (1799-1845) into Chinese and published it in the same magazine. And in 1922, Guo Moruo offered a Chinese version of *The Selected Poems of Percy Bysshe Shelley*.

Prior to the year when he translated Shelley's poems, he published 《女神》, a collection of his free verse written in the vernacular. "The collection laid a foundation for the Chinese new poetry just as Lu Xun's 《呐喊》 (*Shouting*) did for the newtype fiction in China. This collection of his was a brilliant fruit of new literature in the period of the May 4th Movement... One of the factors that made the poet score such a great achievement was the influence of foreign progressive poets. In his essay *My Experience in*

Writing Poems, he said: ' I was first influenced by Tagore and others, advocating simplicity and plainness and then Walter Whitman, beginning to write in a bold and flowing style. 'Talking of Whitman, he added, ' The poetic style that gets rid of the conventional practice was quite in harmony with the spirit of advance by leaps and bounds in the period of the May 4th movement. I was thoroughly moved and stirred by his profound, unconstrained and sonorous tone. ' " (*On Guo Moruo's Poetry in His Early Period of Writing* by Zhang Guangnian, published in the first issue of *Poetry*, 1957). Among the European poets he mentioned the influence exerted on him by Johann Wolfgang von Goethe and Heinrich Heine From these words, we can easily see the influence of the poetry in the West on the free verse in our country both in content and form. The reform in poetry during the May 4th Movement mainly aimed at breaking the rules and forms of classical poetic composition and expressing the new revolutionary ideas and feelings in a comparatively free form. In their pursuit of some new form the new poets found a fairly available one in the Western poetry and the content that seeks emancipation and revolution expressed in the poems of the West struck a sympathetic chord in the poets' minds. [4]

  The May 4th Movement gave birth to quite a few of schools of poetry, such as school of romanticism (Guo Moruo), school for the masses (Liu Bannong), school of short poems (Xie Bingxin), school of lakeside poets (Hu Xuefeng), school of new elegance (Feng Zhi), school of new metrical poetry (Wan Yiduo), school of prose poems (Lu Xun), school of revolutionary poems (Jiang Guangci), school of symbolism (Dai Wangshu). In one word, we may as well say that all the schools and their representatives were more or less inspired and influenced by foreign poems (including the English poems of the East and West). Take the influence

Xie Bingxin accepted from Tagore for example.

"... Bingxin felt that there were only some very interesting but 'fragmentary' ideas in her mind before she read Tagore's poems. It was the penetration of his belief in the 'natural' sense of beauty and his 'poetry giving full play to the natural sense of beauty' into her mind and their composition into musical chords with her originally 'unutterable' ideas that stroke up soundless and wonderful tunes. This enables her works to be 'similar in spirit' with those of Tagore (1861-1941).

"During the high tide of new culture, Young Xie's desire for knowledge was very strong. Pearly impressions and recollections often occurred in her mind. At first, she only jotted them down on the page tops in her notebook. Although they consisted of merely three or five lines, yet they enabled her to recall some 'loving and true' situations. She read the serial of Zheng Zhenduo's translation of *Tagore's Collection of Flying Birds*. 'The few words which were full of poetic flavor, picturesque scene and philosophic truth' in Tagore's verse impelled her to write many short poems which later constituted the two anthologies respectively entitled *Stars* and *Spring Water*. This artistic agreement made the two poets' poetry strikingly 'similar in form'." [5]

There is no denying the fact that even after the May 4th Movement the Chinese poetry was still infuenced by the foreign. Take, for instance, the English sonnets. There were not only people who translated them, but also people who imitated them. Out of the Chinese sonnets Qian Guangpei (钱光培) compiled a collection entitled *Selections from the Chinese Sonnets*. The so-called ladder-shaped poems written by Vladimir Vladimirovich Mayakovski (1893-1930) once produced great influence on the progressive poets in China as well. Various editions of his *Selected Poems* were published and quite a few people wrote poems in Chinese copying his poetic form. Later, the poetic circles made a response to Imagism as soon as the poems of the imagist poets such as Ezra Pound (1885-1975) and T. S. Eliot (1888-1965) were introduced into this country. Take the so-called menglong shi (obscure poetry) in the 1970's for instance. In my eyes, it is somewhat related to Western modernism.

II. Research on the Methods of Translating English Poetry

Just as Wang Yizhu pointed out, in the early years of this century Su Manshu, Ma Junwu and others rendered Byron's poems in the form of pre-Tang poetry and later lots of people followed their example. A few people translated foreign poems even in the form of ci (poetry written to certain tunes with strict tonal patterns and rime schemes, in fixed numbers of lines and words) and qu (a type of verse for singing). Some of the translation themselves are fairly excellent, indeed; but strictly speaking, what appear before us are only their creations, the original works functioning merely as a sort of reference.[6] Su and Ma had great attainments in both the Chinese and the English language. Their translations of English poetry should have a place in the history of verse translation because they were forerunners in this field. It was they that first introduced English poetry into China, which more or less promoted our new poetry. However, it seems improper now for people to take their example to translate English poetry in the form of old poetry so far as the demand of the present time is concerned. There are two major reasons: 1. The old form of poetry, whether with four characters or with five characters or with seven characters to a line, has limitations so that it can hardly embody the meaning, image and artistic conception of the original. 2. The old form of poetry is rather difficult for the broad masses of young readers to understand and appreciate. Take Su Manshu's four-charactered version of the first stanza of *The Ocean* by Byron.

Original

Roll on, thou deep and dark blue ocean—roll!
Ten Thousand fleets sweep over thee in vain;
Man marks the earth with ruin—his control
Stops with the shore; upon the wat'ry plain
The wrecks are all thy deed, nor doth remain
A Shadow of man's ravage, save his own,
When, for a moment, like a drop of rain,
He sinks into thy depths, with bubbling groan
Without a grave, unknelled, uncoffin'd and unknown.

Translation[7]

皇涛澜汗　灵海黝冥
万艘鼓楫　泛若轻萍
芒芒九围　每有遗虚
旷哉天沼　匪人攸居
大器自运　振荡粤夆
岂伊人力　赫彼神工
罔象乍见　决舟没人
狂矞未几　遂为波臣
掩体无棺　归骨无坟
丧钟声嘶　迹矣谁闻

The Chinese version of this stanza itself reads quite fluently. But judging by the strict criteria of verse translation, there is wilful addition, omission or distortion. For example: 1. The character 灵 in the expression 灵海 in the first line is evidently a wilful addition for the sake of forming an antithesis to the foregoing expression 皇涛. The word ocean means "great body of water" and the character 灵 "holy". According to the original, there is nothing holy in the ocean. 2. The second line 万艘鼓楫/泛若轻萍 gives the reader a feeling of lightheartedness, which is contrary to the original meaning. The misrepresentation comes from the wilful omission of the adverbial "in vain" in the original. The original line "Ten thousand fleets sweep over thee in vain" really signifies "the so many ships fail to cross the ocean". 3. The translation of the fourth line 旷哉天沼/匪人攸居 is inaccurate, for the question does not lie in the fact that the ocean is a place man can't inhabit, but lies in the fact that it is a place man can't control. 4. The image of "a drop of rain" disappears in the seventh line of Su's version. Instead, there appears 罔象, a water monster in the Chinese legend. 5. The word "unknelled" in line nine of the original means "without tolling a knell at all" turns out to be "with a hoarse knell". This may be regarded as a wilful distortion.

What's said above is about the content of Su's translation. How about its language? Such a classical literary language may be very hard for young people to read and understand. Some characters are even strange to them. Take the characters 甹夆 and the character 曻. How to read and explain them? The examples I give here is comparatively typical, no doubt, but generally speaking, there exist such shortcomings as mentioned above in the verse translations in the classical literary Chinese language.

Since the May 4th Movement of Literary Revolution put forth the proposition of "promoting writing in the vernacular and opposing those in classical Chinese", remarkable progress has been made in the work of translating English poetry both in language and in form. That's to say, there have been more and more people who translate in the vernacular and pay attention to keeping close to the form of the original. Here I'd like to quote for reference Guo Moruo's version of *The Tyger* written by William Blake (1759-1827), for I think it is fairly well-done not only in its poetic form, but also in its riming and natural rythm, though its rime scheme is different from that of the original.

The Tyger[8]

Tyger! Tyger! burning bright
In the forests of the night,
What immortal hand or eye
Could frame thy fearful symmetry?

In what distant deeps or skies
Burned the fire of thine eyes?
On what wings dare he aspire?
What the hand dare seize the fire?

And what shoulder, and what art,
Could twist the sinews of thy heart?
And when thy heart began to beat,
What dread hand? and what dread feet?

What the hammer? what the chain?

In what furnace was thy brain?
What the anvil? what dread grasp
Dare its deadly terrors clasp?

When the stars threw down their spears,
And water'd heaven with their tears,
Did he smile his work to see?
Did he who made the Lamb make thee?

Tyger! Tyger! burning bright
In the forests of the night,
What immortal hand or eye
Could frame thy fearful symmetry?

《老 虎》

老虎！老虎！黑夜的森林中
燃烧着的煌煌的火光，
是怎样的神手或天眼
造出了你这样的威武堂堂？

你炯炯两眼中的火
燃烧在多远的天空或深渊？
他乘着怎样的翅膀搏击？
用怎样的手夺来火焰？

又是怎样的膂力，怎样的技巧，
把你心脏的筋肉捏成？

当你的心脏开始搏动时
是用怎样猛的手和脚胫?

是怎样的槌?怎样的链子?
在怎样的熔炉中炼成你的脑筋?
是怎样的铁砧?怎样的铁臂
敢于捉着这可怖的凶神?

群星投下了它们的投枪,
用它们的眼泪润湿了穹苍,
他是否微笑着欣赏他的作品?
他创造了你,也创造了羔羊?

老虎!老虎!黑夜的森林中
燃烧着的煌煌的火光,
是怎样的神手和天眼
造出了你这样的威武堂堂?

In 1950s Bian Zhilin and others published an essay on artistic and literary translation, where they definitely put forward the proposition concerning the method of translating the classical English poetry that dun (sound groups) should be used as rhythm units in place of metric feet. This viewpoint of theirs has been cited and expounded in the preceding lecture. I won't make any more explanation of it. Let's see how Bian's practice is. Take his Chinese version of *The Solitary Reaper* written by William Wordsworth (1770-1850).

The Solitary Reaper

Behold her, single in the field,
Yon solitary Highland Lass!
Reaping and singing by herself;
Stop here or gently pass!
Alone she cuts and binds the grain,
And sings a melancholy strain;
Oh listen! for the vale profound
Is overflowing with the sound.

No nightingale did ever chant
More welcome notes to weary bands
Of travellers in some shady haunt,
Among Arabian sands:
A voice so thrilling ne'er was heard
In spring-time from the cuckoo bird,
Breaking the silence of the seas
Among the farthest Hebrides.

Will no one tell me what she sings? —
Perhaps the plaintive numbers flow
For old, unhappy, far-off things,
And battles long ago:
Or is it some more humble lay,
Familiar matter of to-day?
Some natural sorrow, loss, or pain,
That has been, and may be again?

《孤独的割麦女》

看她,在田地独自一个,
那个苏格兰高原的少女!
独自在收割,独自在唱歌;
停住吧,或者悄悄走过去!
她独自割麦,又把它捆好,
唱着一支忧郁的曲调;
听啊,整个深邃的谷地
都有这一片歌声在洋溢。

从没有夜莺能够唱出
更美的音调来欢迎结队商,
疲倦了,到一个荫凉的去处
就在阿拉伯沙漠的中央:
杜鹃鸟在春天叫得多动人,
也没有这样子荡人心魂,
尽管它惊破了远海的静悄,
响彻了赫伯里底群岛。

她唱的是什么,可有谁说得清?
哀怨的曲调也许在流传
古老,不幸,悠久的事情,
还有长久以前的征战;
或者她唱的并不特殊,
只是今日的家常事故?
那些天然的丧忧,哀痛,
有过的,以后还会有的种种?

Whate'er the theme, the maiden sang	不管她唱的是什么题目,
As if her song could have no ending;	她的歌好像会没完没了;
I saw her singing at her work,	我看见她边唱边干活,
And o'er the sickle bending;——	弯着腰,挥动她的镰刀——
I listened, motionless and still,	我一动也不动,听了许久;
And, as I mounted up the hill,	后来,当我上山的时候,
The music in my heart I bore,	我把歌还记在心上,
Long after it was heard no more.	虽然早已听不见声响。

Through the contrast between the Chinese version and the original, we find that Bian is quite strict in his translation and that he gives a good example of how to make use of the Chinese dun in place of the English metrical feet.

As to how to translate the classical English poetry, Wang Keyi (1925-1968) makes a penetrating analysis in his essay *Some Remarks about Shelley's Comments on Translating Poems*. In his opinion, its most important task is "to reproduce the original artistic conception. In order to achieve this, there are two unnegligible obligations confronting us. One is form-transplanting and the other words-weighing."[10] According to his point of view, he rendered *The Revolt of Islam* by Shelley, strove to reproduce the nine lined Spenserian stanza and marked out the number of dun in each line with vertical lines which is helpful to understanding the use of dun in place of metrical feet. Take the third stanza of the first canto for example:

> Hark! 'tis the rushing of a wind that sweeps
> Earth and the ocean. See! The lightnings yawn
> Deluging Heaven with fire, and the lashed deeps

Glitter and boil beneath; it rages on,
The mighty stream, whirlwind and waves upthrown,
Lightning and hail, and darkness eddying by.
There is a pause—the sea-birds, that were gone
Into their caves to shriek, come forth, to spy
What calm has fallen on earth, what light is in the sky.

听！|那不|就是|飞驰的|疾风，
扫过|大地|和海洋？|瞧！|那闪电，
喷出|火光|来撕裂|淫雨的|天空，
被鞭打的|海洋|掀起|金光|万点，
海底|沸腾了，|旋风|把巨浪|席卷，
闪电，|冰雹，|黑暗，|飞旋|直转，
稍顷|风雨|暂停，|海鸥|出现，
才躲进|洞里|去悲啼，|又出来刺探——
天上|可曾|晴阳，|人间|已否|平安？

Wang's translation of this stanza is in the main in keeping with the requirements he puts forth. For one thing he weighs his words carefully, and for another he basically retains the form of the Spenserian stanza. The Chinese version also consists of nine lines, the first eight are made up of five dun and the ninth six. He makes some change in the line indentation, which seems not quite necessary, for the original indentation can be kept.

In the following I'd like to say a few words about the translation of free verse to conclude this lecture. As the world knows. Walt Whitman (1819-1892) was a very famous American poet who initiated the free verse. Now let's first quote a few lines of his and their translation and then make a comment on the Chinese version.

The Original[11]

To behold the day-break!
　　The little light fades the immense and diaphanous shadows,
　　The air tastes good to my palate...

I hear bravuras of birds, bustle of growing
　　wheat, gossip of flames, clack of
　　sticks cooking my meals...

The glories strung like beads on my smallest
　　sights and hearings, on the walk in the street
　　and the passage over the river—

The Translation

看那东方的破晓！
曦微的光使无边的疏稀的黑暗渐渐消失，
空气的味道很好……
我听见鸟的聒噪，麦在习习摇风，火舌低语，
树枝毕剥着烧我的早餐……
我在街上走，我在河上过，看到和听到的东西都
挂着晶莹如珠的光华——

Generally speaking, free verse is easier to translate than classical poetry. But the basic requirements remain the same. That is to say, first, the translator must be faithful to the content of the original, keeping the original meaning, images and artistic conception; secondly, he must weigh his words so as to be as expressive as the original work; thirdly, he must try his best to make his translation close to the original in form. Judging from these requirements, we may say that there are both strong points and shortcomings in the translation of this poem. They may be defined as follows: Two strong points can be given: One, the free verse form is retained. Two, the words in the last stanza and in the first and third lines of the first stanza are properly chosen so that they are as expressive as the original. The shortcomings lie in the fact that some words are not proper enough. As a result, either the original meaning or the original images are somewhat impaired. For example: 1. The collocation of the words "曦微的光" is improper, for "曦" means "光" as in "晨曦" (first rays of the morning sun). 熹微 should be used to describe the first rays of the morning sun as in "晨光熹微" though the characters "熹" and "曦" are of the same pronunciation. 2. It is too strong in tone to render "shadows" as "黑暗" (darkness). The adjective "diaphanous" modifying the word means "pellucid" (清澈的) or "transparent" (透明的). When put together, the words "diaphanous shadows" seem to make a "neutral" sense which may be interpreted as something like "the dim light of the night" (朦胧的夜色). 3. 鸟的聒噪 is not well-collocated. 聒噪 (noise) which annoys people is a derogatory term. "Bravuras" means "pieces of music requiring great skill and spirit in the performers" (要求演唱家或演奏家发挥其技艺和精神的乐曲). The expression "bravuras of birds" may be translated as "鸟的欢唱" (birds' joyous singing) in a flexible way. 4. "麦在习习摇风" doesn't quite conform to the original meaning. The word "bustle" means "stir" in accordance with *Chambers Twentieth Century Dictionary*. It seems better to render the phrase "bustle of growing wheat" as "生长中的麦子在微微抖动". 5. The line "树枝毕剥着烧我的早餐" may be revised as "树枝毕剥毕剥地烧着我的早餐". Only when the second stanza gets improved somewhat like this can the lively, joyous and harmonious morning scene be reproduced.

From the above analysis we can clearly see that the free verse is not so easy to translate as some people suppose. Words are still to be carefully weighed and refined.

Notes

1. For the original and Dong's translation, see the previous lecture.
2. *The Complete Works of Su Manshu*, 81, Zhongguo Bookstore, Beijing, 1985.
3. *Byron's Seventy Lyrics* translated by Yang Deyu, 149, Hunan People's Publishing House, 1981.
4. Feng Zhi et al., *The Translation and Introduction of Russian Literature and Other European Countries* in Luo Xinzhang's *An Anthology of Essays on Translation*, 492.
5. *A Brief History of the Develotnnent of Foreign Literature* compiled by Chen Shoucheng et al., 571, Sichuan National Press, 1986.
6. Wang Yizhu, *On the Untranslatability of Poetry*, Reference for Compilation and Translation, No. 1, 1987.
7. *The Complete Works of Su Manshu* compiled by LiuYazi (1887-1958), a famous poet in China.
8. 9. The original is quoted from *Selected Readings in English Literature* by Sun Zhu et al., Book One, Shanghai Translations Publishing House, 1981 and its translation is from *Selected Poems of England*, published by the same Publishing House, 1988.
10. Wang Keyi, *Some Remarks about Shelley's Comments on Translating Poems*, Wenhui Bao (a daily newspaper), Oct. 12, 1962.
11. The original and its translations are both quoted from *The Literature of the United States* by Marcus Cunliffe, 119, Today's World Press, Hong Kong, 1976.

序　言

　　刘重德教授邀我为其《文学翻译十讲》一书作序,我欣然应命,不仅因为自他求学于西南联大时,我就与他相识,而且因为我在中国大学教过西洋文学,在美国大学里教过中国文学,对翻译这个话题本身,不管是英译汉,还是汉译英,长期以来一直觉得饶有兴趣。诚然,专攻文学者,不能以译作替代原作,我常敦促学生尽可能多学几门外语,然而,译作对广大读者颇有用处,他们希望在世界范围内获取文学、文化、科学、技术等领域的知识,但是,没有能力和机会阅读原作。

　　翻译艺术集文学技巧与有关语法、语言原理的知识之大成,前者需要长期不懈的实践才能掌握、完善,后者的应用有助于语言表达的正确、精密。在《文学翻译十讲》中,作者详细阐述了翻译的双重性,即艺术性与技术性,引用了大量的文献和例证,对初学者很有帮助。在论述了翻译的原则和标准,如"信、达、切",之后,作者深入探讨了直译与意译这一富有争议而又引人入胜的问题,并对这两派在中国文论史上的发展及其倡导者进行了论述。他还对各种翻译方法提出了有益的建议,就其语法和语言等方方面面进行了探讨。尤其令我感兴趣的是最后三章,即翻译中的文学风格问题、英诗汉译与汉诗英译问题。

　　最近数十年来,在我从事汉语文学和英语文学教学、写作和翻译的职业生涯中,我也研究过同样的问题,承朋友、同事和先前的学生协助供稿,编撰出版了一部综合性的汉语诗歌英译选集。[1] 这段经历使我特别能够体会刘重德教授有关诗歌翻译的导言和总体观点。我赞同他的意见：诗歌尽管难译，但是还是可以译得令人满意，译得成功。这里我想补充一点，在"译诗问题"一讲，论及了诗歌翻译的三个流派，即古典派、创作派和自由派，这最后一派一出现即最受欢迎，在西方学者兼译者中吸引了大批追随者。自阿瑟·韦利之后，涌现了有能力的、杰出的新一代译者，他们接手汉英翻译领域，为西方读者极大地拓展了中国诗歌的视野。

然而，令人遗憾的是，中国国内的情况不可同日而语，只有少数译者做过一些零星的尝试，将中国诗歌翻译成外文。我心怀此念，以赞赏与期待的心情，拜读了刘重德教授的专著，此书对翻译方法与技巧能提供有益、实用的指导。刘教授就翻译发表过不少文章，出过专著，也是一位资深翻译家，他在《文学翻译十讲》一书中，对后辈译者谆谆教诲与启迪。我希望，该书的出版不仅能向读者传授翻译的艺术，还能吸引读者从事翻译工作，特别是将汉语文学翻译成英语或将英语文学翻译成汉语，从而促进东西文化交流。我期待刘重德教授的著作在此领域产生预期的影响，做出宝贵的贡献。

柳无忌

注释1：

  Sunflower Splendor: *Three Thousand Years of Chinese Poetry*（1975）(《葵晔集：中国诗歌三千年》)，柳无忌，罗郁正编。"《葵晔集》是最大的，总体来说，也是目前用西方语言翻译出版的一部最好的中国诗歌选集。"（——《纽约时报》书评）

前　言

20世纪40年代,我出乎意料地当上了翻译教员,感觉就像没带指南针在一片未知的海域航行。能依靠的只是一些零星的汉语和英语知识,既没有受过翻译训练,也没有接受过教学培训。

像其他年轻英语教员一样,我求助于中文书籍。我去图书馆查找,去旧书店搜寻。遗憾的是,找到的参考书籍极少,信息不多而且出处不详。诚然,长久以来关于直译、意译都有激烈的争论,但是一些参与者带着情绪,进行论战,而不讲条理,缺少启发意义。

由于对中国学者颇感失望,我转而求助西方专家。其中有亚历山大·弗雷泽·泰特勒(Alexander Fraser Tytler),他提出了简洁明了的翻译原则,但所举的例子与中文没有关系,因此,对中国学生没多大用处;有马修·阿诺德,他对《荷马》以往的译者进行了尖锐的批评,但是,因为原著是希腊文,他的许多评论我看不懂。

以前的翻译课堂上,老师和学生都为练习忙得满头大汗,到了20世纪80年代,教翻译的与学翻译的都能说自己很幸运了。近年来发表了大量关于英汉语对比的文章,也出版了不少有关翻译实践的中文教科书。而且还介绍了一批外国翻译理论家,如萨沃里(Savory)、纽马克(Newmark)和奈达(Nida),他们的著作比以往的更容易懂,也更系统。现在来了一位刘重德教授,带着他长期研究和反复尝试得出的成果——《文学翻译十讲》。

读者翻开这本书，很快就会觉得该书作者格外勤勉，博览群书。他极其耐心地研究各种翻译理论，新旧都有，从严复一直到20世纪80年代的众多翻译著作。他还深挖国外出版的许多翻译著作，从中挖出来的是精要的综述和生动的评价。

　　讲解翻译的书没有译例是不行的，在这方面该书作者提供的帮助特别大。其他书籍只将原文和译文中孤立的短语和句子进行比较，而该书在必要之时都会给出完整的段落。提供完整的语境能让读者对正在审视的用语的意义和文体风格看得更清楚，对作者的论述也看得更加明白。

　　刘教授认为，翻译既是一门科学，又是一门艺术。说它是科学，是因为不同语言系统的比较表明，翻译时译者有规则可循，例如，"The horse is a useful animal."这句话翻译成汉语是"马是有用的动物。"，英语的冠词必须省去。这么做是有道理的，也易于赢得大家的认可。

　　但是，正如第一讲中所言，翻译也是一门艺术，这方面的理论可谓多矣。当代著名翻译理论家之一尤金·奈达承认："尽管对翻译的基本原则和步骤有所探讨，但是全面的翻译理论尚不存在。"因此，该书中如果有些观点不好理解，或难以认同，想必不至于令人愕然。

　　感谢刘重德教授为我提供了许多令人深思的问题。

王宗炎

鸣　谢

　　本书作者衷心感谢那些有助于改善本书的人们,其中特别感谢他的老师柳无忌教授和老友王宗炎教授,他们慨然为本书撰写序言和前言,并就书稿提出了宝贵而又详细的意见。作者还要感谢翻译学领域的一些专家,特别是马祖毅教授、顾延龄教授、彭京教授、谭载喜教授、林基海教授、萧立明教授、楚至大教授和熊希龄教授,他们给作者提出了宝贵的修改意见。

湖南师范大学外国语学院
英语教授
刘重德

目 录

第一讲　翻译的性质…………………………………………… 001
第二讲　翻译的原则…………………………………………… 011
第三讲　翻译的忠实性………………………………………… 024
第四讲　直译和意译…………………………………………… 036
第五讲　常用译法……………………………………………… 052
第六讲　怎样翻译英语定语从句……………………………… 064
第七讲　汉译英中的形象翻译和断句………………………… 076
第八讲　文学风格的可译性…………………………………… 085
第九讲　译诗问题……………………………………………… 106
第十讲　英诗汉译……………………………………………… 128
译后记…………………………………………………………… 142

第一讲 ｜ 翻译的性质

我们这里所说的"翻译",特指"翻译行为",即"翻译某些文字的过程",不是指译本。关于翻译的定义,我们可以从字典中很容易地抄下一个,即"从一种语言到另一种语言的转换",但此定义似乎太过笼统简单。其他还有各种各样为翻译所下的定义,我在此引述数种:

翻译是科学。

翻译是艺术。

翻译是技巧。

翻译是技术。

翻译是操作。

翻译是语言活动。

翻译是交流。

上述定义都可以作为我们的参考,因为每一种说法从某一个特定的角度来看都是正确的。

其中,头两种定义尤为重要,分别代表两个流派:科学派与艺术派。前者认为翻译应当通过语言上的对等转换复制原文的信息,因此强调对翻译过程的描述与语言的结构与形式进行研究,以此来揭示翻译的固有规律。而后者则主张运用译语的表达方式来重新创造一部文学作品,因此强调翻译的效果。林语堂(1895—1976)曾是此流派的代表人物。在《论翻译》一文中，他声称翻译是艺术，能否译好，取决于译者的艺术才华，同时也取决于是否有足够的训练。除此之外，翻译没有定规，亦无捷径可走。

我认为，对于文学翻译来说，两个流派的观点各有千秋，也都存在不足之处。现今则倾向于将两个流派的观点结合起来，形成一个综合性的理论。实际上，文学翻译本身具有双重性。换言之，一方面它是一门科学，有着自身独特的规律与方法；另一方面它也是一门艺术。下面我们来具体探讨一下文学翻译的双重性：

翻译是科学

我们说翻译是科学，是因为它有自己的规律。拿汉英互译来说，要想译好，除应完全熟悉原文内容以及牵涉的各方面的知识这个前提之外，我们起码还必须对这两种语言具有较深的造诣，然后翻译起来，才会得心应手。

汉语和英语各有各的特点，既有类似和共同之处，例如句法上主谓的词序和动宾或介宾的词序；又有大相径庭的地方，例如英语有定冠词"the"，不定冠词"a"和"an"，汉语无冠词。以具有不尽相同特点的汉英两种语言来进行互译，总的说来，是可能的，一则因为语言是思想的直接现实，而且现实—思维—语言这一人类反映客观存在的基本规律也是共同的，从而使不同的语言外壳表达同一的思想感情成为可能；二则因为大量翻译作品的存在，翻译的可能性已从事实上得到了明证。

但同时也要承认，各民族用来进行思维和表达思想的语言却是各有其特点和表达习惯的，而这也正是译者甚至资深翻译家的困难所在，绝不是略通皮毛的人所能解决的。要想做个胜任的译者，首先就必须深入研究和认真比较这两种语言的异同，从而找出两种语言互译对应的规律与方法，才能有效地进行翻译，才能保证译作的质量。

对应的规律是存在的。试举一例如下：

The horse is a useful animal.

这是个很简单的句子，翻译起来在词序上是完全相同的，但在冠词的译法上却很值得研究。遗憾的是，不少初学者往往将句子译成：

这马是一个有用的动物。

乍一看，这个译文似乎十分忠实于原文，每个字都翻译成了汉语，但实际上没有将原文内在的意思传达出来，因此完全译错了。在这种情况下，中国人谁也不会这么说。正确的译法应该是："马是一种有用的动物。"句子现在通了。但为了要达到汉语"言简意赅"的境界，还可以进一步修改为："马是有用的动物。"也就是说，两个冠词都应该略而不译，才符合汉语习惯用法。同样的，如把这句汉语回译成英语，逐词翻译是不行的，而必须把这两个冠词分别用上去，这才符合英语惯用法的要求。当然，如果两个名词都用复数形式，即"Horses are useful animals"的话，就不必使用冠词了。

这个句子的翻译，有增有减。但这种增减并非任意而为，而取决于这两种语言固有的内在特征。就意义与功能而言，汉语"马是有用的动物"与英语"The horse is a useful animal" or "Horses are useful animals"完全一致，达到矛盾的辩证统一。不妨说"适当增减"是汉英互译的对应规律之一，这样的规律可以通过对两种语言进行全面而仔细的对比研究而找出来。

以上所讨论的冠词有无问题是英汉语言之间一个最基本的差异，另一个基本差异则是顾延龄教授与熊希龄教授在《英汉汉英翻译教程》一书中所提到的：汉语中动词的使用频率比英语要高，而名词与介词的使用频率则低于英语。这种现象表面上看来只是不同词性使用情况的差异，但实质上却显示出两种语言在措词、句法、表达习惯等方面的特点。其次，英语中不少名词与形容词常用来表示动作意义，起动词的作用。事实上，这种词并非罕见。而且这种具有动词意义与特性的词作为中心词所构成的搭配也是随处可见。

下面用偶西《英译汉理论与实例》一书中的一个例句，来具体分析上述观点是否正确。

Gates Avenue families carried their pails to the hydrant at the curb.

住在盖茨街的家家户户都得提小桶到街边水龙头去取水。

英语句子中只有一个动词，但汉语译文中一共有六个。这样一对比，我们又发现一个重要的翻译方法——词性转换。

通过以上两个简单句的分析，可以得知翻译简单的句子尚且有这么讲究；不言而喻，翻译整篇作品，就更需要渊博的知识和熟练的技巧了。无论如何，不能逐词翻译，不能拘泥于一个个单词、词组、语法结构的表面上的相似，必须严格遵循从"透彻理解"到"准确表达"这个科学程序。换言之，译者必须先深刻领会全书的思想内容与风格，然后灵活地运用翻译的对应规律和适当方法把原文如实地加以创造性再现，力求译文不仅达意，而且传神。

发现了有关的两种语言的特点和异同之后，自然就能找到其内在规律和相互关系，从而也就必定会归纳出一些切实可行的翻译方法。可见翻译的确是有其独特规律与方法的科学，与语言学中的词汇学、语法学、修辞学等多种分支有关的科学。

翻译是艺术

接下来我们来谈谈翻译的艺术性。关于这一点，有些人尚缺乏正确的认识。一种常见的误解是"翻译比创作容易得多；"另一种是"翻译佶屈聱牙，难以卒读。"既然存在这样的误解，讨论一下下列问题，有必要，也有价值：

1. 翻译难道真的比创作容易得多吗？

创作的确不容易，好的作品也不是人人都能写得出来的。下笔之前，作者必须体验生活，积累大量素材。

而且，他还必须善于概括和创造。只有这样才写得出好的作品来。但是翻译也并不像某些非翻译界人士所认为的那样简单。可以说翻译相当不易。一名合格的译者必须具备以下三个条件：

第一，精通相关的两种语言，十分熟悉其表达特点和异同；

第二，透彻了解原文的思想内容、艺术特点和艺术风格，以及创作的历史背景；

第三，熟悉翻译的基本原则和方法，并有实践经验。

"一名之立，旬月踟蹰"，这是多年以前严复（1853—1921）的名言，我想，这也是许多老翻译家共同的切身体会。连列宁（1870—1924）与鲁迅也不例外。列宁曾经为了翻译一个专门术语在一本详解词典里查找达五次之多，鲁迅也曾遇到某些难译之处而浑身冒冷汗。由此可以想象，要将一部完整的文学作品翻译成另外一种语言何其困难。翻译的难处，正在于有了现成的思想内容，要你用另一种语言外壳恰如其分地予以重现。纵使翻译时遇到再大的障碍，也要设法一个个跨越。有时甚至不得不"标新立异"，例如"资产阶级"和"无产阶级"两个词都是经过音译"布尔乔亚"与"普罗列塔利亚"之后才创立的。同样的，还有汉语的"民主"与"科学"二词也是由 democracy 的音译"德谟克拉西"与 science 的音译"赛恩斯"演变而来的。另外句法方面也有创新。例如，由"假若"引导的条件从句与由"尽管"引导的让步从句置于复合句末尾，最初出现时读者觉得异常，现在已经习以为常了。

由此可见，翻译过程，实际上也就是一种再创造再表现的过程。创作和翻译各有各的难处与前提。怎能厚此薄彼呢？

我们大家都知道,鲁迅和郭沫若(1892—1978)是中国文学史上伟大的作家,同时也是中国文学史上伟大的翻译家。关于翻译与创作的孰难孰易,他们的意见应该是公允而令人信服的。让我们虚心地听一听他们的经验之谈吧:

鲁迅在《且介亭杂文二集"题未定"草(一)》中说过:"我向来总以为翻译比创作容易,因为至少是无须构想。但到真的一译,就会遇着难关,譬如一个名词或动词,写不出,创作时候可以回避,翻译上却不成,也还得想,一直弄到头昏眼花,好像在脑子里面摸一个急于要开箱子的钥匙,却没有。"甚至到了晚年,他对翻译仍然感到困难。他说:"《死魂灵》很难译……真好像在做苦工,日子不好过。"(见1935年3月13日致萧红信)"译果戈理,颇以为苦,每译两章,好像生一场病。"(见1935年6月8日致胡风信)[1]

1954年,郭沫若在全国文学翻译工作会议上所做的《谈文学翻译工作》的报告中指出:"翻译是一种创作性的工作,好的翻译等于创作。……有时候翻译比创作还要困难。创作要有生活体验,翻译却要体验别人所体验的生活。翻译工作者要精通本国的语文,而且要有很好的外文基础,所以它并不比创作容易。"

秉公而论,应该是像鲁迅先生所指出的那样,"创作难,翻译也不易。"[2]

2. 翻译难道真的是佶屈聱牙难以卒读吗?

佶屈聱牙难以卒读的这类所谓翻译,确实出现过,新中国成立前有,新中国成立后也有。但严格说来,这类东西算不得翻译,只不过是一些粗制滥造的货色而已,并非出自具备"翻译是科学"一节中提到的条件的称职译者之手。以其昏昏,怎能使人昭昭?不过这类所谓翻译仍居少数,而绝大部分翻译还是好的,或者说基本上是好的,其中还有一部分是比较优秀的。在我国翻译界,颇有一些名家,如朱光潜（1897—1986）、吕叔湘等。他们的译文既"信"且"顺"，读起来令人觉得津津有味，爱不释手。外国翻译名家的译文也是如此。例如恩格斯（1820—1895）就称赞过劳拉·拉法格的法文译文"忠实流畅"，足证所谓佶屈聱牙难以卒读同翻译并无本质上的联系。事实上，佶屈聱牙难以卒读的创作也是有的，关键在于作者和译者的艺术水平和表达技巧的优劣。

请比较下面引的两个译例，一个翻译得很糟糕，一个翻译得很成功。

例 1. My hands are clean. I have no blood on them.
我的双手是清白的！它们上面没有沾满鲜血。

这两句是从报纸上发表的一篇译文摘引来的，原文标题是 *Judges Will Be Judged*。

显而易见，这两句话的翻译有三个毛病。

首先是搭配不当。"clean"这个词固然有"清白"的意思，如"He has a clean record"可以译为"他历史清白"。但按汉语惯用法，"清白"不能用来描写人的手。人人都知道，"clean"还有"干净"的意思。译者本应选用这个意思。因此，第一句的正确译文应为"我的双手是干净的"。此外，也没有必要把句号改为惊叹号。

其次是措词生硬。"它们上面"是从介词词组"on them"逐字翻译过来的。因此第二句译文读起来就不顺口。有两个办法可以解决这个措辞生硬的问题：一是重复名词"手"，译为"手上没沾鲜血"。二是省略代词"它们"，译为"上面没沾鲜血"，意思就十分清楚了。

再次是语意欠妥。"沾满鲜血"如果用于肯定式是完全可以的，例如说"那些法西斯分子手上沾满了人民的鲜血"。但用于否定式则不妥当，因为"没有沾满鲜血"这么一个表现法可能引起误解，它暗含这个人的双手还是沾有一点血迹。所以"满"字实属多余。

根据上述理由和汉语的表达习惯,这两句英语合译为一句为好:我的双手是干净的,上面没沾鲜血。

例2. 匪军所至,杀戮人民,奸淫妇女,焚毁村庄,掠夺财物,无所不用其极。

Wherever the bandit troops went, they massacred and raped, burned and looted, and stopped at nothing.

原文摘自《毛泽东选集》,是描写反动军队残暴行为的一句话。中间连用四个排比结构,简洁而紧凑有力,全句读来十分顺畅,一气呵成。译者把这句话也译得十分精确,不仅恰如其分地表达了原文的思想感情,而且成功地保全了原文简洁而紧凑有力的风格。译者在这里采取了两种手法:一是适当增减,"人民"、"妇女"、"村庄"和"财物"这几个宾语均有意地略而未译;与此同时,采用了一种修辞手法,即以两个"and"将四个动词连接为两对,构成排比结构。二是将及物动词"massacre","rape","burn"和"loot"转化为不及物动词,隐含宾语。但从上下文来看,意思仍是一清二楚。当然,换个译者也许会翻译成不同的样子,比如有的译者可能会将这些动词照原样译为四个及物动词,宾语一一译出,并在最后只用一个 and 把几个并列谓语加以连接。这样的译法在语法上当然是正确的,但有损于原文简洁紧凑的风格。

文章或书籍的标题翻译也可以反映出译者的艺术感知能力。有些书名译得好,有些译得糟。例如,将查尔斯·狄更斯(1812—1870)的小说 *Oliver Twist* 意译为《雾都孤儿》,威廉·莎士比亚的戏剧 *Hamlet* 意译为《王子复仇记》要远远好过音译的名称《奥列佛·推斯特》和《哈姆莱特》,音译名称虽然无可责备,但是《雾都孤儿》的书名向读者展示了小说主角的鲜明形象和故事的背景,而《王子复仇记》这个名称揭示了故事的内容。我在杂志上读过一篇译文,标题是《我们是怎样过母亲节的》的，原文的标题为 *How We Kept Mother's Day*。我认为译文标题译得并不好，原因有二：首先，英语动词"keep"在这里并不是"度过"，而是指"庆祝"。其次，作者在行文中略带一丝讽刺的意味，原文标题也有所体现，但是译者的误解使得读者根本没有机会去感受文中的讽刺含义。在我看来，标题应当直译为《我们是怎样庆祝母亲节的》。

从上面所举例子的分析，可以看出，翻译要求译者具有渊博的知识，换言之，译者应当对文艺学、修辞学以至美学等等都要有所了解；否则就很难完成重现原作的任务。

"凡上乘译品，不啻创造。"[3] 这话讲得很有道理。我相信，只要通过一些优秀译文的对照研究和进行认真的翻译实践，就不难发现"翻译是一种艺术，一种双重语言的艺术，像绘画一样它使我们能够再现别人的美好思想；不过，不是用颜色，而是用词，用一种不同语言的词。"[4] 译者也好比是演员，能够进入"角色"，以高超的表演艺术，把所扮演的人物演得惟妙惟肖，而译者也必须透彻了解和深刻体会原著的思想内容及其写作特点，以熟练的翻译艺术恰如其分地创造性地予以再现。鲁迅先生指出，翻译要做到"不但移情，也要益智"，又说："一则当然力求其易解，一则保存着原作的丰姿。"[5]

对于翻译的价值和功用，鲁迅先生作过很高的评价。他说："翻译并不比随便的创作容易，然而于新文学的发展却有功，于大家更有益。"并说"翻译是再创作"。普希金（A. S. Pushkin，1799—1837）也说过，翻译创作的目的是"再现"艺术作品。

根据上述论证，我们可以做出如下结论：

译文质量之好坏，顺畅与否，同翻译本身并无关联，关键在于译者的艺术水准和翻译技巧。掌握了翻译理论与技巧，当然就有可能译出让人满意的译文。正如本讲开头所述，这是因为翻译不仅是一门有着独特法则与方法的科学，同时也是一门再现与再创作的艺术。

注释：

1. 参看《翻译通讯》1981 年第 4 期戈宝权《鲁迅——杰出的翻译家》。
2. 见鲁迅《集外集拾遗"新的世故"》。
3. 见张其春著《翻译之艺术》自序，1949 年开明书店出版。
4. 见陆殿扬著《英汉翻译理论与技巧》导言，1958 年时代出版社出版。
5. 见鲁迅《且介亭杂文二集"题未定"草（二）》。

第二讲 | 翻译的原则

翻译的原则与翻译的标准是同一事物的两面。所谓原则，是就译者来说的，即译者在翻译时所应遵循的原则。所谓标准，是就读者或评论家来说的，即评论译文优劣的标准。对于翻译标准的重要性与它所具有的双重功用方面，一位翻译理论家曾这样精辟地论述道：翻译标准是一根铅垂线，用来衡量译文的专业水平，也为译者设立了一个努力的标杆。因此，确立清晰、规范的翻译标准与译文的风味和质量关系重大。本讲着重从译者的立场出发，提出"信、达、切"这个三字原则，以供参考。

数十年来，翻译界一提到翻译的原则，总会想到严复在《天演论·译例言》中所提出的"信达雅"，而且不少人仍然奉为圭臬。

严复在中国资产阶级启蒙运动中，是有贡献的。他和康有为（1858—1927）、梁启超（1873—1929），谭嗣同（1865—1898）等人是1898年戊戌变法的领袖人物。他们"或著书立说，创立维新变法理论；或翻译西方著述，传播欧洲资产阶级思想。他们还成立学会，建立学堂，创办报纸。各地学会、学堂、报纸、竟如雨后春笋，纷纷兴起，分布于江苏、湖南、直隶、广东等省。使传统的中国思想界受到巨大冲击。当时许多爱国知识分子都被席卷进去，影响了整整一代人"。[1]1898年的戊戌变法，虽然寿命不长，终告失败，但在解放思想这一意义上来看，不妨说，它为孙中山（1866—1925）领导的辛亥革命做了准备。

至于翻译西方著述方面,严复的贡献尤其突出。他所译赫胥黎著《天演论》一书头两章的译文,最初就是他于1897年在天津创刊的《国闻报》上发表的。"甲午战争后,紧接着各国强夺海口,对中国人的刺激是太深了。《天演论》阐发弱肉强食,适者生存,保种保群自强进化之公理,给失望悲观的人士指出新希望。《天演论》风行全国,被称为中译本之善本无有过于此书者,在维新运动中起了极大的作用。当时上海《时务报》、天津《国闻报》分掌南北舆论界领导地位,严复思想的影响不下于梁启超。"[2]

但严复为翻译所定的三原则,特别是与三原则有关的一些办法,并不能完全适用于当今的翻译实践,似有重新商榷的必要。我认为,不可不加评论或修正就一概否定,也不能全盘接受。正确的态度是批判地予以继承,吸收其对我们继续有用的部分。为了便于讨论起见,特将他为所译《天演论》写的"译例言"中头三条摘引于下:

(一)译事三难:信、达、雅。求其信已大难矣!顾信矣不达,虽译犹不译也,则达尚焉。……译文取明深义,故词句之间,时有所颠到附益,不斤斤于字比句次,而意义则不倍本文。题曰达旨,不云笔译,取便发挥,实非正法……

(二)西文句中名物字,多随举随释,如中文之旁支,后乃遥接前文,足意成句。故西文句法,少者二三字,多者数十百言。假令仿此为译,则恐必不可通,而删削取径,又恐意义有漏。此在译者将全文神理融会于心,则下笔抒词,自善互备。至原文词理本深,难于共喻,则当前后引衬,以显其意。凡此经营,皆以为达,为达即所以为信也。

(三)《易》曰:"修辞立诚"。子曰:"辞达而已"。又曰:"言之无文,行之不远"。三者乃文章正轨,亦即为译事楷模。故信达而外,求其尔雅。此不仅期以行远已耳,实则精理微言,用汉以前字法句法，则为达易；用近世利俗文字，则求达难。往往抑义就词，毫厘千里……

从上引三例，不难看出，严复学识渊博，文字典雅，对于译述，也深有体会，但所讲方法，从目前的观点来看，有些不能适用于真正的翻译，现逐条剖析于后：

首先，谈谈严复译作的性质问题。

严复译作《天演论》，正如他自己所说，只不过是一种"达诣"，他自己也称之为"实非正法"，也就是说，他的所谓译作不能算名副其实的翻译，只能叫译述或编译。只消把《导言》第一句的原文与译文拿来对比一下，就十分明白。

原文：

It may be safely assumed that, two thousand years ago, before Caesar (100B. C. -44B. C.) set foot in southern Britain, the whole countryside visible from the windows of the room in which I write, was in what is called "the state of nature."

严译：

赫胥黎独处一室之中，在英伦之南，背山而面野，槛外诸境，历历如在几下。乃悬想两千年前，当罗马大将恺撒来到时，此间有何景物。计惟有天造草昧，人功未施。

在严的译文中，可以发现，既有人称的改变，例如把第一人称"我"改作了第三人称"赫胥黎"；也有意义的"附益"，例如"罗马大将"和"背山而面野"等等。这类现象，就严格的翻译来说是不行的。特别是就文艺作品的翻译来说，更是不许可的；否则，就会失真。

其次，谈谈字比句次的问题。

所谓译述或编译，根据情况需要，改变一下字比句次，未可厚非；但就真正的翻译来说，只允许根据原语与目标语的内在规律改变一下"字比"。例如：

Out rushed the man and his wife. (Jespersen)

那个人和他的妻子冲出去了。

这个简单的英语句子，如果不彻底改变"字比"，就无法译成看得懂的汉语。至于"句次"，则必需十分慎重。如果指的是一个复合句中分句的次序，有时是不得不加以重新调整的。例如：

Gone are the days when they ran wild in our country and lorded it over the people.

他们在我国胡作非为、对人民称王称霸的日子已经一去不复返了。

如果指的是带有句号的各句的次序（照理严复应该指的是这类句子的次序），我认为在一般情况下是不能任意"颠倒"的，实际上，也很少有这种必要，因为无论就什么语言来说，一个带有句号的句子都表达一个完整的意义，只要逐句翻译，即可成为前后连贯的段落。当然，译者同时应对全文了然于心。

句次不能任意"颠倒"的原则，用于英译汉，可以说是屡试不爽。不过，汉译英，有时要考虑英语句法结构比较谨严的特点，必要时不妨把某些逗号、分号或冒号，主要是逗号，改为句号。限于篇幅，仅举一例如下：

我们的民族将再也不是一个被人侮辱的民族了，我们已经站起来了。（毛选五卷第一篇《中国人民站起来了》）

Ours will no longer be a nation subject to insult and humiliation. We have stood up. (*English Version of the Selected Works of Mao Zedong*: The Chinese People Have Stood Up).

从英语句法结构的特点来看，英译本把原文一句断成两句是完全正确的，否则句子结构就难免松散。但两个英语句子的顺序未变，与汉语原文中未用连词连接的两个分句顺序相同。反过来说，英译汉，有时在某种情况下，也就有了把一些英语简单句并为一句的必要。例如：

We have utterly lost touch. We have nothing at all to say. We gaze at each other as dumb animals gaze at human beings. (*Seeing People Off* by Max Beerbohm.)

这三个句子可以有以下两种译法：

1. 我们完全失去了联系。我们根本无话可说。我们就像不会讲话的牲畜呆呆地望人那样地你望着我我望着你。

2. 我们完全失去了联系，根本无话可说，就像不会讲话的牲畜呆呆地望人那样地你望着我我望着你。

第一种是逐句译法，第二种则是三句并为一句。二者都忠实于原文，而且文从字顺。但比较起来，前者终嫌有些啰唆冗赘，而后者则使人觉得言简意赅，这是由于汉语很少重复同一主语的缘故，除非有意强调。

第三，谈谈"前后引衬以显其意"的问题。

严复不仅在"译例言"中这么说，而且他在"翻译"《天演论》的过程中也是这么做的。例如在他的第一句的所谓译文中就出现了"罗马大将"（the Roman general）和"背山"（with hills at the back）。此外，在每章"译文"之后，都加了一段"复按"，抒发个人体会，形成了他的个人风格。但就真正的翻译来说，则不能采用这种办法。不论原文难易，译者都只能将全文神理融会于心，如实翻译。同时必须注意句与句以及段与段之间的承上启下，前后呼应，使人读起来有浑然一体之感。至若遇到"词理本深"、"难于共喻"的原文，也只能附加适当的注释予以说明，至于在译文中插入"译者按"，则完全是多此一举。

第四，翻译中用什么体文字的问题。

在这个问题上，严复主张并实行用汉以前字法句法，因为他认为只有这样,才易于表达"精理微言"并能传得久远。这一点提法,也未免有些主观,因为我们知道事物是不断发展的,而语言文字也是不断随着事物的发展而发展的。严复出生以前很久,汉语就已经发展到像《水浒传》和《红楼梦》所使用的那样"利俗文字"。两部名著描绘的生动,刻画的细腻,已是有口皆碑,足证近代语体文字已经具有很好的表达能力。他译的是用近代英语写的著作,为什么非用汉以前的字法句法不可呢?难道用"利俗文字"或"白话文"无法表达像《天演论》那样的"精理微言"吗?实际上,近代纷繁的事物和思想,只有用"利俗文字"或"白话文",而不是文言文,才能较好地表达。所以瞿秋白(1899—1935)明确地提出他的主张说:"我们对于翻译,就不能够不要求:绝对的正确和绝对的中国白话文。这是要把新的文化的言语介绍给大众。"(见鲁迅全集四卷《关于翻译的通信》)不仅如此,而且必要时还不得不创造一些新词,例如"无产阶级"、"人民民主专政",特别是化学元素的名称等。在古汉语中能找到相应的表现法吗?就拿我们最熟悉的"社会主义"一词来说,也还是直到 1902 年才在《新民丛报》上首次出现。科学出版社 1971 年用白话文为广大读者重新翻译出版了赫胥黎的《进化论与伦理学》,因为如今能透彻理解严译的读者已经不多,更不用说欣赏了。其实,严复用古文翻译,足以说明他文字方面的保守思想。他曾在一封信中写道,"吾译非以饷学童,而望其受益也,吾译正以待多读中国古书之人,羞效报馆之文章"。[3]

严复在译事三原则的提法上,固然有些不足之处,但据史论事,应当承认,他当时无论是在翻译理论上,还是在实践上,都是开一代风气之先并做出了巨大贡献的。至于不足之处,乃是由于他的历史局限性所致。做上述剖析与评论,旨在更好地吸收其精华。

关于严复的译事三原则,先谈到这里。下面再介绍一下 18 世纪英国翻译理论家泰特勒(Alexander Fraser Tytler,1749—1814)在

《论翻译的原则》[4]中所提出的三个总则：

1. 翻译应该是原著思想内容的完整的再现。
2. 风格与手法应该和原著属于同一性质。
3. 翻译应该具备原著所有的通顺。①

严格说来，一篇或一部文学作品的思想内容、语言表达和风格特点是一个完整的统一体，而文学翻译也必须是其完整的统一体的如实再现。但为了研究方便起见，这个统一体可分为内容、表达和风格三个方面，这是可行的，而且也反映了一个认真负责的翻译家进行翻译工作的实际过程。

这个过程，可分三个步骤：

第一步，译者应仔细通读全文，认真领会作者所要表达的思想内容，不仅弄清字面意义，而且还要弄清字里行间的含义。

第二步，由于有关的两种语言表达习惯不尽相同，在行文措词方面，往往会出现如下三种情况：（1）有时可以找到完全等值的词语，例如英语 Strike while the iron is hot 和汉语"趁热打铁"等值；（2）有时不得不转换形象，例如英语 as lean as a rake，最好译成'骨瘦如柴'，不能直译成"瘦得像耙"，因为前者通过替换形象，既保存了

---

① 译者注：本书作者所列出的泰特勒的第三条法则是：3. The Translation should have the ease of the original composition，而泰特勒的第三条法则原文本来是：III. That the Translation should have all the ease of original composition.（3rd edition, 1813：p9）。这个 original 前没有定冠词，这是与前两条中的 the original work 和 the original 的重大区别。这是因为 original composition 是表示类指的抽象名词，指具有"独创性"（original）这种性质的"写作"（composition）这一类行为，即"创作"这种行为，而不是与某一译文联系在一起的特指的"原著、原文"。此种理解，有泰特勒在解释第三条法则时所说的话为证：The more he (the translator) studies a scrupulous imitation, the less his copy will reflect the ease and spirit of the original... To use a bold expression, he must adopt the very soul of his author, which must **speak through his own organs.**（3rd edition, 1813：p113）事实上，泰特勒认为译者必须以写自己的作品一样的 ease（即"流畅"，或"达"或"顺"）来传达作者的心灵（思想感情）。由此可见，刘老说"泰特勒所讲的三条法则全面而实用，可全部采纳"，仿佛他的"信达切"三字全部来源于泰特勒，是太谦虚了。其实"达如其分"完全是刘老的创造。

原文生动的表达方式，又符合译语习惯，而后者虽然保存了原文的形象，但却违反了译文的习惯；(3) 有时不得不在字面上作较大的改变，另找能够表达其真正含义的恰当表现法，例如英语谚语 Every dog has its day 只能灵活地译成"人人都有自己得意的时候"。这就是奈达所说的与原文"动态对等"。这个谚语假如逐字翻译，当然会不知所云。

第三步，译者还必须掌握作者在原文中所刻画的人物形象和写作风格，只有这样，翻译时选词造句，才有依据。词句的选择和安排，都以能否比较圆满地再现人物形象和原作风格为标准。就是说，同一句话，应因人物身份和作者风格的不同而采用不同的译法。例如 More haste, less speed。如果出自一个文化水平较低的人物之口或者出自一个风格淳朴的作家之手，就不妨译为"越快就越慢"。如果是出自一个文化水平较高的人物之口，那就最好译为"欲速则不达"。否则，就可能损害原文形象和风格。

一个认真负责的翻译工作者，在动笔之前，必须通过这三个步骤做好充分准备。如果一个译者不从这三个方面进行考虑，碰到作品就逐字翻译，由于违背了翻译原则，难免会失败。正像俄国批评家别林斯基（1811—1848）所指出的那样："贴近原作不是换字母，而是要传达原作的精神"。而车尔尼雪夫斯基（1828—1889）更进一步明确地说："逐字翻译不但不能贴近原文，反而让原文难以理解。"事实证明，的确如此。

逐字翻译究竟是怎样产生的呢？苏联翻译理论家 L. N·索伯列夫在《用形象翻译形象》一文中讲得好："逐字翻译一般是译者无能、不懂翻译技巧与理论的结果。"

在翻译原则方面，严复的头两个字，即"信"与"达"，仍可沿用，而泰特勒所讲的三条法则全面而实用，可全部采纳。

参考上述两家意见，取其精华，拟将翻译原则修订为比较全面而

实用的"信达切"三字:

1. 信——信于内容;
2. 达——达如其分;
3. 切——切合风格。

信于原文内容的"信",即严复所谓意义"不倍本文",亦即泰特勒所谓"翻译应当是原著思想内容的完整的再现"。这自然是翻译的第一个最重要的原则。译者应当忠实而准确地传达作者的思想,不可凭个人的好恶,擅自改变原文意义。鲁迅曾经指出,"翻译绝对不容许错误。"即便是所谓的"编译"和"译述",严格说来,也不能违背或偏离原文的中心意义,只不过是可以"不斤斤于字比句次"、"前后引衬以显其意"罢了。

做到了信于原文内容,译者还得瞄着达如其分的"达"这个目标,因为这译文是给读者看的。译文如果是结里结巴,不知所云,那就失去了翻译的意义。正如严复所说,"顾信矣不达,虽译犹不译也"。

在 20 世纪 30 年代关于翻译原则的论战中,出现过针锋相对的两派。一派主张"宁顺而不信",一派则主张"宁信而不顺"。按前者办事,难免因词害义;依后者行文,可能造成译文不顺畅。这已为双方的翻译实践所证明,我们应该引以为戒。只要在翻译理论和实践上狠下工夫,就能最终把"信"、"顺"这对表面上的矛盾辩证地统一起来,不少高明的翻译家已经为我们树立了可以效法的榜样。

我们可以这么说,"忠实"和"通顺",即"信"与"顺"或"达",是每个翻译工作者所必须遵守的最起码的两项原则。

译者在达到既忠实又通顺的程度之后,才可以进一步追求风格的"切合"。

我为何不采用严复所讲的"雅"字,而改用"切"字呢?那是因为"雅"实际上只不过是各种风格中的一种。显然,翻译起来,不能一律要"雅",而应该准确地再现原文风格。"切"是个中性词,适用于各种不同的风格。张其春(1913—1967)论述过中外文学的各种风格。他说:"风格(style)者,表现之艺术也。……风格为个性之流露;如……李白'诗豪而逸',杜甫'诗雄而正'。"[5]亨利·詹姆斯(1843—1916)与海明威(1899—1961)的风格也截然不同,前者华丽晦涩,后者简洁含蓄。

法国博物学家布丰(1707—1788)曾说"文如其人(Le style, c'est l'homme)"。也就是说,风格因作家各异而有所不同。有些作家风格典雅,有些则相对粗俗;有些辞藻华丽、有些则文字朴实。译者必须尽力使译文风格尽可能切合原文风格。具体说来,如果原文风格典雅,则译文也应当典雅。如果原文不典雅,则译文也不应当典雅。

所谓风格,就是作家的写作特点。作家的风格不尽相同,这已是毋庸置疑的事实。比如说,运用典故,调动读者的形象思维,是列宁政论文章的本质特点。而鲁迅先生杂文的写作特点,则是短小精悍,一针见血,冷嘲热讽。翻译他们的作品的时候,除力求保全原文意义并做到明白通顺外,还必须尽可能重现他们各自的写作特点,即风格。只有这样,其译品才称得上是合乎信、达、切三原则的翻译。

其次再就文艺作品中的人物对话加以讨论,就更可以看出"雅"字作为应用于风格的普遍原则是不恰当的。小说和戏剧中的对话,由于人物身份的不同,十分明显,语言风格是有雅俗之分的,这是不容否认的事实。既然如此,译者应该力求保全所有人物说话的语气与方式,而不应该让俗者雅,雅者俗。如果把所有俗的表达方式都变为雅的表达方式,文学作品中人物的形象就会受损,因为人物角色的典型性一方面表现在其行动上,另一方面表现在其言语上。假设在你要翻译的文学作品中,有一些粗俗话,如:"Damned, you son of a bitch, go to the devil!"这样的话如何能译得雅?只能照原样译为:"该死,你这个狗崽子;见鬼去吧!"否则,便会落得个对原文不忠的骂名!

一般来说，小说与戏剧当中经常会有粗俗的言词，有时甚至诗歌中也会出现。

毛泽东的诗词大家都很熟悉，他的《念奴娇·鸟儿问答》当中有一句十分粗俗的话："不须放屁！""放屁"一词是俗还是雅？毫无疑问是俗词。这一粗俗之词该如何翻译成英语呢？译者是否可以变俗为雅呢？当然不行，译者无权这样做。他必须保留原文粗俗的特点。试比较下面两个译文：一个是"Stop your windy nonsense！"，另一个是"None of your shit！"相比而言，第二种译法要好一些，因为它保留了原文粗俗的特点。第一种译法不如第二种。我这句话，有两个理由：其一，"windy nonsense"不是英语地道的表达方式，我们常常遇到英语中用"sheer nonsense"来进行强调，但很可能难得碰到"windy nonsense"这种说法。这种说法是译者杜撰生造的，因而必不为广大读者所接受。其二，"windy nonsense"这个说法不合逻辑。"windy"这个形容词令人想起风，表示虚无的或空的，而名词"nonsense"指毫无意义的话或夸夸其谈，"windy"显得累赘、多余。当然用"Stop your nonsense"来译"不须放屁"，也可以，但语气不如原文强烈，因此风格与原文不相符。

关于风格，英国18世纪名作家斯威夫特（Jonathan Swift，1667—1745）有句名言：

"适当的词用于适当的场合，这就是风格的确切定义。"

他讲的这句话不仅适用于写作，也适用于翻译。

翻译工作者，若想使自己的译作值得读者赏识，还必须在切合原文风格和人物形象上狠下工夫。但是，这种成功，是不易达到的。阿诺德（M. Arnold，1822—1888）曾评论荷马所著《伊利亚特》与《奥德赛》两部史诗的几种译文，从中可以看出切合风格之难：

"在节奏上荷马是轻快的，在文字和风格上荷马是清晰的，在意义上荷马总是单纯的；在作法上荷马是庄严的。考珀（Cowper）把他翻糟了,因为在节奏上他是迟钝的,在风格上是雕琢的;蒲伯(Pope)把他翻糟了,因为在风格和文字上他是矫揉造作的;查普曼(Chapman)把他翻糟了,因为在意义上他是充满幻想的;纽曼先生(Mr. Newman)也把他翻糟了,因为在文字上他是怪僻的,在作法上也是低劣的。除掉上面所举的那些地方,所有四个译者又都在别的地方背离了他们的原著,只不过是在上面所举的那些地方他们背离的程度最大罢了。"[6]

圆满地实现"信、达、切"三原则,诚然不易,但又必须千方百计地贯彻这些原则,否则便永远达不到别林斯基所说的"再现"艺术作品这个翻译目标。只有圆满地实现上述三原则,才能达到别林斯基提出的标准:"翻译是用本民族的语言完整无缺地再现另一民族的文学作品的艺术。"也只有这样,才能达到译作对原作的忠实。

要想能够圆满地实现"信、达、切"三原则,一个文学翻译工作者就必须在语言学与文学方面具备足够的修养。早在1852年,杜勃罗留波夫就指出:"他要翻译的语言不言而喻是他应该精通的,也就是说,精通词在意义上、在搭配上的细微区别,精通本身并不重要的小品词之间的细微区别。不仅如此,一个译者还应当极其熟练地掌握译文语言,不仅写得正确而优美,而且写得轻松而流畅;能在翻译中运用语言的全部财富,避免使用不正确的措词和不纯洁的词汇,结果在确切地表达原文的思想时,使读者看不出一点儿生硬的地方。"从这位批评家的话中可以看出,一个文学翻译工作者既要全面掌握外语,又要精通祖国语言。此外,还要具有一定的语言学和文艺学的知识,因为正像伊万·卡什金在《为现实主义翻译而斗争》一文中所指出的那样:"预先应通过文艺理论的分析,弄清作者的基本修辞特点,并通过语言学角度的分析,应指出其语言方面的特征。然后,决定性的一步就是按照文学要求和尺度选择所需要的表达手段……"

在实现"信、达、切"三原则的过程中,要实现"切合原文风格"这一条,的确是难上加难。但是我们翻译工作者,无论如何,都必须迎难而上,不能知难而退。毛泽东早就指出:"语言这东西,不是随便可以学好的,非下苦功不可。"何况翻译工作同时要运用两种语言,要译得好,困难程度是不难想象的。我们翻译工作者应该像茅盾(1886—1981)在1954年的全国文学翻译工作会议上所指出的那样,"对原作进行严格的科学研究,这是翻译一部作品时所必须做的工作。"与此同时,在翻译过程中,译者应该严格按照"信、达、切"三原则的要求,在选词炼句上反复推敲,一丝不苟,力求保存原作的"丰姿"和风格。

  总而言之,此讲所论"信、达、切"三原则实际上是一个有机整体,"切"总是体现于风格。"信"、"达"存于"切",反之亦然。"信"是"达"和"切"的前提"达"是"信"和"切"的表现,而"切"则是"信"和"达"的具体体现。"信"、"达"、"切"三者合一的原则至关重要,不可忽视。

注释:

1. 引自一九七九年十二月一日《光明日报》杨东梁、王俊义"评戚本禹的'爱国主义还是卖国主义?'"。
2. 引自范文澜《中国近代史》上册。
3. 参看严复《与梁启超论所译〈原富〉书》。
4. Alexander Fraser Tytler, 1749—1814, *Essay on the Principles of Translation*.
5. 引自张其春《翻译之艺术》。
6. Mathew Arnold, 1822—1888, On Translating Homer in *Essays—Literary and Critical*.

第三讲 | 翻译的忠实性

忠实性是翻译的重大原则问题。所有的理论家都主张翻译应该忠实于原文，一切翻译工作者也无不认为自己的译作忠实于原文。但事实上，有的做到了忠实；有的并未做到。关键显然在于对翻译的忠实性有无正确的理解。严格说来，忠实性乃是信、达、切三原则的概括，也就是说，忠实性既要求译者做到保全原文意义的信，又要求译文做到达如其分的达和切合原文风格的切。对原文意义和风格的忠实并不是逐词逐句进行直译，而是要做到忠实于整个原文。只有这样，才能达到不仅达意而且传神的标准。如不这样考虑，翻译的结果只能是事与愿违。一个译者，如果对翻译的忠实性缺乏理解，不顾上下文的内在联系，只是追求孤立的字面意义，那他就永远也实现不了翻译的忠实性。请看下列一些词句究竟应该怎么译才符合忠实性的要求。

1. No, I didn't.

这是只包括三个词的一句话。表面上看起来，十分简单，似乎不值一提，但从翻译的角度看来，实有推敲的必要。这句话既可用于回答肯定问句，也可用于回答否定问句。假如有人问："Did you go to see the film last night?"（昨晚你去看电影了吗？）如果你没有去看，就可以回答说："No, I didn't."如果有人问："Didn't you go to see the film last night?"（昨晚你没有看电影吗？）如果你待在家里没有去看，同样可以用上面的话来回答。可是怎么译成汉语呢？如果不加区分地翻译"No, I didn't"这个英语句子,那就错了。英汉词典上都把"No"注解为"不",但这种解释对翻译上面的两个答语全无用处。第一种情况下,"no"必须省略不译,整句话应该译为:"我没有去"或者"没有去"。第二种情况下,"No"应该一反其意,译为"是的"。你能从哪本英汉词典中找到"no"有"是的"这个注解吗?肯定找不着。但是在这种情形下"是的"又的的确确与"No"这个英语单词是对应词语。

通过对这个简单句翻译的探讨,我们可以清楚地认识翻译忠实性的本质,还认识到任何时候都完全信赖词典是行不通的。孟子老早就说过,"尽信书不如无书。"在使用字典和其他参考书时我们必须采取一个批判的态度,做出自己的判断。

2. They call themselves Englishmen; and they are afraid to fight.

这是摘自萧伯纳(1856—1950)戏剧中的一句话。如果连词"and"用其常规意义来翻译,译文则会逻辑不通,因此也就不忠实于原文,因为"and"这个词在本句中实际上意为"but"。全句可译为:

他们都称自己为英国人,(而他们)却害怕打仗。

在萧伯纳看来,英国人骁勇善战,没有哪个英国人竟然会害怕打仗,谁要是害怕的话就不配做英国人。他瞧不起那些害怕打仗的人。

3. One step further and you will be lost.

这是个常见的句型。在形式上,它是由并列连词"and"连接的并列句,但从意义上看,它却是个复合句。第一个分句"one step further"是个省略分句,起条件从句的作用,而由"and"连接的第二个分句起表示结果的主句的作用。全句可转换为"If you take (or move) one step further, you will be lost."

因此,翻译本句时,我们可以用"(只要)……就……"这个汉语句型把它译为:

（只要）再走一步，你就完蛋。

4. I am in good health now and I can resume my work.

与例3类似，形式上，这个句子是由并列连词"and"连接的并列句，但意义上却是表示因果的复合句。句中的"and"相当于从属连词"so that"。所以，这个句子的意思实际上是：I am in good health now so that I can resume my work. 恰当的译文应是：

我现在身体很好，（因此我）可以恢复工作了。

5. I cannot keep these flowers alive and I have watered them well, too.

这个句子里的"and"也不能用"而且"或"并且"之类的通常意义来译。必须明白，并列连词"and"实际上起从属连词"though"或"although"的作用。因此恰当的译文应是：

这些花，虽然我也好好浇了，但仍然养不活。

例2~5，都是由并列连词"and"连接的句子，句法分析和翻译之间似乎有些不一致，照以下方式解释这种语言现象，问题就可迎刃而解：

进行句法分析时，我们仍然可以说，这些句子在语法结构上是由"and"连接的并列句，同时必须进一步说明：在实际意义和作用上，这四个句子中的"and"一词却分别引导了不同类型的分句，如例2中是表示对比关系的并列句，例3中是表示结果的主句、例4中是结果状语从句，例5中是让步状语从句。

而翻译则只能以上下文所表达的真正含义为准。我们绝不可为看来简单词语的外表所迷惑，而必须对上下文和单词的涵义彻底研究一番，切实掌握。要不然就会被一些看起来很简单的词引入歧途。在以上四个句子中，如果坚持按常规将"and"译为"而且"或者"并且"，一方面别人理解不了，另一方面也表明你没有完全理解这些句子的意思，哪里还谈得上翻译的忠实性？

6. It never rains but it pours.[1]

本句中有个"but"。你如何解释这个词？意思仍然是"但是"吗？不对。这个"but"相当于"unless"（除非）或"if…not"（如果不），引导一个条件从句。这个句子可有两层意思，其字面意义是描写天气，意为"it never rains unless it pours（if it does not pour）"，可译为：

不下则已，一下就是倾盆大雨。

就其比喻意义来说，这个句子一般指坏事一波未平，一波又起，也就是说坏事接踵而至。可译为"祸不单行"。例如：

John fell ill, then his brothers and sisters all fell ill. It never rains but it pours.

约翰病了，接着他的弟兄和姐妹都病了。真是祸不单行啊！

7. The boy sat down to do his homework when he saw his playmate coming.

一般而言，"when"是个引导时间状语从句的从属连词。但是在这句话里意义和功能相当于"and then suddenly"。也就是说，实际上"when"引导的是一个并列分句。按照汉语简洁凝练的特点，最好把"and then"略去不译，但是要把随后发生事件之突然在译文中表达出来，这样才能完全传达原文的精神。整句可译为："那个男孩坐下去做家庭作业，突然看见自己的玩伴来了。"第一个分句中的谓语动词"sat"用的是一般过去时，有时，这个谓语动词也会用过去进行时。例如，"I was writing a letter when the lights went out."对应的汉语是"（当时）我正在写信，灯突然熄了"。短语动词词组"be about to do something"也常用于这一句型中。例如，"They were about to start when it began to rain heavily."对应的汉语为"他们正要动身，突然下起雨来了"。

再举个例子来说明连词"when"的特殊用法：

Augustus returns and is about to close the door when the voice of the clerk is heard from below.

这句话摘自萧伯纳的一部戏剧，与上例的句型一样。要注意的是句中一般现在时的用法。为什么句子中的谓语动词要用一般现在时呢？原因就在于这句话是剧中的舞台说明。众所周知，舞台说明皆用现在时。全句可译为：

奥古斯塔回来，正要关门，突然从下面传来了那个办事员的声音。

请看下面三个句子中由 who 引导的从句是如何翻译的。

8. Don't you feel it strange that she should be so much ungrateful to Jack, who did so much for her when she was in poverty?

从形式上看，who 引导的是一个非限制性定语从句，但在意义上却是一个让步状语从句。who 这个关系代词的功能相当于 although he。因此本句可译为：

虽然杰克在她穷困时帮了她那么多的忙，她却对杰克如此忘恩负义，难道你不觉得奇怪吗？

9. Some teachers of English will be engaged from America who should strengthen our teaching work.

在形式上，这个句子中的先行词和关系代词之间没有用逗号隔开，故 who 引导的是个限制性的定语从句，但就意义来说，who should 相当于 so that they might…，具有目的状语的意义。全句可译为：

我们将从美国聘请一些英语教师来加强教学工作。

10. Her refusal to obey him greatly incensed him who had never met that kind of opposition before.

形式上 who 引导的也是一个限制性定语从句，但实际上含有原因状语的意义。关系代词"who"可以用"as he"替换。因此，全句可译为：

她拒绝服从他，这使他大为生气，因为他从来没有遭到过那样的反对。

上面所有由 who 引导的从句是定语从句的特例。英语语法学家 R. W·赞德福特（R. W. Zandvoort）在其《英语语法手册》（*A Handbook of English Grammar*）一书中把这种定语从句称为半状语从句。依我看，也可以称之为状语性定语从句，意思是指这些句子在功能上是状语从句，在形式上是定语从句。

11. For the moment, we are discussing nothing but the adoption of agenda.²

这个句子有人译为"我们目前讨论的是通过议程，绝非其他的什么"。你认为译得怎么样？译得完全恰当吗？我认为不太恰当，因为汉语译文听上去不地道。问题在于译者对 nothing but 这个英语习惯用语领会不深。这个说法可以和副词 only 互换，相当于汉语"只是"或者"只不过是"的意思。例如，"他只不过是个白痴"这个汉语句子可以用 nothing but 这个对应的说法译成："He is nothing but an idiot"。例 11 可以改译为：

我们目前正在讨论的只（不过）是通过议程。

12. The origin of the shells was Portuguese; that is to say they come from Portuguese Guinea or Guinea (Bissau).³

请想想"or"这个连词怎么译。译成"或（者）"那就错了，因为葡属几内亚和几内亚（比绍）实际上指的是同一个国家，并非两个国家。"or"在这里的意思是"namely"（即）。因此，本句应译为：

这些炮弹的来源是葡萄牙，也就是说，它们来自葡属几内亚即几内亚（比绍）。

13. We can only wonder why it should be claimed it (the draft) has a history of a whole week behind it.

想想"should"一词应该怎样译。如果译成"应该",惊异的语气就消失了,因为"should"与"why"连用,常表示惊异。"should"相当于汉语"竟然"、"居然"或"偏偏"。本句可译为:

为什么竟然(有人)说草案拖了整整一个星期之久,对此我们不能不觉得奇怪。

14. An old dog like him never barks in vain. Whenever he barks, he always has some wise counsel worth listening to.

仔细想想"old dog"应该怎么译。首先,我们必须了解,英语中"dog"一词既有褒义,也有贬义。如果在英国称别人为 old dog,那是在夸奖他是一个老手或者专家;如果称别人为 running dog,那是在骂他。"牛"、"马"两个汉字也有类似的情况。例如称别人为"千里马"、"识途老马"或者"人民的老黄牛",都有褒义,说"当牛当马"、"牛脾气",则有贬义。有时人们甚至会用这些动物的名称来称呼自己,例如,鲁迅在一首诗中把自己描述为"俯首甘为孺子牛"。别人夸你"老马识途"时,你可以谦虚地答道"马齿徒增"。英语单词"dog",汉字"马"和"牛"在这里所用的都是比喻意义。因此,上例中两个句子可以译为:

像他这样的老狗是从不乱叫的。一叫他总有高见值得一听。

由此可见,做翻译时必须把社会风俗和词汇的比喻用法考虑进去。

15. All is not gold that glitters.

"that glitters"这个分句虽然与其所修饰的先行词隔离开来了,但仍然是限制性定语从句。请注意副词"not"的特殊用法。如果按"This is not a book"和"He is not a worker"之类句子中"is not"的译法来翻译本句中的"is not",就会译出"闪闪发光的东西都不是金子"这种不合逻辑的句子,因为"not"在本句中用于特殊意义,表示部分否定。因此,本句的正确译法是:

闪闪发光的东西并不都是金子。

换句话说，在所有闪闪发光的东西中，有些是金子，有些不是。

16. He did not come to see her.

这个句子，如果脱离语境，有两种译法。一是"他没有来看她"；二是"他并不是来看她的"。后者意味着他来的目的不是看她，而是做别的什么事。这个句子如果意思是"他没有来看她"，说的时候用降调；若意思是"他并不是来看她的"，则用降升调。这两种不同的含义，在书面语中由上下文确定。

17. I'm sorry, but I disagree with you all.

连词"but"前面部分表达的是一种歉意。跟在表示歉意的话语后面的"but"该如何翻译呢？如果考虑汉语在此类情形下的表达习惯，翻译"but"的最好办法是根本不译。所以这句话恰当的汉语译文应该是：

对不起，你们大家的意见，我全不同意。

"Excuse me, but can you tell me how to get to Sloane Square?"这句话情形相同。其中"but"这个词也应该用上述办法来处理，而且在翻译该句时可以更灵活一些。依我看，可以译为"请问，去斯隆广场怎么走？"或者"劳驾，请您告诉我去斯隆广场怎么走。"

18. As time wore on, the old hunger brought him to his old despair.

这个例子与其两种恰当的译法出自一位教授之手。我们研究一下看应该如何翻译这个句子。如果生硬地译成：

随着光阴的消逝，那老饥饿又把他带到他的老绝望。

听起来觉得别扭，不舒服。有时译者必须首先排除表层词汇意义和句法结构的影响或干扰，再在措词和结构上提供一个巧妙的表达方式，这样才能传达出原文的精神实质和文学意味。因此，上面提到的这个英语句子可恰当地翻译如下：

A. 挨过了一段时间之后，旧日的忍饥挨饿的滋味又引起了他旧日的绝望。

B. 挨过了一段时间之后，往昔的饥饿痛苦又使他陷入往昔的绝望心情之中。

A、B 两种译法都很好，读起来自然、顺畅。

值得讨论的具体例句是不胜枚举的。在此我只举十几个例子，希望读者能做到举一反三。尽管例子为数不多，我们也已经能够看出，译者要想圆满地实现翻译的忠实性，就必须：（1）深刻领会语言的实际情景，（2）辩证地运用有关的两种语言的对应规律；（3）考虑自己为之翻译的读者属于哪一种类型；（4）灵活地处理句法结构和实际涵义的矛盾；（5）熟练掌握"and"，"or"，"but"，"when"，"who"之类常见词的特殊用法；（6）以等值或相似的成语来译成语；（7）重视不同的表达手法；（8）掌握形象的译法，或直译，或意译，或转换形象；（9）区分部分否定和全部否定，注意双重否定句，冗余否定，多重否定和累积否定等各类否定句的翻译方法，这些都是让译者头疼的问题；（10）重现原文的精神和语气；（11）注意行文合乎逻辑，自然流畅；（12）反复推敲，精益求精。

简而言之，译者考虑诸如意义、功能、时态、逻辑、文学形式等多种因素是至关重要的，即便是翻译文学作品里的几个句子，几行文字也是如此。不难想象，翻译整篇文章或者整本书我们要进行多么全面的考虑。

为了使译者更进一步理解翻译的忠实性，特从罗斯玛丽·泰勒（Rosemary Taylor）所著《母亲和她的房客们》（*Mother and Her Boarders*）一书中摘引几段和吕叔湘先生的译文做个对照，以供参考：

But then a few days later Mr. Sawyer came to Mother, his face beaming, and said they'd be leaving for Michigan the next day. And Mrs. Sawyer looked radiant, too, and for the first time gobbled up her dinner like a little pig.

Afterward she took Mother into her room for a long talk.

"What do you suppose struck them?" Father asked Mother when they went to bed. "All this time they couldn't leave, just had to stay here, and now they're off in this awful hurry, it sure is a mystery."

"No, it isn't," said Mother, "She told me why. She's going to have a baby."

"Oh, she is. Well, that's good. That'll cheer her up. But it's still no reason for this hasty exit."

"I think she's a little crazy," said Mother. "She told me she had to stay here until she got pregnant, that if she went away before, she knew she would not get pregnant."

"Of all the loony ideas!" snorted Father. "Couldn't she get pregnant back in Michigan? Any particular magic in this house?"

"Maybe," said Mother.

Father pondered on that. "What do you mean by 'maybe'?"

"Well… Rose Kane is going to have one."

"Oh, well, that's fine."

"And," added Mother, "we are, too."

"Great jumping grasshoppers!" cried Father. "Why don't you tell a fellow?"

可是过不了几天，索先生满脸春风的⁴来找母亲来了，他说他们再过一天就回密希根去了，索太太也是一团高兴，吃起饭来也一口等不及一口，像一只小猪。

吃过饭她把母亲请到她屋子里去谈了老大半天。

"你看他们怎么回事？"睡觉的时候父亲问母亲。"一向以来他们只是不愿意走，只是非住这儿不可，这会儿说走就走，真是怪事。"

"不，一点儿也不怪，"母亲说，"索太太告诉我来着，她怀了娃娃了。"

"哦，原来如此，这是好消息。她从此可以快活起来了，可是也不必这么急于要走哇。"

"我看她有点神经，"母亲说。"她告诉我，她当初打定了主意，非在这儿怀了孕不走，她说她若空着肚皮走了，以后就不会再怀孕了。"

"也没听见过这种傻话！"父亲鼻子里哼了声。"她在密希根就怀不了孕吗？咱们这个房子里有仙气吗？"

"也许，"母亲说。

父亲想了想。"你这个'也许'是什么意思？"

"这个……甘太太也有了。"

"喔！有意思。"

"再还有，"母亲随随便便的找补一句，"咱们也有了。"

"乖乖龙底东！"父亲直叫唤。"你怎么不直爽点儿说哇？"

正如中国一句谚语所说的：一叶而之秋。将吕叔湘先生的译文与原文对照之后，我们可以说，他圆满地实现了翻译的忠实性，达到了翻译的标准。理由如下：

第一，他成功地传达了作者的思想感情，保全了原文的意义。

第二，译文行文畅达，一如原文。

第三，译文风格切合原文。原文是生动活泼通俗易懂的口语，译文也是如此。"great jumping grasshoppers"这个感叹语译为苏北方言"乖乖龙底东"尤其精彩，不仅十分切合人物身份和对话场合，而且把一个做丈夫的喜出望外的心情表达得活灵活现。如果把它照字面死译成"蹦跳的大蚂蚱"之类，那就会成为笑柄。

然而，严格说来，也有两处可以改进的地方。一是应该把 Mr. Sawyer, Mrs. Sawyer 和 Rose Kane 译为索耶先生、索耶太太和罗斯·凯恩。没有必要把外国人名译得像是中国人的名字。二是"Why don't you tell a fellow?"这个问句应该直译为"你为啥不告诉人家呢?",这样更加接近原文的语气。大家知道,"a fellow"是第三人称单数,但此处意为"我",也就是说,指说话人自己。汉语里也有同样的语言现象。换言之,与英语"a fellow"一样,汉语的第三人称"人家"或者"别人"也可以代替第一人称。

现在可以得出结论:译者在翻译过程中必须认真注意翻译的忠实性,或者说严格遵守信达切三原则,力求自己的译文信于内容,达如其分,切合风格。

注释

1. M. T. Boatner, J. E. Gates, et al., *A Dictionary of American Idioms*, 1975.
2. *Journal of UN Documents Translation*. No. 1.
3. 同上。No. 3.
4. "的"字在当时,既是汉语白话文形容词的标志,也是副词的标志。

第四讲 | 直译和意译

在中国，直译和意译之争已有悠久的历史。第一次争论发生于梵文佛经汉译的过程中。东晋前秦时代高僧道安（314—385）是坚定地主张直译的代表人物。他虽然不懂梵文，没有亲自参与翻译，但他主持译事，厘定标准，供译人遵循。他唯恐翻译失真，所以主张严格的直译，以保存梵文的原来面貌。在他领导下翻译的佛经，成了逐字翻译的典型，除了偶尔改动一下词序之外，对原文未作任何更动。

与道安同时代的鸠摩罗什（344—413），是坚决主张意译的。他精通梵文，又懂汉语，因此他所译的一切，都照汉语习惯行文。他觉得该增则增，该删则删，以便更好地传达佛经原意。他译的经典，流传很广，对中国哲学与文学都产生了巨大的影响。

直译、意译的争论，一直持续到玄奘（602—664）时期。玄奘是唐朝高僧和大翻译家。他本人并没有明确地提出自己的翻译方法，是主张直译还是意译，但后人称他的翻译为"新译"，其实质就是灵活地使用直译和意译。在当时他已经能够运用增益、删略等方法处理各种语言现象，而且不背原意。不仅如此，玄奘的翻译态度认真负责，孜孜不倦，为同时代的人和后辈树立了光辉的榜样。

玄奘翻译佛经的经验值得梳理总结。例如，他主张采用音译法翻译多义词，如"薄伽"，其原文意思多达六种；对于表示中国没有的东西的词语，如阎浮树（一种树），以及一些难以准确翻译的术语，他也主张采用音译。此外，根据印度学者柏乐天（P. Pradhan）和中国学者张建木的总结，他在翻译佛经时使用了以下一些方法：（1）补充法，（2）省略法，（3）移位法，（4）分合法，（5）假借法，（6）代词还原法。[1]六种方法中有些与词法相关，有些则与句法相关。和玄奘同时代的理论家道宣（596—667），对玄奘的翻译推崇备至，他说道：

"今所翻传，都由奘旨，意思独断，出语成章。词人随写，即可披玩。"

正如罗新璋所言，玄奘明于佛法，兼通梵汉语言，译笔严谨，多用直译，善参意译。罗新璋还引用了梁启超（1873—1929）的话："若玄奘者，则意译直译，圆满调和，斯道之极轨也。"[2]

梁启超在《翻译文学与佛典》一文中接着说："翻译文体之问题，则直译意译之得失，实为焦点……新本日出，玉石混淆。于是求真之念骤炽，而尊尚直译之论起。然而矫枉太过，诘鞠为病；复生反动，则意译论转昌。卒乃两者调和，而中外醇化之新文体出焉。此殆凡治译事者所例经之阶级，一而佛典文学之发达，亦其显证也。"梁启超的这段话，可视为对中国历史上直译意译此消彼长，以及交相为用，孕育玄奘之"新译"这一辩证发展过程的极其宝贵的归结。

上述事实，涉及的是佛经翻译时期关于直译和意译的争论及其发展。到了20世纪30年代，又曾一度发生过一场同样的论战，百家争鸣，各抒己见。有的主张意译，例如赵景深，他甚至说："宁顺而不信。"有的主张直译，例如鲁迅，他与赵景深的观点截然相反，声称："宁信而不顺。"如果拿来当作实用或可以遵循的翻译原则，两种观点皆有失偏颇。我们都明白，一个合格的、令人满意的译文必须做到思想忠实，语言通顺，这是对译者的起码要求。

然而，在此问题上有不少学者的观点还是很值得借鉴的。可以茅盾的观点为例。首先，他对直译和"死译"进行了区分。他的观点如下：

直译的意义若就浅处说，只是"不妄改原文的字句"；就深处说，还求"能保留原文的情调与风格"。同一字的意义，用在某段文中的和注在字典上的，常常有些出入；直译时必须就其在文中的意义觅一个相当的词语来翻译，方才对；如果把字典里的解释直用在译文里，不管其在译语中搭配恰当与否，那便是"死译"。死译出来的译文中一切字都失了适当的位置。这样的译文，自然看不懂了。颇多死译的东西，读者不察，以为是直译的毛病，未免太冤枉了直译。茅盾相信直译在理论上是根本不错的。[3]

其次，他给直译下了一个定义。他认为所谓的直译并非一定是"字对字"，一个不多，一个也不少。因为中西文字组织的不同，这种字对字，一个不多一个也不少的翻译，在实际上是不可能的。张崧年曾经做过一个字对字的翻译尝试，结果以失败告终。直译的定义就是"不要歪曲了原作的面目"。假设同一原文有两种译本在这里，一个是"字对字"的翻译，然而没有原作的精神；另一个是并非"字对字"的翻译，可是原作的精神基本上得以再现。对于这两种译本，我们怎么评判呢？在茅盾看来，后者才可以称为"直译"，这样才是"直译"的正解。[4]

傅斯年也赞同直译，他的理由如下：

"作者的思想，必不能脱离作者的语言而独立。我们想存留作者的思想，必须存留作者的语法；若果换另一副腔调，定不是作者的思想。所以，直译一种办法，是"存真"的"必由之径"。一字一字的直译，或者做不到的，因为中西语言太隔阂，——一句一句的直译，却是做得到的。因为句的次序，正是思想的次序。"[5]

在20世纪30年代，直译派和意译派之间的这场激烈论战中，鲁迅是坚定的直译派，但是也不反对无法避免的意译。实际上，他建议在翻译实践中要遵循忠实和通顺两个主要的标准。鲁迅公开主张

"宁信而不顺",目的是反对赵景深所提倡的"宁顺而不信"的片面观点。就像李季(1922—1980)所指出的那样,鲁迅在实践中,从来没有把直译和意译对立起来,排斥意译,尽管他强调的是前者。正好相反,他认为应该在必要的时候使用意译。李季引用了鲁迅翻译的《小彼得》的前言中的话为据:

"凡学习外国文字的……开手就翻译童话,却很有些不相宜的地方,因为每容易拘泥原文,不敢意译,令读者看得费力。这译本原先就很有这弊病,所以我当校改之际,就大加改译了一通,比较的近于流畅了。"(《鲁迅全集》,第14卷第237页)

为了证明鲁迅并不反对意译,李季给出的另一个有力证据是鲁迅为自己翻译的《艺术论》写的《小序》中的一段话,他说:

"其中涉及生物,生理,心理,物理,化学,哲学……至于美学和科学底社会主义则更不俟言。凡这些,译者都并无素养,因此每多窒滞……费时颇多,而仍只成一本诘屈枯涩的书……倘有潜心研究者,解散原来句法,并将术语改浅,意译为近于解释,才好。"(《鲁迅全集》,第15卷第175页)

李季总结道,直译和意译在鲁迅的译文中是融合在一起的,只是前者为主,后者为辅。[6]

现在简要谈一谈西方有关直译和意译的争论,有意思的是,在西方对这两种方法的观点也是意见不一。例如,在古代,哲罗姆(St. Jerome, 347—420)主张在文学翻译中应当采用意译的方法,而在《圣经》翻译中应当采用直译。马尔库斯·图留斯·西塞罗(Marcus Tullius Cicero, 公元前106—43)说他不是作为讲解员,而是作为演说家进行翻译的,他不赞成字比句次的翻译。在西方直译意译的争论也像在中国一样一直持续到现代。我高兴地发现,中西方有关直译意译的争论发展方向是一致的。换句话说,越来越多的人几乎达到了同一认识:应该把直译作为主要的方法,而把意译作为次要或辅助的方法。

通过对历史上有关直译和意译两场争论的深入研究，我再次发现，从先辈手里传下来的这两种翻译方法并不像有些人想象的那样陈旧过时了，相反，只要我们深入认识直译和意译的本质，实事求是地加以灵活运用，这两种方法对翻译仍旧很有用。我对自己的看法作如下说明：

一方面，直译和意译这两种译法，自有翻译以来就是一对"双胞胎姐妹"，这是历史事实，中外皆然。另一方面，先辈成功的翻译经验，如玄奘和鲁迅，应该继承和发扬。现在有必要为这两种翻译方法做出相对精确而全面的定义了。

直译的特点如下：

Ⅰ. 在翻译过程中，直译以句子为翻译基本单位，同时兼顾整个文本。

Ⅱ. 直译力求再现整个原文的思想内容和风格，尽可能地保全修辞手法和主要的句子结构或者句式，如 SV、SVO、SVC、SVA、SVOO、SVOC、SVOA，这些句式是由《英语语法大全》的作者之一伦道夫·夸克（Randolph Quirk）提出来的。

直译举例

1. A. Still waiting here? Seems you have waited a long time.

   B. Have to wait. C told me he would come, and I have something to tell him. It won't wait.

   A：还等在这儿？好像你已经等了很久时间。B：不得不等。C 对我说他会来，我也有件事要告诉他。那可不能等。

2. He walked at the head of the funeral procession, and every now and then wiped his crocodile tears with a big handkerchief.

他走在送葬队伍的前头，还不时用一条大手绢抹去他那鳄鱼的眼泪。

以上两个例子摘自冯世则《直译·意译·逐字译》[7]一文，但笔者对例1稍微作了一些改动。从这两个例子可以看到译文不仅很好地传达了原文的意思和语气，而且还成功地再现了原文的句式和修辞手法。

那么，什么是意译呢？可以界定如下：意译是一种辅助性的翻译手段，在不能再现原文的句式结构和修辞手法时，用来传达原文的意思和精神实质。只有直译行不通时才采用意译。

例1. No admittance!（单部句）

闲人免进。（主谓句）

例2. It rains cats and dogs.（主谓宾句）

大雨滂沱。（主谓句）

例3. Where there is a will, there is a way.（复合句）

有志者事竟成。（简单句）

例4. It's an ill wind that blows nobody good.（复合句）

对于某些人有害的事可能对于另外一些人有利。（简单句）[8]

这些译例中的句型结构都改变了，例4中原文的比喻在译文中也不复存在。

无论使用直译还是意译，前提都是必须遵循信达切三原则。能保全原文句子结构和修辞手法的意义和精神，这样的翻译才称得上正当的直译，否则只能叫做"死译"或"硬译"。同样，改变原文句子结构和修辞手法，但不对原文意义任意增删，这样的译法才称得上正当的意译，否则就只能叫做"胡译"。

在着手翻译之前，首先必须把要译的文本从头到尾仔细阅读一遍。如果要译的是文学作品，不到对原文的思想内容以及文体风格已经心领神会，绝对不要动笔。在翻译的过程中，你可以使用直译法，条件是，虽保全了原文的句子结构和修辞手法，但读者读了能懂而且读起来通顺。例如，"Mary is a worker"可以采用直译法译为"玛丽是个工人"，"John studies well"可以直译为"约翰学得很好"和"Though the colonialists were armed to the teeth, yet the local people still fight with them"可以直译为"虽然殖民主义者武装到了牙齿，但是当地人民仍然敢于同他们战斗"。

但在许多情况下，全用直译行不通。这时就必须将原文的精神实质融会于心，再根据两种有关语言的特点，采用恰当的意译。例如"Practice makes perfect"可以采用意译法译为"熟能生巧"或者"业精于勤"。再如：It goes very much against the grain with me that the name of the witness should never be suppressed. (J. Galsworthy) 这句话，厦门大学外语系编译的《英语成语词典》是采用意译法这样译的：

不发表证人的名字，实在大大地违反我的本意。

这个句子译得十分恰当。因为第一，"go against the grain with somebody"是个成语，意为"违背某人的意愿"，因此无法逐字翻译；第二，that-分句中的谓语是被动态，编译者把它变换成主动态，这样中文读者读起来更习惯。

由此可见，我们翻译的时候，应该从实际出发，即从具体的句法结构或者修辞手段出发。也就是说，哪些句子或修辞手法用直译法翻译比较好，就用直译法；哪些用意译法翻译比较好，就用意译法。翻译一篇文章或一本书，不可能全用一种译法，必须采取灵活的态度，以免措词生硬，文不达意。其实，即使只译一个句子，有时也不得不把这两种方法结合起来，例如：

例1. Every dog has his day.

人人都有得意的日子。

例2. The oppressed people in the world would rather go through fire and water to fight against imperialists and colonialists than be turned round their little fingers.

世界上被压迫的人民宁肯赴汤蹈火同帝国主义者和殖民主义者进行斗争,也不愿任人摆布。

例1的译文保留了原文的句型结构(主谓宾),但"狗"这个形象改成了"人"。例2的译文再现了原文的句法结构,原文中有两个暗喻,第一个"go through fire and water",基本保留在译文中,而第二个却消失了。显然,以上两句的翻译,既不是百分之百的直译,也不是百分之百的意译,而是一种直译和意译的结合。

不论直译或意译,都有个限度。过了限度,即成荒谬。直译过了限度,就会闹出笑话,如把"the Milky Way"译为"牛奶路",把"lie on one's back"死译为"躺在自己的背上"。正确的译文应该分别是"天河／银河",和"仰卧／仰面躺着"。意译过了限度,也难免张冠李戴。譬如说,林纾(1852—1924)曾经译过一百五十多部文学作品,的确在把外国文学引入中国方面作过巨大的贡献,但就翻译论翻译,他的"翻译",只能叫做"半译半写"。因为第一,他自己不懂外文,只能凭借别人的口述。他不仅在内容上增添或删节了很多,同时在作品体裁上也加以改变。因此,怎能奢望他完全忠实于原文呢?其次,他一律用汉语古文来译。正如茅盾所说的,"这种译法是免不了两重的歪曲的:口译者把原文译为口语,光景不免有多少歪曲,再由林氏将口语译为文言,那就是第二次歪曲了。"⁹ 尽管林纾对外文一无所知,但是他的译作甚丰。林纾的译作尽管不完善,但他为我们存留了一种翻译方式——"注译",促进了当年外国文学在中国的传播。

再举两个例子来进一步说明直译和意译。直译和意译,在一般情况下,取决于两种语言内在的相互关系。拿汉英两种语言来说,表达方式有异有同。我们应该根据具体情形和上下文采用恰当的翻译方法。可能有以下三种情况:A)必须采用直译;B)必须采用意译;

C）必须把两种方法结合起来加以运用。

还有些句子可以运用多种不同的方法翻译，例如，

例1. It means killing two birds with one stone.

作为孤立的句子来看，可以有三种译法：

A. 这意味着一石二鸟。（直译）

B. 这意味着一举两得。（意译）

C. 这意味着一箭双雕。（直译加意译）

译文 A 听起来虽不十分习惯，但同时保留了原文中"石头"和"鸟"的形象，既达意，又新鲜。译文 B 虽然失去了形象，但原文的真正含义，却表达得很好。译文 C 虽然替换了形象，"石头"换成了"箭"，"鸟"换成了"雕"，但仍然形象生动，而且读起来很流畅。三种译法易读好懂，但究竟哪一种好些，取决于整个上下文，以及全文或全书的风格。

例2. 你不要班门弄斧了。

这句汉语，也可以容许三种不同的译法：

A. Don't display your ax at Lu Ban's door. （直译）

B. Don't teach your grandmother to suck eggs. （意译）

C. Never offer to teach a fish to swim. （意译）

三种译文都不错，但哪种最好呢？这要看实际的场合而定。如果你是译给中国人看的，那就不妨采用直译法。如果是译给外国人看的，那就最好采用意译法，他们一看就明白你要表达的意思。否则，你就不得不给这个典故加上详细的注解，因为一般说来，很多外国人既不知道 Lu Ban 是什么样的人，也不懂"display one's axe at sb' door"到底是什么意思。

从上述论证来看，不论是主张直译还是主张意译为唯一译法的观点，都不符合两种语言有异也有同的实际情况，因而难免片面性。翻译一篇文章或者一本书的时候，句句直译通常是行不通的；句句意

译,也不必要。正确的态度应该是:对那些结构近似、取譬相当的句子,一般说来,就应该采用直译法;对那些结构和取譬悬殊的句子,就应当采用意译法;对那些句子结构与取譬部分相同、部分不同的句子,则最好把两种方法灵活而巧妙地结合起来。须知翻译方法是为圆满实现"信、达、切"翻译三原则服务的。[10]

因此,在翻译过程中,信达切三字原则一刻也不能忘记。我们必须心有全文,在字法、句法、章法方面尽最大努力实现这些原则。例如《基辛格传》中有这么一句话:"Nixon was smiling and Kissinger smiling more broadly."这句话翻译起来颇费斟酌。第一,我们不能简单地把动词"smile"译为"笑",因为汉语"笑"既可指"微笑",又可指"大笑",而英语"smile"一词却只相当于汉语的"微笑";第二,副词broadly必须同动词"smile"结合起来考虑,否则恐怕翻遍所有英汉词典也找不到一个恰当的等值词。考虑到传记是一种文学形式,这个句子可译为:"尼克松满面春风,基辛格更是笑容可掬"。大家知道,"满面春风"和"笑容可掬"是汉语描写一个人脸上露出得意或高兴神情的两个文学用语。

总之,采用何种译法,取决于所译的句子结构与修辞手法,取决于信达切三原则的要求。我对直译和意译的看法可以简单地归结为:两种译法缺一不可,相互补充,直译为主,意译为辅,应当从实际出发灵活运用。

我为何把直译看成通常情况下主要或基本的译法?这是因为这种译法更容易使翻译达到以下三个目的:(1)忠实于原文的思想内容,(2)反映异国风情,(3)吸收新的表达方式。翻译这种语言活动要求译者客观公正,不带主观偏见,而直译能有效地达到这个目的。但同时我们应该清楚直译并不是唯一可行和普遍适用的译法,也有其局限性。由于语言、种族、习俗、文化或者历史因素的影响,直译行不通时,自然该想到意译这种次要的或者作为补充的译法,以有效地摆脱面临的困境。

为证明我的结论确实符合英汉翻译,特别是英译汉的实际情况和内在规律,我尝试着把路易·拉穆尔(Louis L'Amour)的作品《黑石棺制作人》(The Black Rock Coffin Makers)最后一部分译成汉语,并对直译,意译和两者结合的手法各自在该翻译中所占的比例加以分析。在译文中,每句话后面都用符号作了标记,lt 表示直译,ft 表示意译,comb. 表示直译意译结合。

所摘选的原文[11]及其译文对照如下:

Tucker's street was more crowded than usual when they rode up to Ashton's office and swung down. Jim Gatlin pulled open the door and stepped in. The tall gray-haired man behind the desk looked up. "You are Ashton?" Gatlin demanded.

他们骑马到艾什顿事务所跃身下马时,塔克镇街上比往常更拥挤。(lt)吉姆·加特林拉开门走进去。(lt)坐在办公桌那里那位苍白头发的人抬起头。(lt)"你是艾什顿吗?"加特林问。(lt)

At the answering nod, he opened his shirt and unbuckled his money belt. "There's ten thousand there. Bid in the XY for Cochrane an' Gatlin."

艾什顿一点头,他就敞开衬衫,解开钱袋。(comb.)"这里有一万。(lt)是为科克伦和加特林购进 XY 农场出的钱。"(comb.)

Ashton's eyes sparkled with sudden satisfaction. "You're her partner?" he asked. "You're putting up the money? It's a fine thing you're doing, man."

艾什顿的眼睛突然闪出满意的神色。(comb.)"你是她的合股人吗?"他问。(lt)"你出这笔钱?(lt)你在做好事啊,伙计。"(ft)

"I'm a partner only in name. My gun backs the brand, that's all. She may need a gun behind her for a little while, an' I've got it."

"我只是名义上的合股人。(lt) 我的枪用来维护农场所有权,就是这样。(comb.) 她可能暂时需要一支枪保卫她,我也刚好有一枝。"(lt)

He turned to Doc, but the man was gone. Briefly, Gatlin explained what they had found and added, "Wing Cary headed for town now."

他转身向多克,但那人走掉了。(lt) 扼要地,加特林说明了他们发现的情况,并补充说:"温·卡里现在就来镇上。"(ft)

"Headed for town?" Ashton's head jerked around. "He's here. Came in twenty minutes ago!"

"就来镇上?"(lt) 艾什顿摇了摇头。(ft) "他在这儿。(lt) 二十分钟以前来过!(lt)"

Jim Gatlin spun on his heel and strode from the office. On the street, pulling his hat brim low against the glare, he stared left, then right. There were men on the street, but they were drifting inside now. There was no sign of the man called Doc or of Cary.

吉姆·加特林急转身,大步离开事务所。(lt) 在街上,他把帽檐拉低,避免刺目的阳光,左看看,右看看。(comb.) 街上有人,但他们此刻都在漫步回到户内去。(comb.) 没有多克或卡里的踪影。(basically lt)

Gatlin's heels were sharp and hard on the boardwalk. He moved swiftly, his hands swinging alongside his guns. His hard brown face was cool, and his lips were tight. At the Barrelhouse, he paused, put up his left hand, and stepped in. All faces turned toward him, but none was that of Cary. "Seen Wing Cary?" he demanded. "He murdered Jim Walker."

加特林的马靴敏捷而坚实地踏在板道上。(ft) 他走得很快,双手随着两支枪前后摆动。(lt) 他结实的棕色面孔表现镇静,嘴唇紧闭。(comb.) 他在那家廉价小酒店门前停下来,举起左手走进去。

(lt) 所有的面孔都转向他，但就是不见卡里。(comb.)"看到温·卡里吗？"他问。(lt) 他谋杀了吉姆·沃克。(lt)"

Nobody replied, and then an oldish man turned his head and jerked it down the street. "He's gettin' his hair cut, right next to the livery barn. Waitin' for the auction to start up."

没人应声，然后一位老人转过头来，向街上努嘴示意。(comb.)"他正在理发，就在马车店隔壁。(lt) 在等拍卖开场。(ft)"

Gatlin stepped back through the door. A dark figure, hunched near the blacksmith shop, jerked back from sight. Jim hesitated, alert to danger, then quickly pushed on.

加特林退出门来。(lt) 一个模糊的人影，靠近那家铁匠铺弯腰站着，往后一缩便不见了。(lt) 吉姆警惕危险，停了一下，接着迅速前进。(lt)

The red and white barber pole marked the frame building. Jim opened the door and stepped in. A sleeping man snored with his mouth open, his back to the street wall. The bald barber looked up, swallowed, and stepped back.

那根红白相间的理发店标杆标明了那座木屋。(lt) 吉姆打开门走进去，(lt) 一个正在睡觉的人打着鼾，口张着，背向临街墙。(lt) 那个秃顶理发师抬起头，吸了口气，向后退。(lt)

Wing Cary sat in the chair, his hair halftrimmed, the white cloth draped around him. The opening door and sudden silence made him look up. "You, is it?" he said.

温·卡里坐在椅子上，头发理了一半，围着白布。(comb.) 开着的门和突然的沉静使他抬起头。(lt)"是你，对吗？"他问. (ft)

"It's me. We found Jim Walker. He marked your name, Cary, as his killer."

"是我。(ft) 我们发现了占姆·沃克。(lt) 他划下了你的名字，卡里，是谋杀者。(lt)"

Cary's lips tightened, and suddenly a gun bellowed and something slammed Jim Gatlin in the shoulder and spun him like a top smashing him sidewise into the door. That first shot saved him from the second. Wing Cary had held a gun in his lap and fired through the white cloth. There was sneering triumph in his eyes, and as though time stood still, Jim Gatlin saw the smoldering of the black-rimmed circles of the holes in the cloth.

卡里的双唇紧闭，而且突然枪响了，什么东西击中吉姆·加特林的肩膀并使他像陀螺一样转了一下，打得他侧着身子倒向门口。(lt) 那击中的第一弹使他未中第二弹。(ft) 温·卡里原来在膝部放着一支枪并隔白布开了火。(lt) 他眼睛里流露出一种胜利的狞笑，而且好像时间停止了走动，吉姆·加特林看见白布上两个洞眼烧焦的边缘还在冒烟。(comb.)

He never remembered firing, but suddenly Cary's body jerked sharply, and Jim felt the gun buck in his hand. He fired again then, and Wing's face twisted and his gun exploded into the floor, narrowly missing his own feet.

他不记得开了火，但突然卡里的身子剧烈地抖动了一下，同时吉姆感到枪托在手里。(lt) 于是他又开了一枪，温的脸抽搐起来，枪也响了，打进地板，差一点儿打中自己的脚。(lt)

Wing started to get up, and Gatlin fired the third time, the shot nicking Wing's ear and smashing a shaving cup, spattering lather. The barber was on his knees in one corner, holding a chair in front of him. The sleeping man had dived through the window, glass and all.

温开始站起来，加特林第三次开枪，那颗子弹射穿了温的耳朵，打碎了刮脸剃胡须用的杯子，肥皂泡沫也溅掉了。(comb.) 在一个

屋角里，那个理发师跪着，拿起椅子挡在前面。(lt) 正在睡觉的那个人也早已冲开玻璃窗逃走了。(ft)

Men came running and Jim leaned back against the door. One of the men was Doc, and he saw Sheriff Eaton, and then Lisa tore them aside and ran to him. "Oh, you're hurt! You've been shot! You've…!"

人们跑着来了，吉姆背靠着门。(lt) 其中有一个是多克，他还看到了司法行政长官伊顿，接着是莉莎把他们扯开，向他跑去。(basically lt)."哦，你受伤了！(lt) 你已经被打中！(lt) 你已经……"(lt)

His feet gave away slowly, and slid down the door to the floor. Wing Cary still sat in the barbershop, his hair halfclipped.

他的脚慢慢站不住了，他从门上滑到地上。(comb.) 温·卡里仍然坐在理发店，头发剪了一半。(lt)

Doc stepped in and glanced at him, then at the barber. "You can't charge him for it, Tony. You never finished."

多克走进来；望了他一眼，然后望着理发师。(lt) "你不能要他的理发费，托尼。(comb.) 你没理完！(lt)"

所选材料共 64 个句子。42 个句子直译（占 65.5$^+$%），8 个句子意译（占 12.5%），其余 14 个是直译意译相结合（占 22$^-$%）。当然，这个比率并非适用于所有的翻译材料。但是，不管如何，它令人信服地说明了这样一个道理：我们应该从实际出发，灵活运用直译和意译，以直译为主，厚此薄彼是绝对错误的。

注释

1. 马祖毅：《中国翻译简史》，中国对外翻译出版公司，1984 年：第 58 - 60 页。
2. 罗新璋：《翻译论集·自序'我国自成体系的翻译理论'》，商务印书馆：1984 年。

3. 茅盾:"直译"与"死译",《小说月报》1922年8月,第13卷第8期。
4. 茅盾:直译·顺译·歪译,《文学》,1934年3月,第二卷第三期。
5. 傅斯年:译书感言,《新潮》,1919年,第一卷第三号。
6. 李季:鲁迅对于翻译工作的贡献,《翻译通讯》,1952年第1期。
7. 冯世则:意译·直译·逐字译,《翻译通讯》,1981年第2期。
8. 《英语成语词典》,商务印书馆,1972年。
9. 见注释4。
10. 刘重德:《翻译漫谈》,陕西人民出版社,1984年:第45-47页。
11. 材料选自路易·拉穆尔(Louis L'Amour)的短篇故事集《沙漠土著的法律》(*Law of the Desert Born*),1983年由Louis L'Amour's Enterprise, Inc. 出版。

第五讲 | 常用译法

谈到各种具体译法，当然是不胜枚举的。在此我们只打算介绍几种常用译法：

一、句型对应

大家知道，熟练地掌握对应句型及其使用的场合是学习英语的一种很好的方法。就翻译来说，掌握有关两种语言的对应句型，是必不可少的一种基本功，因为它们不仅使你反应迅速，而且还能保证你的译文在句法结构上符合习惯用法。对应句型很多，在此只略举数例：

1. As soon as he came to Changsha, he paid a visit to Yuelu Academy.

如果熟悉各种句型的话，一看到这个英语句型，人就一定会在头脑里自然而然地马上想到"……一……就……"这个对应的汉语句型，能够立即正确地把它译成如下汉语句子：

他一到长沙，就访问了岳麓书院。

2. 你书读得越多，就会越有学问。

"……越……越……"是个汉语句型，和它相对应的英语句型是"The more…, the more…"。熟练掌握了这个对应的句型，你会觉得能轻而易举把这个句子译成：

The more you read, the more learned you will become.

3. But for your help, we could not have accomplished our task in

time.

"But for..."是个英语句型，相当于汉语"要是没有……"或"要不是……"。因此本句可译为：

要是没有你的帮助，我们便不能按时完成任务。

4. 他直到成年才开始读书。

"……直到……才……"是个汉语句型，其对应英语句型为"... not... until..."。本句可译成：

He did not start to read until he came of age.

运用这个句型时，要注意否定词 not 后跟的一般是表示瞬间动作的动词。

上述数例，已足以显示句型在翻译工作中的重要性。在学习过程中，我们应随时把所学外语与母语的对应句型加以比较、分析和总结，并牢记在心。这样，到了翻译的时候就会收到良好的效果。

二、词序调整

我们进行英汉翻译的时候，不得不时常调整词序。这是因为这两种语言各有各的特点。譬如说，定语词组和定语从句，在英语中，通常出现在所修饰的词语之后，而在汉语中却通常放在前面，英国人美国人喜欢把时间状语和地点状语放在句末，而我们中国人却喜欢放在句首；如果两种状语并存于一个句子之中，英语一般次序是先地点后时间，而汉语则恰恰与之相反。在英语句子中，物主代词往往出现在其指代的名词之前，人称代词也常出现在主句前的从句里，而汉语则总是先提名词。所有上述特点和其他没有提到的特点就决定了英汉互译时经常调整次序的必要性。例如：

1. The suggestion *put forward by the teacher* was accepted by his students.

教师提的建议被学生接受了。

2. The National Science Conference was held *in Beijing in 1977*.

全国科学会议是一九七七年在北京举行的。

3. When *he* was twelve, *Mark Twain* lost his father.

马克·吐温十二岁时失去了（他）父亲。

4. In *her* novel *Jane Eyre* Charlotte Brontë gives a very vivid description of the ill-treatment of the girls at Lowood.

夏洛特·布朗蒂在（她的）小说《简·爱》里生动地描绘了罗伍德学校女学生受虐待的情形。

5. *His* sympathy for the Chinese revolution and his friendship for the Chinese people gained *Edgar Snow* many enemies.

埃德加·斯诺，由于对中国革命同情并对中国人民友好，引起很多人对他的仇视。

三、词类转化

词类转化也是常用的译法。例如：

1. The *use* of bacteriological weapons is a *clear violation* of the international law.

使用细菌武器显然违反国际法。

英语名词"use"和"violation"转换成了相应的汉语动词"使用"和"违反"，随着"violation"这一名词的转化，形容词"clear"也就转化成副词"显然"。当然，即使逐字翻译，不进行词类转换，这个句子仍然是可以理解的：

细菌武器的使用是对国际法的明显违反。

但听起来无论如何都不如前一种译文自然。

2. At the meeting, some *were for* the proposal and others *against* it.

会上，有的赞成那个提议，有的反对那个提议。

英语"动词 to be + 介词"这一结构转化成了汉语的及物动词"赞成"和"反对"。

3. He dialed the *wrong* number.

他拨错了电话号码。

在英语句子里，起定语作用的修饰名词 number 的 wrong 这个形容词，在译文中却转化成了副词"错"，修饰谓语动词"拨"。

仅从上举三例，即可看出词类转化在翻译中很有用。必要时，我们应该灵活地加以应用。有些译文读起来之所以十分别扭，原因之一就在于译者死扣原文词类，不遗余力地保持不变。

四、恰当增减

很多情况下，逐词翻译既不可能，也不必要。在翻译过程中，时常需要根据有关两种语言的对应规律，对于个别词语酌情有所增减。但要注意，"酌情"增减与"任意"增减截然不同，前者旨在保全并且更好地表达原文意义，而后者则是主观的，是对原文不负责任。请看下列各例，观察究竟怎样才算"酌情增减"：

1. We don't *retreat*, we never have and never will.

我们不后退，我们不曾后退，我们也永远不后退。

动词"retreat"在原文中只出现一次，但在译文中却重复三次。译文中有所增加，但对于传达原文的真正含义，非常必要而恰当，并非任意增减。如果这句汉语回译成英文，那就必须有所删减。

2. John got up very early *in* the morning. He put on *his* jacket, (*his*) trousers and (*his*) shoes, sat down at (*his*) desk and began to do his homework.

清晨约翰起得很早。他穿上夹克、裤子和鞋子，就在书桌前坐下来开始做家庭作业。

在译文中，介词"in"、"at"以及第二个连词"and"都省略未译。至于第三人称物主代词"his"，用一个用五个都行，而译为汉语时，对应的"他的"通常一个也不需要。如果回译为英语，必须把省译的词全都表达出来，使英语句子语法通顺，符合习惯。

五、必要重复

表达同一概念或行为、重复出现的名词或动词，英汉两种语言所采用的办法是不同的。英国人往往采用替代法，中国人则往往采用重复法。英译汉时，应重复前面出现过的名词或动词，汉译英时，则应用代词或代动词替换前面出现过的名词或动词。例如：

1. A functionary in the leading post must be able to discover *problems* and good at analyzing and solving *them*.

领导干部必须能够发现问题，并善于分析问题，解决问题。

2. Parents should not only love their *children* but (also) help *them* and educate them.

父母不仅应当爱护自己的子女，还应当帮助自己的子女，教育自己的子女。

在这两个英语句子中，"problems"和"children"这两个名词只出现一次，而在汉语译文中，"问题"和"子女"这两个名词却重复出现三次，以求更加明确。

3. The *grammar* of Russian is much more complicated than *that* of English.

俄语语法比英语语法复杂得多。

4. The *silks* of China are better and cheaper than *those* of any other country.

中国的绸缎比任何其他国家的绸缎都价廉物美。

在这两个英语例句中，为了避免重复，用指示代词单复数形式 that 和 those 分别替代前面的名词 grammar 和 silks，而汉语句子中，指示代词无此用法，只能重复同样的名词。

5. He *studies* English as hard as she *does* Chinese.

他学英语跟她学汉语一样用功。

6. A. I *appreciate* this film very much.

我很欣赏这部电影。

B. So *do* all the young people.

所有青年人都很欣赏（这部电影）。

在5、6两句中，英语用替代词 do 来代替前面的动词 studies 和 appreciate，而汉语则重复同样的动词。

六、借助"有人……"[1]

对于"It is (was) thought（或者其他类似动词）that..."这类句型，我们不妨借助汉语"有人……"这个句型来克服不便直译的困难。例如：

1. *It was thought that* he was a good teacher.

当时有人认为他是个好老师。

2. *It was believed that* she would never come back again.

当时有人相信她永远都不会回来了。

3. *It is announced that* there will be a new film tomorrow.

有人通知明天放映新影片。

4. *It is maintained that* the criminal should be punished sternly.

有人主张这个罪犯要严加惩处。

七、用"祝"或"愿"[2]

对于以 May 引导的表示祝愿的句型，可以用"祝""愿"两个字来译。例如：

1. *May* you enjoy a splendid health!

祝（愿）您（你）健康！

2. *May* you come back with merits!

祝（愿）您（你）立功归来！

3. *May* the favorable wind accompany you!

祝（愿）您（你）一帆风顺！

4. *May* success attend you!

祝（愿）您（你）成功！

八、利用外位[3]

我们知道，一个句子一般都由几部分构成。英译汉时，如遇到主语部分、定语部分或宾语部分过长，不好按原来句子结构安排的时候，可以考虑利用汉语外位成分的办法加以解决。所谓外位成分，即是先把上述过长的主、定、宾部分译出，放在前面，然后再用汉语的代词"这"、"这些"或"其"复指其含义，有点像英语的关系代词 whose，前面的分句是它的先行词，接着再把其余部分译出来。例如：

1. ... it may be advisable *in the course of the consultations to envisage yet another alternative, namely, that we should consider this question as the fourth item on the agenda and the question of Korea as the third.*

……在磋商过程中设想另外一种可供选择的方案，即我们把这个问题作为议程上的第四个项目来审议，而朝鲜问题则作为第三个项目，这可能是可取的。

在这个句子里，从 in the course 起直到 as the third 都属于主语部分，其中心词是动词不定式 to envisage。这个中心词除带有状语和宾语外，还带有宾语同位语从句。整个主语部分相当长，因此，译者把这个主语部分译为汉语，置于译句之首，然后用"这"字译语法主语 it，再译 it 后的谓语。在"It + 动词 to be + 形容词 + 不定式短语或 that 从句"这个句型中，如果实际主语部分相对较长，都可仿上述办法进行翻译。如果实际主语部分不长，则可将全句译为如下句型："实际主语 + 语法主语 it 引出的谓语"。请看下面的例子：

It is quite necessary (important) for technical personnel to master a foreign language.

技术人员掌握一门外语十分必要（重要）。

2. The questions of *international security, the invitations of representatives of the two parts, disarmament, substantive consideration of the question of the sea-bed* are the questions to be considered in this anniversary

session.

国际安全,邀请两个部分的代表、裁军、海床问题的实质性的审议,这些都是在这届(周年)纪念会议上要审议的问题。

在这个句子里,仅就主语而论,是比较简单的,那就是"the questions",但加上它的介词短语,便构成了一个较长的主语部分。因此,译者采取了利用外位成分的办法,先把几个对主语起同位语作用的介词 of 的宾语译了出来,放在句首,然后又用"这些"综提一下,顺便带出整句的谓语。这样处理,既比较醒目,又更符合汉语表达习惯。

3. We feel that the proper procedure *to resolve the issue of which items should follow it* is through consultation.

我们认为,要解决接下去应是哪些项目这个问题,其适当程序是通过协商。

在这个句子中,动词不定式"to resolve"是修饰 that 从句主语"the proper procedure"的定语,但加上宾语"the issue"和修饰宾语的关系分句,便构成了较长的定语部分。因此,在译完主句 We feel 之后,就利用外位成分先把这个定语部分译出来,接着用"其"字(有点像个关系代词)作为关联词,一方面复指前面的"问题",另一方面把后面的"适当程序"引入译文。这样一来,这个汉语句子就很地道了。

九、正、反转变[4]

英汉语中都有肯定与否定的表达方式。英语中的一些肯定性的词语、短语或句子,翻译为汉语时,可能变为否定表达,反之亦然。

A. 正说反译

1. 动词

(1) If the weather *holds* a couple of days, the plane will take off.

要是天气三两天内保持不变,飞机就起飞。

(2) Such a chance was *denied* me.

我没有得到这样一个机会。

2. 副词

(1) We may *safely* say so.

我们这样说万无一失。

(2) The subversion attempts proved *predictably* futile.

不出所料，颠覆活动证明无效。

3. 形容词

(1) It would be most *disastrous* if even a rumor of it were given out.

甚至只要有一点风声泄漏出去，其结果就不堪设想。

(2) His refusal is not *final*.

他的拒绝并不是不可改变的。

4. 介词

(1) This problem is *above* me.

这个问题我不懂（或：我解决不了）。

(2) It was *beyond* his power to sign such a contract.

他无权签订这种合同。

5. 连词

(1) The guerrillas would fight to death *before* they surrendered.

游击队员宁肯战死，也不投降。

(2) He'd rather die standing *than* live kneeling.

他宁肯站着死，也不愿跪着生。

6. 词组

(1) The islanders found themselves *far from* ready to fight the war.

岛民们发现自己远远没有做好作战准备。

(2) When Philip missed the last bus, he was *at a loss to know* what to do.

菲利普误了最后一班公共汽车，茫然不知该怎么办。

7. 从句或句子

(1) He was 75, but *he carried his years lightly*.

他七十五岁了，可是并不显老。

(2) *My guess is as good as yours.*

我的猜测并不比你高明。

B. 反说正译

1. He *carelessly* glanced through the note and got away.

他马马虎虎地看了看那张便条就走了。

2. *Don't lose time* in posting this letter.

赶快把这封信寄出去。

3. *The significance of these incidents wasn't lost on us.*

这些事件引起了我们的重视。

十、被动译法

人们普遍承认，语态分主动和被动两种。被动语态，在汉语中使用较少，而在英语中则使用极为广泛。现就以下原文摘录及其译文进行比较分析：

Child Laborers in a Country

In a certain country, millions of working-class children are forced to work as child laborers. Child labor is mostly used in agriculture. It is reported that more than eight hundred thousand children are hired on plantations and farms. They are cruelly exploited by the monopoly capitalists.

...

Child laborers are badly treated by the big farmers. They are made to do what is usually done by grown-ups, but they are paid very much less. In one county in a state of that country, as many as 4,000 children are forced every summer to go and work for the capitalists. They are made to work in the burning sun from seven o'clock in the morning until four in the afternoon...

In recent years monopoly capitalism has been hit harder and harder by economic crises. More and more children have been hired to work in factories and on farms, because the monopoly capitalists are trying very hard to keep the wages low.

......

某一个国家的童工

在某个国家，有数百万工人阶级的子女被迫当童工。童工劳动大多用于农业。据说有八十多万儿童受雇于种植园和农场，受着垄断资本家的残酷剥削。

……

童工受着大农场主的虐待。他们被迫来干通常是成年人干的工作，但收入却少得多。在某州的一个县里，每年夏季竟多达四千儿童被迫为资本家劳动，从早上七点直到下午四点都不得不在烤人的太阳下做事……

近年来，垄断资本主义已经遭到经济危机的越来越严重的打击。越来越多的儿童被雇到工厂和农场劳动，因为垄断资本家正在极力设法使工资保持低水平。

……

上引英语摘录包含 3 段，共 11 个句子。除一句外，其余全是被动语态，但读起来仍感自然流畅。假如机械地拿汉语"被+动词"这个形式来翻译这些被动态的谓语，译文必定会非常别扭。在所引译文中，译者采用了下述四种办法来消除这种别扭：（1）"被+动词"；

（2）其他被动形式"受"或"遭到"；（3）用相应的习惯说法，例如"据说"；（4）用语态变换，例如用"收入"换"被付款"，"不得不……做事"换"被强迫工作"。上面提出的几种常用译法，并非主观臆造，而是产生于英汉两种语言内部固有的互相对应的特点。

注释：

1. 参考陆殿扬《翻译理论与实践》第 137 – 138 页，1958 年时代出版社出版。
2. 同上：第 160 页。
3. 参考徐盛桓《外位成分在翻译中的应用》，联合国文件翻译工作简报第二期。
4. 参考张培基等著《英汉翻译教程》第 103 – 110 页，1980 年上海外语教育出版社出版。

第六讲 | 怎样翻译英语定语从句

在英语中，复合句计有三种：包含着形容词性质的定语从句；包含着名词性质的主语、宾语、表语或同位语从句；包含着副词性质的各种状语从句。在这三种复合句中，以第一种的译法较为复杂，特在此加以讨论。首先，我们要了解，汉语里有些定语往往要译为英语定语从句的形式。例如：

这就是说，我们不但要把一个政治上受压边，经济上受剥削的中国变为一个政治上自由与经济上繁荣的中国，而且要把一个被旧文化统治因而愚昧落后的中国，变为一个被新文化统治因而聪明先进的中国。[1]

对应的英语译文如下：

In other words, not only do we want to change a China *that is politically oppressed and economically exploited* into a China *that is politically free and economically prosperous*, we also want to change the China *which is being kept ignorant and backward under the sway of the old culture into an enlightened and progressive China under the sway of a new culture*.

其次，我们必须明白，一个句子流畅还是别扭，并不在于它本身的长短，而在于是否组织得好。上面这个例子很长，但原文和译文都很流畅。另一方面，下面两个句子本身并不太长，但如果译者处理不当，译文也会显得十分别扭。

1. My plan, which I have used many times, is very simple.
我的我已经用过它多次的方案是很简单的。
2. Toward evening, we stopped at an inn, where we passed the night.
傍晚，我们停在一家我们在那里过了夜的旅店。

毫无疑问，这两个句子的汉语译文听起来都很别扭。一方面，它们违反了不同定语从句各自的翻译原则和方法，另一方面，也不符合汉语习惯。以上两个句子中的定语从句都是非限制性定语从句。根据恰当的翻译原则和方法，以及汉语的习惯，这两个定语从句不能按照原文逐字译出并置于原来所修饰的词语之前，同时也不必把两个定语从句的主语在汉译中都表达出来。因此这两个句子的正确译文应该是：

1. 我的方案，已经用过多次，很简单。
2. 傍晚，我们停留在一家旅店，在那里过了夜。

结果，这两个包含有定语从句的英语复合句转换成了两个带并列谓语的简单句。

通过以上分析可以看出，译者必须时刻遵守定语从句翻译的原则和方法。从语法上讲，定语从句分为两类：限制性定语从句和非制性定语从句。但翻译时，得增加三种，R.W·赞德福特在其《英语语法手册》中称之为"半状语性从句"，我则称之为"状语性定语从句"。

第一类：限制性定语从句 [3]

英语限制性定语从句，是用来限制它所修饰的先行词的意义的。这类从句具有三个特点：（1）位于先行词之后；（2）前面通常没有逗号与所修饰的先行词隔开；（3）是全句完整意义的组成部分，如果去掉这类从句，全句意义就会改变，甚至不通。例如：

1. This is a book (that) I like best.
2. This is the book (that) I like best.

去掉定语从句，第一个句子还是一个独立的简单句，但意思就大不相同了。而第二个句子，如果把定语从句去掉，那就不通了。没有适当的上下文或谈话语境，听到你讲"This is the book"这句话，谁也不懂你要表达什么意思。

翻译这类定语从句的时候，一般应按照汉语习惯把它作为定语置于所修饰的词语之前。我这里所讲的定语相当于英语中的定语从句，因为汉语中这些修饰语不一定具有分句的形式，有时会以词或词组的形式出现。这适用于以下所有句子。

1. This is *the place where the workers' and peasants' Red Army made the crossing in* 1934.

这就是工农红军1934年渡江的地方。

2. A. Do you know *the man who spoke to your father yesterday*?

你认识昨天对你父亲讲话的那个人吗？

B. No, I don't know who he is.

不，我不晓得他是谁。

3. Here is *the man you are looking for*.

你正在寻找的那个人就在这儿。

4. *Everything he said* seemed quite reasonable.

他说的话似乎都很有道理。

5. That is *the first book of the kind I have never come across*.

这是我碰见的第一本这样的书。

6. She made a list of *all the articles there are on the subject*.

她把有关这个题目的现有的一切文章列了一个单子。

7. There is no *difficulty we can't overcome*.

没有我们不能克服的困难。

8. This is *the problem which remains to be solved.*

这就是那个尚待解决的问题。

9. That's *the way they study.*

这就是他们学习的方法。

10. Who is *the man you visited yesterday?*

你昨天访问的那个人是谁?

11. *Such people as they are* will never do that sort of thing.

像他们那样的人永远都不会做那种事情。

12. Have you got *the same pen as I bought last week?*

你已经得到像我上周买的那样的钢笔吗?

上面所用的把限制性定语从句置于所修饰的词语之前的这种办法，在绝大多数情况下都是适用的。但在个别情况下，比方说，在"There is（are）"句型中，把限制性定语从句的译文放在它所修饰的词语之前或者之后，两种语序都是可以的。例如：

（1）But there are still *people who have failed to memorize the lessons of the past.*

（2）How many *students* are there in your class *whose homes are in the countryside?*

试比较每个句子的两种汉语译文：

（1）但仍然有人没有记取过去的教训。

但仍然有没有记取过去教训的人。

（2）你们班上有多少同学家在乡下？

你们班上家在乡下的同学有多少？

两种译文都是合乎语法规范的。但第一种译文采用的兼语式结构，似乎显得更自然一些，因而也就更好一些。

第二类　非限定性定语从句

非限制性定语从句，或称补叙性定语从句，用来对被修饰的词语进行进一步或补充说明。英译汉时，一般不必对调先行词与定语从句的位置，也就是说，可以英译汉时保留与原文相同的词序。例如：

1. Someone proposed the name of *Mr. Smith*, *whom we elected as representative.* (= and we elected him...)

有人提史密斯先生的名，我们选他当了代表。

2. Last week I saw *Modern Times* with Charles Chaplin playing the leading role, *which I think one of the most amusing films.* (= and I think it...)

上周我看了查理·卓别林主演的《摩登时代》，我认为是最有趣的影片之一。

3. *His article*, *which I have just read*, is very instructive.

他的文章，我刚才读过，很有教育意义。

4. Westminster Abbey, which is one of the oldest churches in Great Britain, contains the graves of many famous Englishmen.

威斯敏斯特教堂，大不列颠最古老的教堂之一，里面有许多知名英国人士的坟墓。

5. It rained *all night and all day*, during which time the ship broke into pieces. (= and during that time.)

雨整整下了一天一夜，在那段时间里，那条船破碎了。

6. Jack is *a scholar*, *in whose study there are lots of books*, (= and in his study...)

杰克是个学者，他书房里有很多书。

7. *John won the race*, *which made him very happy.* (= and it...)

约翰赛跑获胜，这使他很高兴。

8. *The relations between China and the United States of America have been improved, which will contribute to our four modernizations and world peace.* (= and it...)

中美两国关系已经得到改善,这将有利于我们的四个现代化和世界和平。

这类定语从句,均可将关系代词改成人称代词并用"and"与主句连接起来。不过,句序有两种情况:(1)定语从句原来在整个从句之后的(例句1、2、5、6、7、8),句序依旧;(2)定语从句原来插在主句主语和它的谓语之间的(例句3,4),改造后,则必须把and-分句移到原主句谓语之后,而译文的语序,则与原句保持一致。

纵观上述八个例句的译法,这种定语从句的译文均处于它们所修饰的词语之后。但关系代词的处理不尽相同:(1)关系代词如在从句中作主语或宾语(例1、2、3),均可省略不译;(2)如作其他成分,则须译出,例如在例5、6两句中,关系代词"which"和"whose"都作定语;(3)例7、8两句又有自己的特点:第一,关系代词总是用"which",而且它所代表的不是某个名词或名词词组,而是整个主句所表达的概念;第二,which 在从句中总是作主语,可译为汉语中的"这"字。

第三类　半状语性定语从句

这类状语性的定语从句,赞德福特(R. W. Zandvoort)在《英语语法手册》中叫作半状语性定语从句。这个术语意味着这种从句在形式上是定语从句,但在作用和意义上则是状语从句。姚善友在《英语语法学》一书中则称这类定语从句为"具有状语从句意义的定语从句形式"。这类从句英译汉时一般可根据其实际作用和意义译成表示原因、目的、条件等状语从句。例如:

1. *Premier Zhou who was busy all day long never knew what* fatigue was. (who = though or although he)

周总理虽然整天很忙，却从不知疲倦。（让步）

2. *My uncle, who will be seventy tomorrow,* is still a keen sportsman. [4] (who = though or although he).

我伯父虽然明天就满七十岁了，但仍爱好运动。（让步）

3. *Envoys* were sent *who should strengthen our international position.* (who should = so that they should) [5]

派了使节，以便加强我们的国际地位。（目的）

4. *Anybody who should do that* would be laughed at. (who = if he)

无论是谁，只要做那种事情，都一定会受到嘲笑。（条件）

5. For further particulars you had better apply to *my brother, who has paid particular attention to the subject.* (who = because he)

关于细节，你最好询问我弟弟，因为他对这个问题特别留意。（原因）

这类定语从句，都可以直接置于所修饰的词语之后，用表示各种作用的从属连接词，如"虽然"、"以便"、"只要"、"因为"等加以连接。同时，如果从句主语和主句主语相同，从句主语可以省略不译，如例1、2、3、4所示。如果不同，则必须在汉语译文中加以保留，如例5所示。不过，汉译中有时表示原因的从属连词也可以省略，读者仍能体会出因果关系。例如：

6. *Our teacher, who is getting old,* will soon retire. (who = as he)

我们的老师，越来越老，不久就要退休。（原因）

7. The people's war in Russia, *which inflicted heavy losses on Napolem's army,* incensed *the conqueror, who had never met that kind of opposition anywhere in Europe.* (which = because it; who = as he)

俄国的人民战争，使拿破仑的军队受到重大的损失，激怒了这位征服者，（因为）他在欧洲任何地方都从来没有遭到过那样的反抗。（原因）

第四类　as 引导的定语从句

as 在定语从句中单独用作关系代词的时候，其先行词可能有五种情况。

此处仅举例说明其中三种。请注意关系代词 as 在从句中的作用和译法。

Ⅰ．"as"代表有关分句中的一种行为的概念。

1. *To write a dull book*, *as* any poor writer could do, was unworthy of him.

写一本枯燥无味的书，这是任何一个蹩脚的作家都会做的，但对他来说，是不相称的。

2. It is absolutely wrong *to think foreign languages useless*, as quite a few people did before.

认为外语无用是绝对错误的，不少人过去有这种想法。

例 1 中"as"代表不定式短语"to write a dull book"这个行为的概念，在例 2 中则代表不定式短语"to think foreign languages useless"这个行为的概念。两个不定式短语都在句中作主语，因此，这种 as 是关系代词，在从句中作动词 do 的宾语。翻译这类句型时，as 可译为"这"或"这种"。

Ⅱ．"as"代表有关分句中一个相同或类似的名词或名词词组可以推论出来的概念。

在这种句型中，关系代词 as 可译为"这"（例1）或"这种"（例2）。

1. Now many young people wish to be *scientists*, as (= scientists) it is possible for them to be on condition that they work hard.

现在许多青年都想当科学家,在自己刻苦努力的条件下,这是大有可能如愿以偿的。

2. His grandfather was *a simple-mannered man*, as (= simple mannered man in its plural form) the large-hearted and large-minded men are apt to be.

他祖父质朴大方,慷慨而心胸开阔的人也往往是这样。

3. He seems *a foreigner*, as (= a foreigner) in fact he is.

他似乎是个外国人,事实上,他也是个外国人。

Ⅲ. "as"代表有关分句中一个形容词所表达的概念。

1. He was not *sick*, as (= sick) some of the other passengers were.

他并没有病,其余乘客有些人倒是病了。

2. He thinks her answer *incorrect*, as (= = incorrect) it probably is.

他认为她的回答不正确,她的回答大概也是不正确的。

Ⅱ、Ⅲ两种用法的 as,有两个共同的特点:(1) 都在从句中作表语;(2) as 在其中充当关系代词的从句中必定有动词 to be。翻译这种句型中的"as"时,可用"这"或"这样",或者重复前面的名词或形容词。

第五类　需作特殊处理的定语从句

1. In short, we are for a world *in which every people rooted in their national cultural values, will be receptive to the abundant benefits of other nations.*

一句话,我们赞成这样的世界:每个国家的人民都扎根于自己的民族文化宝库之中,又汲取其他国家的丰富滋养。[7]

2. But it has the big disadvantages that we have no large and disciplined army of socialist leaders *who understand the objectives in all their complexity, and who have clear ideas about how to promote the movement towards them.*

但它的一大缺点是使我们缺少这样一大批受过训练的社会主义领导人，他们懂得我们目标的全部复杂含义，并且明确地知道怎样才能推动运动朝着这些目标前进。

3. He unselfishly contributed his uncommon talents and indefatigable spirit to the struggle *which today brings them (those aims) within the reach of a majority of the human race.*

他把自己非凡的才智和不倦的精力无私地献给了这种斗争，它今天已使人类中大多数人可以达到这些目标。[8]

这三个例子中的限制性定语从句的译文没有以"的"字结尾并置于被修饰的词之前，而是作为后置的解释性分句。同时，先行词前面的英语冠词应转换为汉语修饰语"这样的"（例1）、"这样"（例2）或"这种"（例3），其目的是更清楚地显示有待解释的词与分句间的关系，这些分句的目标就是用来解释原文中的先行词。之所以对以上三例中的限制性定语从句作特殊处理，是因为例1和例2中有多个定语从句，例3中的定语从句则相当长。如果按我们平常的方法进行翻译，听起来既不自然，又不地道。

4. He liked his sister, *who was warm and pleasant*, but he did not like his brother, *who was aloof and arrogant.*

他喜欢热情愉快的妹妹，而不喜欢冷漠高傲的哥哥。

5. But his laugh, *which was very infectious*, broke the silence.

但他富有感染力的笑声打破了沉默。

以上两个定语从句形式上虽是非限制性的，但在翻译时，却如限制性定语从句一样译为前置修饰语，这是因为这些从句较短且与先行词关系紧密。如果按照非限制性定语从句的一般译法来译，整个句子则会显得结构松散，磕磕巴巴。

6. We are peoples *that have inherited ancient wisdom, that know the worth of biding one's time and recognized opportunity for combat.*

我们的人民继承了古代的智慧，懂得如何等待并善于抓住战机。

7. In a word, a true revolution is one *that is devoted to human progress in all domains and that makes human progress the supreme and final object.*

总之，真正的革命，致力于人的全面发展，并以此作为行动的最高指标。

8. We live in a world *where relations between states are relations of forces.*

在我们所处的世界上，国家之间的关系是力量对比的关系。

例6、7、8中的定语从句都是限制性的，但翻译处理的方式却比较特殊：前两句中，主句被压缩成名词词组，作为句子的主语，而从句则去掉关系代词，转换为句子的谓语；第三句中，主句被压缩为一个状语词组，而限制性定语从句则转换成汉语的系表结构，关系副词则与状语词组合为一体，置于句首。

9. He had talked to vice-president Nixon, *who assured him that everything that could be done would be done.*

他同副总统尼克松谈过话。副总统向他担保，凡是能够做到的都将竭尽全力去做。

10. He is with his youngest son, *who is accompanying him on his lecture tour in China.*

他带着小儿子。小儿子陪他在中国进行巡回演讲。[9]

在这两个例子中，动作的发出者和承受者数量相同，性别一样。汉语译文中第二个分句，如果不重复原文中的先行词，读者将难以分辨谁是动作的发出者，因为汉语中没有所谓的关系代词。既然要重复名词，最好是把第二个分句译为独立句，这样更自然，更地道。

上面介绍的几种定语从句的译法，并不完备，但较典型。如能适当参考，对初学者可能有所帮助。

注释：

1. 引自毛泽东《新民主主义论（中文版本）》。
2. 引自毛泽东《新民主主义论（英文版本）》。
3. 部分例句摘自张道真《实用英语语法》。
4. 本句原文引自桑得伏《英语语法手册》。
5. 3～7句例原文引自姚善友《英语语法学》。
6. 参考刘重德《英语 as 的用法研究》，1979 年湖南人民出版社出版。
7. 例句 1、2、6、7、8 引自马祖毅《英译汉技巧浅谈》，1980 年江苏人民出版社出版。
8. 例句 3、4、9、10 引自卢红梅《英语定语从句的翻译》，1990 年 7 月江西举行的《英汉语比较与翻译研讨会》宣读论文。
9. 例 5 引自顾延龄，熊希龄《英汉汉英翻译教程》，1989 年湖南省科教语言音像出版社出版。

第七讲 | 汉译英中的形象翻译和断句

汉译英，值得注意和探讨的问题，当然很多。但在本讲中，笔者将仅谈谈毛泽东的《反对党八股》[1]一文中的形象翻译和断句这两个问题。

Ⅰ. 形象翻译

形象、比喻，是文学作品语言的重要组成部分，但在某些论文和讲演中，亦是屡见不鲜。毛泽东著作中的语言富于形象与比喻，美国作家斯特朗（Anna Louis Strong）早就赞扬备至。仅就他的《反对党八股》一文而论，其中形象与比喻俯拾即是。现只摘引十处并附译文，加以对照分析，找出几条普遍适用的规律，以供参考。

1. 如果我们连党八股也打倒了，那就算对于主观主义和宗派主义最后地"将一军"，弄得这两个怪物原形毕露，"老鼠过街，人人喊打"，这两个怪物也就容易消灭了。

If we destroy that (referring to the stereotyped party writing) too, we shall "*checkmate*" subjectivism and sectarianism and make both these *monsters* show themselves in their true colours, and then we shall easily be able to annihilate them, like "*rats* running across the street with every one yelling, kill them! Kill them!"

2. 中国是一个小资产阶级成分极其广大的国家，我们党是处在这个广大阶级的包围中，我们又有很大数量的党员是出身于这个阶级的，他们都不免或长或短地拖着一条小资产阶级的尾巴进党来。

China is a country with a very large petty bourgeoisie and our Party is surrounded by this enormous class; a great number of our Party members come from this class, and when they join the Party they inevitably drag in with them a petty-bourgeois *tail*, be it long or short.

3. 说理的首要方法，就是重重给病患者一个刺激，向他们大喝一声，说："你有病呀！"使患者为之一惊，出一身汗，然后好好地叫他们治疗。

The first thing to do in this reasoning process is to give the *patient* a good shake-up by shouting at him, "You are ill!" so as to administer a shock and make him break out in a sweat, and then to give him sincere advice on getting treatment.

4. 我们有些同志喜欢写长文章，但是没有内容，真是"懒婆娘的裹脚，又长又臭"。

Some of our comrades love to write long articles with no substance, very much like the *foot-bindings of a slattern* long as well as smelly.

5. "对牛弹琴"这句话，含有讥笑对象的意思。

The saying "*to play the flute to a cow*" implies a gibe at the audience.

6. 何况这是党八股，简直是老鸦声调，却偏要向人民群众哇哇地叫。

What is worse, he is producing a Party stereotype *as raucous as a crow*, and yet he insists on *cawing* at the masses.

7. 党八股的第五条罪状是：甲乙丙丁，开中药铺。

The fifth indictment against stereotyped writing is that it arranges items under a complicated set of headings, *as if starting a Chinese pharmacy.*

8. 主观主义和宗派主义的东西，表现在党八股式的文章和演说里面，却生怕人家驳，非常胆怯，于是就靠样子吓人，以为这一吓，人家就会闭口，自己就可以"得胜回朝"了。

But those who write subjectivist and sectarian articles and speeches in the form of Party stereotypes fear refutation, are very cowardly and therefore rely on pretentiousness to overawe others, believing that they can thereby silence people and "*win the day*".

在这个句子里，毛泽东引用了"得胜回朝"这个成语，原意是指一个将军打了胜仗回到朝廷。翻译时，译者保留了前半部分"得胜"（win the day），丢掉了后半部分"回朝"（return to the court）。其实，这个成语最好还是照字面译成"win the field and return to the court"为好。理由有三点：（1）这个说法本身可以整体译出；（2）直译在上下文中可以理解；（3）符合尽可能保留原形象的原则。我们应该慎重对待形象或比喻，应尽可能保留，因为牺牲形象与比喻，就必然会或多或少损害甚至完全丧失语言的生动性。

9. 俗话说："到什么山上唱什么歌，"又说："看菜吃饭，量体裁衣。"

As the sayings go, "Sing different songs on different mountains" and "fit the dress to the figure and fit the appetite to the dishes".

在这个句子中，译者既用了保留形象的直译法，例如"到什么山上唱什么歌"译为"Sing different *songs* on different *mountains*"，"量体裁衣"译为"fit the *dress* to the *figure*"；又用了转换形象的活译法，例如"看菜吃饭"译为"fit the appetite to the dishes"，其中"菜"字仍然直译为"dishes"，而"吃饭"则转换成"appetite"。

10. 党八股的第四条罪状是：语言无味，像个瘪三。上海人叫瘪三的那批角色，也很像我们的党八股，干瘪得很，样子十分难看。如果一篇文章，一个演说，颠来倒去，总是那几个名词，一套"学生腔"，没有一点生动活泼的语言，这岂不是语言无味，面目可憎，像个瘪三吗？……我们很多人没有学好语言，所以我们在写文章做演说时没有几句生动活泼切实有力的话，只有死板板的几条筋，像瘪三一样，瘦得难看，不像一个健康的人。

The fourth indictment against stereotyped Party writing is its drab language that reminds one of a *Piehsan*.² Like our stereotyped writing, the creatures known in Shanghai as "little piehsan" are wizened and ugly. If an article or a speech merely rings the changes on a few terms in a *classroom tone* without a shred of vigour or spirit, is it not like a piehsan, drab of speech and repulsive in appearance? ... It is because many of us have not mastered language that our articles and speeches contain few vigorous, vivid and effective expressions and *resemble not a hale and healthy person but an emaciated piehsan, a mere bag of bones.*

在这个例子中，翻译形象与比喻时，既用了保留形象的直译法，例如"不像一个健康的人"译为"resemble not a hale and healthy person"，又用了活译法，如"学生腔"译为"classroom tone"，其中"学生"形象转换成了"课堂"形象。此外，还使用了音译法，例如"瘪三"译为"piehsan"。

概括说来，这篇文章中的形象与比喻共使用了四种译法，这些译法既适用于汉译英，又适用于英译汉。

第一种译法是直译法。这种译法，在所引十例中占90%，可见其对形象与比喻翻译的重要性。正如鲁迅所言，这种译法可以保存原作的"情调"和"丰姿"。

第二种是形象转换译法。这种译法，尽管原形象转换成了新形象，但译文语言仍然生动活泼。转换形象有两种情况：一是局部转换，例如"看菜吃饭"；二是全部转换，例如"只有死板板的几条筋"。

第三种译法是保存原形象所具有的意义的意译法。我们必须慎重，不可滥用这种译法，以免损害以至丧失形象，让译文失去原语的生动活泼。有时这种情况不可避免，但使用这种译法时，务必做到完全传达原文形象所包含的真正意义。比方说，"逼上梁山"译为"to join the rebels as the last resort"仍是佳译。但在一般情况下，宜力求保存形象，或者至少用别的恰当的形象取代原形象，使译文语言生动活泼。现谈谈如何翻译"同声相应，同气相求"这个汉语成语。如采用保留原有形象的方法进行直译，外国读者就很难领会其真正喻义；如采用意译法来表达其中的意义，那又会干巴巴的，毫无生气。根据上述应力求与原文一样栩栩如生这一原则，不妨考虑采用转换形象的活译法将这个汉语成语译成英语成语 Birds of a feather flock together。这两个成语含义相同，均喻指"同类互相吸引。"

第四种译法是音译法。例如"瘪三"译为"piehsan"。使用音译法时，要注意意思明了。例如，原文作者已经在上下文中说明了"瘪三"是什么，因此音译"piehsan"的意义已经够清楚了。否则就必须给音译加上脚注，让外国读者看得懂。这种译法虽很少使用，只占全部译例的10%，但也不可偏废。其实，这种译法，由来已久。例如我国封建社会的"衙门"和"叩头"，在英美出版的词典里均可找到"yamen"和"kotow"这两个相应的音译词。

Ⅱ. 断句

由于汉英两种语言属于不同语系，标点符号的用法也有差异。比方说，汉语有顿号（、），而英语则无此种符号。又如翻译外国人姓名时，名与姓之间本无任何符号，但英译汉时，则需要在名姓之间插入一个形如英语句号的实心圆点"·"，如"William Shakespeare"

音译为"威廉·莎士比亚"。这里只想着重讨论一下逗号和句号的用法。对比起来,汉语逗号用得多,而英语则是句号用得多。也就是说,汉译英时,汉语中的某些逗号(在个别情况下是分号)于必要时要在译文中改为句号,结果汉语原句至少变成两句,这自然就引起断句这个问题。请对比下面选自《反对党八股》的句子及其译文:

1. 因为长而且空,群众见了就摇头,(逗号)哪里还会看下去呢?

Because the articles are long and empty, the masses shake their heads at the very sight of them. (以句号替换原文中的逗号) How can they be expected to read them?

2. 延安虽然还没有战争,但军队天天在前方打仗,后方也唤工作忙,(逗号)文章太长了,有谁来看呢?

Although there is as yet no fighting here in Yen'an,[3] our troops at the front are daily engaged in battle, and the people in the rear are busy at work. (以句号替换原文中的逗号) If articles are too long, who will read them?

3. 比如军事指挥员,(逗号)他们并不对外发宣言,但是他们要和士兵讲话,要和人民接洽,(逗号)这不是宣传是什么?

The military commanders, for instance. (以句号替换原文中的逗号) Though they make no public statements, they have to talk to the soldiers and have dealings with people. (再以句号替换原文中的逗号) What is this if not propaganda?

4. 提出问题,首先就要对于问题即矛盾两个基本方面加以大略的调查和研究,才能懂得矛盾的性质是什么,(逗号)这就是发现问题的过程。

To pose the problem, you must first make a preliminary investigation and study of the two aspects of the problem or contradiction before you can understand the nature of the contradiction. (以句号替换原文中的逗号)

This is the process of discovering the problem.

5. 要解决问题，还须作系统的周密的调查工作和研究工作，(逗号) 这就是分析的过程。

In order to solve the problem it is necessary to make a systematic and thorough investigation and study. （以句号替换原文中的逗号）This is the process of analysis.

6. 拿洗脸作比方，(逗号) 我们每天都要洗脸，许多人并且不止洗一次，洗完之后还要拿镜子照一照，要调查研究一番，(大笑) 生怕有什么不妥当的地方。

Let us take washing the face to illustrate the point. （以句号替换原文中的逗号）We all wash our faces every day, many of us more than once, and inspect ourselves in the mirror afterwards by way of "investigation and study" (loud laughter) for fear that something may not be quite right.

7. 其结果，往往是下笔千言，离题万里，(逗号) 仿佛像个才子，实在到处害人。

Often the result is "A thousand words from the pen in a stream, but ten thousand li away from the theme". （以句号替换原文中的逗号）Talented though these writers may appear, they actually harm people.

8. 总之，不看实际情形，死守着呆板的形式、旧习惯，(逗号) 这种现象，不是也应该加以改革吗？

In short, there is a disregard for actual conditions and deadly adherence to rigid forms and old habits. （以句号替换原文中的逗号）Should we not correct all these things too?

9. 所以我劝这些同志先办"少许"，再去办"化"，不然，仍旧脱离不了教条主义和党八股，(逗号) 这叫做眼高手低，志大才疏，没有结果的。

I would therefore advise these comrades to begin just a little change before they go on to "transform", or else they will remain entangled in dogmatism and stereotyped Party writing. （以句号替换原文中的逗号）This can be described as having grandiose aims but puny abilities, great ambition but little talent, and it will accomplish nothing.

10. 有些天天喊大众化的人，连三句老百姓的话都讲不来，（逗号）可见他就没有下过决心跟老百姓学，（逗号）实在他的意思仍是小众化。

There are some who keep clamouring for transformation to a mass style but cannot speak three sentences of the common people. （以句号替换原文中的逗号）It shows they are not really determined to learn from the masses. （以句号替换原文中的逗号）Their minds are still confined to their own small circles.

11. 孔夫子提倡"再思"，韩愈也说"行成于思"，（逗号）那是古代的事情。

Confucius advised, "Think twice". And Han Yu said, "A deed is accomplished through taking thought." （以句号替换原文中的逗号）That was in ancient times.

12. 鲁迅说"至少看两遍"，（逗号）至多呢？

Lu Hsun[4] said, "Read it over twice at least". （以句号替换原文中的逗号）And at most?

13. 把国际主义的内容和民族形式分离起来，是一点也不懂国际主义的人们的做法，（逗号）我们要把二者紧密地结合起来。

To separate internationalist content from national form is the practice of those who do not understand the first thing about internationalism. （以句号替换原文中的逗号）We, on the contrary, must link the two closely.

14. 但是"化"者，彻头彻尾彻里彻外之谓也；（分号）有些人则连"少许"还没有实行，却在那里提倡"化"呢！

But "transformation" means thorough change, from top to bottom and inside out. （以句号替换原文中的分号）Yet some people who have not made even a slight change are calling for a transformation.

上引十四例，每例在汉语都是一句，但译成英语时，却全断成了两句以至三句。仅就这十四例所包括的语言现象加以分析归纳，即可得出下述结论：

汉译英时，一般说来，汉语原文中的逗号（有时是分号，但没有逗号这么常见）在英语译文中可以替换成句号，句号后面的句子有下列五种：（1）疑问句（例1，2，3，8，12）；（2）举例句（例3，6）。"Take sth. (for example or instance)"以及"(Let us) take A to illustrate B"等英语说法，均可归入此类；（3）概括句（例4，5，9，10），英语"This or That 加系动词 be"、"This or That can be described (or defined) as…"以及"this shows"之类说法，均可归入此类；（4）对立句（例13，14）；（5）解说句（例7），在英译文中，第二个句子的作用是对第一个句子作进一步说明。

汉译英既有断句现象存在，那么，英译汉就必然会有合句的情况，例如：

There is a dictionary on the desk. It is very useful. 这两句，翻译的时候可以合并成一句：书桌上有本字典，很有用。

注释

1. 原文引自1969年人民出版社出版的《毛泽东选集》合订本；译文引自1965年北京外文出版社出版的《毛泽东选集》三卷的英文版。
2. 3. 4. 根据汉语拼音方案，"瘪三"、"延安"和"鲁迅"应拼写为"biesan"、"Yan'an"和"Lu Xun"，而不是"Piehsan"、"Yenan"和"Lu Hsun"，但为了保存原来的音译形式，仍按威妥玛式拼音方案拼写。

第八讲 文学风格的可译性

1. 风格的定义与识别

谈及文学风格的可译性,我们必须首先弄清楚风格是什么。根据修订版《文学术语词典》(J. A. Cuddon, 1979)的定义,风格是"散文或诗歌特有的表达方式;是作者叙事的方式。风格的分析和评价包括考察作品的措词、比喻、手法(是否采用修辞)、句子形式(属于松散句还是掉尾句)、段落形式——作者所用语言的方方面面及其运用方式。"风格或许可以比作"作者的语气和口音,这与作者的笑声、走路的姿势、笔迹以及面部表情一样独特。"[1]

在西奥多·萨沃里(Theodore Savory)看来,"风格是每篇作品的重要特征,是作者的个性及当时情绪的产物。散句一旦成章,就必然在一定程度上显示作者的性情。"(Theodore Savory, 1957)[2]

简言之,正如18世纪法国思想家、文学家布封所言:"文如其人"。

作家各有各的风格,反映在其作品之中,这已是普遍共识。人人皆知,李白和杜甫同为中国唐代大诗人,但各有各的风格。李诗飘逸豪放,而杜甫则深沉忧思。詹姆斯和海明威两人的风格也不大一样。前者繁芜隐晦,后者简约含蓄。(张英进,1986)[3]

上述两例，已充分证明布封于 18 世纪提出的"文如其人"这一名言之正确。读一篇业已形成独特风格的作品，即使用笔名发表，也能即刻识别作者是谁。有鲁迅的一则逸事为证：1918 年，周树人在《新青年》杂志上发表了《狂人日记》，第一次采用了"鲁迅"这个笔名。好友许寿裳在江西南昌读到了这篇作品，被深深地吸引打动了。他想：这篇作品内容这么深刻，笔法又是如此简练而冷峻，一定是老友周树人写的。但一看，标题下的署名却是从来未听说过的"鲁迅"，于是写信问周树人："你读到《狂人日记》了吗？认不认得文章的作者？"周树人回信告诉许寿裳，鲁迅是他的笔名。[4]

毫无疑问，不同的文学作品，风格不同，清晰可辨，但一提到原作风格是否可译的问题，意见就不一致了。西奥多·萨沃里在《翻译的艺术》一书中指出：有人说"译文应该反映原作的风格"，有人说"译文应该具有译者的风格"。萨沃里本人主张译文应该反映原作的风格，并借李契（Liche）和莫尔（Moore）的话说明再现原作风格的可能性："假定我们忠实地翻译了拉斯金富有特色的一页文章，交给两位受过良好教育的法国朋友提意见。一个只略识英语，另一个则精通英语。要是第一个说'多么漂亮的描写啊！作者是谁？'第二个说'这必定是拉斯金写的，尽管我不记得这段文字'，那么，我们便可以相信，在风格方面，我们的译文已离我们的理想不远。我们写下的法语译文符合法语习惯，同时仍然保存着原作的风味。"[5]

2. 风格的可译性

在我国翻译界，虽然许多人认为应该再现，也能够再现原文的文学风格，但是也有不少人认为原文文学风格不可译。看来，可译性问题值得深入探讨。在本节，我想介绍赞成风格可译的观点。至于认为风格不可译的观点，将在接下来的三节中予以分析。

可译论者的宝贵意见很多。限于篇幅，不能在此一一引证，仅选录茅盾讲话中的一段作为代表。他在1954年《全国文学翻译工作会议》上指出：

"文学作品是用语言创造的艺术，我们要求于文学作品的，不单单是事物的概念和情节的记叙，而是在这些以外，更具有能够吸引读者的艺术意境，即通过艺术的形象，使读者对书中人物的思想和行为发生强烈的感情。文学的翻译是用另一种语言，把原作的艺术意境传达出来，使读者在读译文的时候能够像读原作时一样得到启发、感动和美的享受。

"这样的翻译，自然不是单纯技术性的语言外形的变易，而是要求译者通过原作的语言外形，深刻地体会了原作者的艺术创造的过程，把握住原作的精神，在自己的思想、感情、生活体验中找到最适合的印证，然后运用适合于原作风格的文学语言，把原作的内容与形式正确无遗地再现出来……文学翻译的主要任务，既然在于把原作的精神、面貌忠实地复制出来，那么，这种艺术创造性的翻译就完全是必要的。世界文学翻译中的许多卓越的范例，就证明了这是可能的；在我国，像鲁迅译果戈理的《死魂灵》，瞿秋白译普希金的《茨冈》和高尔基的一些短篇，也证明了艺术创造性的翻译，是完全可能的。"[6]

"瞿秋白的译作质量之高，一直受到翻译界的推崇。他的译作的最大特色是高度忠实于原作，不仅在内容上，而且在形式上包括句子结构、风格上都酷似原作。他译谁就象谁，译普希金就给读者以普希金的风格，译高尔基就给读者以高尔基的风格。"（李蟠，1984）[7]

西方许多著名的翻译理论家坚信再现原作风格的必要性与可能性。例如亚历山大·弗雷泽·泰特勒在《论翻译的原则》第一章中说：

"因此，我认为好的译文就是将原文的优点完整无缺地输送到译文中，使译文的读者能像原文的读者一样清楚地领悟和强烈地感受到这种优点。"[8]

上述中西理论家均认为译者再现原作的文学风格是必要的，也是可能的，但必须承认这确实是难以完成的任务。以荷马史诗翻译为例。从马修·阿诺德对一些荷马史诗译本的批评，我们可以看出再现荷马风格十分困难。"译者应该对于荷马的四种特点有深刻的体会。第一，荷马是特别敏捷轻快的；第二，在思想进展和思想表达上，也就是在句法和措词上，荷马是特别明白清晰和直截了当的；第三，在思想内容上，荷马也是特别明白清晰和直截了当的；第四，荷马是特别崇高庄重。我这样说似嫌过于笼统，对谁都用处不大，但珂珀和赖特先生翻译荷马史诗的失误源于他们对上述第一个特点，即荷马的节奏轻快，缺乏深刻的体会；蒲伯和索思比的失误源于对上述第二个特点，即荷马风格上和措词上的明白清晰和直截了当，缺乏认识；查普曼的失误源于对上述第三个特点，即荷马思想明白清晰而直截了当，缺乏认识；而纽曼的失误源于对上述第四个特点，即荷马的崇高庄重，缺乏认识。纽曼虽然对于前人的失误有所觉察，但自己的失误却比他们之中谁都更为明显。"[9]

尽管再现原作风格十分困难，但我非常赞同奈达博士在《语言结构与翻译》中的观点：

"译者不会觉得翻译不可能，"他说，"相反，任何从事翻译实践，处理多种语言间转换的译者都会深有感触——尽管语言结构与文化特征似乎存在巨大差异，但有效的语际交流总是可能的。关于语际间能充分交流的印象基于两个根本的因素：（1）语言之间语义相似，这无疑是因为在很大程度上人类经历的核心相似；（2）句法结构中所谓核心句层面根本上相似。"[10]那么奈达提出的动态对等原则（或功能对等）似乎值得研究，因为它有助于翻译中原作风格的再现。

3. 风格不可译论论点之一分析

认为原作风格不可译的人究竟有些什么样的论点？归纳起来，主要有三种，下面我们逐一加以讨论。

有一种论点是不同的语言不可能表达相同的风格。我们承认不同的语言具有不同的特点。我们可以比较一下英汉两种语言来说明这一点。英语有冠词，而汉语没有这种东西；物主代词、连接词和被动态，英语比汉语用得多得多；在这两种语言中"是非疑问句"的答法有时也不同。但其中的确存在着对应的规律。例如英语 The horse is a useful animal 和汉语"马是有用的动物"，英语 He put on his coat and his cat and went out 和汉语"他穿上上衣，戴上帽子就出去了"，英语 Isn't she at home? No, she isn't 和汉语"她不在家吗？是的，她不在家"等，都是符合习惯、达意传神、旗鼓相当的句子。如果我们能很好地掌握这些现存的对应的语言规律，翻译起来就会容易一些。所有的语言，在功能上基本相同。换句话说，不论什么语言，都能够表达思想，反映生活，描绘环境，刻画形象，创造新词语，创造不同风格的文学作品。

谈到风格，我们必须考虑整篇作品，而不能局限于个别词语。风格不可译论者常常拿双关、诗歌及其他难译的问题来佐证自己的论点。"从广义上说，这种不可译性分为两类：一是语言上的困难，一是文化上的困难。"（Catford, 1965）[11] 但称职的译者既然决定翻译某篇文章或某部作品了，通常掌握了啃这些硬骨头的恰当办法。譬如说双关语，有时仍能译为双关语，例如张谷若译《大卫·科波菲尔》时便成功地做到了这一点。不可讳言，有些双关确实难以保留，那么译者可以传达主要意思，再加注释予以补偿。例如：

杨柳青青江水平，闻郎江上唱歌声。

东边日出西边雨,道是无晴却有晴。

——刘禹锡《竹枝词》

The willows are green, green;

The river is serene;

There's his song wafted to me.

In the east the sun is rising;

In the west rain is falling;

Can you see if it's fair or foul?

这是张其春的译作。[12] 但为了让读者更好地理解这首诗,最好能再加如下脚注:

Footnote: "晴" (qing) here is a pun. On the one hand it means "fairness of the weather", and on the other it implies "情" (qing), a homophone, which means "love". (脚注:"晴"[qíng]是双关语。一层意思为"天气晴朗",另一层意思为"情"[qíng],与"晴"同音,意为"爱"。)

其他难译词语,有时也可以处理得很好,例如钱歌川巧妙地把汉语谐音"委员"和"桂圆"译为英语谐音"committee"与"common tea"。以下再举一些如何处理同音异义词的例子:

例一:

(This paper is our passport to the gallows. But there's no backing out now.) If we don't hang together, we shall most assuredly *hang* separately.

(这张纸片儿就是咱们上绞架的通行证。今儿个谁都不准往后缩。)咱们要是不摽到一块儿,保准会吊到一块儿。 (范守义,1978)[13]

原文中"hang"出现了两次。"hang"(together)意为"团结(在一起)","hang"(separately)意为"(分开)吊在绞刑架上"。翻译时很难保留原文的同音异义特征。但译者巧妙地将中文"摽"(biao)

与"吊"（diao）加以利用，克服了这一困难。"摽"在北京方言中意为"绑在一起"，原文的意思得以保留。

例二：

Julia：… Best sing it to the tune of 'light of love.'

Lucetta：It is too heavy for so light a tune.

——*The Two Gentlemen of Verona*, Act I, Scene II.

朱丽娅：……可是你要唱就按《爱的清光》那个调子去唱吧。

露西塔：这个歌儿太沉重了，和轻狂的调子不配。——朱生豪译莎剧《维洛那二绅士》

原文两个 light 构成谐音，译文中"清光"与"轻狂"读音相近，也构成谐音，而且意义也与两个 light 的意义基本相当。（彭长江，1987）[14]

总之，碰到实在不可能直译的词语时，可根据上下文的需要，找个恰当的替代品，即奈达博士所说的动态对等。这样的词语在一般的文学作品中十分罕见，不可能构成再现原作整体风格时不可逾越的障碍。因此，可以有把握地说，见树不见林的观点是不太妥当的。

人人都知道，诗歌较散文难译，但也不能匆匆下结论说诗歌全都不可译。实际上，也有不少译得好的诗歌。现举一例，以资证明：

《春怨》

金昌绪

打起黄莺儿，

莫教枝上啼。

啼时惊妾梦，

不得到辽西。

A Lover's Dream

By Jin Changm

Oh, drive the golden orioles

From off our garden tree!

Their warbling broke the dream wherein

My lover smiled to me.

——W. J. B. Fletcher

在为这首诗所做的注释中，吕叔湘（1980）就这首诗的译文作过精辟的分析。注释如下：

"英语诗和中文诗一样也是押韵的，如这首诗的 tree 和 me。英文诗也有跟中文诗平仄相当的节奏，就是轻音和重音的配置，如第一行：'Oh drí ve/ the gól/ den ór/ ióles'。英诗的字数不定，粗看起来似乎不整齐，要知道，英文一字往往不止一个音节，要是计算诗行里头的重音，仍然是很整齐的，如这首的第一行和第三行各有四个重音，第二行第四行各有三个重音。

"用诗体译诗，因为受韵脚和节拍的牵制，词语方面就不得不更加活泼些，增添、减少，以及换一种说法的地方都更多。如这首'莫叫啼'三字就省译了，第四行也换了说法，但原诗的意义仍然很忠实地表达出来了。如不能谨守原诗的意思和精神，就不算译得好。"15

事实上，翻译这首诗时字面上有所增减，也有改换说法来表达同一意思，但这些译法基于原诗内容，因而没有背离原诗意境。既然黄莺儿已经被赶离园中树枝，也就没有必要再译出"莫教啼"了：这个意思已经暗含在上一行中了。原诗"到辽西"和译诗"smile to me"的表层结构说法虽不同，但在深层结构中均指梦中相会，因而原诗的形象通过另一种说法或者说动态对等得以保留。最后，就这首译诗的分析再多说一句。所有词典中，orioles 只有一个重音，落在第一个字母"o"上，但分析节奏时，两个字母"o"均重读。诗人或诗歌的译者这样做是可行的，因为有所谓诗的破格，即允许诗歌不受一般语言规则的约束。

即使翻译散文体的文学作品，有时也采用上述译法。不过要时刻牢记，运用这种译法，主要是为了更好地表达原诗和原文的意思和精神。《春怨》这首译诗，无论就形式、措词、节奏来说，还是就意思、形象、精神来说，都可说是译得精彩。原诗平易委婉的风格也在译诗中基本上得到了再现。

表明合格的译者能成功地翻译诗歌的例子,并非仅此一例,要引成百上千也做得到。为进一步证明该说法的正确性,再举如下一例:

《月下独酌》	**Last Words**
李　白	
花间一壶酒,	An arbour of flowers and a kettle of wine:
独酌无相亲。	Alas! In the bowers no companion is mine.
举杯邀明月,	Then the moon sheds her rays on my goblet and me,
对影成三人。	And my shadow betrays we're a party of three!
月既不解饮,	Though the moon cannot swallow her share of the grog,
影徒随我身;	And my shadow must follow wherever I jog.
暂伴月将影,	Yet their friendship I'll borrow and gaily carouse,
行乐须及春。	And laugh away sorrow while springtime allows.
我歌月徘徊.	See the moon—how she glances response to my song;
我舞影零乱。	See my shadow—it dances so lightly along!
醒时同交欢,	While sober I feel, you are both my good friends;
醉后各分散。	When drunken I reel, our companionship ends,
永结无情游,	But we'll soon have a greeting without a goodbye,
相期邈云汉!	At our next merry meeting away in the sky.
	—Herbert A. Giles

原诗典雅简洁,格律整齐,富有浪漫色彩,Giles 此译,兼而有之。这是张其春对 Giles 翻译李白《月下独酌》的评价,我基本赞同,但译文的最后两行并不十分准确,可稍加改进。先引用日本诗人小畑薰良最后两行的翻译,以作参考:

Let us pledge a friendship no mortal knows
And often hail each other at evening,
Far across the vast and vaporous space!

小畑薰良的译文听起来有点儿啰唆，但更接近原文。笔者在此译文基础之上将最后两句译为：

Let's keep companions each other abiding by,
Meeting at night far across the broad and vast sky.

4. 风格不可译论论点之二分析

认为原作风格不可译者的另一个论点是，译者各有各的风格。不可否认，优秀的译者在创作自己的作品时有自己的风格，但译者也知道，在翻译文学作品时，应该放弃自己的写作风格，力争以另一种适当的文学语言再现原作的风格。这个道理，《翻译的艺术》一书的作者西奥多·萨沃里讲得透彻生动。他说："译者从来没有允许忘记自己是译者。他得承认，自己不是原作者，手头的作品也不是自己的作品；自己是阐释者，职责是充当沟通作者和读者思想的桥梁或渠道。他必须使自己不露面，让罗马或柏林直接同伦敦或巴黎通话。假若他觉得已经这么做了，那他就可以对自己的成就感到自豪。"[17]

在我国，努力模仿、再现原作的优秀的译品，为数不少。以杨必所译《名利场》为例，请看南木对杨译的简短总结与评价：

萨克雷操着十足的江湖口吻向读者揭开名利场的序幕。译者为了传达这种意境，不论是对通过领班目睹市场上光怪陆离的情景以及他的举止言行，还是对作者插入妙趣横生的道白或评议，都以与原文色调吻合的文学语言传译出来，使全文笼罩着一派江湖气息，弥漫着

(名利)场上的一股乌烟瘴气,收到吸引着读者要把这"名利场"看个究竟的艺术效果。全文一气呵成,宛如行云流水,句式变化多端,词序错落有致,句子成分转换自如。将原著丰满的文学内容与诙谐的艺术风格如实地或近似地复制出来。[18]

孙致礼(1984:37)也对杨译《名利场》给予了很高的评价:

"文学是语言的艺术。文学翻译是语言艺术的再创造。《名利场》中译本之所以称为一部优秀译作,是因为它在力求保持原著丰姿的基础上,充分考虑到祖国语言的规律和习惯,译出了地地道道而又丰富有文采的汉语译文,读起来毫无生硬拗口之弊病,确实能够像读原作时一样得到启发、感动和美的感受。"[19]

他同时也指出杨译本个别地方的不足之处。译者有时因归化过了头而有损洋味,例如把 godfather(教父)和 godson(教子)分别归化成"干爹"和"干儿子"。但无论如何,瑕不掩瑜,杨译《名利场》堪称再现了原作风格的佳作之一。

译者如不考虑原作风格而固执地要在译文中表现自己,其结果必然是吃力不讨好。例如蒲伯翻译荷马史诗就是这样。郑振铎指出,荷马史诗的风格是强健而朴素的。他常用想象、暗示及明喻的语法,但是他却极少用什么假借的(metaphorical)词句,所以用假借的语法来翻译荷马是与原文的性质相反对的。蒲伯的译文有时,虽然不是常常的,竟有这个毛病。如他不说"田里满是谷粒(The fields are full of grains)",而说"夏天之山谷装饰着浪形的金色(In wavy gold the summer vales are dressed)";(*Odyssey*, 19, 131)不说"这个士兵哭着[He (the soldier) wept]"(*Iliad*, 11, 486)而说"从他的眼里流下柔弱的露珠(From his eyes pour'd down the tender dew)"。[20]英国著名批评家阿诺德在《论荷马史诗的翻译》一文中也指责蒲伯没译好荷马史诗,因为在风格上和措词上他是矫揉造作的,不合原作风格。

优秀的译者好比优秀的戏剧演员。演员都各有各的个性,但在舞台上扮演人物时，则必须而且能够在表演过程中暂时忘我，进入角色的精神世界，以便把角色演得惟妙惟肖。在现实生活中，有不少演员能扮演任何角色，正角反角都演得很成功。大家知道，刘晓庆就是这样一位出色的演员。

普天之下无人不知，梅兰芳的演唱风格已经而且正在由他的忠实而又有才能的门徒与追随者一代代传下来。许多著名演员的演唱风格也是如此流传下来的。聪慧勤奋的人能掌握书法与绘画风格，进而模仿。同样的，人们能鉴赏且再现各种文学写作风格。

最近我在《中国日报》上读到的一则新闻，进一步证明了我的有关掌握艺术风格，模仿艺术风格说法是对的。这则故事讲述了刘荫茹如何成为面塑大师曹先生的继承者。

去年3月，在埃及的一个展览上，一位31岁的中国女子用小刻刀与竹针现场制作面人。大约15分钟之后，一团生面变成了三厘米高的老寿星。

这位年轻女子就是刘荫茹。从18岁开始，她在北京艺术雕像厂师从曹仪策。曹仪策人称"面人曹"，以面塑《红楼梦》中的美人著称。

刘荫茹每天坐在师父身旁，观看模仿。起初她只是学习如何制作《红楼梦》中的美人。接着，她会用传统方法自己制作，并且她只是反复练习，有时从黎明练到黄昏。经过三年的努力，刘荫茹终于学会了面塑。

不幸的是，一天，师父突然去世了，这对她来说是个沉重的打击。但是她下定决心要"不辜负师父的期望，将他的技艺流传下去"。她的愿望在多年的努力工作之后终于变为现实。1979年，她的一些作品在北京中山公园展出。许多游人误认为这些是"面人曹"作品，以为他还活着。为什么大家这么认为呢？答案是风格，刘荫茹的展品形似且神似曹先生的作品。

以上的故事进一步生动地表明人们可以很好地掌握与模仿任何形式的艺术风格。从逻辑上讲，谁能说文学写作风格是一种例外呢？

以上所列事实足以说明，称职的译者可以像舞台上表演的演员一样，翻译别人的文学作品时暂时忘记自我，并能尽力学习、模仿，从而再现原文风格。如果译者的写作风格与原作者相同，由这样的译者来翻译，当然是再理想不过了，至少从理论上来说是如此。但这个原则难以实行。

5. 风格不可译论论点之三分析

认为原作风格不可译者的第三种论点是，译文优劣，见仁见智，无客观标准。就一些孤立的词语或句子来说，有时确实难以判断，但就整篇译品的行文与风格来说，还是有比较客观的标准可以遵循的。一经对比，优劣立见。请看下面两例：

例一，伍光健与李霁野《简·爱》译本比较。

原文：There was no possibility of taking a walk that day. We had been wandering, indeed, in the leafless shrubbery an hour in the morning; but since dinner (Mrs. Reed, when there was no company, dined early) the cold winter wind had brought with it clouds so sombre, and rain so penetrating, that further outdoor exercises was now out of the question.

伍译：那一天是不能出门散步的了。当天的早上，我们在那已经落叶小丛树堆里溜过有一点钟了；不料饭后（李特太太，没有客人来，吃饭是早的）刮起冬天的寒风，满天都是乌云，又落雨，是绝对不能出门运动的了。

李译：那一天是没有散步的可能了，不错，早晨我们在无叶的丛林中漫游过一点钟了，但是午饭之后——在没有客人的时候，里德夫人是早早吃饭的——寒冷的冬风刮来这样阴沉的云，和这样侵人的雨，再做户外的活动是不可能的了。

茅盾（1937）对这两段译文的分析如下：

"这两段译文都是直译，但有一同中之异，即李译是尽可能地迻译了原文的句法的。如果细较量起来，我们应该说李译更为"字对字"；第二句中间的"indeed"一字，两个助词"so"，以及"penetrating"一字，在伍译是省过了。然而这是小节。如果我们将这两段译文读着读着，回过去再读原文，我们就不能不承认李译更近于原文那种柔美的情调。伍译的第二句后半，"刮起冬天的寒风，满天都是乌云，又落雨，是绝不能出门运动的了，"诚然明快，可是我们总觉得缺少了委婉。"[22]

上面提到的所谓柔美，所谓委婉，指的都是风格。就再现这一段原文的风格来说，显而易见，李译优于伍译，但茅盾的评论客观而公正，因为对另一段译文，他高度赞扬了伍译。

例二，罗伯特·彭斯（1759—1796）《红玫瑰》两个译本比较：

原文：	译文一
O my Luve's like a red red rose	吾爱吾爱玫瑰红，
That's newly sprung in June;	六月初开韵晓风；
O my Luve's like the melodie	吾爱吾爱如管弦，
That's sweetly played in tune.	其声悠扬而玲珑。
……	……
And fare thee weel, my only Luve!	暂时告别我心肝。
And fare thee weel awhile!	请你不要把心耽，
And I will come again, my Luve,	纵使相隔十万里，
Tho' it were ten thousand mile.	踏破地皮也要还。

第一节诗，正如楚至大（楚至大，1986）指出的那样雅则雅了，

却脱离了原诗的民歌风。"吾爱"这种称呼，古代中国民歌中已属罕见，用来翻译苏格兰方言 my Luve 实在不妥。其他如"韵晓风"和"如管弦"也与原诗不合。我们认为，译者用"玲珑"来形容曲调也不妥。再谈最后一节，听起来很俗。原诗平易清新，没有什么顺口溜的味道。改用"心肝"来译"my Luve"太俚俗，"踏破地皮也要还"也与原诗"I will come again"意境不合。

译文二
啊，我爱人像红红的玫瑰
　　它在六月里初开；
啊，我爱人像一支乐曲
美妙地演奏起来。
……
再见吧，我唯一的爱人，
　　我和你小别片刻。
我要回来的，亲爱的，
　　　即使是万里相隔。

译文二出自袁可嘉的手笔，不但再现了原诗的形式，也体现了原诗的风格。[23]

例三，李煜《相见欢》这首词两个译本比较。李煜（937—978）是五代时期南唐的末代皇帝，擅写诗词，以词著称。

原文：
剪不断，
理还乱，
是离愁，

别是一般滋味在心头。

克拉拉·坎德林（Clara Candlin）的译文：
Unsevered
Though sundered.
In chaos, yet
In order set.
This strange commotion in the heart
Is but the wanderer's woe.
　　　——*The Herald Wind*, P. 34.

初大告的译文：
Cut it, yet unsevered,
Order it, the more tangled—
Such is parting sorrow,
Which dwells in my heart, too subtle a feeling to tell.
　　　Chinese Lyrics, P. 7[24]

两个译本，哪个更好？显而易见。我相信能欣赏原文、读懂译文的读者看一眼就会说第二个译文好得多，因为译文意思更精确，而且形式更自然。

众所周知，不同的文学作品有不同的风格。译作的风格必须与原作的风格相当，或者至少与原作风格相近。译者在译作中必须尽可能再现原作的风格。

严格地说，文学作品的思想内容、语言表达以及风格特征是一个统一的整体。译者也必须把这三个要素当做一个整体来再现。但为了方便起见，严复与泰特勒都将这个整体分为三个成分：内容、表达与风格。这是可行的，也反映了每个兢兢业业的译者实际的工作过程。

大家都承认，文学是一种语言艺术。高尔基在《和青年作家谈话》中也明确指出："文学就是用语言来创造形象和典型人物，用语言来反映现实事件、自然景象和思维过程。"他的意思是说，语言在文学创作中是不可少的工具。换言之，没有语言，就没有文学。没有文学，也就没有（文学）风格。

6. 文学观点与语言学观点

要想比较好地再现原作风格，我认为，译者在着手翻译之前必须具备两个观点：

首先是宏观的观点，即文学的观点。译者要时刻记得自己所译的乃是别人写的文学作品，因而应该尽力使自己的译文成为符合原作思想、感情和语言风格的另一件艺术品。这样，译文就会同样感人，同样生动，读者能够得到同样的美的享受。

其次，译者必须具有微观的观点，即语言学的观点。在翻译过程中，章章句句字字，都要仔细推敲，选择最佳的用语来满足再现原作思想、感情和风格的要求。风格，从语言学观点看，主要是通过章、句、字的巧妙配合而成的。因此，即使有个别字句译得不够令人满意，也影响不了整篇或整部作品的风格大局。只要字句章所配合形成的总的情调或神韵再现出来了，也就可以说基本上再现了原作的风格。

风格离不开语言，换句话说，也就是离不开章法、句法和字法。章、句、字为风格依托的基础。《文心雕龙》的作者刘勰早在一千多年前就阐明了章、句、字和整篇文章气势神韵的关系。他说，"因字而成句，积句而成章，积章而成篇；篇之彪炳，章无疵也；章之明靡，句无玷也；句之菁英，字不妄也。"这历来是文章家追求的目标，而今天的翻译工作者也应全力以赴，既力求切合，至少接近，原作的神韵风格而达到神似，同时译好字、句、章而达到形似。神形俱似，方臻上乘。

现对章法、句法、字法问题，稍作详谈。

先谈章法。我在这里所讲的章法，是指小说的章回和自然段落，戏剧的幕、场和人物对话，散文的段和诗歌的节等等。这些均须按原作次序进行翻译，不必也不得任意颠倒。

再谈句法。句序及句式应尽量保留，如上文所引李霁野译的《简·爱》，袁可嘉译的《红玫瑰》，都基本上符合这一原则，但有时不得不根据表达习惯之不同而有所变通。例如 Good-bye was said 就不必再按原句的被动式直译了；又如以代表时间或地点的词为主语，以 saw 或 witnessed 之类词为谓语动词再加直接宾语的英语句式，翻译时也要加以改变。在必要的情况下，只有这样灵活处理，才能说是达到了意思清晰、文从字顺的起码要求。

第三，谈谈字法。字法在这里指措词和修辞。根据上下文和风格的要求，字字须仔细推敲，每个比喻要认真处理。例如 as lean as a rake 这个明喻，可有两种译法："瘦得像耙"（直译）与"骨瘦如柴"（改换形象）。显而易见，后者比前者要好很多。这说明遣词时的搭配是多么重要。英国讽刺作家乔纳森·斯威夫特说："适当的词用于适当的场合，就是风格的确切定义。"这个简明的定义不仅适用于写作，也适用于翻译。

7. 结论

现在我们可以得出结论：

译作是好是坏，是否顺畅，与原作和原作者没有任何关系，相反,这取决于译者的理论知识与翻译实践技巧。精通理论擅长实践自然能译出令人满意的作品。这是因为翻译不仅是科学——拥有自己独特规则与方法的科学,而且还是艺术——再现与再创作的艺术。

总之,原语中的字、句、章忠实、灵活、令人满意地移入了目标语或曰接受语,思想、感情和风格也就随之再现出来了。形似和神似是相辅相成的。形似是神似的基础,神似则为形似的结晶。作者写作的程序是:从形(字、句、章)到神,也就是说,作品一旦写完,就自然而然地形成了某种风格。但译者应该有两道工序:第一道工序是:通过字、句、章去细心体会全篇的神韵,从文学和语言学的观点来辨别原作反映出什么样的风格。第二道工序是:再从头到尾逐步译好字、句、章,同时念念不忘再现原作风格。"面对一段原语文字,"萨沃里说,"他(译者)必须问问自己:

1. 作者说了什么?
2. 作者的意思是什么?
3. 作者是如何说的?

这个分析方法可运用于翻译段落、句子甚至短语……"[26]

同时,译者必须注意话语的三个方面。茨维坦·托多洛夫(1970)将其分为:词语、句法与语义层面。"词语层面包括构成文章的具体句子。句法层面涉及文章各部分之间的关系。语义层面涵盖话语的整体意义及相关主题。"[27]

本文证明了文学风格可译,提出了其指导原则,举出了令人信服的译例,提出了恰当译法。文学译者应当坚持再现原作风格这个共同目标,为之奋斗终生。

注释:

1. Cuddon, J. A. , 1979, *A Dictionary of Literary Terms*, 663. W. & J. Mackay Limited, Chatham, Great Britain.

2. Savory, Theodore, 1957, *The Art of Translation*, 54. Jonathan Cape, Thirty Bedford Square, London.
3. 张英进，1986 年，从现代文体学看文学风格与翻译，《外国语》第 1 期.
4. 鲁迅这个笔名的用意，1982 年，《名人轶事 600 篇》，中国青年出版社，327 – 328.
5. Savory, *The Art of Translation*, 55.
6. 茅盾，1954 年，为发展文学翻译事业和提高翻译质量而奋斗，《翻译论集》，罗新璋，1984 年：511 – 512。
7. 李蟠，1984 年，李蟠谈我国历代翻译概况，刘重德《翻译漫谈》附录一，陕西人民出版社。
8. Tytler, Alexander Fraser, 1813, *Essay on the Principles of Translation*, Every man's Liberty ed. By Ernest Rhys.
9. Arnold, Mathew, 1919, *On Translating Homer*, *in Essays—Literary and Critical*, 215. Everyman's Library.
10. Nida, Eugene A., 1975, *Language Structure and Translation*, 98. Standford University Press, Standford, California.
11. Catford, J. C., 1978, *A Linguistic Theory of Translation*, 94. Oxford University Press.
12. 张其春，1949 年，《翻译之艺术》，开明书店，第 56 页。
13. 范守义，1987 年，模糊数学与译文评价，《中国翻译》第 4 期，第 5 页。
14. 彭长江，1987 年，语音变革与文学翻译，《中国翻译》第 4 期，第 18 页。
15. 吕叔湘（编注），1980 年，《英译唐人绝句百首》，湖南人民出版社，注释 96。
16. 张其春，1949 年，《翻译之艺术》，第 196 – 197 页。
17. Savory, *The Art of Translation*, 50.
18. 南木，1980 年，《名利场》中译本选介，《中国翻译》第 2 期。
19. 孙致礼，1984 年，评《名利场》中译本的语言特色，《中国翻译》第 10 期，第 37 页。
20. 郑振铎，1921 年，译文学书的方法如何?，《小说月报》第 3 期。

21. 参见 1987 年 8 月 11 日 China Daily 题为"Artist in Dough Is Model of Dedication"的报道。
22. 茅盾，1937 年，《简·爱》的两个译本，《译文》新 2 卷第 5 期。
23. 楚至大，1986 年，译诗须像原诗，《外国语》第 1 期。
24. 见张其春，1949 年，《翻译之艺术》，第 108 页。
25. 刘勰："因字而成句，积句而成章，积章而成篇；篇之彪炳，章无疵也；章之明靡，句无玷也；句之菁英，字不妄也。"
26. 参见 Savory, *The Art of Translation*, 第 25 页。
27. Todorov, Tzvetan. 1971, "The Place of the Style in the Structure of the Text", in *Literary Style, a Symposium*, Oxford University Press.

第九讲 ｜ 译诗问题

关于译诗问题，中外都有不少人探讨。有的认为诗可译，有的认为诗不可译。在诗可译的提倡者中，译为自由体还是格律体，哪种好一点，也是众说纷纭。

此事至今仍无共识。我不揣冒昧，也想发表一点意见，对此进行初步的探索。

我认为，诗要译得满意译得成功，是可能的，但很难。

我为什么这样说？这首先是因为人类互相之间存在着大同。例如，不论是哪个民族，都有逻辑推理的思维能力，都有表示喜怒哀乐爱憎的感情，拥有同一大自然、世界和宇宙。换句话说，就是人同此心，心同此理，心有灵犀一点通。因此，诗歌作为心灵的产物，是可理解，可欣赏，可翻译的。其次，大量的历史事实已充分证明诗歌的可译性。世界著名诗人如英国的莎士比亚、弥尔顿、雪莱、拜伦；美国的朗费罗、惠特曼；法国的雨果；德国的歌德；俄国的普希金以及印度的泰戈尔等人的诗歌，早就译成了各种语言，而且很多译得很好。拿中国唐诗来说，早就有了外国文字的译本。吕叔湘编注的《英译唐人绝句百首》选了五十余位诗人，其中有最有名的两位诗人杜甫与李白；译者多达八人，包括英国的东方文化研究学者翟理斯，英国领事 W. J. B · 弗莱彻[1]。此外，把中国古诗词译成英文出版的现代中国文人亦大有人在，例如蔡廷干的《唐诗英韵》，翁显良的《古诗英译》，许渊冲、陆佩弦、吴钧陶合编的《唐诗三百首新译》，杨宪益夫妇的《唐宋诗文选》。[2]

至于各国当代诗歌，也有不少译成了中文。中文当代诗歌，也有不少译成了外文。

写诗讲求形音义三美，诗歌译者决不可满足于达原文之意，而必须再现原作之美。为达此目标，首先是必须保留原诗的意义和意境；其次，必要时，还应尽力使译诗具有一定的诗的形式、节奏和韵律。由于不同语言的特点存在着种种差异，逐词照搬是行不通的，也是不必要的。但译者有责任千方百计克服难点，甚至克服原语与译语的不同特点造成的个别不可译之处。译者可以对全诗上文或下文某处的词语丢失的意义予以补偿。翻译诗歌时，最重要的是保全原诗的意境和风格。在前一讲我们已经讨论过弗莱彻翻译金昌绪《春怨》的英语译文 *A Lover's Dream*，用来证明我的观点。吕叔湘对弗莱彻的译文给予了高度的评价，认为是极为成功的译文。在第八讲里已详细引述了吕叔湘的分析，也附上了我对译文的评价，这里不再重复。仅就该诗的翻译再补充几句。

最近收到一位青年朋友寄来论文，标题是《试论文学翻译中的作者风格与译者风格》[3]，其中也提到《春怨》这首诗的英译问题，对弗莱彻的翻译基本上是肯定的，但同时指出 lover 一词系译者的误用。他的理由是汉字"妾"与 concubine 并非完全对应，有时也用作已婚妇女的自谦词。他言之有理。因此原诗标题《春怨》应该直译为 *Complaint in Spring* 之类，而不是 *A Lover's Dream*。尽管如此，我们认为，弗莱彻《春怨》这首译诗，无论就形式、措词、节奏说，还是就意思、形象、精神说，都算译得好。而且原诗平易委婉的风格也可以说在译诗中基本上得到了再现。

弗莱彻译本诗时已经运用了"补偿法"。一般来说，补偿法乃是一般有经验的译者译文学作品，特别是译诗时常用来解决局部难点或局部不可译之处的有效变通办法。增词法、引申法、拆译法、溶合法、替代法、转移法等[4]，都属于补偿法之列。译者一旦无法直译某些词语，就可以使用这种可那种补偿法，更好地达原作之神，再现原作的风格。

我认为，应将"减词法"置于补偿法之列，因为增与减一般互相关联。试以冠词为例，英译汉时不得不用减词法，汉译英时不得不用增词法。物主代词在英汉互译中也有类似情况。我曾发表过题为《常用译法例解》[5]一文，归纳总结了九种译法，其中第四项就是"酌情增减"，这事实上包括了上述互相关联的一对译法。

补偿法，是解决翻译文学作品特别是诗歌、诗词中的难点不可缺少的方法。翻译中的补偿，就是用译入语语言形式补足转换原文语言形式造成的语义损失。补偿这一方法，自有翻译以来就得以广泛运用，并且有人加以理论上的总结。宋代僧人法云（1088—1158）就说过："译之言易也，谓以其所有易其所无。"犹太裔学者 G·斯坦纳在《通天塔之后》（*After Babel*）一书中说："翻译而不加补偿，则事难成……"。苏联学者巴尔胡达罗夫指出："当译语中没有原语中某些成分的等值成分，也无适当的表达手段时，常用这种方法（补偿法）。"（《语言与翻译》）国际译联会刊 BABEL 主编在他的一篇文章中，明确指出补偿是再现原文的一种有效方法。（参见《翻译通讯》1984 年第 12 期罗进德文《翻译单位——现代翻译学的一个研究课题》）[6]

克服困难的方法，除补偿法外，还有许多方法，我们稍后再加以讨论。

为了更深入地阐述诗歌的可译性，提出更多的补偿方法，这里我想就彭斯的诗歌 *A Red, Red Rose* 及袁可嘉的译文再说几点意见。前一讲我引用了袁可嘉的译文，作为直译的典范。原诗的作者罗伯特·彭斯是一位苏格兰诗人，他自幼受民歌熏陶，因而他的诗富有乡土气息与民歌风味，语言通俗流畅。袁可嘉的汉语译文非常成功，达到了形美、音美、意美的标准，因为第一，它保留了原诗的意义和意境；第二，基本上保留了跟原诗相当的形式，每节同为四行，每行的长短也比较匀称；第三，语言通俗流畅，节奏自然，韵式也相似，原诗和译诗首节都是 ABCB，只末节稍有差异，原诗是 ABAB，而译诗则为 ABCB。此外，原诗平易活泼的风格比较令人满意地得到了再现。这两节诗简直是直译过来的，即使如此，也同样使用了减词法。例如，首节第一行减去了不定冠词"a"，第三行减去了定冠词"the"，末节第三行减去了物主代词"my"，末节头三行中的三个连词"and"完全减去，第四行表示距离的非人称代词"it"也消失了。否则译文会显得累赘，不合习惯。

诗的可译性就谈这些。

为什么又说诗难译呢？首先是因为各民族的大同中还存在着不少小异。比如说，除开语言文字特点的差异之外，还有当地环境的差异，社会风俗习惯的差异，文化背景的差异等等。第二个原因是诗最讲究文字精练，意境清新，风格鲜明；换句话说，即讲究形美、音美、意美。毋庸置疑，在译文中要再现这三美，实乃不易。此处引用一下马修·阿诺德对荷马的《伊利亚特》和《奥德赛》四个英译本的评论，我相信会有助于阐明这一问题。

"Cowper's diction is not as Homer's diction, nor his nobleness as Homer's nobleness; but it is in movement and grammatical style that he is most unlike Homer. Pope's rapidity is not of the same sort as Homer's rapidity, nor are his plainness of ideas and his nobleness as Homer's plainness of ideas and nobleness; but it is in the artificial character of his style and diction that he is most unlike Homer. Chapman's movement, words, style, and manner are often far enough from resembling Homer's movement, words, style, and manner; but it is the fantasticality of his

ideas which puts him farthest from resembling Homer. Mr. Newman's movement, grammatical style, and ideas are a thousand times in strong contrast with Homer's ; still it is by the oddness of his diction and the ignobleness of his manner that he contrasts with Homer the most violently."
("柯珀的措词不像荷马的措词,他的庄严也不像荷马的庄严,只不过是在节奏上和文法的风格上,他最不像荷马。蒲伯的轻快与荷马的轻快也属于不同的类型,他的思想明白清晰与态度庄严也与荷马的明白清晰与庄严属于不同的类型,他最不像荷马的方面是风格和句法的矫揉造作。查普曼的节奏、文字、风格和作法,已十分不像荷马的节奏、文字、风格和作法;但使他最不像荷马的,则是他的意义上的幻想性。纽曼先生的节奏、文法的风格和意义是一千倍地与荷马形成了强烈的对比;然而他与荷马对比得最厉害的,则是他的句法上的怪僻性和他的作法上的低劣性。"[7])

再举唐诗英译三例,以见译诗之难。

《宿建德江》　　**A Night-Mooring on the Jiande River**
孟浩然　　　　　　*by Meng Haoran*
移舟泊烟渚,　While my little boat moves on its mooring of mist,
日暮客愁新。　And daylight wanes, old memories begin…
野旷天低树,　How wide the world was, how close the trees to heaven,
江清月近人。　And how clear in the water the nearness of the moon!
　　　　　　　　　　　　　　　—Bynner

吕叔湘指出,译者用"begin"译"新"字,亏他想着,试想此"新"字更有何字可译?

"第三行不用'is'用'was',大概是承'old memories'而来;然而目前景色一变而为往日游痕,大失原作情趣;这一字所差太大了!"

《塞下曲》　　　　　　　**Border Songs**
　卢纶　　　　　　　　　*By Lu Lun*
　其三　　　　　　　　　　　Ⅲ
月黑雁飞高，　　High in the faint moonlight, wild geese are soaring
单于夜遁逃。　　Tartar chieftains are fleeing through the dark—
欲将轻骑逐，　　And we chase them, with horses lightly burdened
大雪满弓刀。　　And a burden of snow on our bows and oar swords.
　　　　　　　　　　　　　　　　—Henry H. Hart

　　编注者评论说："最后两行'欲将轻骑逐，大雪满弓刀'，欲逐而终未逐也。译文改作实有其事。原诗状边塞之苦寒，译文写将士之豪劲。"

　　意义、意境是一首诗的重要组成部分，译者只有力求再现的义务，绝无作任何更改的权利。

《赠别》　　　　　　　　**Parting**
　杜牧　　　　　　　　　*by Du Mu*
　其二　　　　　　　　　　　Ⅱ
多情却似总无情，　How can a deep love seem a deep love,
唯觉尊前笑不成。　How can it smile, at a farewell feast?
蜡烛有心还惜别，　Even the candle, feeling our sadness,
替人垂泪到天明。　Weeps, as we do, all night long.
　　　　　　　　　　　　　　　　　　—Bynner

　　吕叔湘对这首诗作了比较详尽的分析。他说：
　　"第一行 seem 是 show itself 的意思。第四行 do 代 weep。

"这一首的第一行译文相当成功：seem a deep love 指笑语殷情，做出多情的样子，真正多情的人这样吗？这样反言以明之，用来翻译'却似总无情'，不可不说是相当成功。但是连第二行一同看，就觉得比原诗浅了。真正多情的人怎么能把多情搁在面子上呢？怎么能在快分别的时候还有说有笑呢？译者之意，正唯多情故笑不成而已。原诗要比这个曲折得多。多情者可以不作态，无情者也可以不作态，这个人对我似有情又似无情，一直是个闷葫芦，现在才知道不是无情。何以见得？'尊前笑不成'也；若真是无情，平时还有个三言二语，何以今日之下而沉默起来了呢？译者只见到真多情者不作寻常儿女情态这一点，却没有把握到多情貌似无情而一往情深自然流露的意思，所以浅了。

"译文用 as we do，便把'替'字译成'伴'，又比原文粗了。他认为，既然笑不成，自然只有淌眼泪了。但既然垂泪，岂非多情之情依然和盘托出？这是译诗立意前后参差之处。而尊前这位姑娘，不但不会强为欢笑，而且也不知道可以寄情于一笑，只会黯然相对。

"总之，原诗写一个十四五岁小儿女含情脉脉，欲用情而不知从何用起，天真羞怯之态，恰到好处。译诗里头的感情就更加浓厚更加成熟了。虽然就诗论诗仍不失为一首好诗。倘若拿画来比，原诗好像一幅粉画，译诗便近于油画；倘若拿酒来比，原诗是黄酒，译诗就有点像白干了。"[8]

分析精当，令人信服。但根据笔者素来主张的信达切三原则之中的"达如其分"这一标准来看，这首诗，作为译诗来看，是不能作为佳译的，因为诚如编注者所批评的那样，它比原诗浅了、粗了，也比原诗多了。

译诗的困难，从上面的讨论，已可从一斑而窥全豹。

然而，究竟有没有完全不可译的诗呢？我想，这样的诗一般是不存在的。即使像中国回文诗，其意义仍可译，但其形式则不能完全保留，不得不一分为二，甚至一分为多种译文。现将王融的《春游回文诗》中的两句试译如下：

池莲照晓月

幔锦拂朝风

这两句诗不管是正读还是倒读都有意义。

译文 A 正读

The lotus in the pond is being shone upon by the dawn moon,

And the curtains of silk stirred by the early morn breeze.

译文 B 倒读

The breeze is stirring the silk curtains at dawn,

And the moon shining upon the lotus pond in the early morn.

十六国时期前秦女诗人苏惠织锦为《回文璇图诗》以赠其因罪被戍流沙的丈夫。这首诗的读法就更复杂了。唐武则天对此大为赞赏，作《璇玑画序》，说它"五色相宜，纵横八寸，题诗二百余首，纵横反复，皆成章句。"尽管如此复杂，但其各种意义仍可翻译，只是不得不译成更多的译文罢了。译诗，要想象原诗一样保留其浑然一体的回文形式，是绝对办不到的。不过，也不能因此专断地说回文诗完全不可译，仍然只能说是难译，难译的程度是有大小之分的。

下面我们来探讨一下诗怎样译的问题。

关于诗怎么译才好的问题，意见很不一致。许渊冲说：

"《比录》（指吕叔湘先生《中诗英译比录》）旧本中的译者大致可以分为三派：第一派是'以诗体翻译'的'初期诗人'，可以说是'格律派'，代表人物是翟理斯（Giles）。第二派是'以散体翻译'的'后期诗人'，可以说是自由诗体派或'自由派'，代表人物是韦利（Waley）。第三派是根据原诗内容进行创造性改写的译者，可以叫做'创造派'，代表人物是庞德（Pound）。《比录》新本中增选的国外译者基本上是这三派的继承人……"，许同时指出，中国译者也同样存在着上述三派译法，并各有代表人物。[9]

说到国外三大流派的发展，柳无忌教授指出，以韦利为代表的自由派在1950年后大为繁荣，近年来出现了不少翻译中国诗歌的译者，如傅乐山（J. D. Frodsham）、大卫·霍克斯（David Hawkes）、伯顿·沃森（Burton Watson）、齐皎瀚（Jonathan Chaves）、史蒂芬·欧文（Stephen Owen）、刘若愚（James J. Y. Liu）等，他们翻译了大量的中国诗歌，成就超过了前辈。在所有这些译作中，最重要、最全面的当属柳无忌和罗郁正编辑的《葵晔集：三千年中国诗歌》（印第安纳大学出版社，1975，1990）。

在评论上述三种译法主张或流派之前，我想，最好还是先论述一下翻译的基本特征和基本要求是什么，然后才有评论的可靠依据和准则。

"原作的内容对译者来说是客观存在的，译者的任务是把这种客观存在的东西而不是把自己的什么东西传达给读者。从这个意义上说，翻译不是自己创作，不是译者自己写文章，也不是借用原作的思想来写文章。对这一点有任何相反的理解，都是与翻译这一概念不能相容的。这是翻译的一个基本特征。"[10] 诗的翻译也同样应该具有这个基本特征，也就是说，译诗也不是自己创作，不是译者自己写诗，不是借用原诗的思想来写诗。

基本要求又是什么呢？成仿吾早就提出过，"译诗应当也是诗，这是我们所最不可忘记的。其次，译诗应当忠于原作。"[11]

这两个基本要求缺一不可。因为第一，原诗是一件形神兼备的艺术品，译诗也必须是一件形神兼备的艺术品，也就是说，保存诗的艺术性，形音意三美均须追求；第二，既然是译诗，不是创作，忠于原作，理所当然。所谓忠于原作，根据我的意见，就是译诗应传原诗的内容，应取原诗的形式。只有符合这两条要求的译诗，才算是成功的译诗。

我曾于1979年提出过信达切三原则。[12]所谓信，即"信于内容"；所谓达，即"达如其分"；所谓切，即"切合风格"。[13]内容与形式，思想性与艺术性，或内容、文字与风格既是统一的整体，又是可以用两分法或三分法加以分析的。就译诗说，信于内容，就是要保留原诗的意义和意境。达如其分，是就原诗文字表达的深浅程度来说的，换言之，假若原诗行文浅易，译文在文字表达上亦应力求浅易；假若原诗行文艰深，译文亦应力求艰深。原诗风格，多种多样，有通俗与典雅之分，有质朴与华丽之分，有庄严与诙谐之分，等等。译诗的风格应力求切合，至少接近原诗的风格。

对于翻译的特征、要求和原则有了正确的认识，便不难看出，创造派的主张和译法是不宜提倡推广的，因为它超越了翻译的范畴，脱离了翻译的轨道。请看下例：

朗费罗《生之颂》第一、五节　　　　　　　　董恂译诗
Tell me not, in mournful numbers,　　　　　莫将烦恼著诗篇
Life is but an empty dream!　　　　　　　　百岁原如一觉眠
For the soul is dead that slumbers,　　　　　梦短梦长同是梦
And things are not what they seem.　　　　　独留真气满坤乾

In the world's broad field of battle,　　　　扰扰红尘听鼓鼙
In the bivouac of life.　　　　　　　　　　风吹大漠草萋萋
Be not like dumb, driven cattle!　　　　　　驾驼甘待鞭笞下
Be a hero in the strife!　　　　　　　　　　骐骥谁能辔勒羁[14]

原诗第一节的主旨本来是"不要以悲哀的诗篇告诉我人生如梦"，而译者却硬说"百岁原如一觉眠，梦长梦短同是梦"。原诗第五节中战场、野营的情景和牛羊、英雄等形象在译诗中也统统消失不

见了。译者用红尘代替了战场,大漠代替了野营,驽骀代替了牛羊,骐骥代替了英雄。在我看来,这种不负责任地随自己所需篡改原诗的主旨、情境和形象的翻译,是不可取的。

汉译英时,创造派也有类似做法。许渊冲指出:"创造派的代表作是英国伦敦出版的《东方诗选》。《东方诗选》的译者们把中国古诗译成了现代派新诗,把一句分译成几行,第一个字母不大写,行末也没有标点。有时译者诗兴大发,就'再创作'一番,如李商隐的《锦瑟》译文,除了'主题'之外,还加上了36行'变奏'。"[15]

美国现代派诗人庞德译诗,也有跑野马的情况,余光中对此十分愤慨。他说:"庞德的好多翻译,与其称为翻译,不如称为'改写','重组',或者是'剽窃的创造',艾略特甚至厚颜宣称庞德'发明了中国诗'。这当然是英雄欺人,不足为训,但某些诗人'寓创造于翻译'的意图,是昭然可见的。"他紧接着又说:"假李白之名抒庞德之情,这种偷天换日式的'翻译',我非常不赞成。"[16]

严格说来,这种偷天换日式的翻译,或者说跑野马式的翻译,是不能称为"意译"的,因为诗的意译是要力求保留原诗的意义、意境以及神韵风格的,而不是任意篡改原作的风貌和神采。茅盾主张有制限的意译。他首先列举了原诗和译诗:

原诗	译诗
美人卷珠帘,	A fair girl draws the blind aside
深坐颦蛾眉;	And sadly sits with the dropping head;
但见泪痕湿,	I see her burning tear drops glide
不知心恨谁。	But know not why those tears are shed.

紧接着加了评语,并为有制限的意译规定了"三要"。他说,这首英译诗"则神韵十九仿佛,也是意译的。……但是意译似乎

也应该有些制限。(1) 要不是节译；任意把原文节删许多，是'不足为训'的。英译的《木兰词》好虽好了，就可惜犯了'太象节译'这毛病。(2) 要有原诗的神韵；神韵是超乎修辞技术之上的一些'奥妙的精神'，是某首诗的个性，最重要最难传达，可不是一定不能传达的。(3) 要合乎原诗的风格；原诗是悲壮的，焉能把他译为清丽。"[17]

在我个人看来，译诗不一定非意译不可，须视具体情况而定。应该是：适于直译者直译之，例如前引袁可嘉所译《红玫瑰》一诗，总体上是直译过来的，非但句法未变，即字面意义也未作任何变更；适于意译者则意译之，例如茅盾所举的这首诗，可以说基本上是意译的，有好几处字面意义作了较大的变更，如"卷珠帘"变成了"draws the blind aside"，"颦蛾眉"变成了"sadly... with the dropping head"，"泪痕湿"变成了"burning tear drops glide"，"心恨谁"变成了"why those tears are shed"，但译诗仍然再现了原诗所表现的"美女愁坐空闺"的意象和情景。上述变换说法含有"再创造"之意，但并非创造派那样的借题发挥。就整个译诗说，它力图表原诗之意（主要指形象和意象），传原诗之神（独守空闺的情绪）。在多数情况下，应灵活或结合运用直译和意译。我之所以说这首译诗"基本上"而非"完全"是意译的，因为它并未改变原诗的句法。

关于创造派的主张的译法之不可取，业已充分讨论，不再赘述。

格律派和自由派（指自由诗体派），目前情况又怎样呢？

目前，就杜诗英译而论，正如周维新、周燕在《杜诗与翻译》一文中所说："虽然是百花齐放，因人而译，但归纳起来，不外两个典型流派。其一是：无拘无束的自由派。其二是：工整贴切的严谨派。两派虽然异曲同工，但最近的趋势则是：各自向纵深发展，不断强化，引出了互相对立的理论依据，从而产生出差异显著的译文。这可以从最近问世的两部代表作中看出。前者是翁显良先生的《古诗英译》（人民出版社，1985年5月），后者是吴钧陶先生的《杜甫诗英译》(陕西人民出版社，1985年9月)。二人都是行家，二书都是佳作。但二人的翻译观针锋相对。翁显良主张把诗译成散体。他说：'译诗不是临摹，似或不似，在神不在貌。更不必受传统形式的束缚，押韵不押韵，分行不分行，一概无所谓，岂不自由得很？'（翁显良：《古诗英译》小序 p.1）相反，吴钧陶则说，'要比较完善地传达原著的精神和面貌，就必须尽最大努力接近原著的精神和面貌。原著是诗，最好不要把它翻译成散文。原著是严谨的古典格律诗，最好不要把它翻译成现代自由诗。'（吴钧陶：《杜甫诗英译》序 p.31）"[18]

紧接着，上述引文作者还把翁、吴译文作了五点比较。虽然前面称赞"二人都是行家，二书都是佳作"，但从五点比较来看，实际上对吴是真褒，而对翁则是褒中有贬，举其第三点比较，即可见一斑：

3. 翁诗自由发挥，失之于荡；吴译憨厚详实，不卑不亢，以《野望》（*A View in the Open*）为例：

清秋望不极，
迢递起层阴。

翁译

The autumn air ought to be clear; yet the prospect is circumscribed by dark masses looming in the distance.

（翁显良：《古诗英译》p.26）

吴译

The autumnal view is infinite for one's gaze.
And far away somewhere roll up the wreaths of haze.

（吴钧陶：《杜甫诗英译》p.130）

"两相比较，吴译严格掌握分寸，恰到好处，无懈可击……而翁译则过于自由,反而疏忽了'望'字,把'望不极'译成了'空气应当是清晰的(air ought to be clear)',与原诗句不够吻合。"与此同时,两位作者还引用了闻一多先生告诫翻译者的一段话:"不能太滥用自己的自由了。译者应当格外小心,不要损伤了原作的意味。"

总之,他们是提倡"韵体译法"的。他们说:

"为了更好地保存原诗情趣,采用韵体译法,即兼顾意美、音美、形美'三合一'的译法。所谓'三合一'是指:(1)译词精确、缜密、俏美。侧重表达深层内容的意味,不拘泥表层形式的'意美'。(2)以押韵、重复、节奏表达原诗的'音美'。(3)以工整、对仗使译文句子的长短与原诗句子的长短相若等方法表达原诗的'形美'。也就是:译者善于将词义和韵律巧妙地结合起来。"并举了一首"三合一"的佳译为例:

《登高》[19]　　　　译文
风急天高猿啸哀,　The wind so swift, the sky so steep, and gibbons cry;
渚清沙白鸟飞回。　Water so clear and sand so white, backwards birds fly.
无边落木萧萧下,　The boundless forest sheds its leaves shower by shower.
不尽长江滚滚来。　The endless river rolls its waves hour after hour.

(许渊冲:《谈唐诗的英译》,载于《翻译通讯》,1983 年第 3 期,p.22)[20]

总体来说,这首诗的译文是非常好的,但还是有一些值得讨论的地方。例如,将"鸟飞回"译为"backwards birds fly"似乎不尽如人意,因为(1)这里的"回"是"迴"的简体形式①,意思是"盘

---

① 译者注:作者的英文原文说:"回"here is the simplified form of "昉" which means "circle" or "wheel"。但权威辞典《汉典》对"昉"的解释是:①明亮,②起始。并无"盘旋"之意。并说"回"的繁体字是"迴"。这个"昉"字很可能由本书原著付梓时打字输入之误造成。故将"昉"改为"迴"。

旋"或"旋转";(2) 即使将"鸟飞回"理解为"鸟儿往回飞"(birds fly back),也不能用 backwards 这个副词替换 back,两个词的意思不一样。我认为,将"鸟飞回"理解为"鸟儿盘旋",译为"birds circle or wheel",更好一些。为了保留原有的韵律,"backwards birds fly"可以改为"birds circlingly fly"或者"birds wheelingly fly"。

关于中国古诗和唐诗的英译,上述"韵体译法"的主张,我是赞成的。在《西奥多·萨沃里所论述的翻译原则》一文中,我曾说过:

"关于怎样译和对原作能否增减的问题,萨沃里赞成以诗译诗的主张,赞成原文押韵的诗也最好押韵;但不赞成为了押韵而对原诗任意有所增减,他认为于必要时可以用现代的散文诗或诗的散文来译,这样,既不受韵的限制,又不受严格的重读规则的限制,因而能够把原诗的意义和情感表达出来。

"……用格律诗译格律诗,如能既讲求格律,又无损原意,自属上乘;但在确实不能用格律诗来译的某些具体情况下,则不妨考虑运用自由诗体来译,以便尽量保留原诗的思想、情节、意境和形象,总比死守诗行的长度和韵脚而对原诗的内容任意增删好得多。"[21]

用自由体译唐诗,亦不乏佳译,例如宾纳所译贺知章《回乡偶书》,现在让我们欣赏一下:

《回乡偶书》
贺知章

少小离家老大回,
乡音无改鬓毛衰;
儿童相见不相识,
笑问"客从何处来?"

Coming Home

by He Zhizhang

I left home young. I return old,
Speaking as then, but with hair grown thin;
And my children, meeting, do not know me.
They smile and say: "Stranger, where do you come from?"

—Bynner

吕叔湘指出:"此'儿童'无论是家中的儿童,或村中的儿童,似均可用'the children',除这一点外,全诗都和原诗密合,而读起来仍是一首很好的诗。"[22]

吕先生对这首自由体译诗的好评,是客观公允的,因为一则它基本上保留了原诗的意美,二则词句排列同为四行,就重读音节看,基本上是匀称的,也可以说译者照顾到了形美,三则译诗具有流畅的自然节奏,读起来上口,听起来悦耳,怎能说它缺乏音美? 韵当然是押韵诗音美的要素,但自然节奏也同样是诗的音美的成分。而且,原诗自然质朴的风格也在译诗中得到了再现。"用自由体来译格律诗也可以产生好译品。外国也有用这种方法而产生好译品的。用意是提防把外国格律诗译成了不相当的本国格律体,特别是带了随本国格律体旧诗而来的陈腔滥调,叫读者一点也感觉不到外国诗的本来气息。英国人詹姆士·雷格用英国格律体翻译我国的《诗经》就远不如他的同国人阿瑟·韦利用自由体(或像我们所说的'半自由体')翻译的见长。当然,这和译者个人才能和语言艺术工夫的高低也或多或少有关系。从此也可以看出:具有足够的语言修养才能用格律体译诗,而另一方面,不借助于适当的形式,相当的格律,而能在译诗中见长,更需要高度的语言艺术水平。"[23]

以上主要谈了中国格律诗英译的问题。英国格律诗的中译,曾提到董恂以五言诗译朗费罗《人生颂》失败的例子，也同时提到袁可嘉以押韵的白话诗（即所谓的半自由体）译彭斯《红玫瑰》成功的例子。中国有不少人曾经试过用中国五言或七言古诗来译英文格律诗，但以"忠于原诗"这一基本要求来说，总令人觉得多少有画蛇添足之嫌，难免因韵害义。王以铸也有同感，他说："我国早些年苏曼殊、马君武等人用古诗译拜伦的诗，后来也不乏仿效的人，也有人把外国诗译成中国的词曲，译文本身有些确是相当精彩，但严格地说，我们读到的只是译者的创作，原作只起个参考作用罢了。"[24]

以中国五言或七言古诗译英国格律诗之所以难得成功，其原因如下：

"第一，我国语言已经从以单字为准的古代文言进而以词为准的现代口语，译诗以单字为准显然违背现代口语的特点；第二，外国语言的音缀以元音为准，一个字包含几个元音就算几个音缀，而我国语言若以单字为准，一个字在任何情况下都只能构成一个音缀，这样中文的单音和外文的多音缀无论怎样也搭配不好；第三，即使在形式上译诗各相应行包含与原诗音缀相等的整齐字数，诵读起来却必须两个字、三个字连在一起念，每个字在时间上的间歇和听觉上的效果也不可能与原作的音缀相等。"[25]

笔者认为，还有一个原因，那就是：中文古诗，言简意赅，概括性强，而英文格律诗精确细致，因而在表意上，时相扞格。

卞之琳等主张以顿（音组）为节奏单位来译外国格律诗。他们说：

"以顿为节奏单位既符合我国古典诗歌和民歌的传统，又适应现代口语的特点。我国的方块字是单音字，我们的语言却不是单音语言。我们平常说话以两个字、三个字连着说为最多，而不是一个字一个字分开说的，因此在现代口语中，顿的节奏也很明显。欧洲（包括苏联）格律诗每行音缀（单音）数虽然也大致固定，每行音步性质和音步数却是关键（法国格律诗是例外，它另有一套）。我们的顿法（音组内部性质和相互之间的关系）也还可以有种种进一步的研究，我们首先用相当顿数（音组数）抵音步而不拘字数来译这种格律诗，既较灵活，又在形式上和节奏上能基本上做到相当，促成效果上的接近。事实上，十年来这种作法也已经产生了一些比较成功的作品，已经显示进一步发展的可能性。"[26]

这种用以顿代步并讲求一定押韵的口语体新诗的形式来译外国格律诗，新中国成立初期已显示优势。发展到今天，更是形成了主流，有湖南人民出版社编印的丛书（《诗苑译林》）中多本译诗为证，例如杨德豫译的《拜伦抒情诗七十首》，便是支持以顿代步的代表作。我们不妨从七十首中选出一首欣赏一下：

She Walks in Beauty

She walks in beauty, like the night
    Of cloudless climes and starry skies;
And all that's best of dark and bright
    Meet in her aspect and her eyes:
Thus mellow'd to that tender light
    Which heaven to gaudy day denies.

One shade the more, one ray the less,
    Had half impair'd the nameless grace
Which waves in every raven tress,
    Or softly lightens o'er her face;
Where thoughts serenely sweet express
    How pure, how dear their dwelling place.

《她走在美的光影里》

她走在美的光影里，好像
    无云的夜空，繁星闪烁；
明与暗的最美的形象
    交会于她的容颜和眼波，
融成一片恬淡的清光——
    浓艳的白天得不到的恩泽。

多一道阴影，少一缕光芒，
    都会损害那难言的优美；
美在她绺绺黑发上飘荡，
    在她的腮颊上洒布柔辉；
愉悦的思想在那儿颂扬
    这神圣寓所的纯洁高贵。

And on that cheek, and o'er that brow,	那脸颊，那眉宇，幽娴、沉静，
So soft, so calm, yet eloquent,	情意却胜似万语千言；
The smiles that win, the tints that glow.	迷人的笑容，灼人的红晕，
But tell of days in goodness spent,	显示温情伴送着芳年；
A mind at peace with all below,	和平的、涵容一切的灵魂！
A heart whose love is innocent.	蕴蓄着真纯爱情的心田！

英诗的音步有抑扬（短长）、扬抑（长短）、扬抑抑（长短短）、抑抑扬（短短长）四种格式。正像中国诗词的平仄不能移入英语译诗一样，英语这四种格式也难以移入中文译诗。"但是，把英语格律诗译成汉语时，第一，使译诗每行的顿数与原诗的步数一致，第二，译诗韵式完全按照原诗，这两条却是可以做到的。做到这两条，有利于使原诗的音乐美（整齐匀称、疾徐有致的鲜明节奏，适应于思想内容需要多样化的优美韵律）在另一种语言中尽可能相似地再现出来。"[27]

杨德豫翻译的《拜伦抒情诗七十首》，译诗有三千四百七十三行，韵式全部按照原诗；就"以顿代步"这一点来说，也至少有百分之九十六以上的诗行做到了与原诗步数相等，只有不足百分之四的诗行，根据具体情况，作了一些变通。可以说，译者杨德豫已经基本上实现了诗人兼诗译家雪莱关于译诗的主张：译诗一定要用与原诗同样的形式来译，才算真正对得起原作者。

译者翻译这七十首抒情诗值得赞赏。笔者认为，对译诗要用"与原诗同样的形式"一语，我们应抱着辩证的实事求是的宽厚的态度予以正当的理解。要亲自试译一下，才知道译诗的甘苦。

最后，探讨一下自由诗的英汉互译问题。自由诗自惠特曼确立于美国以来，盛行于全世界。其主要特点是：诗的分节、分行、押韵等都没有一定的限制，但一般仍分节、分行，多半不讲求押韵，更注重内在的节奏。眼下,这已形成英美当代诗的主要倾向。译英美不讲求押韵的现代派的诗,根据雪莱提出的译诗应像原诗的原则,最好也用不讲求押韵的口语体新诗的形式来译,例如:

Several Voices out of a Cloud
by Louise Bogan

Come, drunks and drug-takers; come perverts unnerved!

Receive the laurel given, though late, on merit; to whom and wherever deserved

Parochial punks, trimmers, nice people, joiners true-blue.

Get the hell out of the way of the laurel. It is deathless. And it isn't for you.[28]

《美国的文学》的作者马库斯·堪利夫指出:

"诗中的俗语用得有些夸张,目的在于使读者吃惊,可是在别处也有数不尽的例证,把俗语用得很有把握,一点也不莽撞。博根小姐这首诗发表于1938年,那时 W.H.奥登正在写对话式的诗,这至少表示这个英国诗人也已经听到了一种声音。随后他移民美国,并归化美籍,也许可以说明,他觉得美国那种雅俗结合的文字对他特别合适。"(p.306)

现在我们来看译文:

《一片云中的几种声音》
张芳杰 原译

来吧,醉鬼和吸毒的人们;来吧,丧失勇气的堕落者!

接受这桂冠吧,给的虽迟,却是论功行赏;给的是受之无愧的人,褊狭的无聊人物,随风转舵者,雅人,高贵的名流。

你们都滚开,不要碰这桂冠,它是没有死亡的,也不是给你们的。[29]

原诗在词汇上,有夸张的俗语,行有长短,亦不押韵。译诗从整体上来讲翻译得很好,因为无论是在措词上、在词序、行序上,还是在思想内容上,都是十分忠于原诗的。只有一点可以加以改进。在这里,应取 deathless 一词的喻义"不朽"而不是其表面意义"没有死亡"。这样,就可以同主语"桂冠"相容无间。由此可再一次看出,即使是翻译这样完全不讲格律的自由诗,要达到比较完美的程度,亦属不易。

中国新诗,从五四运动发展到现在,就形式和韵律说仍有两派。一派是自由的程度大,也像英美当代诗一样,不押韵;而另一派仍讲求一定形式的匀称和一定形式的押韵。这类诗的英译,其基本要求和原则规定如下:

译诗应当也是诗,译诗应当忠于原诗;换言之,译诗必须信于内容,达如其分,切合风格。一言以蔽之:译诗全随原诗而异。

注释:

1. 吕叔湘编注《英译唐人绝句百首》,湖南人民出版社,1980 年。
2. 许渊冲《诗词英译漫谈》,《中国翻译》1988 年第 3 期。
3. 袁洪庚《试论文学翻译中的作者风格和译者风格》,兰州大学学报(社会科学版),1988 年第 2 期。
4. 关于补偿法,参看王恩冕《翻译补偿法初探》,《中国翻译》1988 年第 2、3 期。
5. 刘重德《翻译漫谈》,陕西人民出版社,1984。
6. 见注 4。
7. 见注 5。
8. 见注 1。
9. 见注 2。

10. 何匡《论翻译标准》,《俄文教学》1955年第6期。
11. 成仿吾《论译诗》,罗新璋编《翻译论集》,商务印书馆,1984年333页。
12. 刘重德《试论翻译的原则》,《湖南师院学报》1979年第1期。
13. "达如其分"是笔者对其"信达切"三原则中的"达"所下的新定义。
14. 译诗引自钱钟书《汉译第一首英语诗〈人生颂〉》,罗新璋编《翻译论集》,244-245页。
15. 见注2。
16. 余光中《翻译与创作》,罗新璋编《翻译论集》743页。
17. 茅盾《译诗的一些意见》,《时事新报》附刊《文学旬刊》52期,1922年。原诗是李白的《怨情》。
18. 周维新、周燕《杜诗与翻译》,《外国语》1987年第6期。
19. 《登高》是杜甫所写的一首七律,其后四句为:"万里悲秋常作客,百年多病独登台。艰难苦恨繁霜鬓,潦倒新停浊酒杯。"
20. 见注18。
21. 刘重德《西奥多·萨沃里所论述的翻译原则》,《外国语》1986年第4期。
22. 见注1。
23. 卞之琳等《艺术性翻译问题和诗歌翻译问题》,罗新璋编《翻译论集》。
24. 王以铸《论诗之不可译》,《编译参考》1981年第1期。
25. 26. 见注23。
27. 杨德豫《拜伦抒情诗七十首·译后琐记》,湖南人民出版社,1981年。
28. 马库斯·堪利夫《美国的文学》英汉对照版306-307页,香港今日世界出版社,1979年。

第十讲 | 英诗汉译

一、英诗汉译及其对中国新诗之影响

这里所谓英诗,系指英语诗,并不以英国诗为限。汉译第一首英语诗,乃是清朝董恂所译美国诗人朗费罗(Henry Wadsworth Longfellow)所写的《人生颂》(*A Psalm of Life*, 1839)。

我国文学翻译史上,董恂与林纾颇为相似。(1)两人均不懂外语,但林纾翻译了150多部外国小说,如斯各特(1771—1832)的《劫后英雄传》(1820),斯陀夫人(1811—1896)的《黑奴吁天录》(1852),系借助合作者的口译;而董恂只译了一首诗,即《人生颂》,是在英国驻华公使威妥玛(Sir Thomas Francis Wade, 1818—1895)的汉译[1]基础上提炼而成。(2)两人翻译均用文言。由于不能直接阅读欣赏原著,两人均难免误译之处。尽管如此,林纾的外国文学翻译,对中国的新文学仍有显著的贡献。而董恂则贡献不大,因为只"翻译"了这么一首诗,而且他的译文《人生颂》中[1],有些明显的错误。在前一讲已对他的作品进行了详细分析,这里不再重复。

到20世纪初,英诗也像其他形式的外国文学一样,才开始被行家翻译过来。1909年,苏曼殊(1884—1918)就译了《拜伦诗选》,其中包括《去国行》(*My Native Land—Good Night*)、《赞大海》(*The*

Ocean），《哀希腊》（*The Isles of Greece*）等名篇。兹选录《哀希腊》原诗及苏译第六节，以窥苏曼殊等前辈译者用古诗翻译英诗之一斑：

原文
'Tis something in the dearth of fame,
　　Though link'd among a fetter'd race,
To feel at least a patriot's shame,
　　Even as I sing, suffuse my face;
For what is left the poet here?
For Greeks a blush — for Greece a tear.

译文[2]
威名尽坠地　举族供奴畜
知尔忧国士　中心亦以恧
而我独行谣　我犹无面目
我为希人羞　我为希腊哭

为了使读者易于领会原诗精神，特选录杨德豫用现代汉语和以顿代步的方法翻译[3]的《哀希腊》的对应诗节如下：

置身于披枷带锁的民族，
　　与荣誉无缘，也心甘情愿；
至少，能痛感邦家的屈辱，
　　歌唱的时候，我羞惭满面；
诗人在这里有什么作用？
为祖国落泪，为同胞脸红？

五四运动期间及其前后，翻译英诗的人越来越多，例如 1915 年陈独秀（1879—1942）翻译了由英语转译过来的泰戈尔的四首诗，发表在《青年杂志》（后改名《新青年》）上。紧接着刘半农（1891—1934）在同一杂志发表了英国胡德（Thomas Hood，1799—1845）的《缝衣曲》（*The Song of the Shirt*）的汉语译文。1922 年郭沫若译了《雪莱诗选》。

在译《雪莱诗选》前一年，郭沫若就出版了白话新诗集《女神》。"和小说里的《呐喊》一样，奠定中国新诗基础的是郭沫若的《女神》。这部诗集是五四时代新文艺的一个灿烂果实。诗人之所以取得巨大的成就……还有一个因素，那就是外国进步诗人的影响。诗人在《我的作诗的经过》一文中说过：'在我自己的作诗的经验上，是先受泰戈尔诸人的影响，力主冲淡，后来又受了惠特曼的影响才奔放起来的。'谈到惠特曼，诗人又说，'那种把一切的旧套摆脱干净了的诗风和五四时代的暴风突进的精神十分合拍，我是彻底地为他那雄浑的豪放的宏朗的调子所动荡了。'（张光年《论郭沫若早期的诗》，《诗刊》1957 年 01 期）……在欧洲诗人中，他也提到歌德和海涅给他的影响。从这些话中，我们不难看出，西方诗歌在内容和形式上对我国新诗的影响。五四时代的诗歌运动，主要是打破旧诗格律的枷锁，要用比较自由的形式表达新的革命的思想感情，新诗人在追求新形式时，他们在西方诗歌中找到了比较可用的形式，而西方进步诗歌中所表现的追求解放和革命的内容，也在中国新诗人的心中得到了共鸣。"[4]

五四时代产生了不少新诗流派，如浪漫派（郭沫若），大众派（刘半农），小诗派（冰心），湖畔诗派（冯雪峰），新婉约派（冯至），新格律诗派（闻一多），散文诗派（鲁迅），革命诗派（蒋光慈）和象征诗派（戴望舒）。总而言之，不妨这样说，这些新诗流派及其代表人物，都或多或少地受了外国诗（包括东西方英语诗）的启发和影响。以谢冰心受泰戈尔影响为例。

"冰心感到：在读泰戈尔的作品以前，她的头脑中只有一些很有意思，但又'零碎'的思想，是泰戈尔的信仰'天然'的美感和'发挥天然美感的诗词'渗入她的脑海，和她原来'不能言说'的思想，一缕缕地合成琴弦，奏出缥渺神奇无调无声的音乐。这形成了泰戈尔与冰心作品的'神似'。

"在新文化的高潮中，年轻的冰心求知欲很旺盛。她脑海中经常浮现一些珍珠般的感想与回忆。最初只是将这些感想与回忆歪歪斜斜写在笔记本的眉批上，虽然不过三、五行，却能叫她回想起一些'很亲切，很真实'的情景。偶尔她读到了郑振铎译的《飞鸟集》的连载，泰戈尔《飞鸟集》中那些'很短的充满诗情画意和哲理的三言两语'，给了冰心很大的启发。于是她头脑那些'零碎'的思想由'很短的充满诗情画意和哲理的三言两语'组成了《繁星》和《春水》。这种艺术上的契合，使泰戈尔和冰心的诗又惊人地'形似'。"[5]

五四运动以后的新诗，毋庸讳言，仍然在受外国诗歌的影响。譬如说，英国的十四行诗，不仅有人译过，还有人摹写过。中国诗人钱光培就曾编辑过一本《中国十四行诗选》。苏联马雅可夫斯基（1893—1930）的梯形诗，也对中国的进步诗人产生过极大影响，不仅翻译出版各种版本的马雅可夫斯基选集，也有人仿照他的诗体写过汉语诗。随着以庞德（1885—1975）和艾略特（1888—1965）为代表的现代意象派诗歌的引进，在中国诗坛上亦有所反映，例如70年代盛行的朦胧诗，我认为，就同现代派有一定的关系。

二、关于英诗译法的探索

正如王以铸所指出的那样，我国早些年苏曼殊、马君武等人用古诗译拜伦的诗，后来也不乏仿效的人，也有人把外国诗歌译成中国的词曲，译文本身有些确实相当精彩，但严格地说，我们读到的只是译者的创作，原作只起个参考作用罢了。⁶ 苏马两人在中英两种文字方面，造诣修养都很深，他们译的英诗应在英诗汉译的历史上占有一席地位，因为他们是译诗的先驱，首先把英诗介绍进来，这或多或少促进了我国新诗的发展。但就当前时代的要求来说，再仿效他们用古诗来译英诗似不妥当。主要原因有两点：（1）古诗，无论四言、五言或七言，用来译英诗，都有较大的局限性，难以包容原诗全部意义、意象和意境；（2）古诗，无论四言、五言或七言，用来译英诗，对今天的广大青年读者来说，都比较难懂，不易欣赏接受。以苏曼殊用四言诗译的拜伦的《赞大海》（*The Ocean*）第一段为例：

拜伦原诗
Roll on, thou deep and dark blue ocean—roll!
Ten Thousand fleets sweep over thee in vain;
Man marks the earth with ruin—his control
Stops with the shore; upon the wat'ry plain
The wrecks are all thy deed, nor doth remain
A Shadow of man's ravage, save his own,
When, for a moment, like a drop of rain,
He sinks into thy depths, with bubbling groan
Without a grave, unknelled, uncoffin'd and unknown.

苏曼殊译文⁷
皇涛澜汗 灵海黝冥
万艘鼓楫 泛若轻萍
芒芒九围 每有遗虚

旷哉天沼　匪人攸居
大器自运　振荡皇夲
岂伊人力　赫彼神工
罔象乍见　决舟没人
狂暑未几　遂为波臣
掩体无棺　归骨无坟
丧钟声嘶　逖矣谁闻

这节译诗本身读起来朗朗上口，声调铿锵，但严格以译诗的标准来衡量，就有任意增删以词害义之处：（1）第一行二句"灵海"中的"灵"字系为了与一句"皇涛"对仗而无中生有的增字，根据原诗本意，ocean 意为"海洋"，而"灵"意为 holy。按原文，海洋何"灵"之有？（2）第二行"万艘鼓揖／泛若轻萍"，给人以轻快的感觉，有违原义。这一表达失误源自任意删减原文中的状语"in vain"。原诗"Ten thousand fleets sweep over thee in vain"的真正含义是"上万舰只未能掠过海洋"。（3）第四行"旷哉天沼／匪人攸居"亦意犹未尽，因为不是人不能居住的问题而是非人所能控制的问题。（4）第七行原诗中"a drop of rain"（雨滴）的意象消失了，译诗中却出现了中国传说中的水怪"罔象"。（5）原诗第九行"unknelled（未敲丧钟）"到了译文里却变成了"丧钟声嘶"，与事实不符，可谓以词害义。

以上是就苏的译诗的内容说的，那么译文的语言又怎么样呢？像这样的古文，对广大青年读者来说是很难读懂的，甚至有些字都很生僻，如"皇夲"和"暑"，这些字怎么读音，是什么意思？当然，我选的例子比较典型。但一般说来，用文言文译诗，都或多或少存在类似毛病。

自从五四文学革命运动明确提出"反对文言文，提倡白话文"

的主张以来，英诗汉译的工作，无论在语言上，还是在形式上，都有所前进，也就是说，用白话文译诗的人越来越多了，并开始注意接近原诗的形式。兹转录郭沫若译的英国诗人布莱克（William Blake, 1759—1827）的《老虎》（*The Tyger*），以供欣赏，因为这首译诗，不管在自然节奏方面，在押韵方面，还是在整诗的形式方面，我认为，都做得相当好，尽管译文韵式不同于原文。

The Tyger[8]

Tyger! Tyger! burning bright
In the forests of the night,
What immortal hand or eye
Could frame thy fearful symmetry?

In what distant deeps or skies
Burned the fire of thine eyes?
On what wings dare he aspire?
What the hand dare seize the fire?

And what shoulder, and what art,
Could twist the sinews of thy heart?
And when thy heart began to beat,
What dread hand? and what dread feet?

What the hammer? what the chain?
In what furnace was thy brain?
What the anvil? what dread grasp
Dare its deadly terrors clasp?

《老虎》

老虎！老虎！黑夜的森林中
燃烧着的煌煌的火光，
是怎样的神手或天眼
造出了你这样的威武堂堂？

你炯炯两眼中的火
燃烧在多远的天空或深渊？
他乘着怎样的翅膀搏击？
用怎样的手夺来火焰？

又是怎样的膂力，怎样的技巧，
把你心脏的筋肉捏成？
当你的心脏开始搏动时
是用怎样猛的手和脚胫？

是怎样的槌？怎样的链子？
在怎样的熔炉中炼成你的脑筋？
是怎样的铁砧？怎样的铁臂
敢于捉着这可怖的凶神？

When the stars threw down their spears,	群星投下了它们的投枪,
And water'd heaven with their tears,	用它们的眼泪润湿了穹苍,
Did he smile his work to see?	他是否微笑着欣赏他的作品?
Did he who made the Lamb make thee?	他创造了你,也创造了羔羊?
Tyger! Tyger! burning bright	老虎!老虎!黑夜的森林中
In the forests of the night,	燃烧着的煌煌的火光,
What immortal hand or eye	是怎样的神手和天眼
Could frame thy fearful symmetry?	造出了你这样的威武堂堂?

到了20世纪50年代,卞之琳等在《文学评论》上发表了论艺术翻译和诗歌翻译的文章,关于格律诗的译法,明确地提出了"以顿代步"的主张。这一观点在前一讲已作引用并加以详细说明,这里不再赘述。我们且看卞之琳是如何身体力行自己的主张的。以他所译的华兹华斯(William Wordsworth, 1770—1850)的《孤独的割麦女》(*The Solitary Reaper*)为例。

The Solitary Reaper

Behold her, single in the field,
Yon solitary Highland Lass!
Reaping and singing by herself;
Stop here or gently pass!
Alone she cuts and binds the grain,
And sings a melancholy strain;
Oh listen! for the vale profound
Is overflowing with the sound.

No nightingale did ever chant

More welcome notes to weary bands
Of travellers in some shady haunt,
Among Arabian sands:
A voice so thrilling ne'er was heard
In spring-time from the cuckoo-bird,
Breaking the silence of the seas
Among the farthest Hebrides.

Will no one tell me what she sings? —
Perhaps the plaintive numbers flow
For old, unhappy, far-off things,
And battles long ago:
Or is it some more humble lay,
Familiar matter of to-day?
Some natural sorrow, loss, or pain,
That has been, and may be again?

Whatever the theme, the maiden sang
As if her song could have no ending;
I saw her singing at her work,
And o'er the sickle bending; —
I listened, motionless and still,
And, as I mounted up the hill,
The music in my heart I bore,
Long after it was heard no more.

孤独的割麦女

看她,在田地独自一个,
那个苏格兰高原的少女!
独自在收割,独自在唱歌;
停住吧,或者悄悄走过去!
她独自割麦,又把它捆好,
唱着一支忧郁的曲调;
听啊,整个深邃的谷地
都有这一片歌声在洋溢。

从没有夜莺能够唱出
更美的音调来欢迎结队商,
疲倦了,到一个荫凉的去处
就在阿拉伯沙漠的中央:
杜鹃鸟在春天叫得多动人,
也没有这样子荡人心魂,
尽管它惊破了远海的静悄,
响彻了赫伯里底群岛。

她唱的是什么,可有谁说得清?
哀怨的曲调也许在流传
古老,不幸,悠久的事情,
还有长久以前的征战;
或者她唱的并不特殊,
只是今日的家常事故?
那些天然的丧忧,哀痛,
有过的,以后还会有的种种?

> 不管她唱的是什么题目，
> 她的歌好像会没完没了；
> 我看见她边唱边干活，
> 弯着腰，挥动她的镰刀——
> 我一动也不动，听了许久；
> 后来，当我上山的时候，
> 我把歌还记在心上，
> 虽然早已听不见声响。

这样一对比汉译与原文，不难看出，卞译十分严谨，他为以顿代步翻译英语格律诗树立了一个良好榜样。

关于如何翻译英语律诗，王科一（1925—1968）在《从雪莱论译诗谈起》一文中作了精辟分析。他认为"首要任务是再现原作的境界。要再现境界，就面临着两重不可忽视的具体职责，一曰移植形式，二曰用字遣词的分寸"。[10] 按照自己的见解，他译了雪莱的《伊斯兰的起义》（The Revolt of Islam），并在译诗中用垂直线标出了每行的顿数，对于理解以顿代步的译法，颇有帮助。现以第一章第三节为例：

Hark! 'tis the rushing of a wind that sweeps
　　Earth and the ocean. See! The lightnings yawn
Deluging Heaven with fire, and the lashed deeps
　　Glitter and boil beneath: it rages on,
　　The mighty stream, whirlwind and waves upthrown,
Lightning and hail, and darkness eddying by.
　　There is a pause—the sea-birds, that were gone
Into their caves to shriek, come forth, to spy

What calm has fallen on earth, what light is in the sky.

听！｜那不｜就是｜飞驰的｜疾风，
扫过｜大地｜和海洋？瞧！｜那闪电，
　　喷出｜火光｜来撕裂｜淫雨的｜天空，
被鞭打的｜海洋｜掀起｜金光｜万点，
海底｜沸腾了，｜旋风｜把巨浪｜席卷，
　　闪电，｜冰雹，｜黑暗，｜飞旋｜直转，
稍顷｜风雨｜暂停，｜海鸥｜出现，
　　才躲进｜洞里｜去悲啼，｜又出来刺探——
天上｜可曾｜晴阳，｜人间｜已否｜平安？

这节诗译得基本上符合他自己提的要求。一是遣词较有分寸，二是大体上保留了斯宾塞诗体的形式。每节九行，1～8行每节5顿，第9行则为6顿。但译者改变了缩进的行次，这似乎不太必要，原诗的缩进行次是可以保留的。

下面略谈一下自由体诗歌的翻译以结束这一讲。美国惠特曼（Walt Whitman, 1819—1892）是倡导自由体的最知名的诗人。众所周知，著名美国诗人惠特曼（1819—1892）是自由体的首创者。我们首先引他的几行小诗和译文，然后再就译文进行评论。

原文[11]
To behold the day-break!
　　The little light fades the immense and diaphanous shadows,
　　The air tastes good to my palate...

I hear bravuras of birds, bustle of growing

    wheat, gossip of flames, clack of
     sticks cooking my meals...

    The glories strung like beads on my smallest
     sights and hearings, on the walk in the street
     and the passage over the river—

译文
看那东方的破晓！
曦微的光使无边的稀疏的黑暗渐渐消失，
空气的味道很好……
我听见鸟的聒噪，麦在习习摇风，火舌低语，
树枝毕剥着烧我的早餐……
我在街上走，我在河上过，看到和听到的东西都
挂着晶莹如珠的光华——

  翻译自由诗，一般说来，要比翻译格律诗容易一些，但基本要求仍是一样。那就是说，第一，必须信于内容，保留原诗意义、意象和意境，第二，必须锤炼文字，达如其分；第三，必须尽量切合原诗形式。拿这些标准衡量这几行译诗，它既有可取之处，又有不足之处。两方面的具体情况如下：可取之处是：（1）保留了原诗自由体的形式，（2）第一节一、三两行和最后一节措辞恰当，达如其分。不足之处是有些词炼得不够，或有损原诗意义，或有损原诗意象。例如：（1）"曦微的光"有语病。"曦"就是"光"的意思，如"晨曦"。形容早晨最初的阳光应用"熹微"两字，如"晨光熹微"。（2）把"shadows"译成黑暗，分量太重。修饰这个词的形容词"diaphanous"意为"清澈的"或"透明的"。合在一起，"Diaphanous shadows"似

乎带有"中性"色彩,可译成"朦胧的夜色",较能表达原意。(3)"鸟的聒噪",用词不当。"聒噪"之声,令人心烦,应是贬义词,而"bravuras"的意思是要求演唱家或演奏家发挥其技艺和精神的乐曲,华丽雄壮的乐曲。"Bravuras of birds"似可灵活译为"鸟的欢唱"。(4)"麦在习习摇风"与原意不合。"bustle"一词,《钱伯斯20世纪词典》注有"stir"(微动)之意,把"bustle of growing wheat"译成"生长中的麦子在微微抖动"似乎好一些。(5)"树枝毕剥着烧我的早餐"一行可修订为"树枝毕剥毕剥地烧着我的早餐"。整个第二节经过这么一修改,才能重现原诗所描绘的一幅生机勃勃、欢快和谐的晨景。

从上述分析可以看出,即使翻译自由诗也并不像人们所认为的那么容易,也需要下一番字斟句酌的锤炼功夫。

注释:
1. 原文和董恂的译文,参见前一讲。
2. 柳亚子编《苏曼殊全集》,北京中国书店出版社,1985,81页。
3. 杨德豫译《拜伦抒情诗七十首》,湖南人民出版社,1981,149页。
4. 冯至等,《五四时期俄罗斯文学和其他欧洲国家文学的翻译和介绍》,见罗新璋编《翻译论集》,492页。
5. 见陈守成等编《外国文学发展简史》,第571页,四川民族出版社,1986年。
6. 王以铸《论诗之不可译》,《编译参考》1987年第1期。
7. 柳亚子(1887—1958),中国著名诗人,编有《苏曼殊全集》。
8. 9. 原文引自孙铢等编《英语文学选读》第一册,上海译文出版社,1981;译文引自《英国诗歌选集》,上海译文出版社,1988。
10. 王科一,"从雪莱论译诗谈起——雪莱作品学习小札",《文汇报》,1962年10月12日。
11. 原诗和译诗均引自马库斯·堪利夫著张芳杰原译李培同增订的《美国的文学》(*The Literature of the United States* by Marcus Cunliffe),香港今日世界出版社,1976,119页。

译后记

刘重德教授,河南滑县人,生于1914年,1931年考入开封高中文科,在校刊上发表他翻译的雪莱抒情短诗数首,1934年入北京大学,先后从朱光潜先生学英诗,从叶公超学翻译。毕业后相继执教于河南大学、国立师范学院、湖南大学、湖南师范大学,曾任湖南省译协会长、中国译协副会长、中国英汉语比较研究会会长。刘重德教授因病医治无效,于2008年2月11日在长沙逝世,享年94岁。

刘老是我国有名的翻译家与翻译理论家。主要译作有:英国奥斯汀的《爱玛》、赫士列特的《莎士比亚戏剧人物论》;美国斯陀夫人的《黑奴吁天录》和盖斯特的《寻常人家》。主要翻译论著有:《试论翻译的原则》《翻译原则刍议》《谈翻译的忠实性》《理解、表达与文学翻译》《常用译法例解》《谈谈直译和意译》《英语定语从句的译法》《阿诺德评荷马史诗的翻译》《托尔曼教授谈翻译的艺术》《翻译漫谈》《文学翻译十讲》等。

《文学翻译十讲》一书用英文写成。我应湖南师范大学外国语学院之邀,将该书译为中文,感到十分荣幸。书中大部分内容都以刘老发表过的中文文章为基础。对于该书的汉译来说,这既提供了很大的便利,也造成相当棘手的问题。便利之处是,书中英文与发表过的文章的行文十分吻合者,将后者中的原文移过来即可。棘手之处是,首先必须想方设法找到有关中文文章。找到文章一看,发现刘老有时修改了中文文章中的行文顺序与具体措词。碰到这种情况,译者应把中文文章中的说法直接搬过来,还是按照刘老的英文著作自己翻译呢?经过思考,我认为,作为英文著作的作者,刘老有权修改自己发表过的文章的说法;我作为译者,同样要按照"信达切"的原则,忠实于他的英文原作,即:两种文本中都有者则采用中文文章的行文,中文文章中所无而英文原作中所有者则增,中文文章中所有而英文原作中所无者则减。中文文章中完全找不到的文字,则自己翻译,当然也参照刘老的行文习惯。另外一个问题是,本书英文原作中引用了许多别的中国学者的话,翻译时尽量以被引用的中文原话为准。

由于水平所限,译文中肯定还有许多不尽如人意之处,望行家不吝斧正。